Masterman Ready
Or, The Wreck of the "Pacific"

by

Frederick Marryat

Masterman Ready
Or, The Wreck of the "Pacific"
by Frederick Marryat

ISBN: 978-93-63057-73-9

Published by

DOUBLE 9 BOOKS

2/13-B, Ansari Road
Daryaganj, New Delhi – 110002
info@double9books.com
www.double9books.com
Tel. 011-40042856

ABOUT THE AUTHOR

Captain Frederick Marryat (an early innovator of the sea story) was a British Royal Navy Officer and novelist. He gained the Royal Human Society's gold medal for bravery, before leaving the services in 1830 to write books. He is mainly remembered for his stories of the sea, many written from his own experiences. He started a series of adventure novels marked by a brilliant, direct narrative style and an absolute fund of incident and fun. These have The King's Own (1830), Peter Simple (1834), and Mr. Midshipman Easy (1836). He also created a number of children's books, among which The Children of the New Forest (1847), a story of the English Civil Wars is a classic of children literature. A Life and Letters was processed by his daughter Florence (1872). He is recognized also for a broadly used system of maritime flag signalling known as Marryat's Code. Familiar for his adventurous novels, his works are known for their representation of deep family bonds and social structure beside naval action. Marryat died in 1848 at the age of fifty.

CONTENTS

Chapter One

It was in the month of October, 18—, that the *Pacific*, a large ship, was running before a heavy gale of wind in the middle of the vast Atlantic Ocean. She had but little sail, for the wind was so strong, that the canvas would have been split into pieces by the furious blasts before which she was driven through the waves, which were very high, and following her almost as fast as she darted through their boiling waters; sometimes heaving up her stern and sinking her bows down so deep into the hollow of the sea, that it appeared as if she would have dived down underneath the waves; but she was a fine vessel, and the captain was a good seaman, who did what he considered best for the safety of his vessel, and then put his trust in that Providence who is ever watchful over us.

The captain stood before the wheel, watching the men who were steering the ship; for when you are running before a heavy gale, it requires great attention to the helm: and as he looked around him and up at the heavens, he sang in a low voice the words of a sea song:

"One wide water all around us,
All above us one black sky."

And so it was with them;—they were in the middle of the Atlantic, not another vessel to be seen, and the heavens were covered with black clouds, which were borne along furiously by the gale; the sea ran mountains high, and broke into large white foaming crests, while the fierce wind howled through the rigging of the vessel.

Besides the captain of the ship and the two men at the wheel, there were two other personages on deck: one was a young lad about twelve years old, and the other a weather-beaten old seaman, whose grisly locks were streaming in the wind, as he paced aft and looked over the taffrail of the vessel.

The young lad, observing a heavy sea coming up to the stern of the vessel, caught hold of the old man's arm, crying out—"Won't that great wave come into us, Ready?"

"No, Master William, it will not: don't you see how the ship lifts her quarters to it?—and now it has passed underneath us. But it might happen, and then what would become of you, if I did not hold on, and hold you on also? You would be washed overboard."

"I don't like the sea much, Ready; I wish we were safe on shore again," replied the lad. "Don't the waves look as if they wished to beat the ship all to pieces?"

"Yes, they do; and they roar as if angry because they cannot bury the vessel beneath them: but I am used to them, and with a good ship like this, and a good captain and crew, I don't care for them."

"But sometimes ships do sink, and then everybody is drowned."

"Yes; and very often the very ships sink which those on board think are most safe. We can only do our best, and after that we must submit to the will of Heaven."

"What little birds are those flying about so close to the water?"

"Those are Mother Carey's chickens. You seldom see them except in a storm, or when a storm is coming on."

The birds which William referred to were the stormy petrels.

"Were you ever shipwrecked on a desolate island like Robinson Crusoe?"

"Yes, Master William, I have been shipwrecked; but I never heard of Robinson Crusoe. So many have been wrecked and undergone great hardships, and so many more have never lived to tell what they have suffered, that it's not very likely that I should have known that one man you speak of, out of so many."

"Oh! but it's all in a book which I have read. I could tell you all about it—and so I will when the ship is quiet again; but now I wish you would help me down below, for I promised mamma not to stay up long."

"Then always keep your promise like a good lad," replied the old man; "now give me your hand, and I'll answer for it that we will fetch the hatchway without a tumble; and when the weather is fine again, I'll tell you how I was wrecked, and you shall tell me all about Robinson Crusoe."

Having seen William safe to the cabin door, the old seaman returned to the deck, for it was his watch.

Masterman Ready, for such was his name, had been more than fifty years at sea, having been bound apprentice to a collier which sailed from South Shields, when he was only ten years old. His face was browned from long exposure, and there were deep furrows on his cheeks, but he was still a hale and active man. He had served many years on board of a man-of-war, and had been in every climate: he had many strange stories to tell, and he might be believed even when his stories were strange, for he would not tell an untruth. He could navigate a vessel, and, of course, he could read and write. The name of Ready was very well suited to him, for he was seldom at a loss; and in cases of difficulty and danger, the captain would not hesitate to ask his opinion, and frequently take his advice. He was second mate of the vessel.

The *Pacific* was, as we have observed, a very fine ship, and well able to contend with the most violent storm. She was of more than four hundred tons burthen, and was then making a passage out to New South Wales, with a valuable cargo of English hardware, cutlery, and other manufactures. The captain was a good navigator and seaman, and moreover a good man, of a cheerful, happy disposition, always making the best of everything, and when accidents did happen, always more inclined to laugh than to look grave. His name was Osborn. The first mate, whose name was Mackintosh, was a Scotsman, rough and ill-tempered, but paying strict attention to his duty—a man that Captain Osborn could trust, but whom he did not like.

Ready we have already spoken of, and it will not be necessary to say anything about the seamen on board, except that there were thirteen of them, hardly a sufficient number to man so large a vessel; but just as they were about to sail, five of the seamen, who did not like the treatment they had received from Mackintosh, the first mate, had left the ship, and Captain Osborn did not choose to wait until he could obtain others in their stead. This proved unfortunate, as the events which we shall hereafter relate will show.

Chapter Two

Master William, whom we have introduced to the reader, was the eldest boy of a family who were passengers on board, consisting of the father, mother, and four children: his father was a Mr Seagrave, a very well-informed, clever man, who having for many years held an office under government at Sydney, the capital of New South Wales, was now returning from a leave of absence of three years. He had purchased from the government several thousand acres of land; it had since risen very much in value, and the sheep and cattle which he had put on it were proving a source of great profit. His property had been well managed by the person who had charge of it during his absence in England, and he was now taking out with him a variety of articles of every description for its improvement, and for his own use, such as furniture for his house, implements of agriculture, seeds, plants, cattle, and many other things too numerous to mention.

Mrs Seagrave was an amiable woman, but not in very strong health. The family consisted of William, who was the eldest, a clever, steady boy, but, at the same time, full of mirth and humour; Thomas, who was six years old, a very thoughtless but good-tempered boy, full of mischief, and always in a scrape; Caroline, a little girl of seven years; and Albert, a fine strong little fellow, who was not one year old: he was under the charge of a black girl, who had come from the Cape of Good Hope to Sydney, and had followed Mrs Seagrave to England. We have now mentioned all the people on board of the Pacific: perhaps we ought not to forget two shepherd's dogs, belonging to Mr Seagrave, and a little terrier, which was a great favourite of Captain Osborn, to whom she belonged.

It was not until the fourth day from its commencement that the gale abated, and then it gradually subsided until it was nearly a calm. The men who had been watching night after night during the gale now brought all their clothes which had been drenched by the rain and spray, and hung them up in the rigging to dry: the sails, also, which had been furled, and had been saturated by the wet, were now loosened and spread out that they might not be mildewed. The wind blew mild and soft, the sea had gone down, and the ship was running through the water at the speed of about four miles an hour. Mrs Seagrave, wrapped up in a cloak, was seated upon one of the arm-chests near the stern of the ship, her husband and children were all with her enjoying the fine weather, when Captain Osborn, who had been taking an observation of the sun with his sextant, came up to them.

"Well, Master Tommy, you are very glad that the gale is over?"

"I didn't care," replied Tommy, "only I spilt all my soup. But Juno tumbled off her chair, and rolled away with the baby, till papa picked them both up."

"It was a mercy that poor Albert was not killed," observed Mrs Seagrave.

"And so he might have been, if Juno had not thought only of him and nothing at all about herself," replied Mr Seagrave.

"That's very true, sir," replied Captain Osborn. "She saved the child, and, I fear, hurt herself."

"I thump my head very hard," said Juno, smiling.

"Yes, and it's lucky that you have a good thick woolly coat over it," replied Captain Osborn, laughing.

"It is 12 o'clock by the sun, sir," said Mackintosh, the first mate, to the captain.

"Then bring me up the latitude, Mr Mackintosh, while I work out the longitude from the sights which I took this morning. In five minutes, Mr Seagrave, I shall be ready to prick off over our place on the chart."

"Here are the dogs come up on deck," said William; "I dare say they are as glad of the fine weather as we are. Come here, Romulus! Here, Remus!— Remus!"

"Well, sir," said Ready, who was standing by them with his quadrant in his hand, "I should like to ask you a question. Those dogs of yours have two very odd names which I never heard before. Who were Romulus and Remus?"

"Romulus and Remus," replied Mr Seagrave, "were the names of two shepherds, brothers, who in ancient days founded the city of Rome, which eventually became the largest and most celebrated empire in the world. They were the first kings of Rome, and reigned together. History says that Remus affronted Romulus by leaping over a wall he had raised, and Romulus, in his anger, took away his life; but the history of early days is not to be depended upon."

"No, nor the brothers either, it appears," replied Ready; "however, it is the old story—two of a trade can never agree. One sometimes hears of Rome now—is that the same place?"

"Yes," replied William, "it is the remains of the old city."

"Well, one lives and learns," said Ready. "I have learnt something to-day, which everyone will to the last day of his life, if he will only ask questions. I'm an old man, and perhaps don't know much, except in the seafaring way; but I should have known much less if I did not ask for information, and was not ashamed to acknowledge my ignorance; that's the way to learn, Master William."

"Very good advice, Ready,—and, William, I hope you will profit by it," said Mr Seagrave; "never be ashamed to ask the meaning of what you do not understand."

"I always do, papa. Do I not ask you questions, Ready?"

"Yes, you do, and very clever questions for a boy of your age; and I only wish that I could answer them better than I can sometimes."

"I should like to go down now, my dear," said Mrs Seagrave; "perhaps Ready will see the baby down safe."

"That I will, ma'am," said Ready, putting his quadrant on the capstan: "now, Juno, give me the child, and go down first;—backwards, you stupid girl! how often do I tell you that? Some day or another you will come down with a run."

"And break my head," said Juno.

"Yes, or break your arm; and then who is to hold the child?"

As soon as they were all down in the cabin, the captain and Mr Seagrave marked the position of the vessel on the chart, and found that they were one hundred and thirty miles from the Cape of Good Hope.

"If the wind holds, we shall be in to-morrow," said Mr Seagrave to his wife. "Juno, perhaps you may see your father and mother."

Poor Juno shook her head, and a tear or two stole down her dark cheek. With a mournful face she told them, that her father and mother belonged to a Dutch boer, who had gone with them many miles into the interior: she had been parted from them when quite a little child, and had been left at Cape Town.

Chapter Three

The next morning the *Pacific* arrived at the Cape and anchored in Table Bay.

"Why do they call this Table Bay, Ready?" said William.

"I suppose it's because they call that great mountain the Table Mountain, Master William; you see how flat the mountain is on the top."

"Yes, it is quite as flat as a table."

"Yes, and sometimes you will see the white clouds rolling down over the top of it in a very curious manner, and that the sailors call spreading the tablecloth: it is a sign of bad weather."

"Then I hope they will not spread the tablecloth while we are here, Ready," said William, "for I shall certainly have no appetite. We have had bad weather enough already, and mamma suffers so much from it. What a pretty place it is!"

"We shall remain here two days, sir," said Captain Osborn to Mr Seagrave, "if you and Mrs Seagrave would like to go on shore."

"I will go down and ask Mrs Seagrave," said her husband, who went down the ladder, followed by William.

Upon the question being put to Mrs Seagrave, she replied that she was quite satisfied with the ship having no motion, and did not feel herself equal to going on shore; it was therefore decided that she should remain on board with the two younger children, and that, on the following day, Mr Seagrave should take William and Tommy to see Cape Town, and return on board before night.

The next morning, Captain Osborn lowered down one of the large boats, and Mr Seagrave, accompanied by Captain Osborn, went on shore with William and Tommy. Tommy had promised his mamma to be very good; but that he always did, and almost always forgot his promise directly he was out of sight. As soon as they landed, they went up to a gentleman's house, with whom Captain Osborn was acquainted. They stayed for a few minutes to drink a glass of lemonade, for it was very warm; and then it was proposed that they should go to the Company's Gardens and see the wild beasts which were confined there, at which William was much delighted, and Tommy clapped his hands with joy.

"What are the Company's Gardens, papa?" inquired William.

"They were made by the Dutch East India Company, at the time that the Cape of Good Hope was in their possession. They are, properly speaking, Botanical Gardens; but, at the same time, the wild animals are kept there. Formerly there were a great many, but they have not been paid attention to lately, for we have plenty of these animals in England now."

"What shall we see?" said Tommy.

"You will see lions, Tommy, a great many in a large den together," said Captain Osborn.

"Oh! I want to see a lion."

"You must not go too near them, recollect."

"No, I won't," said Tommy.

As soon as they entered the gates, Tommy escaped from Captain Osborn, and ran away in his hurry to see the lions; but Captain Osborn caught him again, and held him fast by the hand.

"Here is a pair of very strange birds," said the gentleman who accompanied them; "they are called Secretaries, on account of the feathers which hang behind their heads, as the feather of a pen does when a clerk puts it behind his ear: but they are very useful, for they are snake-killers; indeed, they would, if they could, live altogether upon snakes, which they are very great enemies to, never letting one escape. They strike them with their feet, and with such force as to kill them immediately."

"Are there many snakes in this country?" inquired William.

"Yes, and very venomous snakes," replied Mr Seagrave; "so that these birds are very useful in destroying them. You observe, William, that the Almighty, in his wisdom, has so arranged it that no animal (especially of a noxious kind) shall be multiplied to excess, but kept under by being preyed upon by some other; indeed, wherever in any country an animal exists in any quantity, there is generally found another animal which destroys it. The Secretary inhabits this country where snakes exist in numbers, that it may destroy them: in England the bird would be of little value."

"But some animals are too large or too fierce to be destroyed by others, papa; for instance, the elephant and the lion."

"Very true; but these larger animals do not breed so fast, and therefore their numbers do not increase so rapidly. For instance, a pair of elephants will not have more than one young one in the space of two years or more; while the rabbits, which are preyed upon and the food of so many other beasts as well as birds, would increase enormously, if they were not destroyed. Examine through the whole of creation, and you will find that there is an unerring hand, which invariably preserves the balance exact; and that there are no more mouths than for which food is provided, although accidental circumstances may for a time occasion a slight alteration."

They continued their walk until they came to the den of the lions. It was a large place, in closed with a strong and high wall of stone, with only one window to it for the visitors to look at them, as it was open above. This window was wide, and with strong iron bars running from the top to the bottom; but the width between the bars was such that a lion could put his paw out with ease; and they were therefore cautioned not to go too near. It was a fine sight to see eight or ten of these noble-looking animals lying down in various attitudes, quite indifferent apparently to the people outside—basking in the sun, and slowly moving their tufted tails to and fro. William examined them at a respectful distance from the bars; and so did Tommy, who had his mouth open with astonishment, in which there was at first not a little fear mixed, but he soon got bolder. The gentleman who had accompanied them, and who had been long at the Cape, was relating to Mr Seagrave and Captain Osborn some very curious anecdotes about the lion. William and they were so interested, that they did not perceive that Tommy had slipped back to the grated window of the den. Tommy looked at the lions, and then he wanted to make them move about: there was one fine full-grown young lion, about three years old, who was lying down nearest to the window; and Tommy took up a stone and threw it at him: the lion appeared not to notice it, for he did not move, although he fixed his eyes upon Tommy; so Tommy became more brave, and threw another, and then another, approaching each time nearer to the bars of the window.

All of a sudden the lion gave a tremendous roar, and sprang at Tommy, bounding against the iron bars of the cage with such force that, had they not been very strong, it must have broken them. As it was, they shook and rattled so that pieces of mortar fell from the stones. Tommy shrieked; and, fortunately for himself, fell back and tumbled head over heels, or the lion's paws would have reached him. Captain Osborn and Mr Seagrave ran up to Tommy, and picked him up: he roared with fright as soon as he could fetch his breath, while the lion stood at the bars, lashing his tail, snarling, and showing his enormous fangs.

"Take me away—take me on board the ship!" cried Tommy, who was terribly frightened.

"What did you do, Tommy?" said Captain Osborn.

"I won't throw any more stones, Mr Lion; I won't indeed!" cried Tommy, looking terrified towards the animal.

Mr Seagrave scolded Tommy well for his foolish conduct, and by degrees he became more composed; but he did not recover himself until they had walked some distance away from the lion's den.

They then looked at the other animals which were to be seen, Tommy keeping a most respectful distance from every one of them. He wouldn't even go near to a Cape sheep with a broad tail.

When they had seen everything, they went back to the gentleman's house to dinner; and, after dinner, they returned on board.

Chapter Four

The following morning the fresh water and provisions were received on board, and once more the *Pacific* stretched her broad canvas to the winds, and there was every prospect of a rapid voyage, as for many days she continued her passage with a fair wind and flowing sheet. But this did not continue: it fell calm, and remained so for nearly three days, during which not a breath of wind was to be seen on the wide expanse of water; all nature appeared as if in repose, except that now and then an albatross would drop down at some distance from the stern of the vessel, and, as he swam lazily along with his wings half-furled, pick up the fragments of food which had been thrown over the side.

"What great bird is that, Ready?" inquired William.

"It is an albatross, the largest sea-bird we have. Their wings are very long. I have seen them shot, and they have measured eleven feet from the tip of one wing to the tip of the other when the wings have been spread out."

"It is the first one that I have seen," said William.

"Because you seldom meet them north of the Cape, sir: people do say that they go to sleep on the wing, balancing themselves high up in the air."

"Papa," said William, turning to Mr Seagrave, who stood by, "why is it that one bird can swim and another cannot? You recollect when Tommy drove the hens into the large pond, they flounced about, and their feathers became wet, and would support them no longer, and then they were drowned. Now, how does a sea-bird contrive to remain so long on the water?"

"Because a sea-bird, William, is provided with a sort of oil on purpose to anoint the outside of its feathers, and this oil prevents the water from penetrating them. Have you not observed the ducks on shore dressing their feathers with their bills? They were then using this oil to make their feathers waterproof."

"How odd!"

"Don't say how odd, William; that is not an expression to use when we talk of the wonderful provisions made by the Almighty hand, who neglects not the meanest of his creatures—say rather, how wonderful!"

"That's very true, sir," observed Ready; "but still you must not be too hard upon Master William, for I have heard many a grownup man make use of the same expression."

On the third day of the calm, the barometer fell so low as to induce Captain Osborn to believe that they should have a severe gale, and every preparation was made to meet it, should it come on. Nor was he mistaken: towards midnight the clouds gathered up fast, and as they gathered up in thick piles, heaped one over the other, the lightning darted through them in every direction; and as the clouds rose up, so did the wind, but at first only in heavy gusts, and then lulling again to a calm.

"Ready," said Captain Osborn, "how do you think we shall have the wind?"

"Why, Captain Osborn, to tell you the truth, I don't think it will be steady to one point long. It may at first blow hard from the north, but it's my idea it will shift soon to some other quarter, and blow still harder."

"What think you, Mackintosh?"

"We'll have plenty of it, and a long steady gale, that's my notion; and the sooner we ship the dead lights the better."

Mr Seagrave, with William, happened to be standing by at the time of this conversation, and at the term *dead* lights Willy's face expressed some anxiety. Ready perceived it, and said—

"That's a foolish name they give to the shutters which go over the cabin windows to prevent the water from breaking into the cabin when a vessel sails before the wind; you know we had them on the last time that we had a gale."

"But, Ready," said Captain Osborn, "why do you think that we shall have a shift of wind?"

"Well, I don't know; perhaps I was wrong," replied the old man, "and Mr Mackintosh is right: the wind does seem to come steady from the northeast, that's certain;" and Ready walked away to the binnacle, and looked at the compass. Mr Seagrave and William then went below, and Mr Mackintosh went forward to give his orders. As soon as they were all gone, Ready went up again to Captain Osborn and said:

"Captain Osborn, it's not for me to contradict Mr Mackintosh, but that's of little consequence in a time like this: I should have held to my opinion, had it not been that the gentleman passenger and his son were standing by, but now, as the coast is clear, I tell you that we shall have something worse than a gale of wind. I have been in these latitudes before, and I am an old seaman, as you know. There's something in the air, and there has been something during the last three days of calm, which reminds me too well of what I have seen here before; and I am sure that we shall have little better than a hurricane, as far as wind goes—and worse in one point, that it will last much longer than hurricanes generally do. I have been watching, and even the birds tell me so, and they are told by their nature, which is never mistaken. That calm has been nothing more than a repose of the winds previous to their being roused up to do their worst; and that is my real opinion?"

"Well, and I'm inclined to agree with you, Ready; so we must send topgallant yards down on deck, and all the small sails and lumber out of the tops. Get the trysail aft and bent, and lower down the gaff. I will go forward."

Their preparations were hardly complete before the wind had settled to a fierce gale from the north-east. The sea rose rapidly; topsail after topsail was furled; and by dusk the *Pacific* was flying through the water with the wind on her quarter, under reefed foresail and storm staysail. It was with difficulty that three men at the wheel could keep the helm, such were the blows which the vessel received from the heavy seas on the quarter. Not one seaman in the ship took advantage of his watch below to go to sleep that night, careless as they generally are; the storm was too dreadful. About three o'clock in the morning the wind suddenly subsided; it was but for a minute or two, and then it again burst on the vessel from another quarter of the compass, as Ready had foretold, splitting the foresail into fragments, which lashed and flogged the wind till they were torn away by it, and carried far to leeward. The heavens above were of a pitchy darkness, and the only light was from the creaming foam of the sea on every side. The shift of wind, which had been to the west-north-west, compelled them to alter the course of the vessel, for they had no chance but to scud, as they now did, under bare poles; but in consequence of the sea having taken its run from the former wind, which had been north-east, it was, as sailors call it, cross, and every minute the waves poured over the ship, sweeping all before their weight of waters. One poor man was washed overboard, and any attempt made to save him would have been unavailing. Captain Osborn was standing by the weather gunnel, holding on by one of the belaying-pins, when he said to Mackintosh:

"How long will this last, think you?"

"Longer than the ship will," replied the mate gravely.

"I should hope not," replied the captain; "still it cannot look worse. What do you think, Ready?"

"Far more fear from above than from below just now," replied Ready, pointing to the yard-arms of the ship, to each of which were little balls of electric matter attached, flaring out to a point. "Look at those two clouds, sir, rushing at each other; if I—"

Ready had not time to finish what he would have said, before a blaze of light, so dazzling that it left them all in utter darkness for some seconds afterwards, burst upon their vision, accompanied with a peal of thunder, at which the whole vessel trembled fore and aft. A crash—a rushing forward—and a shriek were heard, and when they had recovered their eyesight, the foremast had been rent by the lightning as if it had been a lath, and the ship was in flames: the men at the wheel, blinded by the lightning, as well as appalled, could not steer; the ship broached to—away went the mainmast over the side—and all was wreck, confusion, and dismay.

Fortunately the heavy seas which poured over the forecastle soon extinguished the flames, or they all must have perished; but the ship lay now helpless, and at the mercy of the waves beating violently against the wrecks of the masts which floated to leeward, but were still held fast to the vessel by their rigging. As soon as they could recover from the shock, Ready and the first mate hastened to the wheel to try to get the ship before the wind; but this they could not do, as, the foremast and mainmast being gone, the mizenmast prevented her paying off and answering to the helm. Ready, having persuaded two of the men to take the helm, made a sign to Mackintosh (for now the wind was so loud that they could not hear each other speak), and, going aft, they obtained axes, and cut away the mizen-rigging; the mizen-topmast and head of the mizenmast went over the side, and then the stump of the foremast was sufficient to get the ship before the wind again. Still there was much delay and confusion, before they could clear away the wreck of the masts; and, as soon as they could make inquiry, they found that four of the men had been killed by the lightning and the fall of the foremast, and there were now but eight remaining, besides Captain Osborn and his two mates.

Chapter Five

Sailors are never discouraged by danger as long as they have any chance of relieving themselves by their own exertions. The loss of their shipmates, so instantaneously summoned away, — the wrecked state of the vessel, — the wild surges burying them beneath their angry waters, — the howling of the wind, the dazzling of the lightning, and the pealing of the thunder, did not prevent them from doing what their necessity demanded. Mackintosh, the first mate, rallied the men, and contrived to fix a block and strap to the still smoking stump of the foremast; a rope was rove through the block, and the main-topgallant sail hoisted, so that the vessel might run faster before the gale, and answer her helm better than she did.

The ship was again before the wind, and comparatively safe, notwithstanding the heavy blows she now received from the pursuing waves. Night again came on, but there was no repose, and the men were worn out with exposure and fatigue.

The third day of the gale dawned, but the appearances were as alarming as ever: the continual breaking of the seas over the stern had washed away the binnacles, and it was impossible now to be certain of the course the ship had been steered, or the distance which had been run; the leaky state of the vessel proved how much she had already suffered from the violent shocks which she had received, and the certainty was apparent, that if the weather did not abate, she could not possibly withstand the force of the waves much longer.

The countenance of Captain Osborn showed great anxiety: he had a heavy responsibility on his shoulders—he might lose a valuable ship, and still more valuable cargo, even if they did not all lose their lives; for they were now approaching where the sea was studded with low coral islands, upon which they might be thrown by the waves and wind, without having the slightest power to prevent it in their present disabled condition.

Ready was standing by him when Captain Osborn said—

"I don't much like this, Ready; we are now running on danger and have no help for it."

"That's true enough," replied Ready: "we have no help for it; it is God's will, sir, and His will be done."

"Amen!" replied Captain Osborn solemnly; and then he continued, after a pause, "There were many captains who envied me when I obtained command of this fine ship,—would they change with me now?"

"I should rather think not, Captain Osborn, but you never know what the day may bring forth. You sailed with this vessel, full of hope—you now, not without reason, feel something approaching to despair; but who knows? it may please the Almighty to rebuke those angry winds and waves, and to-morrow we may again hope for the best; at all events you have done your duty—no man can do more."

"You are right," replied Captain Osborn; "but hold hard, Ready, that sea's aboard of us."

Ready had just time to cling with both hands to the belaying-pins when the sea poured over the vessel, with a volume of water which for some time swept them off their legs: they clung on firmly, and at last recovered their feet.

"She started a timber or two with that blow, I rather think," said Ready.

"I'm afraid so; the best vessel ever built could not stand such shocks long," replied Captain Osborn; "and at present, with our weak crew, I do not see that we can get more sail upon her."

All that night the ship flew in darkness before the gale. At daybreak the wind abated, and the sea went down: the ship was, however, still kept before the wind, for she had suffered too much to venture to put her broadside to the sea. Preparations were now made for getting up jury-masts; and the worn-out seamen were busily employed, under the direction of Captain Osborn and his two mates, when Mr Seagrave and William came upon deck.

William stared about him: he perceived, to his astonishment, that the tall masts, with all their rigging and sails, had disappeared, and that the whole deck was in a state of confusion and disorder.

"See, my child," said Mr Seagrave, "the wreck and devastation which are here. See how the pride of man is humbled before the elements of the great Jehovah."

"Ay, Master Willy," said old Ready, "look around you, as you well may. Do you remember the verses in the Bible?—if not, I remember them well, for I have often read them, and have often felt the truth of them: 'They that go down to the sea in ships, that do business in great waters, these see the works of the Lord, and his wonders in the deep.'"

"But, father," said Willy, after a pause, "how shall we ever get to Sydney without masts or sails?"

"Why, William," replied Ready, "we must do what we can: we sailors are never much at a loss, and I dare say before night you will find us under some sort of sail again. We have lost our great masts, so we must put up jury-masts, as we call them; that is, little ones, and little sails upon them; and, if it pleases God, we shall see Sydney yet. How is Madam, sir?" continued Ready to Mr Seagrave. "Is she better?"

"I fear she is very weak and ill," replied Mr Seagrave; "nothing but fine weather will do her any good. Do you think that it will be fine now?"

"Why, sir, to tell you the truth, I fear we shall have more of it yet: I have not given my thoughts to the captain, as I might be mistaken; but still I think so—I've not been fifty years at sea without learning something. I don't like the gathering of that bank there, Mr Seagrave, and I shouldn't wonder if it were to blow again from the very same quarter, and that before dark."

"God's will be done," replied Mr Seagrave, "but I am very fearful about my poor wife, who is worn to a shadow."

"I shouldn't think so much about that, sir, as I really never knew of people dying that way, although they suffer much. William, do you know that we have lost some of our men since you were down below?"

"No—I heard the steward say something outside about the foremast."

"We have lost five of our smartest and best men—Wilson was washed overboard, Fennings and Masters struck dead with the lightning, and Jones and Emery crushed by the fall of the foremast. You are young, Master Willy, but you cannot think too early of your Maker, or call to mind what they say in the burial service,—'In the midst of life we are in death.'"

"Thank you, Ready, for the lesson you have given my son," said Mr Seagrave; "and, William, treasure it up in your memory."

"Yes, William, they are the words of an old man who has seen many and many a one who was full of youth and spirits called away before him, and who is grateful to God that he has been pleased to preserve his life, and allow him to amend his ways."

"I have been thinking," said Mr Seagrave, after a silence of a minute or two, "that a sailor has no right to marry."

"I've always thought so, sir," replied Ready; "and I dare say many a poor deserted sailor's wife, when she has listened to the wind and rain in her lonely bed, has thought the same."

"With my permission," continued Mr Seagrave, "my boys shall never go to sea if there is any other profession to be found for them."

"Well, Mr Seagrave, they do say that it's no use baulking a lad if he wishes to go to sea, and that if he is determined, he must go: now I think otherwise—I think a parent has a right to say no, if he pleases, upon that point; for you see, sir, a lad, at the early age at which he goes to sea, does not know his own mind. Every high-spirited boy wishes to go to sea—it's quite natural; but if the most of them were to speak the truth, it is not that they so much want to go to sea, as that they want to go from school or from home, where they are under the control of their masters or their parents."

"Very true, Ready; they wish to be, as they consider they will be, independent."

"And a pretty mistake they make of it, sir. Why, there is not a greater slave in the world than a boy who goes to sea, for the first few years after his shipping: for once they are corrected on shore, they are punished ten times at sea, and they never again meet with the love and affection they have left behind them. It is a hard life, and there have been but few who have not bitterly repented it, and who would not have returned, like the prodigal son, and cast themselves at their fathers' feet, only that they have been ashamed."

"That's the truth, Ready, and it is on that account that I consider that a parent is justified in refusing his consent to his son going to sea, if he can properly provide for him in any other profession. There never will be any want of sailors, for there always will be plenty of poor lads whose friends can do no better for them; and in that case the seafaring life is a good one to choose, as it requires no other capital for their advancement than activity and courage."

Chapter Six

Mr Seagrave and William went down below into the cabin, where they found that there was plenty of employment; the steward had brought a basin of very hot pea-soup for the children. Tommy, who was sitting up in the bed-place with his sister, had snatched it out of Juno's left hand, for she held the baby with the other, and in so doing, had thrown it over Caroline, who was screaming, while Juno, in her hurry to assist Caroline, had slipped down on the deck with the baby, who was also crying with fright, although not hurt. Unfortunately, Juno had fallen down upon Vixen the terrier, who in return had bitten her in the leg, which had made Juno also cry out; while Mrs Seagrave was hanging her head out of her standing bed-place, frightened out of her wits at the accident, but unable to be of any assistance. Fortunately, Mr Seagrave came down just in time to pick up Juno and the baby, and then tried to comfort little Caroline, who after all was not much scalded, as the soup had had time to cool.

"Massa Tommy is a very naughty boy," cried Juno, rubbing her leg. Master Tommy thought it better to say nothing—he was duly admonished—the steward cleaned up the mess, and order was at length restored.

In the meantime, they were not idle upon deck, the carpenter was busy fixing a step for one of the spare topmasts instead of a mainmast, and the men were fitting the rigging; the ship unfortunately had sprung a leak, and four hands at the pumps interfered very much with their task. As Ready had prophesied, before night the gale blew, the sea rose again with the gale, and the leaking of the vessel increased so much, that all other labour was suspended for that at the pump. For two more days did the storm continue, during which time the crew were worn out with fatigue—they could pump no longer: the ship, as she rolled, proved that she had a great deal of water in her hold—when, melancholy as were their prospects already, a new disaster took place, which was attended with most serious results. Captain Osborn was on the forecastle giving some orders to the men, when the strap of the block which hoisted up the main-topgallant yard on the stump of the foremast gave way, the yard and sail came down on the deck, and struck him senseless. As long as Captain Osborn commanded them, the sailors had so high an opinion of his abilities as a seaman, and were so encouraged by his cheerful disposition, that they performed their work well and cheerfully; but now that he was, if not killed, at all events senseless and incapable of action, they no longer felt themselves under control. Mackintosh was too much disliked by the seamen to allow his words to have any weight with them. They were regardless of his injunctions or requests, and they now consulted among themselves.

"The gale is broke, my men, and we shall have fine weather now," observed Ready, going up to the sailors on the forecastle. "The wind is going down fast."

"Yes," replied one of the men, "and the ship is going down fast, that's quite as certain."

"A good spell at the pumps would do us some good now," replied Ready. "What d'ye say, my lads?"

"A glass of grog or two would do us more," replied the seaman. "What d'ye say, my boys? I don't think that the captain would refuse us, poor fellow, if he could speak."

"What do you mean to do, my lads?" inquired Mackintosh: "not get drunk, I hope?"

"Why not?" observed another of the men; "the ship must go down soon."

"Perhaps she may—I will not deny it," said Mackintosh; "but that is no reason why we should not be saved: now, if you get drunk, there is no chance of any one being saved, and my life is precious to me. I'm ready to join with you in anything you please, and you may decide what is to be done; but get drunk you shall not, if I can help it, that's certain."

"And how can you help it?" replied one of the seamen, surlily.

"Because two resolute men can do a great deal—I may say three, for in this instance Ready will be of my side, and I can call to my assistance the cabin passenger—recollect the firearms are all in the cabin. But why should we quarrel?—Say at once what you intend to do; and if you have not made up your minds, will you listen to what I propose?"

As Mackintosh's courage and determination were well known, the seamen again consulted together, and then asked him what he proposed.

"We have one good boat left, the new yawl at the booms: the others, as you know, are washed away, with the exception of the little boat astern, which is useless, as she is knocked almost to pieces. Now we cannot be very far from some of the islands, indeed I think we are among them now. Let us fit out the boat with everything we require, go about our work steadily and quietly, drink as much grog as will not hurt us, and take a good provision of it with us. The boat is complete with her masts, sails, and oars; and it's very hard if we do not save ourselves somewhere. Ready, do I give good advice or not?"

"You give very good advice, Mackintosh—only what is to become of the cabin passengers, the women, and children? and are you going to leave poor Captain Osborn? or what do you mean to do?"

"We won't leave the captain," said one of the seamen.

"No—no!" exclaimed the others.

"And the passengers?"

"Very sorry for them," replied the former spokesman; "but we shall have enough to do to save our own lives."

"Well, my lads, I agree with you," said Mackintosh. "Charity begins at home. What do you say?—shall it be so?"

"Yes," replied the seamen, unanimously; and Ready knew that it was in vain to expostulate. They now set about preparing the boat, and providing for their wants. Biscuits, salt pork, two or three small casks of water, and a barrel of rum were collected at the gangway; Mackintosh brought up his quadrant and a compass, some muskets, powder and shot; the carpenter, with the assistance of another man, cut away the ship's bulwarks down to the gunnel, so as to enable them to launch the boat overboard, for they could not, of course, hoist her out now that the masts were gone. In an hour everything was prepared. A long rope was made fast to the boat, which was brought to the gunnel ready for launching overboard, and the ship's broadside was brought to the wind. As this was done, Mr Seagrave came on deck and looked around him.

He perceived the boat ready for launching, the provisions and water at the gangway, the ship brought to the wind, and rolling slowly to the heave of the sea; at last he saw Ready sitting down by Captain Osborn, who was apparently dead. "What is all this, Ready?" inquired Seagrave. "Are they going to leave the ship? have they killed Captain Osborn?"

"No, sir,—not quite so bad as that. Poor Captain Osborn was struck down by the fall of the yard, and has been insensible ever since; but, as to the other matter, I fear that is decided: you see they are launching the boat."

"But my poor wife, she will never be able to go—she cannot move—she is so ill!"

"I'm afraid, Mr Seagrave, that they have no idea of taking either you, or your wife, or your children, with them."

"What! leave us here to perish! Merciful Heaven! how cruel—how barbarous!"

"It is not kind, Mr Seagrave, but still you see it is the law of nature. When it is a question of life, it is every one for himself, for life is sweet: they are not more unkind than they would be to each other, if there were too many for the boat to hold. I've seen all this before in my time," replied Ready, gravely.

"My wife! my children!" cried Mr Seagrave, covering his face with his hands. "But I will speak to them," continued he after a pause; "surely they will listen to the dictates of humanity; at all events Mr Mackintosh will have some power over them. Don't you think so, Ready?"

"Well, Mr Seagrave, if I must speak, I confess to you that there is not a harder heart among them than that of Mr Mackintosh, and it's useless speaking to him or any one of them; and you must not be too severe upon them neither: the boat is small, and could not hold more people with the provisions which they take with them—that is the fact. If they were to take you and your family into the boat, it might be the cause of all perishing together; if I thought otherwise I would try what I could do to persuade them, but it is useless."

"What must be done, then, Ready?"

"We must put our trust in a merciful God, Mr Seagrave, who will dispose of us as he thinks fit."

"We must? What! do not you go with them?"

"No, Mr Seagrave. I have been thinking about it this last hour, and I have made up my mind to remain with you. They intend to take poor Captain Osborn with them, and give him a chance, and have offered to take me; but I shall stay here."

"To perish?" replied Mr Seagrave, with surprise.

"As God pleases, Mr Seagrave. I am an old man, and it is of little consequence. I care little whether I am taken away a year or two sooner, but I do not like to see blossoms cut off in early spring: I may be of use if I remain, for I've an old head upon my shoulders, and I could not leave you all to perish when you might be saved if you only knew how to act. But here the seamen come—the boat is all ready, and they will now take poor Captain Osborn with them."

The sailors came aft, and lifted up the still insensible captain. As they were going away one of them said, "Come, Ready, there's no time to lose."

"Never mind me, Williams; I shall stick to the ship," replied Ready. "I wish you success with all my heart; and, Mr Mackintosh, I have but one promise to exact from you, and I hope you will not refuse me: which is, that if you are saved, you will not forget those you leave here on board, and take measures for their being searched for among the islands."

"Nonsense, Ready! come into the boat," replied the first mate.

"I shall stay here, Mr Mackintosh; and I only beg that you will promise me what I ask. Acquaint Mr Seagrave's friends with what has happened, and where it is most likely we may be found, if it please God to save us. Do you promise me that?"

"Yes, I do, if you are determined to stay; but," continued he, going up to Ready, and whispering to him, "it is madness:— come away, man!"

"Good-bye, Mr Mackintosh," replied Ready, extending his hand. "You will keep your promise?"

After much further expostulation on the part of Mackintosh and the seamen, to which Ready gave a deaf ear, the boat was pushed off, and they made sail to the north-east.

Chapter Seven

For some time after the boat had shoved off from the ship, old Ready remained with his arms folded, watching it in silence. Mr Seagrave stood by him; his heart was too full for utterance, for he imagined that as the boat increased her distance from the vessel, so did every ray of hope depart, and that his wife and children, himself, and the old man who was by his side were doomed to perish. His countenance was that of a man in utter despair. At last old Ready spoke.

"They think that they will be saved and that we must perish, Mr Seagrave; they forget that there is a Power above, who will himself decide that point—a power compared to which the efforts of weak man are as nought."

"True," replied Mr Seagrave, in a low voice; "but still what chance we can have on a sinking ship, with so many helpless creatures around us, I confess I cannot imagine."

"We must do our best, and submit to His will," replied Ready, who then went aft, and shifted the helm, so as to put the ship again before the wind.

As the old man had foretold to the seamen before they quitted the vessel, the gale was now over, and the sea had gone down considerably. The ship, however, dragged but slowly through the water, and after a short time Ready lashed the wheel, and went forward. On his return to the quarter-deck, he found Mr Seagrave had thrown himself down (apparently in a state of despair) upon the sail on which Captain Osborn had been laid after his accident.

"Mr Seagrave, do not give way," said Ready; "if I thought our situation hopeless, I would candidly say so; but there always is hope, even at the very worst,—and there always ought to be trust in that God without whose knowledge not a sparrow falls to the ground. But, Mr Seagrave, I shall speak as a seaman, and tell you what our probabilities are. The ship is half-full of water, from her seams having opened by the straining in the gale, and the heavy blows which she received; but, now that the gale has abated, she has recovered herself very much. I have sounded the well, and find that she has not made many inches within the last two hours, and probably, as she closes her seams, will make less. If, therefore, it pleases God that the fine weather should continue, there is no fear of the vessel sinking under us for some time; and as we are now amongst the islands, it is not impossible, nay, it is very probable, that we may be able to run her ashore, and thus save our lives. I thought of all this when I refused to go in the boat, and I thought also, Mr Seagrave, that if you were to have been deserted by me as well as by all the rest, you would have been unable yourself to take advantage of any chances which might turn up in your favour, and therefore I have remained, hoping, under God's providence, to be the means of assisting you and your family in this sore position. I think now it would be better that you should go down into the cabin, and with a cheerful face encourage poor Mrs Seagrave with the change in the weather, and the hopes of arriving in some place of safety. If she does not know that the men have quitted the ship, do not tell her; say that the steward is with the other men, which will be true enough, and, if possible, leave her in the dark as to what has taken place. Master William can be trusted, and if you will send him here to me, I will talk to him."

"I hardly know what to think, Ready, or how sufficiently to thank you for your self-devotion, if I may so term it, in this exigency. That your advice is excellent and that I shall follow it, you may be assured; and, should we be saved from the death which at present stares us in the face, my gratitude—"

"Do not speak of that, sir; I am an old man with few wants, and whose life is of little use now. All I wish to feel is, that I am trying to do my duty in that situation into which it has pleased God to call me. What can this world offer to one who has roughed it all his life, and who has neither kith nor kin that he knows of to care about his death?"

Mr Seagrave pressed the hand of Ready, and went down without making any reply. He found that his wife had been asleep for the last hour, and was not yet awake. The children were also quiet in their beds. Juno and William were the only two who were sitting up.

William made a sign to his father that his mother was asleep, and then said in a whisper, "I did not like to leave the cabin while you were on deck, but the steward has not been here these two hours: he went to milk the goat for baby and has not returned. We have had no breakfast, none of us."

"William, go on deck," replied his father; "Ready wishes to speak to you."

William went on deck to Ready, who explained to him the position in which they were placed; he pointed out to him the necessity of his doing all he could to assist his father and him, and not to alarm his mother in her precarious state of health. William, who, as it may be expected, looked very grave, did, however, immediately enter into Ready's views, and proceeded to do his best. "The steward," said he, "has left with the other men, and when my mother wakes she will ask why the children have had no breakfast. What can I do?"

"I think you can milk one of the goats if I show you how, while I go and get the other things ready; I can leave the deck, for you see the ship steers herself very nicely;—and, William, I have sounded the well just before you came up, and I don't think she makes much water; and," continued he, looking round him, and up above, "we shall have fine weather, and a smooth sea before night."

By the united exertions of Ready and William the breakfast was prepared while Mrs Seagrave still continued in a sound sleep. The motion of the ship was now very little: she only rolled very slowly from one side to the other; the sea and wind had gone down, and the sun shone brightly over their heads; the boat had been out of sight some time, and the ship did not go through the water faster than three miles an hour, for she had no other sail upon her than the main-topgallant sail hoisted up on the stump of the foremast. Ready, who had been some time down in the cabin, proposed to Mr Seagrave that Juno and all the children should go on deck. "They cannot be expected to be quiet, sir; and, now that Madam is in such a sweet sleep, it would be a pity to wake her. After so much fatigue she may sleep for hours, and the longer the better, for you know that (in a short time, I trust) she will have to exert herself." Mr Seagrave agreed to the good sense of this proposal, and went on deck with Juno and the children, leaving William in the cabin to watch his mother. Poor Juno was very much astonished when she came up the ladder and perceived the condition of the vessel, and the absence of the men; but Mr Seagrave told her what had happened, and cautioned her against saying a word to Mrs Seagrave. Juno promised that she would not; but the poor girl perceived the danger of their position, and, as she pressed little Albert to her bosom, a tear or two rolled down her cheeks. Even Tommy and Caroline could not help asking where the masts and sails were, and what had become of Captain Osborn.

"Look there, sir," said Ready, pointing out some floating sea-weed to Mr Seagrave.

"I perceive it," said Mr Seagrave; "but what then?"

"That by itself would not be quite proof," replied Ready, "but we sailors have other signs and tokens. Do you see those birds hovering over the waves?"

"I do."

"Well, sir, those birds never go far from land, that's all: and now, sir, I'll go down for my quadrant; for, although I cannot tell the longitude just now, at all events I can find out the latitude we are in, and then by looking at the chart shall be able to give some kind of guess whereabout we are, if we see land soon.

"It is nearly noon now," observed Ready, reading off his quadrant, "the sun rises very slowly. What a happy thing a child is! Look, sir, at those little creatures playing about, and as merry now, and as unaware of danger, as if they were at home in their parlour. I often think, sir, it is a great blessing for a child to be called away early; and that it is selfish in parents to repine."

"Perhaps it is," replied Mr Seagrave, looking mournfully at his children.

"It's twelve o'clock, sir. I'll just go down and work the latitude, and then I'll bring up the chart."

Mr Seagrave remained on deck. He was soon in deep and solemn thought; nor was it to be wondered at—the ship a wreck and deserted—left alone on the wide water with his wife and helpless family, with but one to assist him: had that one deserted as well as the rest, what would have been his position then? Utter helplessness! And now what had they to expect? Their greatest hopes were to gain some island, and, if they succeeded, perhaps a desert island, perhaps an island inhabited by savages—to be murdered, or to perish miserably of hunger and thirst. It was not until some time after these reflections had passed through his mind, that Mr Seagrave could recall himself to a sense of thankfulness to the Almighty for having hitherto preserved them, or could say with humility, "O Lord! thy will, not mine, be done." But, having once succeeded in repressing his murmurs, he then felt that he had courage and faith to undergo every trial which might be imposed upon him.

"Here is the chart, sir," said Ready, "and I have drawn a pencil line through our latitude: you perceive that it passes through this cluster of islands; and I think we must be among them, or very near. Now I must put something on for dinner, and then look sharp out for the land. Will you take a look round, Mr Seagrave, especially a-head and on the bows?"

Ready went down to see what he could procure for dinner, as the seamen, when they left the ship, had collected almost all which came first to hand. He soon procured a piece of salt beef and some potatoes, which he put into the saucepan, and then returned on deck.

Mr Seagrave was forward, looking over the bows, and Ready went there to him.

"Ready, I think I see something, but I can hardly tell what it is: it appears to be in the air, and yet it is not clouds. Look there, where I point my finger."

"You're right, sir," replied Ready, "there is something; it is not the land which you see, but it is the trees upon the land which are refracted, as they call it, so as to appear, as you say, as if they were in the air. That is an island, sir, depend upon it; but I will go down and get my glass."

"It is the land, Mr Seagrave," said Ready, after examining it with his glass—"yes, it is so," continued he, musing; "I wish that we had seen it earlier; and yet we must be thankful."

"Why so, Ready?"

"Only, sir, as the ship forges so slowly through the water, I fear that we shall not reach it before dark, and I should have wished to have had daylight to have laid her nicely on it."

"There is very little wind now."

"Well, let us hope that there will be more," replied Ready; "if not, we must do our best. But I must now go to the helm, for we must steer right for the island; it would not do to pass it, for, Mr Seagrave, although the ship does not leak so much as she did, yet I must now tell you that I do not think that she could be kept more than twenty-four hours above water. I thought otherwise this morning when I sounded the well; but when I went down in the hold for the beef, I perceived that we were in more danger than I had any idea of; however, there is the land, and every chance of escape; so let us thank the Lord for all his mercies."

"Amen!" replied Mr Seagrave.

Ready went to the helm and steered a course for the land, which was not so far distant as he had imagined, for the island was very low: by degrees the wind freshened up, and they went faster through the water; and now, the trees, which had appeared as if in the air, joined on to the land, and they could make out that it was a low coral island covered with groves of cocoa-nuts. Occasionally Ready gave the helm up to Mr Seagrave, and went forward to examine. When they were within three or four miles of it, Ready came back from the forecastle and said, "I think I see my way pretty clear, sir: you see we are to the windward of the island, and there is always deep water to the windward of these sort of isles, and reefs and shoals to leeward; we must, therefore, find some little cleft in the coral rock to dock her in, as it were, or she may fall back into deep water after she has taken the ground, for sometimes these islands run up like a wall, with forty or fifty fathom of water close to the weather-sides of them; but I see a spot where I think she may be put on shore with safety. You see those three cocoa-nut trees close together on the beach? Now, sir, I cannot well see them as I steer, so do you go forward, and if I am to steer more to the right, put out your right hand, and if to the left, the same with your left; and when the ship's head is as it ought to be, then drop the hand which you have raised."

"I understand, Ready," replied Mr Seagrave; who then went forward and directed the steering of the vessel as they neared the island. When they were within half a mile of it, the colour of the water changed, very much to the satisfaction of Ready, who knew that the weather-side of the island would not be so steep as was usually the case: still it was an agitating moment as they ran on to beach. They were now within a cable's length, and still the ship did not ground; a little nearer, and there was a grating at her bottom—it was the breaking off of the coral-trees which grew below like forests under water—again she grated, and more harshly, then struck, and then again; at last she struck violently, as the swell lifted her further on, and then remained fast and quiet. Ready let go the helm to ascertain the position of the ship. He looked over the stern and around the ship, and found that she was firmly fixed, fore and aft, upon a bed of coral rocks.

Chapter Eight

"All's well so far, sir," said Ready to Mr Seagrave; "and now let us return thanks to Heaven."

As they rose to their feet again, after giving thanks to the Almighty, William came up and said, "Father, my mother was awakened by the noise under the ship's bottom, and is frightened—will you go down to her?"

"What is the matter, my dear,—and where have you all been?" exclaimed Mrs Seagrave, when her husband went down below. "I have been so frightened—I was in a sound sleep, and I was awakened with such a dreadful noise."

"Be composed, my dear," replied Mr Seagrave; "we have been in great danger, and are now, I trust, in safety. Tell me, are you not better for your long sleep?"

"Yes, much better—much stronger; but do tell me what has happened."

"Much took place, dearest, before you went to sleep, which was concealed from you; but now, as I expect we shall all go on shore in a short time—"

"Go on shore, my dear?"

"Yes, on shore. Now be calm, and hear what has happened, and how much we have reason to be grateful to Heaven."

Mr Seagrave then entered into a detail of all that had passed. Mrs Seagrave heard him without reply; and when he had finished, she threw herself in his arms and wept bitterly. Mr Seagrave remained with his wife, using all his efforts to console her, until Juno reappeared with the children, for it was now getting late; then he returned on deck.

"Well, sir," said Ready, when Mr Seagrave went up to him, "I have been looking well about me, and I think that we have great reason to be thankful. The ship is fast enough, and will not move until some violent gales come on and break her up; but of that there is no fear at present: the little wind that there is, is going down, and we shall have a calm before morning."

"I grant that there is no immediate danger, Ready; but how are we to get on shore?—and, when on shore, how are we to exist?"

"I have thought of that too, sir, and I must have your assistance, and even that of Master William, to get the little boat on board to repair her: her bottom is stove in, it is true, but I am carpenter enough for that, and with some well-tarred canvas I can make her sufficiently water-tight to land us all in safety. We must set to at daylight."

"And when we get on shore?"

"Why, Mr Seagrave, where there are cocoa-nut trees in such plenty as there are on that island, there is no fear of starvation, even if we had not the ship's provisions. I expect a little difficulty with regard to water, for the island is low and small; but we cannot expect to find everything exactly as we wish."

"I am thankful to the Almighty for our preservation, Ready; but still there are feelings which I cannot get over. Here we are cast away upon a desolate island, which perhaps no ship may ever come near, so that there is little chance of our being taken off. It is a melancholy and cruel fate, Ready, and that you must acknowledge."

"Mr Seagrave, as an old man compared to you, I may venture to say that you are ungrateful to Heaven to give way to these repinings. What is said in the book of Job? 'Shall we receive good of the Lord, and shall we not receive evil?' Besides, who knows whether good may not proceed from what appears evil? I beg your pardon, Mr Seagrave, I hope I have not offended you; but, indeed, sir, I felt that it was my duty to speak as I have done."

"You have reproved me very justly, Ready; and I thank you for it," replied Mr Seagrave; "I will repine no more, but make the best of it."

"And trust in God, sir, who, if he thinks fit, will restore you once more to your friends, and increase tenfold your flocks and herds."

"That quotation becomes very apt, Ready," replied Mr Seagrave, smiling, "considering that all my prospects are in flocks and herds upon my land in New South Wales. I must put myself under your orders; for, in our present position, you are my superior—knowledge is power. Can we do anything to-night?"

"I can do a little, Mr Seagrave; but you cannot assist me till tomorrow morning, except indeed to help me to drag these two spars aft; and then I can rig a pair of sheers, and have them all ready for hoisting up to-morrow morning to get the boat in. You see, with so little strength on board, and no masts, we shall be obliged to contrive."

Mr Seagrave assisted Ready in getting the two spars aft, and laid on the spot which was required. "There now, Mr Seagrave, you may go down below. William had better let loose the two dogs, and give them a little victuals, for we have quite forgot them, poor things. I shall keep watch to-night, for I have plenty to do, and plenty to think of; so, good-night, sir."

Ready remained on deck, lashing the heads of the spars, and fixing his tackles ready for the morrow. When all was done, he sat down upon one of the hen-coops aft, and remained in deep thought. At last, tired with watching and exertion, the old man fell asleep. He was awakened at daylight by the dogs, who had been set at liberty, and who, after walking about the ship and finding nobody, had then gone to sleep at the cabin door. At daybreak they had roused up, and going on deck had found old Ready asleep on the hen-coop, and were licking his face in their joy at having discovered him. "Ay," said the old man, as he got off the hen-coop, "you'll all three be useful, if I mistake not, by and by. Down, Vixen, down—poor creature, you've lost a good master, I'm afraid."

"Stop—now let me see," said Ready, talking to himself; "first—but I'll get the log board and a bit of chalk, and write them down, for my memory is not quite so good as it was."

Ready placed the logboard on the hen-coop, and then wrote on it with the chalk:— "Three dogs, two goats, and Billy the kid (I think there's five pigs); fowls (quite enough); three or four pigeons (I'm sure); the cow (she has lain down and won't get up again, I'm afraid, so we must kill her); and there's the merino ram and sheep belonging to Mr Seagrave—plenty of live stock. Now, what's the first things we must get on shore after we are all landed—a spar and topgallant sail for a tent, a coil or two of rope, a mattress or two for Madam and the children, two axes, hammer and nails, something to eat—yes, and something to cut it with. There, that will do for the present," said old Ready, getting up. "Now, I'll just light the fire, get the water on, and, while I think of it, boil two or three pieces of beef and pork to go on shore with them; and then I'll call up Mr Seagrave, for I reckon it will be a hard day's work."

Chapter Nine

As soon as Ready had executed his intentions, and had fed the animals, he went to the cabin and called Mr Seagrave and William. With their assistance the sheers were raised, and secured in their place; the boat was then hooked on, but, as one person was required to bear it clear of the davits and taffrail, they could not hoist it in.

"Master William, will you run down to Juno, and tell her to come on deck to assist us—we must all work now?"

William soon returned with Juno, who was a strong girl; and, with her assistance, they succeeded in getting the boat in.

The boat was turned over, and Ready commenced his work; while Mr Seagrave, at his request, put the pitch-pot on the galley fire, all ready for pitching the canvas when it was nailed on. It was not till dinner-time that Ready, who had worked hard, could patch up the boat; he then payed the canvas and the seams which he had caulked with pitch both inside and out.

"I think we shall do now, sir," said Ready; "we'll drag her to the gangway and launch her. It's fortunate for us that they did clear away the gunnel, as we shall have no trouble."

A rope was made fast to the boat, to hold her to the ship: she was then launched over the gunnel by the united exertions of Mr Seagrave and Ready, and to their great satisfaction she appeared to leak very little.

"Now, sir," said Ready, "what shall we do first—take some things on shore, or some of the children?"

"What do you say, Ready?"

"I think as the water is as smooth as glass, and we can land anywhere, you and I had better go first to reconnoitre,—it is not two hundred yards to the beach, and we shall lose but little time."

"Very well, Ready, I will first run down and tell my wife."

"And, in the meanwhile, I'll put the sail into the boat, and one or two other things."

Ready put the sail in, an axe, a musket, and some cord; then they both got into the boat and pulled on shore.

When they landed, they found that they could see nothing of the interior of the island, the cocoa-nut groves were so thick; but to their right they perceived, at about a quarter of a mile off, a small sandy cove, with brushwood growing in front of the cocoa-nut trees.

"That," said Ready, pointing to it, "must be our location. Let us get into the boat again and pull to it."

In a few minutes they arrived at the cove; the water was shallow, and as clear as crystal. Beneath the boat's bottom they could see beautiful shells, and the fish darting about in every direction.

The sand extended about forty yards from the water, and then commenced the brushwood, which ran back about forty yards further, intermingled with single cocoa-nut trees, until it joined the cocoa-nut grove. They pulled the boat in and landed.

"What a lovely spot this is!" exclaimed Mr Seagrave; "and perhaps mortal man has never yet visited it till now: those cocoa-nuts have borne their fruit year after year, have died, and others have sprung up in their stead; and here has this spot remained, perhaps for centuries, all ready for man to live in, and to enjoy whenever he should come to it."

"Providence is bountiful, Mr Seagrave," replied Ready, "and supplies our wants when we least expect it. If you please we will walk a little way into the wood: take the gun as a precaution, sir; not that there appears to be much occasion for it—there is seldom anything wild on these small islands, except a pig or two has been put on shore by considerate Christians."

"Well, now that we are in the grove, Ready, what do you think?"

"I was looking for a place to fix a tent up for the present, sir, and I think that on that little rise would be a very good place till we can look about us and do better; but we have no time now, sir, for we have plenty of trips to make before nightfall. If you please, we'll haul the sail and other articles on to the beach, and then return on board."

As they were pulling the boat back, Ready said, "I've been thinking about what is best, Mr Seagrave. Would Mrs Seagrave mind your leaving her?—if not, I should say we should have Juno and William on shore first, as they can be of use."

"I do not think that she will mind being left on board with William and the children, provided that I return for her when she is to come on shore herself with the baby."

"Well then, let William remain on board, if you please, sir. I'll land you and Juno, Tommy, and the dogs, this time, for they will be a protection in case of accidents. You and Juno can be doing something while I return by myself for the other articles we shall require."

As soon as they arrived on board, Mr Seagrave went down to cheer his wife with the account of what they had seen. While he was down below, Ready had cast off the lashings of the two spars which had formed the sheers, and dragging them forward, had launched them over the gunnel, with lines fast to them, ready for towing on shore. In a few minutes Juno and Tommy made their appearance on deck; Ready put some tools into the boat, and a couple of shovels, which he brought up when he went for the dogs, and once more they landed at the sandy cove. Tommy stared about him a great deal, but did not speak, until he saw the shells lying on the beach, when he screamed with delight, and began to pick them up as fast as he could; the dogs barked and galloped about, overjoyed at being once more on shore; and Juno smiled as she looked around her, saying to Ready, "What a nice place!"

"Now, Mr Seagrave, I'll remain on shore with you a little. First, we'll load the musket in case of need, and then you can put it out of the way of Tommy, who fingers everything, I observe. We will take up the sail between us. Juno, you can carry the tools; and then we can come back again for the spars, and the rope, and the other things. Come, Tommy, you can carry a shovel at all events, and that will make you of some use."

Having taken all these things to the little knoll which Ready had pointed out before, they returned for the spars; and in two trips they had carried everything there, Tommy with the second shovel on his shoulder, and very proud to be employed.

"Here are two trees which will answer our purpose pretty well," said Ready, "as they are far enough apart: we must lash the spars up to them, and then throw the sail over, and bring it down to the ground at both ends; that will be a beginning, at all events; and I will bring some more canvas on shore, to set up the other tent between these other trees, and also to shut up the two ends of both of them; then we shall have a shelter for Madam, and Juno, and the younger children, and another for William, Tommy, and ourselves. Now, sir, I'll just help you to lash the spars, and then I'll leave you to finish while I go on board again."

"But how can we reach so high, Ready?"

"Why, sir, we can manage that by first lashing a spar as high as we can conveniently reach, and then standing on that while we lash the other in its proper place. I shall bring another spar on shore, that we may do the same when we set up the other tent."

Having by this plan succeeded in lashing the spar high enough, and throwing the sail over the spar, Ready and Mr Seagrave spread it out, and found that it made a very good-sized tent.

"Now, sir, I'll return on board; in the meantime, if you can cut pegs from the brush-wood to fasten the sail down to the ground, and then with the shovel cover the bottom of it with sand to keep it down, it will be close enough when it is all finished."

"I shall do very well," replied Mr Seagrave; "Juno can help me to pull the canvas out tight when I am ready."

"Yes; and in the meantime, Juno, take a shovel, and level the inside of the tent nice and smooth, and throw out all those old cocoa-nut leaves, and look if you see any vermin lurking among them. Master Tommy, you must not run away; and you must not touch the axes, they will cut you if you do. It may be as well to say, Mr Seagrave, that should anything happen, and you require my assistance, you had better fire off the gun, and I will come on shore to you immediately."

Chapter Ten

When Ready returned on board, he first went down into the cabin to acquaint Mrs Seagrave and William with what they had done. Mrs Seagrave naturally felt anxious about her husband being on shore alone, and Ready informed her that they had agreed that if anything should occur Mr Seagrave would fire the musket. He then went down into the sail-room to get some canvas, a new topgallant sail which was there, and a palm and needles with twine. Scarcely had he got them out, and at the foot of the ladder, when the report of the musket was heard, and Mrs Seagrave rushed out of the cabin in the greatest alarm; Ready seized another musket, jumped into the boat, and pulled on shore as fast as he could. On his arrival, quite out of breath, for as he pulled on shore he had his back towards it, and could see nothing, he found Mr Seagrave and Juno busy with the tent, and Tommy sitting on the ground crying very lustily. It appeared that, while Mr Seagrave and Juno were employed, Tommy had crept away to where the musket was placed up on end against a cocoa-nut tree, and, after pulling it about some little while, had touched the trigger. The musket went off; and, as the muzzle was pointed upwards, the charge had brought down two large cocoa-nuts. Mr Seagrave, who was aware what an alarm this would produce on board the vessel, had been scolding him soundly, and now Master Tommy was crying, to prove how very penitent he was.

"I had better return on board immediately, sir, and tell Mrs Seagrave," said Ready.

"Do, pray," replied Mr Seagrave.

Ready then returned to the ship, and explained matters, and then recommenced his labour.

Having put into the boat the sailmaker's bag, with palm and needles, two mattresses, and blankets from the captain's state room, the saucepan with the beef and pork, and a spar which he towed astern, Ready found that he had as much as he could carry; but, as there was nobody but himself in it, he came on shore very well. Having, with the assistance of Mr Seagrave and Juno, got all the things up to the knoll, Ready lashed the spar up for the second tent, and then leaving them to fix it up like the other, he returned again on board. He made two other trips to the ship, bringing with him more bedding, a bag of ship's biscuits, another of potatoes, plates, knives and forks, spoons, frying-pans and other cooking utensils, and a variety of other articles. He then showed Juno how to fill up the ends of the first tent with the canvas and sails he had brought on shore, so as to inclose it all round; Juno took the needle and twine, and worked very well. Ready, satisfied that she would be able to get on without them, now said: "Mr Seagrave, we have but two hours more daylight, and it is right that Mrs Seagrave should come on shore now; so, if you please, we'll go off and fetch her and the children. I think we shall be able to do very well for the first night; and if it pleases God to give us fine weather, we may do a great deal more to-morrow."

As soon as they arrived on board, Mr Seagrave went down to his wife to propose her going on shore. She was much agitated, and very weak from her illness, but she behaved courageously notwithstanding, and, supported by her husband, gained the deck, William following with the baby, and his little sister Caroline carried by Ready. With some difficulty they were all at last placed in the boat and shoved off; but Mrs Seagrave was so ill, that her husband was obliged to support her in his arms, and William took an oar. They landed very safely, and carried Mrs Seagrave up to the tent, and laid her down on one of the mattresses. She asked for a little water.

"And I have forgotten to bring any with me: well, I am a stupid old man; but I'll go on board directly," said Ready: "to think that I should be so busy in bringing other things on shore and forget the greatest necessary in life! The fact is, I intended to look for it on the island as soon as I could, as it would save a great deal of trouble."

Ready returned on board as fast as he could, and brought on shore two kegs of fresh water, which he and William rolled up to the tent.

Juno had completely finished her task, and Mrs Seagrave having drunk some water, declared that she was much better.

"I shall not return on board any more to-night," said Ready, "I feel tired—very tired indeed."

"You must be," replied Mr Seagrave; "do not think of doing any more."

"And I haven't touched food this day, or even quenched my thirst," replied Ready, sitting down.

"You are ill, are you not, Ready?" said William.

"A little faint, William; I'm not so young as I was. Could you give me a little water?"

"Stop, William, I will," said Mr Seagrave, taking up a tin can which had been filled for his wife: "here, Ready, drink this."

"I shall be better soon, sir; I'll just lie down a little, and then I'll have a biscuit and a little meat."

Poor old Ready was indeed quite tired out; but he ate something, and felt much revived. Juno was very busy; she had given the children some of the salt meat and biscuit to eat. The baby, and Tommy, and Caroline had been put to bed, and the second tent was nearly ready.

"It will do very well for to-night, Juno," said Mr Seagrave; "we have done work enough for this day."

"Yes, sir," replied Ready, "and I think we ought to thank God for his mercies to us before we go to sleep."

"You remind me of my duty, Ready; let us thank him for his goodness, and pray to him for his protection before we go to sleep."

Mr Seagrave then offered up a prayer of thankfulness; and they all retired to rest.

Chapter Eleven

Mr Seagrave was the first who awoke and rose from his bed on the ensuing morning. He stepped out of the tent, and looked around him. The sky was clear and brilliant. A light breeze ruffled o'er the surface of the water, and the tiny waves rippled one after another upon the white sand of the cove. To the left of the cove the land rose, forming small hills, behind which appeared the continuation of the cocoa-nut groves. To the right, a low ridge of coral rocks rose almost as a wall from the sea, and joined the herbage and brushwood at about a hundred paces, while the wreck of the Pacific, lying like some huge stranded monster, formed the prominent feature in the landscape. The sun was powerful where its beams could penetrate; but where Mr Seagrave stood, the cocoa-nuts waved their feathery leaves to the wind, and offered an impervious shade. A feeling of the extreme beauty of the scene, subdued by the melancholy created by the sight of the wrecked vessel, pervaded the mind of Mr Seagrave as he meditated over it.

"Yes," thought he, "if, tired with the world and its anxieties, I had sought an abode of peace and beauty, it would have been on a spot like this. How lovely is the scene!—what calm—what content—what a sweet sadness does it create! How mercifully have we been preserved when all hope appeared to be gone; and how bountifully have we been provided for, now that we have been saved,—and yet I have dared to repine, when I ought to be full of gratitude! May God forgive me! Wife, children, all safe, nothing to regret but a few worldly goods and a seclusion from the world for a time—yes, but for how long a time—What! rebellious still!—for the time that it shall please God in his wisdom to ordain." Mr Seagrave turned back to his tent. William, Tommy, and old Ready still remained fast asleep. "Excellent old man!" thought Mr Seagrave. "What a heart of oak is hid under that rugged bark!—Had it not been for his devotion where might I and all those dear helpless creatures have been now?"

The dogs, who had crept into the tent and laid themselves down upon the mattresses by the side of William and Tommy, now fawned upon Mr Seagrave. William woke up with their whining, and having received a caution from his father not to wake Ready, he dressed himself and came out.

"Had I not better call Juno, father?" said William; "I think I can, without waking mamma, if she is asleep."

"Then do, if you can, my boy; and I will see what cooking utensils Ready has brought on shore."

William soon returned to his father, stating that his mother was in a sound sleep, and that Juno had got up without waking her or the two children.

"Well, we'll see if we cannot get some breakfast ready for them, William. Those dry cocoa-nut leaves will make an excellent fire."

"But, father, how are we to light the fire? we have no tinder-box or matches."

"No; but there are other ways, William, although, in most of them, tinder is necessary. The savages can produce fire by rubbing a soft piece of wood against a hard one. But we have gunpowder; and we have two ways of igniting gunpowder—one is by a flint and steel, and the other is by collecting the sun's rays into one focus by a magnifying-glass."

"But, father, when we have lighted the fire, what have we to cook? we have no tea or coffee."

"No, I do not think we have," replied Mr Seagrave.

"But we have potatoes, father."

"Yes, William, but don't you think it would be better if we made our breakfast off the cold beef and pork and ship's biscuit for once, and not use the potatoes? we may want them all to plant, you know. But why should we not go on board of the ship ourselves? you can pull an oar pretty well, and we must all learn to work now, and not leave everything for poor old Ready to do. Come, William."

Mr Seagrave then went down to the cove; the little boat was lying on the beach, just lifted by the rippling waves; they pushed her off, and got into her. "I know where the steward kept the tea and coffee, father," said William, as they pulled on board; "mamma would like some for breakfast, I'm sure, and I'll milk the goats for baby."

Although they were neither of them very handy at the oar, they were soon alongside of the ship; and, having made the boat fast, they climbed on board.

William first went down to the cabin for the tea and coffee, and then left his father to collect other things while he went to milk the goats, which he did in a tin pan. He then poured the milk into a bottle, which he had washed out, that it might not be spilt, and went back to his father.

"I have filled these two baskets full of a great many things, William, which will be very acceptable to your mamma. What else shall we take?"

"Let us take the telescope, at all events, father; and let us take a whole quantity of clothes—they will please mamma: the clean ones are all in the drawers—we can bring them up in a sheet; and then, father, let us bring some of the books on shore; and I'm sure mamma will long for her Bible and prayer-book;—here they are."

"You are a good boy, William," replied Mr Seagrave. "I will now take those things up to the boat, and then return for the rest."

In a short time everything was put into the boat, and they pulled on shore again. They found Juno, who had been washing herself, waiting for them at the cove, to assist to take up the things.

"Well, Juno, how do you find yourself this morning?"

"Quite well, massa," said Juno: and then pointing to the clear water, she said, "Plenty fish here."

"Yes, if we only had lines," replied Mr Seagrave. "I think Ready has both hooks and lines somewhere. Come, Juno, take up this bundle of linen to your tent: we can manage all the rest."

When they arrived at the tent they found that every one was awake except Ready, who appeared still to sleep very sound. Mrs Seagrave had passed a very good night, and felt herself much refreshed. William made some touch-paper, which he lighted with one of the glasses from the telescope, and they soon had a good fire. Mr Seagrave went to the beach, and procured three large stones to rest the saucepan on; and in half an hour the water was boiling and the tea made.

Chapter Twelve

Juno had taken the children down to the cove, and, walking out into the water up to her knees, had dipped them in all over, as the shortest way of washing them, and had then dressed them and left them with their mother, while she assisted William to get the cups and saucers and plates for breakfast. Everything was laid out nice and tidy between the two tents, and then William proposed that he should awaken Ready.

"Yes, my boy, you may as well now—he will want his breakfast."

William went and pushed Ready on the shoulder. "Ready, have you had sleep enough?" said William, as the old man sat up.

"Yes, William. I have had a good nap, I expect; and now I will get up, and see what I can get for breakfast for you all."

"Do," replied William, laughing.

Ready was soon dressed, for he had only taken off his jacket when he lay down. He put it on, and came out of the tent; when, to his astonishment, he found the whole party (Mrs Seagrave having come out with the children) standing round the breakfast, which was spread on the ground.

"Good-morning, Ready!" said Mrs Seagrave, extending her hand. Mr Seagrave also shook hands with him.

"You have had a good long sleep, Ready," said Mr Seagrave, "and I would not waken you after your fatigue of yesterday."

"I thank you, sir; and I am glad to see that Madam is so well: and I am not sorry to see that you can do so well without me," continued Ready, smiling.

"Indeed, but we cannot, I'm afraid," replied Mrs Seagrave; "had it not been for you and your kindness, where should we have been now?"

"We can get a breakfast ready without you," said Mr Seagrave; "but without you, I think we never should have required another breakfast by this time. But we will tell Ready all we have done while we eat our breakfast: now, my dear, if you please." Mrs Seagrave then read a chapter from the Bible, and afterwards they all knelt down while Mr Seagrave offered up a prayer.

While they were at breakfast, William told Ready how they had gone on board, and what they had brought on shore, and he also mentioned how Juno had dipped all the children in the sea.

"But Juno must not do that again," replied Ready, "until I have made all safe; you know that there are plenty of sharks about these islands, and it is very dangerous to go into the water."

"Oh, what an escape they have had!" cried Mrs Seagrave, shuddering.

"It's very true," continued Ready; "but they don't keep so much to the windward of the islands where we are at present; but still that smooth cove is a very likely place for them to come into; so it's just as well not to go in again, Juno, until I have time to make a place for you to bathe in in safety. As soon as we can get as much as we want from the ship, we must decide whether we shall stay here or not."

"Stay here or not, Ready!—what do you mean?"

"Why, we have not yet found any water, and that is the first necessary of life—if there is no water on this side of the island, we must pitch our tents somewhere else."

"That's very true," replied Mr Seagrave; "I wish we could find time to explore a little."

"So we can, sir; but we must not lose this fine weather to get a few things from the ship. We had better go now. You and William can remain on board to collect the things, and I will land them on the beach for Juno to bring up."

The whole day was spent in landing every variety of article which they thought could be useful. All the small sails, cordage, twine, canvas, small casks, saws, chisels, and large nails, and elm and oak plank, were brought on shore before dinner. After they had taken a hearty dinner, the cabin tables and chairs, all their clothes, some boxes of candles, two bags of coffee, two of rice, two more of biscuits, several pieces of beef and pork and bags of flour, some more water, the grindstone, and Mrs Seagrave's medicine-chest were landed. When Ready came off again, he said, "Our poor boat is getting very leaky, and will not take much more on shore without being repaired; and Juno has not been able to get half the things up—they are too heavy for one person. I think we shall do pretty well now, Mr Seagrave; and we had better, before it is dark, get all the animals on shore. I don't much like to trust them to swim on shore, but they are awkward things in a boat. We'll try a pig, at all events; and while I get one up, do you and William tie the legs of the fowls, and put them into the boat; as for the cow, she cannot be brought on shore, she is still lying down, and, I expect, won't get up again any more; however, I have given her plenty of hay, and if she don't rise, why I will kill her, and we can salt her down."

Ready went below, and the squealing of the pig was soon heard; he came on deck with it hanging over his back by the hind legs, and threw it into the sea over the gunnel: the pig floundered at first; but after a few seconds, turned its head away from the ship and swam for the shore.

"He goes ashore straight enough," said Ready, who, with Mr Seagrave and William, was watching the animal; but a minute afterwards, Ready exclaimed:

"I thought as much—we've lost him!"

"How?" replied Mr Seagrave.

"D'ye see that black thing above water pushing so fast to the animal?— that's the back fin of a shark, and he will have the poor thing—there, he's got him!" said Ready, as the pig disappeared under the water with a heavy splash. "Well, he's gone; better the pig than your little children, Mr Seagrave."

"Yes, indeed, God be praised!—that monster might have been close to them at the time that Juno took them into the water."

"He was not far off; I reckon," replied Ready. "We'll go down now and tie the legs of the other four pigs, and bring them up; with what's already in the boat they will be a good load."

As soon as the pigs were in the boat, Ready sculled it on shore, while Mr Seagrave and William brought up the goats and sheep ready for the next trip. Ready soon returned. "Now this will be our last trip for to-day, and, if I am any judge of the weather, our last trip for some days; it is banking up very thick in the offing. This trip we'll be able to put into the boat a bag of corn for the creatures, in case we require it, and then we may say good-bye to the ship for a day or two at least."

They then all got into the boat, which was very deeply laden, for the corn was heavy, but they got safe on shore, although they leaked very much. Having landed the goats and sheep, William led them up to the tent, where they remained very quietly; the pigs had run away, and so had the fowls.

"That's what I call a good day's work, Mr Seagrave," said Ready; "the little boat has done its duty well; but we must not venture in her again until I have put her into a little better condition."

They were not at all sorry, after their hard day's work, to find that Juno had prepared coffee for them; and while they were drinking it, they narrated to Mrs Seagrave the tragically death of the poor pig by the shark.

Poor Juno appeared quite frightened at the danger which the children had been in, even now that it was all over.

"We shall have plenty to do here to-morrow," observed Mr Seagrave, "in getting things into their places."

"We shall have plenty to do for some time, I expect," replied Ready. "In two months, or thereabouts, we shall have the rainy season come on, and we must be under cover before that time, if we possibly can."

"What's the first thing we must do, Ready?" inquired Mr Seagrave.

"To-morrow we had better fix up another tent or two, to stow away all the articles we have brought on shore: that will be one good day's work; we shall then know where to lay our hands upon everything, and see what we want."

"That's very true; and what shall we do then?"

"Why then, sir, I think we must make a little expedition to explore the island, and find out where we must build our house."

"Can we build a house?" said William.

"Oh, yes, sir, and with more ease than you would think. There's no tree so valuable as the cocoa-nut tree; and the wood is so light that we can easily move it about."

"Why, what are the great merits of the cocoa-nut tree?" said Mrs Seagrave.

"I'll tell you, madam: in the first place, you have the wood to build the house with; then you have the bark with which you can make ropes and lines, and fishing-nets if you please; then you have the leaves for thatching your house; then you have the fruit, which, as a nut, is good to eat, and very useful in cooking; and in the young nut is the milk, which is also very wholesome; then you have the oil to burn, and the shell to make cups of, if you haven't any, and then you can draw toddy from the tree, which is very pleasant to drink when fresh, but will make you tipsy if it is kept too long. There is no tree which yields so many useful things to man, for it supplies him with almost everything."

"At all events, we've plenty of them," said William.

"Yes, William, there's no want of them; and I am glad of it, for had there been but few, I should not have liked to destroy them. People might be wrecked here, as well as ourselves, and without the good fortune that we have had in getting so many necessaries on shore; and they might be obliged to depend wholly upon the cocoa-nut trees for their support."

Chapter Thirteen

When breakfast was over the next morning, Ready observed, "Now, Mr Seagrave, we must hold a council of war, and decide upon an exploring party for to-morrow; and, when we have settled that, we will find some useful way of employing ourselves for the rest of the day. The first question is, of whom is the party to consist?—and upon that I wish to hear your opinion."

"Why, Ready," replied Mr Seagrave, "it appears to me that you and I should go."

"Surely not both of you, my dear," interrupted Mrs Seagrave. "You can do without my husband, can you not, Ready?"

"I certainly should have liked to have Mr Seagrave to advise with, ma'am," replied Ready; "but still I have thought upon it, and do not think that William would be quite sufficient protection for you; or, at all events, you would not feel that he was, which is much the same thing; and so, if Mr Seagrave has no objection, it would perhaps be better that he remained with you."

"Would you go alone, then, Ready?" said Mr Seagrave.

"No, sir, I do not think that would be right either,—some accident might happen; there is no saying what might happen, although there is every appearance of safety. I should like, therefore, to have some one with me; the question is, whether it be William or Juno?"

"Take me," said Tommy.

"Take you, Tommy!" said Ready, laughing; "then I must take Juno to take care of you. No; I think they cannot spare you. Your mamma will want you when we are gone; you are so useful in gathering wood for the fire, and taking care of your little sister and brother, that your mother cannot part with you; so I must have either Juno or William."

"And which would you prefer, Ready?" said Mrs Seagrave.

"William, certainly, ma'am, if you will let him go with me, as you could ill spare the girl."

"Indeed, I do not like it; I would rather lose Juno for a time," replied Mrs Seagrave.

"My dear wife," said Mr Seagrave, "recollect how Providence has preserved us in such awful dangers—how we are landed in safety. And now, will you not put trust in that Providence, when the dangers are, as I trust, only imaginary?"

"I was wrong, my dear husband; but sickness and suffering have made me, I fear, not only nervous and frightened, but selfish: I must and will shake it off. Hitherto I have only been a clog and an incumbrance to you; but I trust I shall soon behave better, and make myself useful. If you think, then, that it would be better that you should go instead of William, I am quite content. Go, then, with Ready, and may Heaven protect you both!"

"No, ma'am," replied Ready, "William will do just as well. Indeed, I would go by myself with pleasure; but we know not what the day may bring forth. I might be taken ill—I might hurt myself—I am an old man, you know; and then I was thinking that if any accident was to happen to me, you might miss me—that's all."

"Pardon me," replied Mrs Seagrave; "a mother is foolish at times."

"Over-anxious, ma'am, perhaps, but not foolish," replied Ready.

"Well, then, William shall go with you, Ready;—that point's settled," observed Mr Seagrave: "what is the next?"

"The next is to prepare for our journey. We must take some provisions and water with us, a gun and some ammunition, a large axe for me, and one of the hatchets for William; and, if you please, Romulus and Remus had better come with us. Juno, put a piece of beef and a piece of pork into the pot. William, will you fill four quart bottles with water, while I sew up a knapsack out of canvas for each of us?"

"And what shall I do, Ready?" said Mr Seagrave.

"Why, sir, if you will sharpen the axe and the hatchet on the grindstone, it would be of great service, and Tommy can turn it, he is so fond of work."

Tommy jumped up directly; he was quite strong enough to turn the grindstone, but he was much fonder of play than work; but as Ready had said that he was fond of it, he wished to prove that such was the case, and worked very hard. Before they went to prayers and retired for the night, the axe was sharpened, the knapsacks made, and everything else ready.

"When do you intend to start, Ready?" said Mr Seagrave.

"Why, sir, I should like to get off at the dawn of day, when the heat is not so great."

"And when do you intend to come back?" said Mrs Seagrave.

"Why, madam, we have provisions enough for three days: if we start to-morrow morning, which is Wednesday, I hope to be back some time on Friday evening; but I won't be later than Saturday morning if I can help it."

"Good-night—and good-bye, mother," said William, "for I shall not see you to-morrow!"

"God bless and protect you, my dear child!" replied Mrs Seagrave. "Take care of him, Ready, and good-bye to you till we meet."

Mrs Seagrave went into the tent to hide the tears which she could not suppress.

Chapter Fourteen

Ready was up before the sun had appeared, and he awakened William. The knapsacks had been already packed, with two bottles of water in each, wrapped round with cocoa-nut leaves, to prevent their breaking, and the beef and pork divided between each knapsack. Ready's, which was larger than William's, held the biscuit and several other things which Ready had prepared in case they might require them.

As soon as the knapsacks were on, Ready took the axe and gun, and asked William if he thought he could carry a small spade on his shoulder, which they had brought on shore along with the shovels. William replied that he could; and the dogs, who appeared to know they were going, were all ready standing by them. Then, just as the sun rose, they turned into the cocoa-nut grove, and were soon out of sight of the tents.

"Now, William, do you know," said Ready, stopping after they had walked twenty yards, "by what means we may find our way back again; for you see this forest of trees is rather puzzling, and there is no path to guide us?"

"No, I am sure I cannot tell; I was thinking of the very same thing when you spoke; and of Tom Thumb, who strewed peas to find his way back, but could not do it, because the birds picked them all up."

"Well, Tom Thumb did not manage well, and we must try to do better; we must do as the Americans always do in their woods,—we must *blaze* the trees."

"Blaze them! what, set fire to them?" replied William.

"No, no, William. Blaze is a term they use when they cut a slice of the bark off the trunk of a tree, just with one blow of a sharp axe, as a mark to find their way back again. They do not *blaze* every tree, but about every tenth tree as they go along, first one to the right, and then one to the left, which is quite sufficient; and it is very little trouble,—they do it as they walk along, without stopping. So now we'll begin: you take the other side, it will be more handy for you to have your hatchet in your right hand; I can use my left. See now—just a slice off the bark—the weight of the axe does it almost."

"What an excellent plan!" observed William.

"But I have another friend in my pocket," replied Ready, "and I must use him soon."

"What is that?"

"Poor Captain Osborn's pocket-compass. You see, William, the *blazing* will direct us how to go back again; but it will not tell us what course we are now to steer. At present, I know we are going right, as I can see through the wood behind us; but by and by we shall not be able, and then I must make use of the compass."

"I understand that very well; but tell me, Ready, why do you bring the spade with us—what will be the use of it? You did not say yesterday that you were going to bring me."

"No, William, I did not, as I did not like to make your mother anxious; but the fact is, I am very anxious myself as to whether there is any water on this island; if there is not, we shall have to quit it sooner or later, for although we may get water by digging in the sand, it would be too brackish to use for any time, and would make us all ill. Very often there will be water if you dig for it, although it does not show above-ground; and therefore I brought the spade."

"You think of everything, Ready."

"No, I do not, William; but, in our present situation, I think of more things than perhaps your father and mother would: they have never known what it is to be put to their shifts; but a man like me, who has been all his life at sea, and who has been wrecked, and suffered hardships and difficulties, and has been obliged to think or die, has a greater knowledge, not only from his own sufferings, but by hearing how others have acted when they were in distress. Necessity sharpens a man's wits; and it is very curious what people do contrive when they are compelled to do so, especially seamen."

"And where are we going to now, Ready?"

"Right to the leeward side of the island."

"Why do you call it the leeward side of the island?"

"Because among these islands the winds almost always blow one way; we landed on the windward side; the wind is at our back; now put up your finger, and you will feel it even among the trees."

"No, I cannot," replied William, as he held up his finger.

"Then wet your finger, and try again."

William wet his finger, and held it up again. "Yes, I feel it now," said he; "but why is that?"

"Because the wind blows against the wet, and you feel the cold."

As Ready said this the dogs growled, then started forward and barked.

"What can be there?" cried William.

"Stand still, William," replied Ready, cocking his gun, "and I will go forward to see." Ready advanced cautiously with the gun to his hip. The dogs barked more furiously; and at last, out of a heap of cocoa-nut leaves collected together, burst all the pigs which had been brought on shore, grunting and galloping away as fast as they could, with the dogs in pursuit of them.

"It's only the pigs," said Ready, smiling; "I never thought I should be half-frightened by a tame pig. Here, Romulus! here, Remus! come back!" continued Ready, calling to the dogs. "Well, William, this is our first adventure."

"I hope we shall not meet with any one more dangerous," replied William, laughing; "but I must say that I was alarmed."

"No wonder; for, although not likely, it is possible there may be wild animals on this island, or even savages; but being alarmed is one thing, and being afraid is another: a man may be alarmed, and stand his ground; but a man that is afraid will run away."

"I do not think I shall ever run away and leave you, Ready, if there is danger."

"I'm sure you will not; but still you must not be rash; and now we will go on again, as soon as I have uncocked my gun. I have seen more accidents happen from people cocking their guns, and forgetting to uncock them afterwards, than you can have any idea of. Recollect, also, until you want to fire, never cock your gun."

Ready and William continued their way through the cocoa-nut grove for more than an hour longer, marking the trees as they went along; they then sat down to take their breakfast.

"Don't give the dogs any water, William, nor any of the salt meat; give them biscuit only."

"But they are very thirsty; may not I give them a little?"

"No: we shall want it all ourselves, in the first place; and, in the next, I wish them to be thirsty. And, William, take my advice, and only drink a small quantity of water at a time. The more you drink, the more you want."

"Then I should not eat so much salt meat."

"Very true; the less you eat the better, unless we find water, and fill our bottles again."

"But we have our axes, and can always cut down a cocoa-nut, and get the milk from the young nuts."

"Very true; and fortunate it is that we have that to resort to; but still we could not do very well on cocoa-nut milk alone, even if it were to be procured all the year round. Now we will go on if you do not feel tired."

"Not in the least; I am tired of seeing nothing but the stems of cocoa-nut trees, and shall be glad when we are through the wood."

"Then the faster we walk the better," said Ready; "as far as I can judge, we must be about half-way across now."

Ready and William recommenced their journey; and, after half-an-hour's walking, they found that the ground was not so level as it had been—sometimes they went gradually up hill, at others down.

"I am very glad to find the island is not so flat here; we have a better chance of finding water."

"It is much steeper before us," replied William; "it's quite a hill."

The ground now became more undulating, although still covered with cocoa-nut trees, even thicker together than before. They continued their march, occasionally looking at the compass, until William showed symptoms of weariness, for the wood had become more difficult to get through than at first.

"How many miles do you think we have walked, Ready?" said Willy.

"About eight, I should think."

"Not more than eight?"

"No; I do not think that we have made more than two miles an hour: it's slow work, travelling by compass and marking the trees; but I think the wood looks lighter before us, now that we are at the top of this hill."

"It does, Ready; I fancy I can see the blue sky again."

"Your eyes are younger than mine, William, and perhaps you may—however, we shall soon find out."

They now descended into a small hollow, and then went up hill again. As soon as they arrived at the top, William cried out, "The sea, Ready! there's the sea!"

"Very true, William, and I'm not sorry for it."

"I thought we never should get out of that nasty wood again," said William, as he impatiently pushed on, and at last stood clear of the cocoa-nut grove. Ready soon joined him, and they surveyed the scene before them in silence.

Chapter Fifteen

"Oh! how beautiful!" exclaimed William, at last; "I'm sure mamma would like to live here. I thought the other side of the island very pretty, but it's nothing compared to this."

"It is very beautiful," replied Ready, thoughtfully.

A more lovely scene could scarcely be imagined. The cocoa-nut grove terminated about a quarter of a mile from the beach, very abruptly, for there was a rapid descent for about thirty feet from where they stood to the land below, on which was a mixture of little grass knolls and brushwood, to about fifty yards from the water's edge, where it was met with dazzling white sand, occasionally divided by narrow ridges of rock which ran inland. The water was a deep blue, except where it was broken into white foam on the reefs, which extended for miles from the beach, and the rocks of which now and then showed themselves above water. On the rocks were perched crowds of gannets and men-of-war birds, while others wheeled in the air, every now and then darting down into the blue sea, and bringing up in their bills a fish out of the shoals which rippled the water, or bounded clear of it in their gambols. The form of the coast was that of a horse-shoe bay—two points of land covered with shrubs extending far out on each side. The line of the horizon, far out at sea, was clear and unbroken.

Ready remained for some time without speaking; he scanned the horizon right and left, and then he turned his eyes along the land. At last William said:

"What are you thinking of, Ready?"

"Why, I am thinking that we must look for water as fast as we can."

"But why are you so anxious?"

"Because I can see no island to leeward of us as I expected, and therefore there is less chance of getting off this island; and this bay, although very beautiful, is full of reefs, and I see no inlet, which makes it awkward for many reasons. But we cannot judge at first sight. Let us now sit down and take our dinner, and after that we will explore a little."

Ready cut two wide marks in the stems of the cocoa-nut trees, and then descended with William to the low ground, where they sat down to eat their dinner. As soon as their meal was finished they first walked down to the water's edge, and Ready turned his eyes inland to see if he could discover any little ravine or hollow which might be likely to contain fresh water. "There are one or two places there," observed Ready, pointing to them with his finger, "where the water has run down in the rainy season: we must examine them carefully, but not now. I want to find out whether there is any means of getting our little boat through this reef of rocks, or otherwise we shall have very hard work (if we change our abode to this spot) to bring all our stores through that wood; so we will pass the rest of this day in examining the coast, and to-morrow we will try for fresh water."

"Look at the dogs, Ready, they are drinking the sea-water, poor things!"

"They won't drink much of that, I expect; you see they don't like it already."

"How beautiful the corals are—look here, they grow like little trees under the water,—and look here, here is really a flower in bloom growing on that rock just below the water."

"Put your finger to it, Master William," said Ready.

William did so, and the flower, as he called it, immediately shut up.

"Why, it's flesh, and alive!"

"Yes, it is; I have often seen them before: they call them sea-anemones—they are animals; but I don't know whether they are shell-fish or not. Now, let us walk out to the end of this point of land, and see if we can discover any opening in the reef. The sun is going down, and we shall not have more than an hour's daylight, and then we must look out for a place to sleep in."

"But what is that?" cried William, pointing to the sand—"that round dark thing?"

"That's what I'm very glad to see, William: it's a turtle. They come up about this time in the evening to drop their eggs, and then they bury them in the sand."

"Can't we catch them?"

"Yes, we can catch them if we go about it quietly; but you must take care not to go behind them, or they will throw such a shower of sand upon you, with their hind flappers or fins, that they would blind you and escape at the same time. The way to catch them is to get at their heads and turn them over on their backs by one of the fore-fins, and then they cannot turn back again."

"Let us go and catch that one."

"I should think it very foolish to do so, as we could not take it away, and it would die to-morrow from the heat of the sun."

"I did not think of that, Ready; if we come to live here, I suppose we shall catch them whenever we want them."

"No, we shall not, for they only come on shore in the breeding-season; but we will make a turtle pond somewhere which they cannot get out of, but which the sea flows into; and then when we catch them we will put them into it, and have them ready for use as we require them."

"That will be a very good plan," replied William.

They now continued their walk, and, forcing their way through the brushwood which grew thick upon the point of land, soon arrived at the end of it.

"What is that out there?" said William, pointing to the right of where they stood.

"That is another island, which I am very glad to see even in that direction, although it will not be so easy to gain it, if we are obliged to leave this for want of water. It is a much larger island than this, at all events," continued Ready, scanning the length of the horizon, along which he could see the tops of the trees. — "Well, we have done very well for our first day, so we will go and look for a place to lie down and pass the night."

They returned to the high ground where the cocoa-nut grove ended, and collecting together several branches and piles of leaves, made a good soft bed under the trees.

"And now we'll go to bed. Look, William, at the long shadow of the trees the sun has nearly set."

"Shall I give the dogs some water now, Ready? See, poor Remus is licking the sides of the bottles."

"No, do not give them any: it appears to be cruel, but I want the intelligence of the poor animals to-morrow, and the want of water will make them very keen, and we shall turn it to good account. So now, William, we must not forget to return thanks to a merciful God, and to beg his care over us for this night. We little know what the day may bring forth. Good-night!"

Chapter Sixteen

William slept as sound as if he had been on shore in England upon a soft bed in a warm room—so did old Ready; and when they awoke the next morning it was broad daylight. The poor dogs were suffering for want of water, and it pained William to see them with their tongues out, panting and whining as they looked up to him. "Now, William," said Ready, "shall we take our breakfast before we start, or have a walk first?"

"Ready, I cannot really drink a drop of water myself, and I am thirsty, unless you give a little to these poor dogs."

"I pity the poor dumb creatures as much as you do, Master Willy; it is kindness to ourselves and them too, which makes me refuse it to them. However, if you like, we will take a walk first, and see if we can find any water. Let us first go to the little dell to the right, and if we do not succeed, we will try farther on where the water has run down during the rainy season." William was very glad to go, and away they went, followed by the dogs, Ready having taken up the spade, which he carried on his shoulder. They soon came to the dell, and the dogs put their noses to the ground, and snuffed about. Ready watched them; at last they lay down panting.

"Let us go on," said Ready, thoughtfully; they went on to where the run of water appeared to have been—the dogs snuffed about more eagerly than before.

"You see, William, these poor dogs are now so eager for water, that if there is any, they will find it out where we never could. I don't expect water above-ground, but there may be some below it. This beach is hardly far enough from the water's edge, or I should try in the sand for it."

"In the sand—but would it not be salt?" replied William.

"No, not if at a good distance from the sea-beach; for you see, William, the sand by degrees filters the sea-water fresh, and very often when the sand runs in a long way from the high-water mark, if you dig down, you will find good fresh water, at other times it is a little brackish, but still fit for use."

"Look, Ready, at Romulus and Remus—how hard they are digging with their paws there in the hollow."

"Thanks to Heaven that they are! You don't know how happy you have made me feel: for, to tell you the truth, I was beginning to be alarmed."

"But why do they dig?"

"Because there is water there, poor animals. Now you see the advantage of having kept them in pain for a few hours; it is in all probability the saving of all of us, for we must either have found water or quitted this island. Now let us help the poor dogs with the spade, and they shall soon be rewarded for their sufferings."

Ready walked quickly to where the dogs continued digging: they had already got down to the moist earth, and were so eagerly at work, that it was with difficulty he could get them out of his way to use his spade. He had not dug two feet before the water trickled down, and in four or five minutes the dogs had sufficient to plunge their noses in, and to drink copiously.

"Look at them! how they enjoy it! I don't think any Israelite felt more grateful when Moses struck the rock than I do now, William. This was the one thing wanting, but it was the one thing indispensable. Now we have everything we can wish for on this island, and if we are only content, we may be happy—ay, much happier than are those who are worrying themselves to heap up riches, not knowing who shall gather them. See, the poor animals have had enough at last. Now, shall we go back to breakfast?"

"Yes," replied William: "I shall enjoy it now, and have a good drink of water myself."

"That is a plenteous spring, depend upon it," said Ready, as they walked back to where they had slept and left their knapsacks; "but we must clear it out further up among the trees, where the sun cannot reach it, and then it will be cool, and not be dried up. We shall have plenty of work for the next year at least, if we remain here. Where we are now will be a capital spot to build our house on."

As soon as the breakfast was over, Ready said, "Now we must go down and explore the other point, for you see, William, I have not yet found a passage through the reef, and as our little boat must come round this side of the island, it is at the point on this side that I must try to find an entrance. When I was on the opposite point it did appear to me that the water was not broken close to this point; and should there be a passage we shall be very fortunate."

They soon arrived at the end of the point of land, and found that Ready was not wrong in his supposition; the water was deep, and there was a passage many yards wide. The sea was so smooth, and the water so clear, that they could see down to the rocky bottom, and watched the fish as they darted along. "Look there!" said Willy, pointing out about fifty yards from the beach, "a great shark, Ready!"

"Yes, I see him, sir," replied Ready: "there's plenty of them here, depend upon it; and you must be very careful how you get into the water: the sharks always keep to the leeward of the island, and for one where Juno bathed your little brother, you will find fifty here. I'm quite satisfied now, William, we shall do very well, and all we have now to think of is moving away from the other side of the island as fast as possible."

"Shall we go back to-day?"

"Yes, I think so, for we shall only be idle here. It is not twelve o'clock, I should think, and we shall have plenty of time. I think we had better start at once; we will leave the spade and axe here, for it is no use taking them back again. The musket I will take along. But first let us go back and look at the spring, and see how the water flows."

As they walked along the edge of the sandy beach they found the sea-birds hovering close to them: all of a sudden a large shoal of fish threw themselves high and dry on the sand, and they were followed by several of a larger size, which also lay flapping on the beach, while the sea-birds, darting down close to the feet of William and Ready, and seizing up the fish, flew away with them.

"How very strange!" said William, surprised.

"Yes, sir; but you see how it is—the small fish were chased by the larger ones, which are bonettas, and in their fright ran upon the beach. These bonettas were so anxious to catch them, that they came on shore also, and then the gannets picked them all up."

They found the hole which Ready had dug quite full of water, and, tasting it, it proved very sweet and good. Overjoyed at this discovery, they covered up the articles they agreed to leave behind them with some boughs under the notched cocoa-nut trees, and, calling the dogs, set off on their journey back again to the cove.

Chapter Seventeen

Guided by the marks made on the trees, William and Ready made rapid progress in their return, and in less than two hours found themselves almost clear of the wood which had taken them nearly eight hours to force their way through the day before.

"I feel the wind now, Ready," observed William, "and we must be nearly through the wood; but it appears to me to be very dark."

"I was just thinking the same," replied Ready. "I should not wonder if there is a storm brewing up; and if so, the sooner we are back again the better."

As they proceeded, the rustling and waving of the boughs of the trees, and ever and anon a gust of wind, followed by a moaning and creaking sound, proved that such was the fact; and as they emerged from the grove, they perceived that the sky, as it became visible to them, was of one dark leaden hue, and no longer of the brilliant blue which it usually had presented to their sight.

"There is indeed a gale coming on," said Ready, as they cleared the wood: "let us go on to the tents as fast as possible, for we must see that all is as secure as we can make it."

The dogs now bounded forward; and at their appearance at the tents Mr Seagrave and Juno came out, and seeing Ready and William advancing, made known the welcome tidings to Mrs Seagrave, who, with the children, had remained within. In a moment more William was pressed in his mother's arms.

"I am glad that you are come back, Ready," said Mr Seagrave, shaking him by the hand after he had embraced William, "for I fear that bad weather is coming on."

"I am sure of it," replied Ready, "and we must expect a blusterous night. This will be one of the storms which are forerunners of the rainy season. However, we have good news for you, and must only take this as a warning to hasten our departure as soon as possible. We shall have fine weather after this for a month or so, although we must expect a breeze now and then. But we must work hard and do our best; and now, if you please, you and Juno, William and I, will go and haul up the boat as far from the beach as we possibly can, for the waves will be high and run a long way up, and our boat will be our main dependence soon."

The four went down as soon as Ready had sawed the ends of the spars which had been cut off, into three rollers, to fix under the keel; with the help afforded by them, the boat was soon hauled up high into the brushwood, where it was considered by Ready to be perfectly safe.

"I meant to have worked upon her immediately," observed Ready; "but I must wait now till the gale is over; and I did hope to have got on board once more, and looked after some things which I have since remembered would have been useful; but I strongly suspect," continued he, looking at the weather, "that we shall never go on board of the poor vessel again. Hear the moaning of the coming storm, sir; look how the sea-birds wheel about and scream, as if to proclaim her doom; but we must not wait here—the tents must be made more secure, for they will have to hold up against no small force of wind, if I mistake not."

Ready, assisted by Mr Seagrave, now got out some heavy canvas and lines, and commenced putting it as a double cover over the tents, to keep out the rain; they also secured the tents with guys and stays of rope, so as to prevent them being blown down; while Juno with a shovel deepened the trench which had been made round the tents, so that the water might run off more easily. During the time they were at work, Ready had made Mr Seagrave acquainted with what they had discovered and done during the exploring expedition, and the adventure with the pigs made them all laugh heartily.

As the sun went down, the weather threatened still more; the wind blew strong, and the rocky beach was lashed by the waves and white with spray, while the surf roared as it poured in and broke upon the sand in the cove. The whole family had retired to bed except Ready, who said that he would watch the weather a little before he turned in. The old man walked towards the beach, and leaned against the gunnel of the boat, and there he remained with his keen grey eye fixed upon the distance, which was now one opaque mass, except where the white foam of the waters gleamed through the darkness of the night! "Yes!" thought he; "the winds and the waves are summoned to do his bidding, and evenly do they work together—as one rises, so does the other; when one howls, the other roars in concert—hand in hand they go in their fury and their force. Had they been called up but one week since, where would have been those who have now been, as it were, intrusted to my weak help? The father, the mother, the children, the infant at the breast, and I, the grey-headed old man,—all buried fathoms deep, awaiting our summons; but they were restrained by his will, and by his will we were saved. Will those timbers which bore us here so miraculously hold together till morning? I should think not. What are the iron bolts and fastenings of weak man, compared with the force of God's elements: they will snap as yarns; and by to-morrow's dawn, the fragments of the stout ship will be washing and tossing on the wild surf. Well, it will be a kindness to us, for the waters will perform the labour which we could not; they will break up the timbers for our use, and throw on shore from the hold those articles which we could not reach with our little strength."

A sharp flash of lightning struck upon the old man's eyes, and obstructed his vision for the moment. "The storm will soon be at its height," thought he; "I will watch the tents, and see how they stand up against its force." Then the rain came pattering down, and the wind howled louder than before. In a minute or two the darkness became so intense that he could hardly find his way back to the tents. He turned round, but could not see, for he was blinded by the heavy rain. As nothing could be done, he went into the tent and sheltered himself from the storm, although he would not lie down, lest his services might be required. The others had retired to bed, but with the exception of Tommy and the children, they had not taken off their clothes.

Chapter Eighteen

The storm now raged furiously, the lightning was accompanied by loud peals of thunder, and the children awoke and cried with fright, till they were hushed to sleep again. The wind howled as it pressed with all its violence against the tents, while the rain poured off in torrents. One moment the canvas of the tents would bulge in, and the cords which held it strain and crack; at another, an eddy of wind would force out the canvas, which would flap and flap, while the rain found many an entrance. The tent in which Mrs Seagrave and the children reposed was on the outside of the others, and therefore the most exposed. About midnight the wind burst on them with greater violence than before. A loud crash was heard by Ready and Mr Seagrave, followed by the shrieks of Mrs Seagrave and Juno; the pegs of the tent had given way, and the inmates were exposed to the fury of the elements. Ready rushed out, followed by Mr Seagrave and William. So strong was the wind and beating rain, and such was the darkness, that it was with some difficulty that by their united efforts the women and children could be extricated. Tommy was the first taken up by Ready: his courage had all gone, and he was bellowing furiously. William took Albert in charge and carried him into the other tent, where Tommy sat in his wet shirt roaring most melodiously. Juno, Mrs Seagrave, and the little girl were at last carried away and taken into the other tent: fortunately no one was hurt, although the frightened children could not be pacified, and joined in chorus with Tommy. Nothing more could be done except to put the children into bed, and then the whole party sat up the remainder of the night listening to the noise of the wind, the roaring of the sea, and the loud patter of the rain against the canvas. At dawn of day, Ready went out, and found that the gale had spent its force, and had already much abated; but it was not one of those bright glorious mornings to which they had been accustomed since their arrival at the island: the sky was still dark, and the clouds were chasing each other wildly; there was neither sun nor blue sky to be seen: it still rained, but only at intervals, and the earth was soft and spongy; the little cove, but the day before so beautiful, was now a mass of foaming and tumultuous waves, and the surf was thrown many yards upon the beach: the horizon was confused—you could not distinguish the line between the water and the sky, and the whole shore of the island was lined with a white foam. Ready turned his eyes to where the ship had been fixed on the rocks: it was no longer there—the whole frame had disappeared; but the fragments of it, and the contents of the holds, were floating about in every direction, or tossing amongst the surf on the beach.

"I thought as much," said Ready, pointing to where the ship had lain, as he turned round and found that Mr Seagrave had followed him; "look, sir, this gale has broken her up entirely. This is a warning to us not to remain here any longer: we must make the most of the fine weather which we may have before the rainy season sets in."

"I agree with you, Ready," replied Mr Seagrave,—"and there is another proof of it," pointing to the tent which had been blown down. "It was a mercy that none of them were hurt."

"Very true, sir; but the gale is breaking, and we shall have fine weather to-morrow. Let us now see what we can do with the tent, while William and Juno try if they can get any breakfast."

They set to work. Ready and Mr Seagrave made it fast with fresh cords and pegs, and very soon had it all ready; but the beds and bedding were wet through. They hauled over the wet canvas, and then left it to go to their breakfast, to which Juno had summoned them.

"We need do no more at present," said Ready, "by night-time it will not be so wet, and we can handle it easier. I see a break in the sky now which promises fine weather soon. And now we had better work hard to-day, for we may save a great many things, which may be dashed to pieces on the rocks, if we do not haul them on the beach."

Chapter Nineteen

They went down to the beach. Ready first procured from the stores a good stout rope; and as the waves threw up casks and timbers of the vessel, they stopped them from being washed back again, and either rolled or hauled them up with the rope until they were safely landed. This occupied them for the major part of the day; and yet they had not collected a quarter of the articles that were in their reach, independent of the quantity which floated about out at sea and at the entrance of the cove.

"I think," said Ready, "we have done a good day's work; tomorrow we shall be able to do much more, for the sea is going down, and the sun is showing himself from the corner of that cloud. Now we will go to supper, and then see if we can make ourselves more comfortable for the night."

The tent which had not been blown down was given to Mrs Seagrave and the children, and the other was fitted up as well as it could be. The bedding being all wet, they procured some sails from the stores, which, being stowed away farther in the grove, had not suffered much from the tempest; and, spreading the canvas, they lay down, and the night passed without any disaster, for the wind was now lulled to a pleasant breeze.

The next morning the sun shone bright—the air was fresh and bracing; but a slight breeze rippled the waters, and there was little or no surf. The various fragments of the wreck were tossed by the little surf that still remained; many things were lying on the beach which had landed during the night, and many more required but a little trouble to secure them. There appeared to be a sort of in draught into the cove, as all the articles which had been floating out at sea were now gradually coming on shore in that direction. Ready and Mr Seagrave worked till breakfast-time, and had by that time saved a great many casks and packages.

After breakfast they went down again to the beach and resumed their labours. "Look, Ready; what is that?" said William, who was with them, as he pointed to a white-looking mass floating in the cove.

"That, sir, is the poor cow; and if you look again, you will see the sharks are around, making a feast of her: don't you see them?"

"Yes, I do—what a quantity!"

"Yes, there's no want of them, William; so be very careful how you get into the water, and never let Tommy go near it, for they don't care how shallow it is when they see their food. But now, sir," said Ready, "I must leave you and William to do what you can in saving any more of the wreck, while I set to and put the boat in proper repair."

Ready left them at their own employment, and went away for his tools. During this time Mr Seagrave and William occupied themselves in collecting the different articles thrown on shore, and rolling up the casks as far as they could.

As it would take some days for Ready to put the boat into proper order, Mr Seagrave determined that he would go to the other side of the island with William, that he might examine it himself; and, as Mrs Seagrave had no objection to be left with Ready and Juno, on the third day after the gale they set off. William led the way, guiding his footsteps through the grove by the blazing of the cocoa-nut trees; and in two hours they reached their destination.

"Is not this beautiful, father?" said William.

"Yes, indeed it is, my dear boy," replied Mr Seagrave. "I fancied that nothing could be more beautiful than the spot where we reside, but this surpasses it, not only in variety, but in extent."

"And now let us examine the spring, father," said William, leading the way to the ravine.

The spring was full and flowing, and the water excellent. They then directed their steps towards the sandy beach, and, having walked some time, sat down upon a coral rock.

"Who would have ever imagined, William," said Mr Seagrave, "that this island, and so many more which abound in the Pacific Ocean, could have been raised by the work of little insects not bigger than a pin's head?"

"Insects, father?" replied William.

"Yes, insects. Give me that piece of dead coral, William. Do you see that on every branch there are a hundred little holes? Well, in every one of these little holes once lived a sea-insect; and as these insects increase, so do the branches of the coral-trees."

"Yes, I understand that; but how do you make out that this island was made by them?"

"Almost all the islands in these seas have been made by the labour and increase of these small animals. The coral grows at first at the bottom of the sea, where it is not disturbed by the winds or waves: by degrees, as it increases, it advances higher and higher to the surface, till at last it comes near to the top of the water; then it is stopped in its growth by the force of the winds and waves, which break it off, and of course it never grows above the water, for if it did the animals would die."

"Then how does it become an island?"

"By very slow degrees; the time, perhaps, much depending upon chance: for instance, a log of wood floating about, and covered with barnacles, may ground upon the coral reefs; that would be a sufficient commencement, for it would remain above water, and then shelter the coral to leeward of it, until a flat rock had formed, level with the edge of the water. The sea-birds are always looking for a place to rest upon, and they would soon find it, and then their droppings would, in course of time, form a little patch above water, and other floating substances would be thrown on it; and land-birds, who are blown out to sea, might rest themselves on it, and the seeds from their stomachs, when dropped, would grow into trees or bushes."

"I understand that."

"Well then, William, you observe there is an island commenced, as it were, and, once commenced, it soon increases, for the coral would then be protected to leeward, and grow up fast. Do you observe how the coral reefs extend at this side of the island, where they are protected from the winds and waves; and how different it is on the weather side, which we have just left? Just so the little patch above water protects the corals to leeward, and there the island increases fast; for the birds not only settle on it, but they make their nests and rear their young, and so every year the soil increases; and then, perhaps, one cocoa-nut in its great outside shell at last is thrown on these little patches—it takes root, and becomes a tree, every year shedding its large branches, which are turned into mould as soon as they decay, and then dropping its nuts, which again take root and grow in this mould; and thus they continue, season after season, and year after year, until the island becomes as large and as thickly covered with trees as the one we are now standing upon. Is not this wonderful, my dear boy? Is not he a great and good God who can make such minute animals as these work his pleasure, and at the time he thinks fit produce such a beautiful island as this?"

"Indeed he is!" exclaimed William.

"We only need use our eyes, William, and we shall love as well as adore. Look at that shell—is it not beautifully marked?—could the best painter in the world equal its colouring?"

"No, indeed,—I should think not."

"And yet there are thousands of them in sight, and perhaps millions more in the water. They have not been coloured in this way to be admired, like the works of man; for this island has been till now probably without any one upon it, and no one has ever seen them. It makes no difference to Him, who has but to wish, and all is complete."

For a few minutes after this conversation, Mr Seagrave and William were both silent. Mr Seagrave then rose from where he was sitting: "Come, William, let us now find our way back again; we have three hours' daylight left, and shall be home in good time."

Chapter Twenty

Everything was now preparing for their removal to the leeward side of the island. Ready had nearly completed the boat; he had given it a thorough repair, and fitted a mast and sail. William and Mr Seagrave continued to collect and secure the various articles thrown on shore, particularly such as would be injured by their exposure to the weather: these they rolled or carried into the cocoa-nut grove, so as to be sheltered from the sun; but there were so many things thrown on shore day after day, that they hardly knew what they had: but they secured case and cask one after another, waiting for a better opportunity to examine their contents. At last they collected a great many articles together, and, with their shovels, covered them over with sand, it being impossible to get them from the beach without more time than they could spare.

Neither was Mrs Seagrave, who was now getting quite strong, or Juno, idle. They had made up everything that they could in packages, ready for moving. On the eighth day after the gale, they were ready, and it was arranged that Ready should put into the boat the bedding and canvas of one tent, and should take William with him on his expedition. Having transported this safe, he should return for a load of the most necessary articles, and then the family should walk through the grove to the other side of the island, and remain there with Mr Seagrave while Ready and William returned for the other tent; and after that, the boat should make as many trips as the weather would permit, till they had brought all the things absolutely required. It was a lovely calm morning when Ready and William pushed off in the boat, which was well loaded; and as soon as they were clear of the cove they hoisted the sail, and went away before the wind along the coast. In two hours they had run to the eastern end of the island, and hauled up close inshore: the point which ran out, and at the end of which there was an inlet, was not a mile from them, and in a very short time they had lowered the sail, and were pulling in for the sandy beach.

"You see, William, it is fortunate for us that we shall always have a fair wind when we come down loaded, and only have to pull our empty boat back again."

"Indeed it is. How many miles do you think it is from the cove to this part of the island?"

"About six or seven, not more: the island, you see, is long and narrow. Now let us get the things out and carry them up, and then we will be back to the cove long before dark."

The boat was soon unloaded, but they had some way to carry up the things. "We shall not mind such a gale as we had the other day when our tents are pitched here, William," said Ready, "for we shall be protected by the whole width of the cocoa-nut grove. We shall hardly feel the wind, although we shall the rain, for that will come down in torrents."

"I must go and see how our spring gets on," said William, "and get a drink from it."

Willy reported the spring to be up to the brim with water, and that he had never drunk water so excellent. They then pushed off the boat, and, after rowing for about two hours or more, found themselves at the entrance of the cove, and Mrs Seagrave, with Tommy by her side, waving her handkerchief to them.

They very soon pulled in to the beach, and, landing, received the congratulations of the whole party at their first successful voyage, and all expressed their delight at its having proved so much shorter than had been anticipated.

"Tommy will go next time," said Master Tommy.

"By and by, when Tommy grows a little taller," replied Ready.

"Massa Tommy, you come help me to milk the goats," said Juno.

"Yes, Tommy milk the goats," said the little urchin, running after Juno.

"You must be almost tired of eating nothing but salt meat and biscuit, ma'am," said Ready, as they sat down to their meal; "but when we are all safe on the other side of the island we hope to feed you better. At present it is hard work and hard fare."

"As long as the children are well, I care very little about it; but I must say that, after the last gale, I am as anxious as you to be on the other side of the island, especially after the account William has given me of it. It must be a paradise! When do we set off?"

"Not till the day after to-morrow, ma'am, I should think; for you see I must have another trip for the cooking utensils and the bundles which you have made up. If you will spare Juno to walk through the wood with William to-morrow, we will then have the tent ready for you and the children."

Chapter Twenty One

Old Ready had his boat loaded and had made sail for the other side of the island long before the family were up; indeed, before they were dressed he had landed his whole cargo on the beach, and was sitting down quietly taking his breakfast. As soon as he had eaten the beef and biscuit which he had taken with him, he carried up the things which he had brought, and commenced arrangements for setting up the tent, intending to await the arrival of William and Juno, that they might assist him in getting up the spars and canvas over it.

About ten o'clock William made his appearance, leading one of the goats by a string, followed by the others. Juno came after with the sheep, also holding one with a cord; the rest had very quietly joined the procession. "Here we are at last!" said William laughing; "we have had terrible work in the woods, for Nanny would run on one side of a tree when I went on the other, and then I had to let go the string. We fell in with the pigs again, and Juno gave such a squall!"

"I tink 'em wild beast," said Juno. "Ah! what a nice place! Missis will like to live here."

"Yes, it is a very nice place, Juno; and you'll be able to wash here, and never mind about saving the water."

"I am thinking," said William, "how we are to get the fowls here; they are not very wild, but still we cannot catch them."

"I'll bring them with me to-morrow, William."

"But how will you catch them?"

"Wait till they are gone to roost, and then you may catch them when you please."

"And I suppose the pigeons and the pigs must run wild?"

"The best thing we can do with them."

"Then we shall have to shoot them, I suppose?"

"Well, William, so we shall; and the pigeons also, when they have become plentiful, if we remain here so long. We shall soon be well stocked and live in plenty. But now you must help me to get the tent up and everything in order, so that your mamma may find things comfortable on her arrival, for she will be very tired, I dare say, walking through the wood."

"Mamma is much better than she was," replied William. "I think she will soon be quite strong again, especially when she comes to live at this beautiful place."

"We have a great deal of work to do, more than we can get through before the rainy season; which is a pity, but it can't helped; by this time next year we shall be more comfortable."

"Why, what have we to do besides putting up the tents and shifting over here?"

"In the first place we have to build a house, and that will take a long while. Then we ought to make a little garden, and sow the seeds which your father brought from England with him."

"Oh! that will be nice; where shall we make it, Ready?"

"We must put a fence across that point of land, and dig up all the brushwood; the mould is very good."

"Then what next?"

"Then we shall want a storehouse for all the things we have got, and all that are in the wood and on the beach: and consider what a many trips we shall have to make with the little boat to bring them all round."

"Yes, that is very true, Ready. Have we anything more to do?"

"Plenty; we have to build a turtle-pond and a fish-pond, and a bathing-place for Juno to wash the children in. But first we must make a proper well at the spring, so as to have plenty of fresh water: now there's enough for a year's hard work at least."

"Well, let us once get mamma and the children here, and we will work hard."

"I should wish very much to see it all done, William," said Ready. "I hope my life will be spared till it is done, at all events."

"But why do you say that, Ready? you are an old man, but you are strong and healthy."

"I am so now; but what does the Book say?—'In the midst of life we are in death.' You are young and healthy, and promise a long life; but who knows but you may be summoned away tomorrow. Can I, then, an old man, worn out with hardships, expect to live long? No—no, William! Still I should like to remain here as long as I can be useful, and then I trust I may depart in peace. I never wish to leave this island; and I have a kind of feeling that my bones will remain on it. God's will be done!"

For some time after Ready had finished, neither of them said a word, but continued their employment, stretching out the canvas of the tent, and fastening it down to the ground with pegs. At last William broke the silence.

"Ready, did you not say your Christian name was Masterman?"

"So it is, William."

"It is a very odd Christian name! You were called after some other person?"

"Yes, I was, William; he was a very rich man."

"Do you know, Ready, I should like very much if you will one day tell me your history—I mean your whole life, from the time you were a boy."

"Well, perhaps I may, William; for there are many parts of my life which would prove a lesson to others: but that must be after we have got through our work."

"How old are you, Ready?"

"I am turned of sixty-four; a very old age for a seaman. I could not obtain employment on board of a vessel if it were not that I am well known to several captains."

"But why do you say 'old for a seaman?'"

"Because sailors live faster than other people, partly from the hardships which they undergo, and partly from their own fault in drinking so much spirits; and then they are too often reckless and care nothing for their healths."

"But you never drink spirits now?"

"No, never, William; but in my early days I was as foolish as others. Now, Juno, you may bring in the bedding. We have two or three hours yet, William; what shall we do next?"

"Had we not better make the fireplace all ready for cooking?"

"It was what I was going to propose, if you had not. I shall be here to-morrow long before any of you, and I will take care that supper is ready on your arrival."

"I brought a bottle of water in my knapsack," replied William, "not so much for the water, as because I want to milk the goats and take back the milk for baby."

"You proved yourself not only thoughtful but kind, William: now while you and Juno fetch the stones for the fireplace, I will stow away under the trees the things I have brought in the boat."

"Shall we let the goats and sheep loose, Ready?"

"Oh, yes,—there is no fear of their straying; the herbage here is better than on the other side, and there is plenty of it."

"Well, I will let Nanny go as soon as Juno has milked her. Now, Juno, let us see how many stones we can carry at once."

In an hour the fireplace was made, Ready had done all that he could, the goats were milked and let loose, and then William and Juno set off on their journey back.

Ready went down to the beach. On his arrival there, he observed a small turtle: creeping up softly he got between it and the water, and succeeded in turning it over. "That will do for to-morrow," said he, as he stepped into the boat; and laying hold of the oars, he pulled out of the bay to return to the cove.

Chapter Twenty Two

Ready arrived at the cove, and proceeded to the tents, where he found the whole party listening to William, who was detailing what had been done. The arrangements for the next day were made as soon as Ready joined them. They then separated for the night, but Ready and William remained until it was dark, to catch the fowls and tie their legs, ready for their being put in the boat the next morning. At daylight all were summoned to dress themselves as soon as possible, as Ready wanted to take down the tent in which Mrs Seagrave and the children had slept. For, with the exception of Tommy, the others had slept upon some canvas, which they had spread out under the cocoa-nut trees. As soon as Mrs Seagrave was dressed, the tent was taken down, and, with all the bedding, put into the boat. Then, when they had breakfasted, the plates, knives and forks, and some other necessaries, were also put in; Ready laid the fowls on the top of all, and set off by himself for their new location.

After he was gone, the rest of the party prepared for their journey through the cocoa-nut grove. William led the way, with the three dogs close to his heels, Mr Seagrave with the baby in his arms, Juno with little Caroline, and Mrs Seagrave with Master Tommy holding her hand. They cast a last look round at the cove, and the fragments of the wreck and cargo, strewed about in every direction, and then turned into the wood. Ready arrived at the point, and was again on shore in less than two hours after he had set off. As soon as the boat was safe in, he did not wait to land his cargo, but going up to the turtle which he had turned the day before, he killed it, and cleaned it on the beach. He then went to where they had built up the fireplace with stones, made a fire, filled the iron saucepan full of water, and set it on to boil; he then cut up a portion of the turtle, and put it into the pot, with some slices of salt pork, covered it up, and left it to boil; and having hung up the rest of the turtle in the shade, he went back to the beach to unload the boat. He released the poor fowls, and they were soon busy seeking for food.

It was two or three hours before he had carried everything up, for it was a good distance, and some of the articles were heavy, and the old man was not sorry when he had finished his task, and could sit down to rest himself.

"It's almost time they arrived," thought Ready; "they must have started nearly four hours ago." Ready remained a quarter of an hour more watching the fire, and occasionally skimming the top of the pot, when the three dogs came bounding towards him.

"Well, they are not far off now," observed Old Ready.

In six or seven minutes afterwards the party made their appearance, very hot and very fatigued. It appeared that poor little Caroline had been tired out, and Juno had to carry her; then Mrs Seagrave complained of fatigue, and they had to rest a quarter of an hour; then Tommy, who refused to remain with his mamma, and had been running backwards and forwards from one to the other, had declared that he was tired, and that someone must carry him; but there was no one to carry him, so he began to cry until they stopped for another quarter of an hour till he was rested; then as soon as they went on again he again complained of being tired. William then carried him pickaback for some time, and in so doing he missed the blaze-cut on the trees, and it was a long while before he could find it again; then baby became hungry, and he cried, and little Caroline was frightened at being so long in the wood, and she cried. But finally they got on better, and arrived at last so warm and exhausted, that Mrs Seagrave went into the tent with the children to repose a little, before she could even look at the place which was to be their future residence.

"I think," said Mr Seagrave, "that this little journey of to-day has been a pretty good proof of how helpless we should have been without you, Ready."

"I am glad that you are here, sir," replied Ready, "it is a weight off my mind; now you will get on better. I think that after a while you may live very comfortably here; but still we have much to do. As soon as Madam has rested, we will have our dinner and then fix up our own tent, which will be quite enough after such a hard day's work."

"Do you go back to the cove to-morrow, Ready?"

"Yes, sir, we want our stores here; it will take about three trips to empty our storehouses; and as to the other things, we can examine them and bring them down at our leisure. As soon as I have made those three trips in the boat, we can then work here altogether."

"But I can do something in the meantime."

"Oh yes, there is plenty for you to do."

Mr Seagrave went into the tent, and found his wife much refreshed; but the children had all fallen fast asleep on the beds. They waited another half-hour, and then woke Tommy and Caroline, that they might all sit down to dinner.

"Dear me," exclaimed William, as Ready took the cover off the saucepan, "what is it that you have so good there?"

"It's a treat I have prepared for you all," replied Ready. "I know that you are tired of salt meat, so now you are going to feed like aldermen."

"Why, what is it, Ready?" said Mrs Seagrave; "it smells very good."

"It is turtle-soup, ma'am; and I hope you will like it; for, if you do, you may often have it, now that you are on this side of the island."

"Indeed, it really is excellent; but it wants a little salt. Have you any salt, Juno?"

"Got a little, ma'am. Very little left," replied Juno.

"What shall we do when all our salt is gone?" said Mrs Seagrave.

"Juno must get some more," replied Ready.

"How I get salt?—hab none left," replied Juno, looking at Ready.

"There's plenty out there, Juno," said Mr Seagrave, pointing to the sea.

"I don't know where," said Juno, looking in that direction.

"What do you mean, my dear?" inquired Mrs Seagrave.

"I only mean if we want salt we can have as much as we please by boiling down salt-water in the kettle, or else making a salt-pan in the rocks, and obtaining it by the sun drying up the water and leaving the salt. Salt is always procured in that way, either by evaporation, or boiling."

"I'll soon arrange that for you, ma'am," said Ready, "and show Juno how to get it when she wants it."

"I am very glad to hear you say so; for I should feel the want of salt very much," replied Mrs Seagrave, "I really never enjoyed a dinner so much as I have to-day."

The soup was pronounced excellent by everybody. As soon as they had finished, Mrs Seagrave remained with the children; and Ready and Mr Seagrave, assisted by Juno and William, got the second tent up, and everything ready for the night. They then all assembled, and returned thanks to God for their having gained their new abode; and, tired out with the fatigue of the day, were soon fast asleep.

Chapter Twenty Three

Mr Seagrave was the first up on the ensuing morning; and when Ready came out of the tent, he said to him, "Do you know, Ready, I feel much happier and my mind much more at ease since I find myself here. On the other side of the island everything reminded me that we had been shipwrecked; and I could not help thinking of home and my own country; but here we appear as if we had been long settled, and as if we had come here by choice."

"I trust that feeling will be stronger every day, sir; for it's no use, and indeed sinful, to repine."

"I acknowledge it, and with all humility. What is the first thing which you wish we should set about?"

"I think, sir, the first object is to have a good supply of fresh water; and I therefore wish you and William—Here he is. Good-morning, William—I was saying that I thought it better that Mr Seagrave and you should clear out the spring while I am away in the boat. I brought another shovel with me yesterday, and you both can work; perhaps we had better go there, as Juno, I see, is getting the breakfast ready. You observe, Mr Seagrave, we must follow up the spring till we get among the cocoa-nut trees, where it will be shaded from the sun; that is easily done by digging towards them, and watching how the water flows. Then, if you will dig out a hole large enough to sink down in the earth one of the water-casks which lie on the beach, I will bring it down with me this afternoon; and then, when it is fixed in the earth in that way, we shall always have the cask full of water for use, and the spring filling it as fast as we empty it."

"I understand," replied Mr Seagrave; "that shall be our task while you are absent."

"Now, I have nothing more to do than to speak to Juno about dinner," replied Ready; "and then I'll just take a mouthful, and be off."

Ready directed Juno to fry some pork in the frying-pan, and then to cut off some slices from the turtle, and cook turtle-steaks for dinner, as well as to warm up the soup which was left; and then, with a biscuit and a piece of beef in his hand, he went down to the boat and set off for the cove. Mr

Seagrave and William worked hard; and, by twelve o'clock, the hole was quite large and deep enough, according to the directions Ready had given. They then left their work and went to the tent.

"You don't know how much happier I am now that I am here," said Mrs Seagrave, taking her husband's hand, as he seated himself by her.

"I trust it is a presentiment of future happiness, my dear," said Mr Seagrave. "I assure you that I feel the same, and was saying so to Ready this morning."

"I feel that I could live here for ever, it is so calm and beautiful; but I miss one thing—there are no birds singing here as at home."

"I have seen no birds except sea-birds, and of them there is plenty. Have you, William?"

"Only once, father. I saw a flight a long way off. Ready was not with me, and I could not tell what they were; but they were large birds, as big as pigeons, I should think. There is Ready coming round the point," continued William. "How fast that little boat sails! It is a long pull, though, for the old man when he goes to the cove."

"Let us go down and help Ready carry up some of the things before dinner," said Mrs Seagrave.

They did so; and William rolled up the empty water-cask which Ready had brought with him.

The turtle-steaks were as much approved of as the turtle-soup; indeed, after having been so long on salt meat, a return to fresh provisions was delightful.

"And now to finish our well," said William, as soon as dinner was over.

"How hard you do work, William!" said his mother.

"So I ought, mother. I must learn to do everything now."

"And that you will very soon," said Ready.

They rolled the cask to the spring, and, to their astonishment, found the great hole which they had dug not two hours before quite full of water.

"Oh dear," said William, "we shall have to throw all the water out to get the cask down."

"Think a little, William," said Mr Seagrave, "for the spring runs so fast that it will not be an easy task. Cannot we do something else?"

"Why, father, the cask will float, you know," replied William.

"To be sure it will as it is; but is there no way of making it sink?"

"Oh yes. I know—we must bore some holes in the bottom, and then it will fill and sink down of itself."

"Exactly," replied Ready. "I expected that we should have to do that, and have the big gimlet with me."

Ready bored three or four holes in the bottom of the cask, and as it floated the water ran into it, and by degrees it gradually sank down. As soon as the top of the cask was level with the surface they filled in all round with the spade and shovel, and the well was completed.

Chapter Twenty Four

The next morning, as soon as breakfast was over, Mr Seagrave observed: "Now that we have so many things to do, I think, Ready, we ought to lay down a plan of operations; method is everything when work is to be done: now tell me what you propose shall be our several occupations for the next week, for to-morrow is Sunday; and although we have not yet been able to honour the day as we should, I think that now we must and ought to keep it holy."

"Yes, sir," replied Ready. "To-morrow we will rest from our labour, and ask God's blessing upon our endeavours during the six days of the week; and now, as to your proposition, Mr Seagrave, shall we begin first with the lady?"

"You must not consider that you have ladies with you now, Ready," said Mrs Seagrave, "at least, not fine ladies. My health and strength are recovering fast, and I mean to be very useful. I propose to assist Juno in all the domestic duties, such as the cookery and washing, to look after and teach the children, mend all the clothes, and make all that is required, to the best of my ability. If I can do more I will."

"I think we may be satisfied with that, Mr Seagrave," replied Ready. "Now, sir, the two most pressing points, with the exception of building the house, are to dig up a piece of ground, and plant our potatoes and seeds; and to make a turtle-pond, so as to catch the turtle and put them in before the season is over."

"You are right," replied Mr Seagrave; "but which ought to be done first?"

"I should say the turtle-pond, as it will be only a few days' work for you, Juno, and William. I shall not want your assistance for this next week. I shall fix upon some spot, not far from here, where the trees are thickest in the grove, and cut them down so as to clear out a space in which we will, by and by, build our storerooms; and, as soon as the rainy season has gone by, we can remove all our stores from the other side of the island. It will occupy me the whole of the week, cutting down the trees and sawing them into proper lengths, ready for building the house, and then we must all join our strength and get it up without delay."

"Can you really manage to get it up in time? How soon do you expect the rains will come on?"

"In three or four weeks. After next week, I shall probably have the assistance of two of you, if not of all. Now I think of it, I must return to the cove."

"What for?"

"Don't you recollect, sir, your two-wheeled carriage, packed up in matting, which was thrown on shore in the gale? You laughed when you saw it, and said it would be of little use now; but the wheels and axle will be very useful, as we can make a wide path to the place when I cut down the trees, and wheel out the logs much more easily than we can drag or carry them."

"That is an excellent idea. It will save a great deal of labour."

"I expect that it will, sir. William and I will go away early on Monday morning, and be back before breakfast. To-day we will fix upon the spots where our garden is to be, our turtle-pond to be made, and the trees to be cut down. That shall be our business, Mr Seagrave; and William and Juno may put things a little more to rights here."

Mr Seagrave and Ready then walked down to the beach, and, after surveying the reefs for some time, Ready said, "You see, Mr Seagrave, we do not want too much water for a turtle-pond, as, if it is too deep, there is a difficulty in catching them when we want them: what we want is a space of water surrounded by a low wall of stones, so that the animals cannot escape, for they cannot climb up, although they can walk on the shelving sand with their flippers. Now the reef here is high out of the water, and the space within the reef and the beach is deep enough, and the rocks on the beach nearly fill up that side and prevent them crawling away by the shore. We have, therefore, little more to do than to fill up the two other sides, and then our pond will be complete."

"I see it will not be a long job either, if we can find loose rocks enough," replied Mr Seagrave.

"Almost all those which are on the beach are loose," replied Ready, "and there are plenty close to us: some of them will be too heavy to carry, but they can be brought here by the aid of handspikes and crowbars. Suppose we make a signal for William and Juno, and set them to work."

Mr Seagrave called and waved his hat, and Juno and William came down to them. Juno was ordered to go back for two handspikes, while Ready explained to William what was to be done. Having stayed with them and assisted them for some time after Juno had returned with the implements, Mr Seagrave and Ready proceeded to the point, to fix upon a spot for a garden, leaving William and Juno to continue their labour.

Chapter Twenty Five

Mr Seagrave and Ready then continued their way along the beach, until they arrived at the point which the latter had considered as a convenient place to make the garden. They found a sufficiency of mould; and as the point was narrow at its joining on to the mainland, no great length of enclosure would be required.

"You see, sir," said Ready, "we can wait till after the rainy season is over before we put up the fence, and we can prepare it in the meantime, when the weather will permit us to work. The seeds and potatoes will not come up until after the rains are finished; so all we have to do is to dig up the ground, and put them in as fast as we can. We cannot make a large garden this year; but our potatoes we must contrive to get in, if we cannot manage anything else."

"If we have no fence to make," replied Mr Seagrave, "I think we shall be able to clear away quite enough ground in a week to put in all that we require."

"The first job will be to pull up the small brushwood," said Ready, "and turn up the ground; the larger plants we must leave, if we have not time. Tommy might be of some use here in taking away the shrubs as you pull them up; but we had better now go on to the grove, and choose the spot for cutting down the trees. I have made my mark."

Ready and Mr Seagrave proceeded in the direction which the former had pointed out, until they arrived at a spot on a rising ground, where the trees were so thick that it was not very easy to pass through them.

"There is the place," said Ready. "I propose to cut all the timber we want for the houses out of this part of the grove, and to leave an open square place, in the centre of which we will build our storerooms. You see, sir, if necessary, with a very little trouble we might turn it into a place of protection and defence, as a few palisades here and there between the trees would make it, what they call in the East Indies, a stockade."

"Very true, but I trust we shall not require it for such a purpose."

"I hope so too, but there is nothing like being prepared; however, we have plenty to do before we can think of that. Now, sir, as dinner is ready, suppose we return, and after dinner we will both commence our tasks."

Juno and William returned to the dinner which Mrs Seagrave had prepared. They were both very warm with their work, which was very hard, but very eager to finish their task. After dinner was over, Mrs Seagrave requested her husband, as he was about to go down to the point, with the spade and a small hatchet in his hand, to take Tommy with him, as she had a great deal to do, and could not watch him as well as the baby and Caroline. So Mr Seagrave took Tommy by the hand, and led him to the point, and made him sit down close to him while he cleared away the brushwood.

Mr Seagrave worked very hard, and when he had cut down and cleared a portion of the ground, he made Tommy carry away to a little distance, and pile in a heap, the bushes which he had cleared away. When Mr Seagrave had cleared away a large piece of ground with his hatchet, he then took his spade to dig at the roots and turn up the mould, leaving Tommy to amuse himself. What Tommy did for about an hour, during which Mr Seagrave worked very diligently, his father did not observe; but all of a sudden he began to cry; and when his father asked him the reason, he did not answer, but only cried the more, until at last he put his hands to his stomach, and roared most lustily. As he appeared to be in very great pain, his father left off work, and led him up to the tent, when Mrs Seagrave came out, alarmed at his cries. Ready, who had heard Tommy screaming for so long a while, thought that there might be something serious, and left his work to ascertain the cause. When he heard what had passed, he said:

"Depend upon it, the child has eaten something which has made him ill. Tell me, Tommy, what did you eat when you were down there?"

"Berries," roared Tommy.

"I thought as much, ma'am," said Ready. "I must go and see what the berries were." And the old man hastened down to the place where Mr Seagrave had been at work. In the meantime Mrs Seagrave was much alarmed lest the child should have poisoned himself, and Mr Seagrave went to search among the medicines for some castor-oil.

Ready returned just as he came back to the tent with the bottle of castor-oil, and he told Ready that he was about to give Tommy a dose.

"Well, sir," replied Ready, who had a plant in his hand, "I don't think you should give him any, for it appears to me that he has taken too much

"I like fried fish," said Tommy; "why don't we have fried fish?"

"Because every one is too busy to catch them just now. Tommy, go and bring your brother Albert back; he has crawled too near to Billy, and he butts sometimes."

Tommy went after the baby, who was crawling towards the kid, which had now grown pretty large, and as he took up his brother he kicked at the goat's head.

"Don't do that, Tommy; he'll butt at you, and hurt you."

"I don't care," replied Tommy, holding the baby by one hand while he continued to kick at Billy. Billy, however, would not stand it; he lowered his head, made a butt at Tommy, and he and Albert rolled on the ground one over the other. The baby roared, and Tommy began to whimper. Mrs Seagrave ran up to them and caught up the baby; and Tommy, alarmed, caught hold of his mother's dress for protection, looking behind him at Billy, who appeared inclined to renew the attack.

"Why don't you mind what is said to you, Tommy? I told you that he would butt you," said Mrs Seagrave, pacifying the child.

"I don't care for him," replied Tommy, who perceived that the goat was walking away.

"No, you are very brave now that he has gone; but you're a very naughty boy not to mind what is said to you."

"Billy never butts at me, mamma," said Caroline.

"No, my dear, because you do not tease him; but your brother is very fond of teasing animals, and so he gets punished and frightened. It is very wrong of him to do so, especially as he is told by his father and me that he ought not."

"You said I was a good boy when I learnt my lesson this morning," replied Tommy.

"Yes, but you should always be good," replied his mother.

"I can't be always good," said Tommy; "I want my dinner."

"It is dinner-time, Tommy, that is certain, but you must wait until they all come home from their work."

"There's Ready coming, with a bag on his shoulder," replied Tommy.

Ready soon came up to where Mrs Seagrave was sitting, and laid down the bag. "I've brought you some young cocoa-nuts, and some old ones also, from the trees that I have been cutting down."

"Oh! cocoa-nuts—I like cocoa-nuts!" cried Tommy.

"I told you, Tommy, that we should have some by and by, and they have come sooner than we thought. You are very warm, Ready."

"Yes, ma'am," replied Ready, wiping his face; "it is rather warm work, for there is no breeze in the grove to cool one. Is there anything you want from the other side of the island, for I shall go there directly after dinner?"

"What for?"

"I must bring the wheels to get the timber out; for I must clear it away as I go, until the path is finished. I must have William to help me."

"William will like the trip, I do not doubt. I do not recollect anything in particular that we want, Ready," replied Mrs Seagrave. "There he comes with Juno, and I see Mr Seagrave has laid down his spade; so Caroline, dear, take care of Albert, while I get the dinner for them."

Ready assisted Mrs Seagrave, and the dinner was spread out on the ground, for they had not brought the chairs and tables with them to their new residence, as they thought that they could do without them till the house was built. William reported that Juno and he would have the turtle-pond complete by the next day. Mr Seagrave had cleared sufficient ground to plant the half-sack of potatoes that they had saved, so that in a day or two they would be able to put all their strength upon the cutting and drawing of the timber.

After dinner, William and Ready set off in the boat, and, before it was dark, returned with the wheels and axle of the carriage, and several other articles to make up their load.

Chapter Twenty Seven

"Now, William," said Ready, "if you are not very sleepy, perhaps you would like to come with me to-night, and see if we cannot turn some of the turtle, for the season is going away fast, and they will leave the island very soon."

As soon as the sun had disappeared, William and Ready went down to the beach, and sat quietly on a rock. In a short time, Ready perceived a turtle crawling on the sand, and, desiring William to follow him without speaking, walked softly down by the water's edge, so as to get between the animal and the sea.

As soon as the turtle perceived them, it made for the water, but they met it; and Ready, seizing hold of one of its fore-flippers, turned it over on its back.

"You see, William, that is the way to turn a turtle: take care that he does not catch you with his mouth, for, if he did, he would bite the piece out. Now the animal cannot get away, for he can't turn over again, and we shall find him here to-morrow morning; so we will now walk along the beach, and see if we cannot find some more."

Ready and William remained till past midnight, and turned sixteen turtle.

"I think that will do, William, for once: we have made a good night's work of it, for we have provided food for many days. Tomorrow we must put them all into the pond."

"How shall we carry such large animals?"

"We need not carry them; we must put some old canvas under them, and haul them along by that means; we can easily do that on the smooth sand."

"Why don't we catch some fish, Ready? We might put them into the turtle-pond."

"They would not stay there long, William, nor could we easily get them out if they did. I have often thought of getting some lines ready, and yet the time has never come, for I feel sleepy after our day's work; but as soon as the house is built, we will have them, and you shall be fisherman-in-chief."

"But the fish will bite at night, will they not?"

"Oh yes, and better than they do in the daytime."

"Well, then, if you will get me a line and show me how, I will fish for an hour or so after the work is done; I know mamma is getting tired of salt meat, and does not think it good for Caroline."

"Well, then, I will get a bit of candle to-morrow night, and fit up two fishing-lines. But I must go with you, William. We don't use much candle, at all events."

"No, we are too glad to go to bed: but there are two or three boxes of one sort or another up in the cove."

The next morning before breakfast all hands were employed in getting the turtle into the pond. After breakfast, William and Juno finished the pond where the walls had not been raised high enough; and, when they returned to dinner, reported that their task was completed. Mr Seagrave also said that he had, he thought, cleared quite ground enough for the present; and as Mrs Seagrave wanted Juno to help her to wash the linen that afternoon, it was agreed that William, Ready, and Mr Seagrave should all go down to the garden, and put in the potatoes.

Ready worked with the spade, while Mr Seagrave and William cut the potatoes in pieces, so as to have an eye in each piece. When they had finished this work, Mr Seagrave said—"Now that we have finished cutting the potatoes, let us go and assist Ready in planting them and the seeds which we have brought down with us."

Chapter Twenty Eight

That night Ready sat up for two or three hours working by candle-light (William keeping him company), very busily engaged fitting up the fishing-lines with leads and hooks. At last two were complete.

"What bait must we use, Ready?"

"I should think that the best would be one of the fish out of the shells which are in the sand; but a piece of pork fat will, I dare say, do as well."

"And whereabouts would you fish, Ready?"

"The best place, I should think, would be at the farthermost end of the point, where I got the boat through the reef—the water is deep there close to the rocks."

"I was thinking, Ready, if those gannets and men-of-war birds would be good eating."

"Not very, William; they are very tough and very fishy: we must try for those when we can get nothing better. Now that we have got in the seeds and potatoes, we must all set to to-morrow morning to fell and carry the timber. I think Mr Seagrave had better use the axe with me; and you and Juno can, when I have shown you how, hang the timber to the axle, and wheel it out to the place where we have decided upon building the house. And now we had better go to bed."

William, however, had made up his mind to do otherwise: he knew that his mother would be very glad to have some fish, and he determined, as the moon shone bright, to try if he could not catch some before he went to bed; so he waited very quietly till he thought Ready was asleep as well as the others, and then went out with the lines, and went down to the beach, where he picked up three or four shells, and, breaking them between two pieces of rock, took out the fish and baited his hooks. He then walked to the point. It was a beautiful night; the water was very smooth, and the moonbeams pierced deep below the surface. William threw in his line, and as soon as the lead touched the bottom he pulled it up about a foot, as Ready had instructed him; and he had not held his line more than half a minute, when it was jerked so forcibly, that not expecting it he was nearly hauled into the water; as it was, the fish was so strong that the line slipped through his hand and scored his fingers; but after a time he was able to pull it in, and he landed on the beach a large silver-scaled fish, weighing nine or ten pounds. As soon as he had dragged it so far away from the edge of the rocks as to prevent its flapping into the water again, William took out the hook and determined to try for another. His line was down as short a time as before, when it was again jerked with violence; but William was this time prepared, and he let out the line and played the fish till it was tired, and then pulled it up, and found that the second fish was even larger than the first. Satisfied with his success, he wound up his lines, and, running a piece of string through the gills of the fish, dragged them back to the tents, and hanged them to the pole, for fear of the dogs eating them; he then went in, and was soon fast asleep. The next morning William was the first up, and showed his prizes with much glee; but Ready was very much displeased with him.

"You did very wrong, William, to run the risk which you did. If you were resolved to catch fish, why did you not tell me, and I would have gone with you? You say, yourself, that the fish nearly hauled you into the water; suppose it had done so, or suppose a small shark instead of one of these gropers (as we call them) had taken the bait, you must have been jerked in; and the rocks are so steep there, that you would not have been able to get out again before a shark had hold of you. Think a moment what would have been the distress of your father and the agony and despair of your poor mother, when this news should have arrived."

"I was very wrong, Ready," replied William, "now that I think of it; but I wanted to surprise and please my mother."

"That reason is almost sufficient to plead your pardon, my dear boy," replied Ready; "but don't do so again. And now let us say no more about it; nobody will know that you have been in danger, and there's no harm done; and you mustn't mind an old man scolding you a little."

"No, indeed, Ready, I do not, for I was very thoughtless; but I had no idea that there was danger."

"There's your mother coming out of her tent," replied Ready. "Good-morning, madam. Do you know what William has done for you last night? Look, here are two beautiful fish, and very excellent eating they are, I can tell you."

"I am quite delighted," replied Mrs Seagrave.

Tommy clapped his hands and danced about, crying, "Fried fish for dinner;" and Juno said, "Have very fine dinner to-day, Missy Caroline."

After breakfast they all set out for the grove, where Ready had been cutting down the trees, taking with them the wheels and axle, and a couple of stout ropes. Mr Seagrave and Ready cut down the trees and slung them to the axle, and Juno and William dragged them to the spot where the house was to be built.

They were not sorry when dinner was ready, for it was very hard work.

That night, tired as they were, Ready and William went out, and turned eight more turtle. They continued felling the cocoa-nut trees and dragging the timber for the remainder of the week, when they considered that they had nearly enough, and on Tuesday morning they commenced building the house.

Chapter Twenty Nine

Ready had cut out and prepared the door-posts and window-frames from timber which he had towed round from the cove. He now fixed four poles in the earth upright at each corner, and then, with the assistance of Mr Seagrave, notched every log of cocoa-nut wood on both sides, where it was to meet with the one crossing it, so that, by laying log upon log alternately, they fitted pretty close, and had only to have the chinks between them filled in with cocoa-nut leaves twisted very tight, and forced between them: this was the work of William and Juno when no more logs were ready for carrying; and, by degrees, the house rose up from its foundation. The fireplace could not be made at once, as they had either to find clay, or to burn shells into lime and build it up with rocks and mortar; but a space was left for it. For three weeks they worked very hard: as soon as the sides were up, they got on the whole of the roof and rafters; and then, with the broad leaves of the cocoa-nut trees which had been cut down, Ready thatched it very strong and securely. At the end of the three weeks the house was secure from the weather; and it was quite time, for the weather had begun to change, the clouds now gathered thick, and the rainy season was commencing.

"We have no time to lose, sir," said Ready to Mr Seagrave. "We have worked hard, but we must for a few days work harder still. We must fit up the inside of the house, so as to enable Madam to get into it as soon as possible."

The earth in the inside of the house was then beaten down hard, so as to make a floor; and a sort of bedstead, about two feet from the ground, running the whole length of the house, was raised on each side of the interior: these were fitted with canvas screens to let down by night. And then Ready and William took the last trip in the boat to fetch the chairs and tables, which they did just before the coming on of the first storm of the season. The bedding and all the utensils were now taken into the house; and a little outhouse was built up to cook in, until the fireplace could be made.

It was late on the Saturday night that the family shifted into the new house; and fortunate it was that they had no further occasion for delay, for on the Sunday the first storm burst upon them; the wind blew with great force; and, although they were shielded from it, still the cocoa-nut trees ground and sawed each other's stems as they bent their heads to its force. The lightning was vivid, and the thunder appalling, while the rain descended in a continual torrent. The animals left the pastures, and sheltered themselves in the grove; and, although noonday, it was so dark that they could not see to read.

"This, then, is the rainy season which you talked about, Ready," said Mrs Seagrave. "Is it always like this? If so, what shall we do?"

"No, madam; the sun will shine sometimes, but not for long at a time. We shall be able to get out and do something every now and then almost every day, but still we shall have rain, perhaps, for many days without intermission, and we must work indoors."

"How thankful we ought to be that we have a house over our heads; we should have been drowned in the tents."

"That I knew, madam, and therefore I was anxious to get a house over your head; let us thank God for it."

"Indeed we ought," observed Mr Seagrave; "and it is, indeed, time for us to read the service."

The morning service was then performed in the new house. Violent as the rain was, it did not penetrate through the thatch which had been put on. Ready and William went out to secure the boat, which they were afraid would be injured, and returned wet to the skin. The storm continued without intermission the whole of the night, but they slept dry and safe; and, when awakened by the noise of the thunder and the pelting of the rain, they thanked God that they had found a dwelling in the wilderness upon which they had been cast.

Chapter Thirty

When they all rose up the next morning, the clouds had cleared off, and the sun was shining bright. Ready and Juno were the first out of the house—Ready with the telescope under his arm, which he always took with him when he went his rounds, as he termed it, in the morning.

"Well, Juno," said Ready, "this is a fine morning after the rain."

"Yes, Massa Ready, very fine morning; but how I get fire light, and make kittle boil for breakfast, I really don't know—stick and cocoa-nut trash all so wet."

"Before I went to bed last night, Juno, I covered up the embers with ashes, put some stones over them, and then some cocoa-nut branches, so I think you will find some fire there yet. I was going my morning's round, but I will stay a little and help you."

"Tank you, Massa Ready; plenty rain fell last night."

"Yes, not a little, Juno; you must not expect to find the water at the well very clear this morning; indeed, I doubt if you will see the well at all. Here's some stuff which is not very wet."

"I got plenty of fire, too," replied Juno, who had removed the branches and stones, and was now on her knees blowing up the embers.

"You'll do very well now, Juno," said Ready; "besides, William will be out directly—so I'll leave you."

Ready whistled to the dogs, who came bounding out, and then set off on his round of inspection. He first directed his steps to the well in the ravine; but, instead of the gushing spring and the limpid clear water, with which the cask sunk for a well had been filled, there was now a muddy torrent, rushing down the ravine, and the well was covered with it, and not to be distinguished.

"I thought as much," said Ready, musing over the impetuous stream; "well, better too much water than too little." Ready waded through, as he wished to examine the turtle-pond, which was on the other side of the stream. Finding all right, he again crossed the water, where it was now spread wide over the sandy beach, until he came to the other point where he had moored his boat, both by the head and stern, with a rope, and a heavy stone made fast to it, as an anchor.

From this point, as usual, he surveyed the horizon with his telescope; not that he thought that there was a chance of a vessel arriving among these islands; but, still, as it was possible, he took the trouble; but never except when he went out in the morning alone, as he was aware that the very circumstance of his so doing would make Mr Seagrave melancholy and unsettled. As usual, he dropped the telescope on his arm, after his survey, saying to himself, "Little use doing that."

The gale having blown offshore, the boat had dragged her moorings, and was so far out that Ready could not get at her.

"Here's a puzzle," said the old man; "how foolish of me not to have made a line fast to the shore! I'll not trust myself to John Shark by swimming to the boat."

"Let me see." Ready took the halyards and sheets belonging to the boat's sails, which he had left on the beach, and bent one on to the other until he had sufficient length of rope. He then made a piece of wood, about two feet long, fast by the middle to the end of the rope, and, after one or two attempts, contrived to throw it into the boat. The piece of wood caught under one of the thwarts, and this enabled him to draw the boat to the shore.

Having baled out the water which had fallen into her during the storm, he then landed again and examined the garden.

"Now to find the sheep and goats," said Ready, "and then my morning's walk is over. Now, Romulus, now, Remus, boys, find them out," continued he; and the dogs, who appeared to know what he was in search of, went away in pursuit, and soon found the sheep and two of the goats, but the third goat was not with them.

"Why, where can Black Nanny be?" muttered Ready, stopping a little while; at last he heard a bleat, in a small copse of brushwood, to which he directed his steps, followed by the dogs. "I thought as much," said he, as he perceived Nanny lying down in the copse with two new-born kids at her side. "Come, my little fellows, we must find some shelter for you," said he, taking one up under each arm. "Come, Nanny."

Ready walked back to the house, and brought in the kids, followed by Nanny. He found Mr and Mrs Seagrave and the children all dressed.

Caroline and Tommy gave a scream of delight when they saw the little kids, and even little Albert clapped his hands. As soon as Ready put them down on the ground, Tommy and Caroline had each their arms round one.

"I've brought an addition to our family, Mrs Seagrave," said Ready: "we must allow them to remain in the house until I can knock up a little shelter for them. This is only a beginning; I expect we shall soon have more."

As soon as the children could be persuaded to part with the kids, Nanny was tied up in a corner, and was very content with fondling and nursing her progeny. Juno and William brought in the breakfast, and as soon as it was over, Mr Seagrave said, "Now, Ready, I think we must hold a council, and make arrangements as to our allotted duties and employments during the rainy season. We have a great deal to do, and must not be idle."

"Yes, sir, we have a great deal to do, and, to get through our work, we must have order and method in our doings. I've lived long enough to know how much can be done by regularity and discipline. Why, sir, there is more work got out of men in a well-conducted man-of-war than there can in the merchant service in double the time. And why so? Because everything is in its place, and there is a place for everything."

"I agree with you," said Mrs Seagrave; "method is everything. While one careless little girl is looking for her thimble, another will have finished her work."

"I assure you I never should have known what can be done by order and arrangement, if I had not been pressed on board of a man-of-war. I found that everything was done in silence. Every man was to his post; everyone had a rope to haul upon, or a rope to let go; the boatswain piped, and in a few seconds every sail was set or taken in as was required. It seemed to me at first like magic. And you observe, Mr Seagrave, that when there is order and discipline, every man becomes of individual importance. If I learnt nothing else on board of a man-of-war, I learnt to make the most of time, and the most of the strength which you could command."

"You are very right, Ready; you must teach us to do the same," replied Mr Seagrave.

"We have so much to do, that I hardly know where to begin; yet, sir, we must work at present how we can, and when we can, until we have got things into a little better order. We have done well up to the present."

"What do you think we ought to do first?"

"Well, sir, our first job will be to haul up the boat and secure her from harm; we will half-dock her in the sand, and cover her over, for I do not think it will be safe to go in her now to the other side of the island, where the sea will always be rough."

"There I perfectly agree with you. Now what is the next?"

"Why, sir, we must not leave the tents where they are, but take them down, and as soon as they are dry, stow them away, for we may want them by and by; then, sir, we must build a large outhouse for our stores and provisions, with a thatched roof, and a floor raised about four feet from the ground; and then, under the floor, the sheep and goats will have a protection from the weather. Then there is the fish-pond to make, and also a salt-pan to cut out of the rock. Then we have two more long jobs. One is, to go through the woods and examine the stores we have left on the other side of the island, sort and arrange them all ready for bringing here after the rains are over; and we must also explore the island a little, and find out what it produces; for at present we know nothing of it: we may find a great many things useful to us, a great many trees and fruits, and I hope and trust we may be able to find some more grass for our live stock."

"I agree with you in all you say, Ready," replied Mr Seagrave; "now how shall we divide our strength?"

"We will not divide at present, sir, if you please. Juno has plenty to do indoors with Mrs Seagrave; William, and you, and I, will first secure the boat and stow away the tents and gear; after that, we will set about the outbuilding, and work at it when we can. If Juno has any time to spare, she had better collect the cocoa-nut leaves, and pile them up for fuel; and Tommy will, I dare say, go with her, and show her how to draw them along."

"Yes, I'll show her," said Tommy, getting on his feet.

"Not just now, Tommy," said Ready, "but as soon as your mamma can spare her to go with you. Come, sir, a few hours of weather like this is not to be lost," continued Ready; "we shall have more rain before the day is over, I expect. I will first go to the tent for the shovels; then I will haul the boat round to the beach and meet you there. You and William can take some cord, tie up a large bundle of cocoa-nut boughs, sling it to the wheels, and draw it down to the beach and meet me."

Chapter Thirty One

As so many cocoa-nut trees had been cut down to build the house, there were plenty of boughs lying in every direction, and William and Mr Seagrave had soon procured sufficient. In a very short time the boat was drawn up about ten yards from the water's edge, which Ready said was quite sufficient; they then dug from under with their shovels until the boat was sunk about half down in the sand.

Having filled in the sand all round her up to her gunnel, the boat was then carefully covered over with the boughs, which were weighed down with sand that they might not be blown away.

"I don't see why you should cover the boat up in this way, Ready; the rain won't hurt her," observed William.

"No, sir, the rain won't do her any harm, but the sun will, when it bursts out occasionally; for it's very powerful when it does shine, and it would split her all to pieces."

"I forgot that," replied William. "What shall we do now?"

"Suppose, as we have two hours to dinner-time, you run for the lines, William, and we'll try for some fish."

"We cannot all three of us fish with only two lines," said Mr Seagrave.

"No, sir; and as William knows how to catch them, suppose you remain with him, and I will go up and collect wood and chips for Juno's fire. She was hard pressed for it this morning, it was so wet; but, if once piled up, it will soon be dry. Be careful, Mr Seagrave, not to hold the lines tight in your hands, or you may be jerked into the water."

Mr Seagrave and William were very fortunate; before the two hours were expired they had caught eight large fish, which they brought up to the house slung on the boat-hook. Tommy hallooed loudly for fish for dinner, and as they had caught so many, it was agreed that the dinner should be put off until some could be got ready, and they were not sorry to eat them instead of salt pork.

They had hardly sat down to table, when the rain came pattering down on the roof, and in a quarter of an hour the storm was as violent, and the thunder and lightning as terrific as on the day before. All outdoor labour was again suspended. Mrs Seagrave, Juno, and Caroline took their work, for there was plenty to do with the needle and thread, and Ready soon found employment for the rest. William and Mr Seagrave unlaid some thick rope, that Ready might make smaller and more useful rope with the yarns. Ready took up his sailing needles, and worked eyelet-holes in the canvas screens (which they had put up in a hurry), so that they might be drawn to and fro as required.

As soon as Ready had hung up the curtains, he looked under the bedsteads for a large bundle, and said, as he opened it, "I shall now decorate Madam Seagrave's sleeping-place. It ought to be handsomer than the others." The bundle was composed of the ship's ensign, which was red, and a large, square, yellow flag with the name of the ship *Pacific* in large black letters upon it. These two flags Ready festooned and tied up round the bed-place, so as to give it a very gay appearance, and also to hide the rough walls of the cottage.

"Indeed, Ready, I am much obliged to you," said Mrs Seagrave, when he had finished; "it is really quite grand for this place."

"It's the best use we can put them to now, madam," said Ready.

"I am afraid so," replied Mr Seagrave, thoughtfully.

"Ready," said William, after the candles were lighted, "you once half-promised me that you would tell me your history; I wish you would tell us some of it now, as it will pass away the evening."

"Well, William, I did say so, and I shall keep my word. When you have heard my story, you will say that I have been very foolish in my time; and so I have; but if it proves a warning to you, it will, at all events, be of some use."

Ready then commenced his history as follows:

History of Old Ready

"Of course, you wish to know who my father and mother were: that is soon told. My father was the captain of a merchant vessel, which traded from South Shields to Hamburg, and my poor mother, God bless her, was the daughter of a half-pay militia captain, who died about two months after their marriage. The property which the old gentleman had bequeathed to my mother was added to that which my father had already vested in the brig, and he then owned one-third of the vessel; the other two-thirds were the property of a very rich ship-builder and owner, of the name of Masterman. What with the profits of the share he held of the vessel and his pay as captain, my father was well to do. Mr Masterman, who had a very high opinion of my father, and gained much money by his exertions and good management, was present at the marriage, and when I was born, about a year afterwards, he stood for me as godfather. Every one considered that this was a most advantageous circumstance for me, and congratulated my father and mother; for Mr Masterman was a bachelor, of nearly sixty years, without any near relations. It is true, that he was very fond of money; but that, they said, was all the better, as he could not take it away with him when he died. An end, however, was soon put to all their worldly ideas, for a year after I was born, my father was drowned at sea, his vessel and the whole of her crew being lost on the Texel sands; and my mother found herself a widow, with a child scarcely weaned, when she was but twenty-two years of age.

"It was supposed that my mother would still have sufficient to live upon, as the ship had been insured at two-thirds of her value; but, to the astonishment of everybody, Mr Masterman contrived to make it appear that it was his two-thirds of the vessel which had been insured."

"What is insurance?" inquired William.

"Insurance, my dear boy, is paying a certain sum to people who are called underwriters, that in case the vessel or cargo is lost or damaged, the loss or damage is made good to the owners of the vessel or cargo. You pay in proportion to the risk incurred. Supposing you wished to insure one thousand pounds on a vessel or cargo, and ten per cent was required, you would, if the vessel came home safe, pay the underwriters one hundred pounds; if, on the contrary, the vessel was lost, the underwriters would have to pay you one thousand pounds, the sum which you had insured. I beg your pardon for the interruption, Ready."

"No need, Mr Seagrave; we never should lose an opportunity of teaching the young. Well, how far the assertion of Mr Masterman was correct or not, it was impossible at the time to say; but I do know that everybody cried out 'shame', and that if he did deprive the widow, he had much to answer for; for the Bible says, 'Pure religion is to visit the fatherless and the widows in their affliction, and to keep yourself unspotted in the world'. The consequence was, that my mother had little or nothing to live upon; but she found friends who assisted her, and she worked embroidery, and contrived to get on somehow until I was eight or nine years of age."

"But did not your godfather come forward to the assistance of your mother?" inquired Mr Seagrave.

"No, sir, strange to say, he did not; and that made people talk the more. I believe it was the abuse of him, which he did not fail to hear, and which he ascribed to my mother, which turned him away from us; perhaps it was his own conscience, for we always dislike those we have injured."

"Unfortunately, there is great truth in that remark of yours, Ready," observed Mr Seagrave; "still, it is strange that he did not do something."

"It was very strange, sir,—at least, so it appeared at the time, but he was very fond of money, and irritated at the reports and observations which were made about him. But, to go on, sir, I was a strong, hardy boy, and, whenever I could escape from my mother or school, was always found by the water-side or on board of the vessels. In the summer-time I was half the day in water, and was a very good swimmer. My mother perceived my fondness for the profession, and tried all she could to divert my thoughts some other way. She told me of the dangers and hardships which sailors went through, and always ended with my father's death and a flood of tears.

"We certainly are of a perverse nature, as I have often heard the clergyman say, for it appears to me that we always wish to do that which we are told not to do. If my mother had not been always persuading me against going to sea, I really believe I might have stayed at home. I've often thought since, how selfish and unfeeling I must have been. I was too young to know what pain I was giving my mother, and how anxiety was preying upon her, all on my account. Children cannot feel it; if they did, they would do otherwise, for our hearts are seldom hard until we grow older."

"I agree with you, Ready," said Mr Seagrave. "If children really knew how much their parents suffer when they behave ill, how alarmed they are at any proofs of wickedness in them, they would be much better."

"We never find that out, sir, till it is too late," continued Ready. "Well, sir, I was little more than nine years old, when, on a very windy day, and the water rough, a hawser, by which a vessel was fast to the wharf, was carried away with a violent jerk, and the broken part, as it flew out, struck a person who was at the edge of the wharf, and knocked him into the sea. I heard the crying out, and the men from the wharf and from the ships were throwing ropes to him, but he could not catch hold of them; indeed, he could not swim well, and the water was rough. I caught a rope that had been hauled in again, and leapt off the wharf.

"Young as I was, I swam like a duck, and put the rope into his hands just as he was going down. He clung to it as drowning men only can cling, and was hauled to the piles, and soon afterwards a boat, which had been lowered from the stern of one of the vessels, picked us both up. We were taken to a public-house, and put into bed till dry clothes could be sent for us; and then I found that the person I had saved was my godfather, Mr Masterman. Everyone was loud in my praise; and, although perhaps I ought not to say it, it was a bold act for so young a boy as I was. The sailors took me home to my mother in a sort of triumphal procession; and she, poor thing, when she heard what I had done, embraced me over and over again, one moment rejoicing at my preservation, and the next weeping bitterly at the thoughts of the danger I had encountered, and the probability that my bold spirit would lead me into still greater."

"But she did not blame you for what you had done?"

"Oh no, William; she felt that I had done my duty towards my neighbour, and perhaps she felt in her own heart that I had returned good for evil; but she did not say so. The next day Mr Masterman called upon us; he certainly looked very foolish and confused when he asked for his godson, whom he had so long neglected. My mother, who felt how useful he might be to me, received him very kindly; but I had been often told of his neglect of me and my mother, and of his supposed unfair conduct towards my father, and had taken a violent dislike to him; his advances towards me were therefore very coolly received. I felt glad that I had saved him; but although I could not exactly understand my own feelings at the time, I am ashamed to say that my pleasure was not derived from having done a good action, so much as indulging a feeling of revenge in having put one under an obligation who had treated me ill; this arose from my proud spirit, which my mother could not check. So you see, William, there was very little merit in what I had done, as, after I had done it, I indulged those feelings which I ought to have checked."

"I think I could not have helped feeling the same, Ready, under such circumstances," replied William.

"The impulse which induced me to act was good," replied Ready; "but the feeling which I indulged in afterwards took away the whole merit of the deed. I am stating what I believe to be the truth; and an old man like me can look upon the past without bias, but not without regret. Mr Masterman made but a short visit; he told my mother that he would now take care of me and bring me up to the business of a ship-builder as soon as I was old enough to leave school, and that in the meantime he would pay all my expenses. My poor mother was very grateful, and shed tears of joy; and when Mr Masterman went away, she embraced me, and said that now she was happy, as I should have a profession on shore and not go to sea. I must do justice to Mr Masterman; he kept his word and sent money to my mother, so that she became quite cheerful and comfortable, and everyone congratulated her, and she used to fondle me, and say, it was all through me that she was relieved from her distress."

"How happy that must have made you, Ready!" said William.

"Yes, it did, but it made me also very proud. Strange to say, I could not conquer my dislike to Mr Masterman; I had nourished the feeling too long. I could not bear that my mother should be under obligations to him, or that he should pay for my schooling; it hurt my foolish pride, young as I then was; and although my mother was happy, I was not. Besides, as I was put to a better school, and was obliged to remain with the other boys, I could no longer run about the wharfs, or go on board the vessels, as before. I did not see then, as I do now, that it was all for my good but I became discontented and unhappy, merely because I was obliged to pay attention to my learning, and could no longer have my own way. The master complained of me; and Mr Masterman called and scolded me well. I became more disobedient, and then I was punished. This irritated me, and I made up my mind that I would run away to sea. You see, William, I was all in the wrong; and so will all boys be who think they know better than those who have charge of them; and now only see what I probably lost by my foolish conduct. I say *probably*, for no one can calculate or foresee what is to take place; but, as far as appearances went, I had every prospect of receiving a good education—of succeeding Mr Masterman in his business, and, very probably, of inheriting his large fortune; so that I might have been at this time a rich and well-educated man, surrounded with all the comforts and luxuries of life; perhaps with an amiable wife and large family round me, to make me still happier, instead of being what I now am, a poor, worn-out old seaman upon a desert isle. I point this out to you, William, to show how one false and foolish step in the young may affect their whole prospects in life; and, instead of enabling them to sail down with the stream of prosperity, may leave them to struggle against the current of adversity, as has been the case with me."

"It is, indeed, a good lesson, Ready," said Mr Seagrave.

"It is; not that I repine at my lot, even while I regret the errors that led to it. An all-wise and gracious God disposes of us as he thinks best; and I can now say with perfect sincerity, 'Thy will, not mine, be done'."

"Your misfortunes have, however, proved an incalculable benefit to us, Ready," observed Mrs Seagrave; "for had you not gone to sea, and been on board the ship when the crew deserted us, what would have become of us?"

"Well, madam, it is some comfort to think that a worn-out old seaman like myself has been of some use."

Chapter Thirty Two

The bleating of the kids woke them the next morning earlier than usual. The weather was again fine, and the sun shining brightly, and Ready turned out Nanny and her progeny. They had an excellent breakfast of fried fish, and then Mr Seagrave, Ready, and William went out to their work: the two first took down the tents, and spread the canvas on the ground, that it might be well dried, while William went in pursuit of the fowls, which had not been seen for a day or two. After half-an-hour's search in the cocoa-nut grove, he heard the cock crow, and soon afterwards found them all. He threw them some split peas, which he had brought with him. They were hungry enough and followed him home to the house, where he left them and went to join Ready and his father.

"William," said Ready, "I think, now that we have spread out the tents, we will, if Mr Seagrave approves, all set to at once and knock up a fowl-house; it won't be more than a day's job, and then the creatures will have a home. There are four very thick cocoa-nut trees close to the house; we will build it under them; it will be a good job over." Mr Seagrave assented, and they set immediately to work. There were many thin poles left, the tops of the cocoa-nut trees which had been cut down to build the house; these they nailed to the trunks of the four trees, so as to make a square, and then they ran up rafters for a pitched roof.

"Now, sir, this is only rough work; we will first put up a perch or two for them, and then close in the side, and thatch the roof with cocoa-nut branches; but there's Juno taking in the dinner, so we'll finish it afterwards."

After their meal the work was renewed; Mr Seagrave collected the branches while William and Ready worked upon the sides and roof, and before the evening closed in, the fowl-house was complete. William enticed the fowls down to it with some more split peas, and then walked away.

"Now, sir, the creatures will soon find their way in; and by and by, when I have time, I'll make a door to the entrance."

"And now," said William, "I think we had better roll up the canvas of the tents; we have had a splendid day, and may not be so fortunate to-morrow."

"Very true; we will get them housed, and stow them away under the bed-places; there is plenty of room." By the time that they had folded up the canvas, and William had brought in Nanny and the kids, the sun had set, and they went into the house. Ready was requested to go on with his history, which he did as follows:—

"I said last night that I determined to run away from school and go to sea, but I did not tell you how I managed it. I had no chance of getting out of the school unperceived, except after the boys were all put to bed. The room that I slept in was at the top of the house—the doors I knew were all locked; but there was a trap-door which led out on the roof, fastened by a bolt inside, and a ladder leading up to it; and I determined that I would make my escape by that way. As soon as all the other boys were fast asleep, I arose and dressed myself very quietly, and then left the room.

"The moon shone bright, which was lucky for me, and I gained the trap-door without any noise. I had some difficulty in forcing it up, as it was heavy for a boy of my age; but I contrived to do so at last, and gained the roof of the house. I then began looking about me, to see how I was to get to the ground, and after walking to and fro several times, I decided that I could slip down by a large water-pipe; it was so far detached from the bricks, that I could get my small fingers round it. I climbed over the parapet, and, clinging to the pipe firmly with my hands and knees, I slid down, and arrived at the bottom in safety."

"It's a wonder you did not break your neck, Ready," observed Mrs Seagrave.

"It was, indeed, ma'am. As soon as I was landed in the flowerbed, which was below, I hastened to the iron gates at the entrance, and soon climbed up and got to the other side into the road. I started as fast as I could towards the port, and when I arrived at the wharf, I perceived that a vessel had her topsails loose, and meant to take advantage of the ebb-tide which had just made; the men were singing 'Yo heave yo,' getting the anchor up; and as I stood watching, almost making up my mind that I would swim off to her, I perceived that a man pushed off in her jolly-boat, and was sculling to a post a little higher up, where a hawser had been made fast; I ran round, and arrived there before he had cast off the rope; without saying a word, I jumped into the boat.

"'What do you want, youngster?' said the seaman.

"'I want to go to sea,' said I, breathless; 'take me on board—pray do.'

"'Well,' said he, 'I heard the captain say he wanted an apprentice, and so you may come.'

"He sculled the boat back again to the vessel, and I climbed up her side.

"'Who are you?' said the captain.

"I told him that I wanted to go to sea.

"'You are too little and too young.'

"'No, I am not,' replied I.

"'Why, do you think that you dare go aloft?'

"'I'll show you,' replied I; and I ran up the rigging like a cat, and went out at the topgallant yard-arm.

"When I came down, the captain said, 'Well, I think you'll make a sharp seaman by and by; so I'll take you, and, as soon as I get to London, I'll bind you apprentice.'

"The ship, which was a collier, was soon out of port, and before the day had dawned I found myself on the wide ocean, which was hereafter to be my home.

"As soon as the hurry and confusion were over, I was examined by the captain, who appeared to me to be a very rough, harsh man; indeed, before the day was over I almost repented of the step which I had taken, and when I sat down cold and wet upon some old sail at night, the thoughts of my mother, and what distress I should occasion her, for the first time rushed into my mind, and I wept bitterly; but it was too late then. I have often thought, Mr Seagrave, that the life of hardship which I have since gone through has been a judgment on me for my cruelty to my mother, in leaving her the way I did. It broke her heart; a poor return, William, for all her care and kindness! God forgive me!"

Old Ready left off for some little time, and the remainder of the party kept silence. Then he said—"I'll leave off now, if you please: I don't feel inclined to go on; my heart is full when I recall that foolish and wicked deed of mine."

Chapter Thirty Three

The next morning was fine, and as soon as breakfast was over, they took the wheels down to the turtle-pond, and Ready having speared one of the largest by means of a pike with a barb to it, which he had made on purpose, they hauled it on shore, slung it under the wheels, and took it up to the house. Having killed the turtle, and cut it up, Juno, under the directions of Ready, chose such portions as were required for the soup; and when the pot was on the fire, Ready, Mr Seagrave, and William set off with the cross-cut saw and hatchets, to commence felling the cocoa-nut trees for the building of the outhouse, which was to hold their stores, as soon as they could be brought round from the other side of the island.

"I mean this to be our place of refuge in case of danger, sir," observed Ready; "and therefore I have selected this thick part of the wood, as it is not very far from the house, and by cutting the path to it in a zigzag, it will be quite hidden from sight; and we must make the path just wide enough to allow the wheels to pass, and stump up the roots of the trees which we are obliged to cut down, otherwise the stumps would attract attention."

"I agree with you, Ready," replied Mr Seagrave; "there is no saying what may happen."

"You see, sir, it is often the custom for the natives, in this part of the world, to come in their canoes from one island to another, merely to get cocoa-nuts. I can't say that the other islands near us are inhabited, but still it is probable, and we cannot tell what the character of the people may be. I tell you this, but we had better not say a word to Mrs Seagrave, as it may distress her."

Mr Seagrave agreed, and Ready continued:

"We are now near the spot, sir. You see, when we have got over this hill, where the trees are so very thick, the fall in the ground will assist in the concealment of the building. I should say we are very near right where we now stand."

"How far are we now from the house? We must not be too distant."

"I reckon we are not 150 yards in a straight line, although the road will, by its turning, make it double the distance."

"Then I think this spot will do very well."

"I'll just mark out the trees which are to stand, Mr Seagrave, and those which are to be cut down, so as to leave about four feet of stump standing."

As soon as they had planned the building, the axes and saw were in full use, and tree after tree fell one upon the other. They worked hard till dinner-time, and were not sorry at the prospect of sitting down to a rich mess of turtle-soup.

"My dear William, and you too, Mr Seagrave, how very warm you are!" said Mrs Seagrave; "you must not work so hard."

"Cutting down trees is very warm work, mother," replied William, "and hard work will never hurt any one, especially when he dines off turtle-soup. Why, Tommy, what's the matter with you?"

"Tommy and I are at variance," replied Mrs Seagrave. "I had my thimble this morning, and had commenced my sewing, when I was called out by Juno, and Caroline went with me, and Tommy was left in the house. When I came back I found him outside, and on going back to my work, there was no thimble to be found; I asked him if he had touched it, and his answer was that he would look for it. He did look, and said he could not find it; I have asked him several times if he took it away, and his only answer is that he will find it by and by."

"Tommy, did you take the thimble?" said Mr Seagrave, gravely.

"I'll find it by and by, papa."

"That's not an answer. Did you take the thimble?"

"I'll find it by and by, papa," said Tommy, whimpering.

"That's all the answer he will give me," said Mrs Seagrave.

"Well, then, he shall have no dinner till the thimble makes its appearance," replied Mr Seagrave.

Master Tommy began to cry at this intelligence. Juno appeared with the turtle-soup; and Tommy cried louder when they had said grace and commenced their dinner. They were all very hungry, and William sent his plate for another portion, which he had not commenced long before he put his finger in his mouth and pulled out something.

"Why, mother, here's the thimble in my soup," cried William.

"No wonder he said he would find it by and by," said Ready, smiling; "he meant to have fished it up, I suppose, from what was left of the soup after dinner. Well, Mrs Seagrave, I don't mean to say that Tommy is a good boy, but still, although he would not tell where the thimble was, he has not told a falsehood about it."

"No, he has not," replied William. "I think, now that the thimble is found, if he begs pardon, papa will forgive him."

"Tommy, come here," said Mr Seagrave. "Tell me why you put that thimble into the soup?"

"I wanted to taste the soup. I wanted to fill the thimble; the soup burnt my fingers, and I let the thimble drop in."

"Well, a thimbleful wasn't much, at all events," observed Ready. "And why didn't you tell your mamma where the thimble was?"

"I was afraid mamma throw all the soup away, and then I get none for dinner."

"Oh! that was it, was it? Well, sir, I said you should have no dinner till the thimble was found, so, as it is found, you may have your dinner; but if you ever refuse to answer a question again, I shall punish you more severely."

Tommy was glad the lecture was over, and more glad to get his turtle-soup; he finished one plate, and, as he asked for another, he said, "Tommy won't put thimble in again; put tin pot in next time."

After dinner they went to their work again, and did not come in again till sunset.

"The clouds are gathering fast, sir," observed Ready; "we shall have rain to-night."

"I fear we shall; but we must expect it now, Ready."

"Yes, sir; and by and by we shall have it for days together."

"Ready," said Mrs Seagrave, "if you are not too tired, perhaps you will go on with your history."

"Certainly, ma'am, if you wish it," replied Ready. "When I left off, I was on board of the collier, bound to London. We had a very fair wind, and a quick passage. I was very sick until we arrived in the Nore, and then I recovered, and, as you may suppose, was astonished at the busy scene, and the quantity of vessels which were going up and down the river. But I did not like my captain; he was very severe and brutal to the men; and the apprentice who was on board told me to run away, and get into another vessel, and not to bind myself apprentice to this captain, or I should be beat all day long, and be treated as bad as he was. I knew this was the case, as the captain kicked and cuffed him twenty times a day. The men said that he did not do so to me, for fear I should refuse to be his apprentice; but that, as soon as my indentures were signed, he would treat me in the same way.

"Well, I made up my mind that I would not remain in the collier; and, as the captain had gone on shore, I had plenty of time to look about me. There was a large ship, which was ready to sail, lying in the stream; I spoke to two boys who were at the stairs in her boat, and they told me that they were very comfortable on board, and that the captain wanted two or three apprentices. I went on board with them, and offered myself. The captain asked me a great many questions, and I told him the truth, and why I did not like to remain in the collier. He agreed to take me; and I went on shore with him, signed my indentures, and received from him a sufficient supply of clothes; and, two days afterwards, we sailed for Bombay and China."

"But you wrote to your mother, Ready, did you not?" said William.

"Yes, I did; for the captain desired me to do so, and he put a few lines at the bottom to comfort her; but, unfortunately, the letter, which was sent on shore by the cook, never arrived. Whether he dropped it, or forgot it till after the ship sailed, and then tore it up, I do not know; but, as I found out afterwards, it never did get to her hands."

"It was not your fault that the letter did not arrive safe," said Mrs Seagrave.

"No, madam, that was not my fault; the fault had been committed before."

"Don't dwell any more upon that portion of your history, Ready; but tell us what took place after you sailed for the East Indies."

"Be it so, if you please. I certainly was very smart and active for my age, and soon became a great favourite on board, especially with the lady passengers, because I was such a little fellow. We arrived safely at Bombay, where our passengers went on shore, and in three weeks afterwards we sailed down the straits for China. It was war time, and we were very often chased by French privateers; but as we had a good crew and plenty of guns, none of them ventured to attack us, and we got safe to Macao, where we unloaded our cargo and took in teas. We had to wait some time for a convoy, and then sailed for England. When we were off the Isle of France, the convoy was dispersed in a gale; and three days afterwards, a French frigate bore down upon us, and after exchanging a few broadsides, we were compelled to haul down our colours. A lieutenant was sent on board with forty men to take charge of us, for we were a very rich prize to them. The captain and most of the crew were taken on board of the frigate, but ten Lascars and the boys were left in the Indiaman, to assist in taking her into the Isle of France, which was at that time in the hands of the French. I thought it hard that I was to go to prison at twelve years old; but I did not care much about it, and very soon I was as gay and merry as ever. We had made the island, and were on a wind beating up to the port, when a vessel was seen to windward, and although I could not understand what the Frenchmen said, I perceived that they were in a great fluster and very busy with their spy-glasses, and Jack Romer, one of my brother 'prentices who had been three years at sea, said to me, 'I don't think we'll go to prison after all, Ready, for that vessel is an English man-of-war, if I'm not mistaken.' At last she came down within three miles of us, and hoisted English colours and fired a gun. The Frenchmen put the ship before the wind, but it was of no use; the man-of-war came up with us very fast, and then the Frenchmen began to pack up their clothes, together with all the other things which they had collected out of the property of our captain and crew; a shot was fired which went clean over our heads, and then they left the helm, and Jack Romer went to it, and, with my help, hove the ship up in the wind; a boat came on board and took possession, and so there was one escape, at all events.

"They sent a midshipman as prize-master on board of the vessel, and left all us, who had been taken prisoners by the French, in the vessel, to help to work her into port, as the captain did not wish to part with any more men of his own than was necessary. We soon made sail for England, quite delighted at having escaped a French prison, but, after all, we only exchanged it for a Dutch one."

"How do you mean?"

"I mean that, two days afterwards, as we were rounding the Cape, another French vessel bore down upon us, and captured us. This time we did not find any friend in need, and were taken into Table Bay; for at that time the Cape of Good Hope was in the possession of the Dutch, who, as well as the French, were at war with England."

"How very unfortunate you were, Ready!" said Mrs Seagrave.

"Yes, madam, we were, and I can't say much in favour of a Dutch prison. However, I was very young at that time, and did not care much—I had a light heart."

Chapter Thirty Four

A heavy storm came on soon after they had retired to rest; the lightning was so vivid that its flashes penetrated through the chinks of the door and windows, and the thunder burst upon them with a noise which prevented them obtaining any sleep. The children cried and trembled as they lay in the arms of Mrs Seagrave and Juno, who were almost as much alarmed themselves.

"This is very awful," said Mr Seagrave to Ready, for they had both risen from their beds.

"It is indeed, sir; I never knew a more terrible storm than this."

"Merciful Heaven!" exclaimed Mr Seagrave.

As he spoke, they were both thrown back half-stunned; a crash of thunder burst over the house, which shook everything in it; a sulphurous smell pervaded the building, and soon afterwards, when they recovered their feet, they perceived that the house was full of smoke, and they heard the wailing of the women and the shrieks of the children in the bed-places on the other side.

"God have mercy on us!" exclaimed Ready, who was the first to recover himself, and who now attempted to ascertain the injury which had been done: "the lightning has struck us, and I fear that the house is on fire somewhere."

"My wife—my children!" exclaimed Mr Seagrave; "are they all safe?"

"Yes, yes!" cried Mrs Seagrave, "all safe; Tommy has come to me; but where is Juno? Juno!"

Juno answered not. William darted to the other side of the house, and found Juno lying on her side, motionless.

"She is dead, father," cried William.

"Help me to carry her out of the house, Mr Seagrave," said Ready, who had lifted up the poor girl; "she may be only stunned."

They carried Juno out of the house, and laid her on the ground; the rain poured down in torrents.

Ready left them for a minute, to ascertain if the house was on fire; he found that it had been in flames at the further corner, but the rain had extinguished it. He then went back to Mr Seagrave and William, who were with Juno.

"I will attend to the girl, sir," said Ready; "go you and Master William into the house; Mrs Seagrave will be too much frightened if she is left alone at such an awful time. See, sir! Juno is not dead—her chest heaves—she will come to very soon; thank God for it!"

William and Mr Seagrave returned to the house; they found Mrs Seagrave fainting with anxiety and fear. The information they brought, that Juno was not killed by the lightning, did much to restore her. William soothed little Albert, and Tommy in a few minutes was fast asleep again in his father's arms. The storm now abated, and as the day began to break, Ready appeared with Juno, who was sufficiently recovered to be able to walk in with his support; she was put into her bed, and then Ready and Mr Seagrave went to examine if further mischief had been done. The lightning had come in at the further end of the house, at the part where the fireplace was intended to have been made.

"We have been most mercifully preserved," said Mr Seagrave.

"Yes, sir, thanks be to God for all his goodness," replied Ready.

"I think we have a large roll of copper wire, Ready; have we not?" said Mr Seagrave.

"Yes, sir, I was just thinking of it myself; we will have a lightning-conductor up the first thing."

It was now broad daylight. Mrs Seagrave dressed herself and the children, and as soon as she was ready, Mr Seagrave read such portions of the Psalms as were appropriate, and they earnestly joined in a prayer of thankfulness and humility. William went out to prepare the breakfast, and Ready procured the coil of copper wire from those stores which were stowed under the bed-places. This he unrolled, and stretched it out straight, and then went for the ladder, which was at the outhouse they had commenced building. As soon as breakfast was over, Ready and Mr Seagrave went out again to fix up the lightning-conductor, leaving William to do the work of Juno, who still remained fast asleep in her bed.

"I think," said Ready, "that one of those two trees which are close together will suit the best; they are not too near the house, and yet quite near enough for the wire to attract the lightning."

"I agree with you, Ready; but we must not leave both standing."

"No, sir, but we shall require them both to get up and fix the wire; after that we will cut down the other."

Ready put his ladder against one of the trees, and, taking with him the hammer and a bag of large spike-nails, drove one of the nails into the trunk of the tree till it was deep enough in to bear his weight; he then drove in another above it, and so he continued to do, standing upon one of them while he drove in another above, till he had reached the top of the tree, close to the boughs; he then descended, and, leaving the hammer behind him, took up a saw and small axe, and in about ten minutes he had cut off the head of the cocoa-nut tree, which remained a tall, bare pole.

"Take care, Ready, how you come down," said Mr Seagrave anxiously.

"Never fear, sir," replied Ready; "I'm not so young as I was, but I have been too often at the mast-head, much higher than this."

Ready came down again, and then cut down a small pole, to fix with a thick piece of pointed wire at the top of it, on the head of the cocoa-nut tree. He then went up, lashed the small pole to the head of the tree, made the end of the copper wire fast to the pointed wire, and then he descended. The other tree near to it was then cut down, and the lower end of the wire buried in the ground at the bottom of the tree on which the lightning-conductor had been fixed.

"That's a good job done, sir," said Ready, wiping his face, for he was warm with the work.

"Yes," replied Mr Seagrave; "and we must put up another near the outhouse, or we may lose our stores."

"Very true, sir."

"You understand this, William, don't you?" said his father.

"O yes, papa; lightning is attracted by metal, and will now strike the point instead of the house, run down the wire, and only tear up the ground below."

"It's coming on again, sir, as thick as ever," observed the old man; "we shall do no work to-day, I'm afraid. I'll just go and see where the stock are."

Juno was now up again, and said that she was quite well, with the exception of a headache. As Ready had predicted, the rain now came on again with great violence, and it was impossible to do any work out of doors. At the request of William he continued his narrative.

Narrative of Old Ready

"Well, William, as soon as they had let go their anchor in Table Bay, we were all ordered on shore, and sent up to a prison close to the Government Gardens. We were not very carefully watched, as it appeared impossible for us to get away, and I must say we were well treated in every respect; but we were told that we should be sent to Holland in the first man-of-war which came into the bay, and we did not much like the idea.

"There were, as I told you, some other boys as well as myself, who belonged to the Indiaman, and we kept very much together, not only because we were more of an age, but because we had been shipmates so long. Two of these boys, one of whom I have mentioned as Jack Romer, and the other Will Hastings, were my particular friends; and one day, as we were sitting under the wall warming ourselves, for it was winter time, Romer said, 'How very easy it would be for us to get away, if we only knew where to go to!'

"'Yes,' replied Hastings; 'but where are we to go to, if it is not to the Hottentots and wild savages; and when we get there, what can we do?—we can't get any further.' 'Well,' said I, 'I would rather be living free among savages, than be shut up in a prison.' That was our first talk on the subject, but we had many others afterwards; and as the one or two Dutch soldiers who stood sentry spoke English, and we could talk a little Dutch, we obtained a good deal of information from them; for they had very often been sent to the frontiers of the colony. We continued to ask questions, and to talk among ourselves for about two months, and at last we resolved that we would make our escape. We should have done much better if we had remained where we were; but there is no putting old heads upon young shoulders. We saved up our provisions, bought some long Dutch knives, tied our few clothes up in bundles, and one dark night we contrived to remain in the yard without being perceived, when the prisoners were locked up; and raising a long pole, which lay in the yard, to the top of the wall, with a good deal of scrambling we contrived to get over it, and made off as fast as we could for the Table Mountain."

"What was your reason for going there, Ready?"

"Why, Hastings, who was the oldest, and, I will say, the sharpest of the three, said that we had better stay up there for a few days, till we had made up our minds what to do, and try if we could not procure a musket or two, and ammunition; for, you see, we had money, as, when the Indiaman was first taken, the captain divided a keg of rupees, which was on board, among the officers and men, in proportion to the wages due to them, thinking it was better for the crew to have the money than to leave it for the Frenchmen; and we had spent very little while in prison. There was also another reason why he persuaded us to go to the Table Mountain, which was, that as soon as our escape was found out, they would send parties to look for us; thinking, of course, that we had made for the interior; and we should have less chance of being retaken if we travelled after the first search was over. The soldiers had told us of the lions, and other wild animals, and how dangerous it was to travel, and Hastings said, that not finding us, they would suppose we had been destroyed by the wild beasts, and would not look for us any more."

"Foolish indeed," observed Mrs Seagrave, "to set off you knew not where, in a country full of wild beasts and savages."

"True enough, madam," replied Ready. "We ran at first until we were out of breath, and then we walked on as fast as we could—not going right up the mountain, but keeping a slanting direction to the south-west, so as to get away from the town, and more towards False Bay.

"We had walked about four hours, and began to feel very tired, when the day dawned, and then we looked out for a place to conceal ourselves in. We soon found a cave with a narrow entrance, large enough inside to hold half-a-dozen of such lads as we were, and we crawled in. It was quite dry, and, as we were very tired, we lay down with our heads on our bundles, intending to take a nap; but we had hardly made ourselves comfortable and shut our eyes, when we heard such a screaming and barking that we were frightened out of our lives almost. We could not think what it could be. At last Hastings peeped out, and began to laugh; so Romer and I looked out also, and there we saw about one hundred and fifty large baboons leaping and tumbling about in such a way as I never saw; they were bigger than we were—indeed, when they stood on their hind legs they were much taller, and they had very large white tusks. Some of them were females, with young ones on their backs, and they were just as active as the males. At last they played such antics, that we all burst out into a loud laugh, and we had not ceased when we found the grinning face of one of the largest of those brutes close to our own. He had dropped from the rock above us, like magic. We all three backed into the cave, very much frightened, for the teeth of the animal were enormous, and he looked very savage. He gave a shrill cry, and we perceived all the rest of the herd coming to him as fast as they could. I said that the cave was large enough to hold six of us; but there was a sort of inner cave which we had not gone into, as the entrance was much smaller. Romer cried out, 'Let us go into the inside cave—we can get in one by one;' and he backed in; Hastings followed with his bundle, and I hurried in after him just in time; for the baboons, who had been chattering to each other for half a minute, came into the outer cave just as I crawled into the inner. Five or six of them came in, all males, and very large. The first thing they did was to lay hold of Romer's bundle, which they soon opened—at once they seized his provisions and rammed them into their pouches, and then they pulled out the other things and tore them all to pieces. As soon as they had done with the bundle, two of them came towards the inner cave and saw us. One put his long paw in to seize us; but Hastings gave him a slash with his knife, and the animal took his paw out again fast enough. It was laughable to see him hold out his hand to the others, and then taste the blood with the tip of his tongue, and such a chattering I never heard—they were evidently very angry, and more came into the cave and joined them; then another put in his hand, and received a cut just as before. At last, two or three at once tried to pull us out, but we beat them all off with our knives, wounding them all very severely. For about an hour they continued their attempts, and then they went away out of the cave, but remained at the mouth shrieking and howling. We began to be very tired of this work, and Romer said that he wished he was back in prison again; and so did I, I can assure you; but there was no getting out, for had we gone out the animals would have torn us to pieces. We agreed that we had no chance but the animals becoming tired and going away; and most anxious we were, for the excitement had made us very thirsty, and we wanted water. We remained for two hours in this way imprisoned by baboons, when all of a sudden a shrill cry was given by one of the animals, and the whole herd went galloping off as fast as they could, screaming louder than ever. We waited for a short time to see if they would return, and then Hastings crawled out first, and looking out of the cave very cautiously, said that they were all gone, and that he could see nothing but a Hottentot sitting down watching some cattle; we therefore all came out, very happy at our release. That was our first adventure; we had plenty afterwards; but I think it is now time we should go to bed. It is my opinion we shall have a fine day to-morrow, sir; but there's no saying."

"I do so want to hear what happened to you afterwards, Ready," said William.

"Well, so you shall; but there's a time for everything, and this is bedtime, unless you like to go with me; the weather has cleared up, and I want to catch a fish or two for to-morrow."

Chapter Thirty Five

As Ready had predicted, the weather set in fine after the violent storm of which we have made mention. For a fortnight, with little intermission, it continued fine, and during that time, Ready, Mr Seagrave, and William worked from daylight till dusk at the storehouse, which they were so anxious to complete, and were so tired when their work was over, that even William did not ask Ready to go on with his history. At last the storehouse was complete, thatched and wattled in on three sides, leaving one open for ventilation; the lower part, which had been arranged for the folding of the stock at night and during the rainy season, was also wattled in with cocoa-nut boughs on three sides, and made a very comfortable retreat for the animals. The winding path to the storehouse was also cut through the cocoa-nut grove, but the stumps were not removed, as they could not spare the time. All the stores that they had brought round were put into the storehouse, and they were now ready to take up some other job. It was, however, agreed that, on the day after the building was finished, they should all have a day's holiday, which they certainly did require. William caught some fish, a turtle was speared and wheeled up to the house; and they not only had a holiday, but a feast. Mr Seagrave and William had been walking on the beach with Mrs Seagrave and the children, while Ready was assisting Juno in cutting up the turtle; they had shown Mrs Seagrave the storehouse, and the goats with the four kids had been led there, as there was no longer any occasion for them to remain in the house. The weather was beautiful, and they agreed to go and examine the garden. They found that the seeds had not yet commenced sprouting, notwithstanding the heavy rains.

"I should have thought that so much rain would have made them come up," said Mrs Seagrave.

"No, my dear," replied Mr Seagrave; "they require more of the sun than they will have till the rainy season is nearly over; a few days like this, and they will soon be above-ground."

"Let us sit down on this knoll, it is quite dry," said Mrs Seagrave. "I little thought," continued she, "that I could have been so happy in a desert island. I thought I should feel the loss of books very severely, but I really do not think that I could have found time to read."

"Employment is a source of happiness, especially when you are usefully employed. An industrious person is always a happy person, provided he is not obliged to work too hard; and even where you have cause for unhappiness, nothing makes you forget it so soon as occupation."

"But, mamma, we shall not always have so much to do as we have now," said William.

"Of course not," replied Mr Seagrave; "and then we shall find our books a great source of enjoyment. I am anxious to go to the other side of the island, and see what have been spared to us, and whether they have been much damaged; but that cannot be until after the rains are over, and we can use the boat again.

"Look at this minute insect which is crawling on my finger," said Mr Seagrave, turning to William: "what a number of legs it has!"

"Yes, I have seen something like it in old books. How fast it runs with its little legs; thinner than hairs—how wonderful!"

"Yes, William," replied Mr Seagrave, "we have only to examine into any portion, however small, of creation, and we are immediately filled with wonder. There is nothing which points out to us the immensity and the omniscience of the Almighty more than the careful provision which has been made by Him for the smallest and most insignificant of created beings. This little animal is perhaps one of many millions, who have their term of existence, and their enjoyment, as well as we have. What is it?—an insect of the minutest kind, a nothing in creation; yet has the same care been bestowed upon its formation: these little legs, hardly visible, have their muscles and their sinews; and every other portion of its body is as complete, as fearfully and wonderfully fashioned, as our own. Such is his will; and what insects we ought to feel ourselves, when compared to the God of power and of love!"

"Let me also point out to you, William," continued Mr Seagrave, "the infinity of his creative power, displayed in endless variety. Amongst the millions of men that have been born, and died, if ever yet were there seen two faces or two bodies exactly alike; nay, if you could examine the leaves upon the trees, although there may be millions upon millions in a forest, you could not discover two leaves of precisely the same form and make."

"I have often tried in vain," replied William; "yet some animals are so much alike, that I cannot perceive any difference between them—sheep, for instance."

"Very true; you cannot tell the difference, because you have not examined them; but a shepherd, if he has seven hundred sheep under his care, will know every one of them from the others; which proves that there must be a great difference between them, although not perceptible to the casual observer; and the same, no doubt, is the case with all other classes of animals."

"Yes, William," observed Ready; "I have often wondered over the things that I have seen, and I have even in my ignorance felt what your papa has now told you; and it has brought into my mind the words of Job: 'When I consider, I am afraid of him.'"

"Papa," said William, after a pause in the conversation, "you have referred to the variety—the wonderful variety—shown in the works of the Deity. Tell me some other prominent feature in creation."

"One of the most remarkable, William, is order."

"Point out to me, papa, where and in what that quality is most observable."

"Everywhere and in everything, my dear boy; whether we cast our eyes up to the heavens above us, or penetrate into the bowels of the earth, the principle of order is everywhere—everything is governed by fixed laws, which cannot be disobeyed: we have order in the seasons, in the tides, in the movement of the heavenly bodies, in the instinct of animals, in the duration of life assigned to each; from the elephant who lives more than a century, to the ephemeral fly, whose whole existence is limited to an hour.

"Inanimate nature is subject to the same unvarying laws. Metals, and rocks, and earths, and all the mineral kingdom follow one law in their crystallisation, never varying from the form assigned to them; each atom depositing itself in the allotted place, until that form is complete: we have order in production, order in decay; but all is simple to him by whom the planets were thrown out into space, and were commanded to roll in their eternal orbits."

"Yes; the stars in the heavens are beautiful," said William, "but they are not placed there in order."

"The fixed stars do not appear to us to be in order—that is, they do not stud the heavens at equal distances from each other as we view them; but you must recollect that they are at very different distances from this earth, spreading over all infinity of space; and we have reason to suppose that this our earth is but a mere unit in the multitude of created worlds, only one single portion of an infinite whole. As the stars now appear to us, they are useful to the mariner, enabling him to cross the trackless seas; and to the astronomer, who calculates the times and seasons."

"What do you mean, papa, by saying that this world of ours is supposed to be but one of a multitude of created worlds?"

"Our little knowledge is bounded to this our own earth, which we have ascertained very satisfactorily to be but one of several planets revolving round our own sun. I say our own sun, because we have every reason to suppose that each of those fixed stars, and myriads now not visible to the naked eye, are all suns, bright and glorious as our own, and of course throwing light and heat upon unseen planets revolving round them. Does not this give you some idea of the vastness, the power, and the immensity of God?"

"One almost loses one's self in the imagination," said Mrs Seagrave.

"Yes," replied Mr Seagrave; "and it has been surmised by some, who have felt in their hearts the magnificence of the Great Architect, that there must be some point of view in space where all those glorious suns, which seem to us confused in the heavens above us, will appear all symmetrically arranged, will there be viewed in regular order, whirling round in one stupendous and perfect system of beauty and design; and where can that be, if it is not in that heaven which we hope to gain?"

There was a silence for a few moments, when William said, "They say that there are people who are atheists, papa. How can they be so if they only look around them? I am sure a mere examination of the works of God ought to make them good Christians."

"No, my child," replied Mr Seagrave; "there you are in error. Few deny the existence of a Deity, and an examination of his works may make them good and devout men, but not Christians. There are good men to be found under every denomination, whether they be Jews, Mahomedans, or Pagans; but they are not Christians."

"Very true, papa."

"Faith in things seen, if I may use the term, my dear child, may induce men to acknowledge the power and goodness of the Almighty, but it will not make them wise to salvation; for that end, it is necessary, as the Apostle saith, to have faith in things not seen."

Chapter Thirty Six

"Well, Ready," said Mr Seagrave, after breakfast, "which is to be our next job?"

"Why, sir, I think we had better all set to, to collect the branches and ends of the cocoa-nut trees cut down, and stack them for fuel. Tommy and Juno have already made a good large pile, and I think, by to-night, we shall have made the stack, and so arranged it that the rain will not get into it much. After that, as the weather will not permit us to leave the house for any time, we will cut our salt-pan and make our fish-pond; they will take a week at least, and then we shall have little more to do near home. I think the strength of the rains is over already, and perhaps in a fortnight we may venture to walk through the wood, and examine what we have saved from the wreck."

"And we are to explore the island; are we not, Ready?" said William. "I long to do that."

"Yes, William, but that must be almost the last job; for we shall be away for two or three nights, perhaps, and we must look out for fine weather. We will, however, do that before we bring the stores round in the boat."

"But how are we to make the salt-pan, Ready? We must cut it out of the solid rock."

"Yes, William; but I have three or four of what they call cold chisels, and with one of them and a hammer, we shall get on faster than you think; for the coral rock, although hard at the surface, is soft a little below it."

The whole of that day was employed in piling up the cocoa-nut branches and wood. Ready made a square stack, like a haystack, with a gable top, over which he tied the long branches, so that the rain would pour off it.

"There," said Ready, as he came down the ladder, "that will be our provision for next year; we have quite enough left to go on with till the rainy season is over, and we shall have no difficulty in collecting it afterwards when the weather is dry."

Mr Seagrave sighed and looked grave; Ready observed it, and said, "Mr Seagrave, it is not that we may want it; but still we must prepare for the next rainy season, in case we do want it. That Captain Osborn, if he lives, will send to look for us, I have no doubt; nay, I believe that Mackintosh will do the same; but still you must not forget that they all may have perished, although we have been so mercifully preserved. We must put our trust in God, sir."

"We must, Ready; and if it is his will, we must not murmur. I have schooled myself as much as possible; but thoughts will come in spite of my endeavours to restrain them."

"Of course they will, sir; that's natural: however, sir, you must hope for the best; fretting is no good, and it is sinful."

"I feel it is, Ready; and when I see how patient, and even happy, my wife is under such privations, I am angry with myself."

"A woman, sir, bears adversity better than a man. A woman is all love, and if she has but her husband and children with her, and in good health, she will make herself happy almost anywhere: but men are different: they cannot bear being shut out of the world as you are now."

"It is our ambition which makes us unhappy, Ready," replied Mr Seagrave; "but let us say no more about it: God must dispose of me as he thinks fit."

After supper, Ready, being requested by William, continued his narrative.

"I left off, if I recollect right, William, just as the Hottentot, with the cattle under his care, had frightened away the baboons who were tormenting us. Well, we came out of the cave and sat down under the rock, so that the Hottentot could not see us, and we had a sort of council of war. Romer was for going back and giving ourselves up again; for he said it was ridiculous to be wandering about without any arms to defend ourselves against wild beasts, and that we might fall in with something worse than the baboons very soon; and he was right. It would have been the wisest thing which we could have done; but Hastings said, that if we went back we should be laughed at, and the idea of being laughed at made us all agree that we would not. Bear this in mind, William, and never let the fear of ridicule induce you to do what is wrong; or if you have done wrong, prevent you from returning to what is your duty."

"Many thanks for your advice, Ready; I hope William will not forget it," said Mr Seagrave.

"Well, sir, such was our reason for not giving up our mad scheme; and having so decided, the next point of consultation between us was, how we were to procure arms and ammunition, which we could not do without. As we were talking this over, I peeped from behind the rock to see where the Hottentot might be; I perceived that he had laid himself down, and wrapped himself up in his kross, a mantle of sheep-skins which they always wear. Now we had observed that he carried his musket in his hand, when we first saw him, as the Hottentots always go out armed, and I pointed out to Hastings and Romer that if he was asleep, we might get possession of his musket without his perceiving it. This was a good idea, and Hastings said he would crawl to him on his hands and knees, while we remained behind the rock. He did so very cautiously, and found the man's head covered up in his kross and fast asleep; so there was no fear, for the Hottentots are very hard to wake at any time; that we knew well. Hastings first took the musket and carried it away out of the reach of the Hottentot, and then he returned to him, cut the leather thong which slung his powder-horn and ammunition, and retreated with all of them without disturbing the man from his sleep. We were quite overjoyed at this piece of good luck, and determined to walk very cautiously some distance from where the Hottentot lay, that in case he awoke he should not see us. Keeping our eyes about in every direction, lest we should meet with anybody else, we proceeded nearly a mile towards Table Bay, when we fell in with a stream of water. This was another happy discovery, for we were very thirsty; so we concealed ourselves near the stream after we had quenched our thirst, and made a dinner off the provisions we had brought with us."

"But, Ready, did you not do wrong to steal the Hottentot's musket?"

"No, William; in that instance it could not be considered as a theft. We were in an enemy's country, trying to escape; we were therefore just as much at war with the country as we were when they took us prisoners, and we no more stole the musket than they could be said to have stolen our ship. Am I not right, Mr Seagrave?"

"I believe you are justified in what may seem extreme acts for the recovery of your liberty, after you have been made prisoners. It has always been so considered."

"Well, sir, to go on: we waited till dusk, and then we continued our march towards False Bay as fast as we could. We knew that there were farmers down in the valley, or rather on the sides of the hills, and we hoped to obtain, by some means or other, two more muskets. It was near twelve o'clock at night, with a bright moon, when we had a sight of the water in False Bay, and soon afterwards we heard the baying of a large dog, and not far from us we distinguished two or three farmhouses, with their cattle-folds and orchards. We then looked for a hiding-place, where we might remain till the morning; we found one between some large pieces of rock. We agreed that one should watch while the other two slept; this Hastings undertook to do, as he was not inclined to sleep. At daylight he woke Romer and me, and we made our breakfast. From the place we were concealed in, we had a bird's-eye view of the farmhouse, and of what was going on.

"The farmhouse and buildings just below us were much smaller than the other two, which were more distant. We watched the people as they went about. In about an hour the Hottentots came out, and we perceived that they were yoking the oxen to the waggon; they yoked twelve pair, and then the Hottentot driver got in and drove off towards Cape Town. Soon after that, another Hottentot drove the cows up the valley to feed; and then a Dutch woman came out of the house with two children, and fed the poultry.

"We watched for another hour, and then the farmer himself made his appearance, with a pipe in his mouth, and sat down on a bench. When his pipe was out, he called to the house, and a Hottentot woman came to him with more tobacco and a light. During the whole of the day we did not see any other people about the house, so we concluded that there were no more than the farmer, his wife, the Hottentot woman, and two children. About two hours after noon the farmer went to the stable and led out his horse, mounted, and rode away; we saw him speak to the Hottentot woman when he rode off, and she soon after went down the valley with a basket on her head, and a long knife in her hand. Then Hastings said it was time that we moved, for there was but one woman in the house, and we could easily overpower her and get what we wanted; still there was a great risk, as she might give the alarm, and we should have to escape in the day-time, and might be seen and taken prisoners again. However, as it was our only chance, we resolved to go down to the farmhouse very cautiously, and be all ready to seize any opportunity. We crept down the hill, and gained the fence, which was at the back of the farmhouse, without being discovered: we remained there for about a quarter of an hour, when, to our great joy, we observed the farmer's wife go out of the house, leading a child in each hand; apparently she was going to visit one of her neighbours, for she went in the direction of one of the other farms. As soon as she was a hundred yards off, Hastings crept softly through the fence, and entered the farmhouse by the back-door; he came out again, and made a sign for us to come in. We found him already in possession of a rifle and a musket, which had been hanging over the fire-place, and we soon handed down the powder-horns and ammunition pouches, which were hung up at a different part of the room, away from the fire-place.

"Having gained these, Hastings set me to watch at the front door, lest anybody should return, while Romer and he looked out for something else in the way of provisions. We got possession of three hams, and a large loaf of bread as big as a small washing-tub. With these articles we made our way safe back to our retreat. We then looked round, and could see nobody in any direction, so we presumed that we were not discovered. As there was a sort of ravine full of rocks dividing the hill, which we were obliged to pass before we could get into the valley, unless we went down close to the farmhouse, we agreed that it would be better at once to cross it during the day-time, so that we should get that difficulty over, and, at the same time, be further from the farmhouse. We did so; and found a very secure hiding-place, where we lay down, waiting for the sun to set before we started on our journey into the interior. I think I had better leave off now, William, as it is getting late."

Chapter Thirty Seven

The fishpond was commenced the next morning. Ready, Mr Seagrave, and William went down together to the beach, and, after much examination, chose a spot about one hundred yards from the turtle-pond as most eligible for the purpose; the water being shallow, so that at the part farthest from the shore there would not be more than three feet.

"Now, sir," said Ready, "this is a very simple job; all we have to do is to collect small rocks and stones, pile them up wall-fashion inside, and with a slope outside, so as to break the force of the waves when the water is a little rough; of course, the water will find its way through the stones, and will be constantly changed. It's very true, that we can at most times catch fish when we want them, but it is not always that we can spare the time, so it's just as well to have always a certain quantity at hand, to take out at a moment's warning; and we can, of course, catch them and put them in here when we have nothing else to do. Juno will be able to come down and take them out with a spear, when we are away and she wants something for dinner."

"But there are few stones about here, Ready; we shall have to fetch them a long way," said William

"Well, then, William, let us get the wheels down here, and then we can carry a quantity at a time."

"But how shall we carry them, Ready?"

"We will sling a tub on the axle; I will go up and get that ready and bring it down; in the meantime, you and Mr Seagrave can collect all the stones which are near at hand."

Ready soon returned with the wheels, and the tub slung with rope on the axle, and by that means they found that they could collect the stones very fast; Mr Seagrave and William bringing them, and Ready in the water, building up the wall.

"We have quite forgot another job which we must put in hand, sir," observed Ready; "but the fish-pond reminds me of it."

"What is that, Ready?"

"A bathing-place for the children, and indeed for us all; we shall want it when the hot weather comes on, but we will put it off till then. I can tell you, sir, that although I don't mind building this wall in the shallow water, I shall be very careful when the water is up to my knees, for you don't know how bold the sharks are in these latitudes. When I was at St. Helena, not very long ago, we had a melancholy proof of it."

"Tell us the story, Ready."

"Well, two soldiers were standing on the rocks at St. Helena; the rocks were out of the water, but the swell just broke over them. Two sharks swam up to them, and one of them, with a blow of his tail, turning round the same way, tripped one of them into the water, which was very deep. His comrade was very much frightened, and ran to the barracks to tell the story. About a week afterwards, a schooner was in Sandy Bay, on the other side of the island, and the people seeing a very large shark under the stern, put out a hook with a piece of pork, and caught him; they opened him, and found inside of him, to their horror, the whole of the body of the soldier, except the legs below the knees: the monster had swallowed him whole, with the exception of his legs, which it had nipped off when it closed its jaws."

"I really had no idea that they were so bold, Ready."

"It is a fact, I assure you; and therefore we cannot be too careful how we go into the water: you saw how soon the poor pig was despatched."

"I wonder how the pigs get on, Ready," said William.

"I dare say they have littered by this time, sir; they have no want of food."

"But can they eat the cocoa-nuts?"

"Not the old ones, but they can the young ones, which are constantly dropping from the trees, and then there's plenty of roots for them. If we stay long here we shall soon have good sport hunting them; but we must be very careful; for although they were tame pigs when we brought them on shore, they will be wild and very savage in a very short time."

"How must we hunt them?" said Mr Seagrave.

"Why, sir, with the dogs, and then shoot them. I am glad that Vixen will have pups soon; we shall want more dogs."

"Shall we not have more mouths than we can find food for?"

"Never fear that, sir, as long as we have the sea to fish in. Dogs live very well upon fish, even if it is raw."

"We shall have some lambs soon, Ready, shall we not?"

"Yes, sir, I expect very soon. I wish we had more food for the animals: they are put rather hard to it just now; but next year, if we find more food on the island, we must keep the grass near home, to make hay and stack it for the winter time—or the rainy season rather, for there is no winter in these latitudes. I'm pretty sure we shall find some clear land on the south of the island, for the cocoa-nut grove does not extend so close to the water on that side as it does on the north."

"I do so long to go on our exploring party," said William.

"We must wait a little," replied Ready; "but I don't know whether you will go; we must not all three go at once, and leave Mrs Seagrave alone."

"No," replied Mr Seagrave, "that would not be fair; either you or I must remain, William."

William made no reply, but it was evident that he was annoyed at the idea of not being of the party. They worked very hard that day, and the walls rose fast out of the water.

After supper, Ready continued his narrative. "We remained concealed until it was dark, and then Hastings and Romer, each with a musket on his shoulders and a ham at his back; and I, being the smallest, with the rifle and the great loaf of bread, set off on our journey. Our intention was to travel north, as we knew that was the road leading from the colony; but Hastings had decided that we should first go to the eastward, so as to make what we sailors call a circumbendibus, which would keep us out of the general track. We passed through the deep sands of False Bay, and after that gradually ascended, getting among brushwood and young trees; but we saw no signs of cultivation, nor did we pass one house after we had left False Bay astern of us. About twelve o'clock we were very much fatigued, and longed for a drink of water, but we did not find any, although the moon shone as bright as day. We distinctly heard, however, what we did not much like, the howling and cries of the wild beasts which increased as we went on; still we did not see any, and that was our comfort. At last we were so tired that we all sat down on the ledge of a rock. We dared not go to sleep, so we remained there till daylight, listening to the howling of the animals. We none of us spoke, and I presume that Hastings' and Romer's thoughts were the same as my own, which were, that I would have given a great deal to find myself safe and sound again within the prison walls. However, daylight came at last; the wild beasts did not prowl any more; we walked on till we found a stream of water, where we sat down and took our breakfast, after which our courage revived, and we talked and laughed as we walked on, just as we had done before. We now began to ascend the mountains, which Hastings said must be the Black Mountains that the soldiers had talked to us about. They were very desolate; and when night came on we collected brushwood, and cut down branches with our knives, that we might make a fire, not only to warm ourselves, but to scare away the wild beasts, whose howling had already commenced. We lighted our fire and ate our supper; the loaf was half gone, and the hams had been well cut into—we knew, therefore, that very soon we should have to trust to our guns for procuring food. As soon as we had finished our meal, we lay down by the fire, with our muskets loaded close to us, and our ammunition placed out of danger. We were so tired that we were soon fast asleep. It had been agreed that Romer should keep the first watch, and Hastings the middle, and I the morning; but Romer fell asleep, and the consequence was, that the fire was not kept up. It was about midnight that I was awakened by something breathing hard in my face, and just as I could recall my senses and open my eyes, I found myself lifted up by my waistband, and the teeth of some animal pinching my flesh. I tried to catch at my musket, but I put out my wrong hand, and laid hold of a still lighted brand out of the fire, which I darted into the animal's face; it let me drop directly, and ran away."

"What a providential escape!" said Mrs Seagrave.

"Yes, it was, ma'am; the animal was a hyena. Fortunately they are a very cowardly sort of beast; still, had it not been for the lighted stick, it would have carried me off, for I was very small then, and it lifted me up as if I was a feather in its mouth. The shout I gave woke Hastings, who seized his musket and fired. I was very much frightened, as you may suppose. As for Romer, he never woke till we pushed him hard, he was so completely knocked up. This affair, of course, made us more cautious, and afterwards we lighted two fires, and slept between them, one always remaining on the watch. For a week we travelled on, and as soon as we were over the mountains, we turned our heads to the northward. Our provisions were all gone, and we were one day without any; but we killed an antelope called a spring-bock, which gave us provisions for three or four days: there was no want of game after we had descended into the plain. I forgot to mention, however, a narrow escape we had, just before we had left an extensive forest on the side of the mountain. We had walked till past noon, and were very much tired; we decided upon taking our dinner under a large tree, and we threw ourselves down in the shade. Hastings was lying on his back, with his eyes looking upwards, when he perceived on the lower branch of the tree a panther, which lay along it, his green eyes fixed upon us, and ready to spring; he seized his musket, and fired it without taking aim, for there was no time; but the ball entered the stomach of the animal, and, as it appeared, divided its back-bone. Down came the beast, within three or four feet of where we lay, with a loud roar, and immediately crouched to spring upon Romer; but it could not, for the back-bone being broken, it had not any power in its hinder quarters, so it raised up its fore quarters, and then dropped down again. I never saw such rage and fury in an animal in my life. At first we were too much frightened to fire; but, perceiving that the beast could not spring, Hastings snatched the musket from Romer and shot it through the head.

"We were now obliged to hunt for our livelihood, and we became bolder than ever. Our clothes were all in rags; but we had plenty of powder and ammunition; there were hundreds and hundreds of antelopes and gnus in the plain—indeed, sometimes it was impossible to count them. But this plentiful supply of game was the cause of our being in greater danger, for now, for the first time, we heard the roar of the lions every night. We made large fires to keep them off, but they often made us tremble when they came near to us."

"Did you ever meet with one in the day time?" said William.

"Yes, sir; we often saw them, but they never attacked us, and we were too much afraid to fire at them. Once we met one face to face. We had killed an antelope called a hartebeest, and, with our muskets on our shoulders, were running to secure it. Just as we came up to the spot, we heard a roar, and found ourselves not ten yards from a lion, who was lying on the top of the beast we had killed, his eyes flashing fire at us, and half raising himself, as if ready for a spring. We all took to our heels as fast as we could. I never looked back till I was out of breath: but the lion was content with our running away, and did not take the trouble to follow us. Well, sir, we had been travelling, we really hardly knew where, but certainly in a northerly direction, for three weeks, and were quite worn out: we now all agreed that we had done a very foolish thing, and would gladly have gone back again. For my part, I declare that I was willing to lie down and die, if I could have so done, and I became quite indifferent to the roaring of the lions, and felt as if I should be glad if one would have made a meal of me. At length, one morning, we fell in with a party of natives. They were of the Karroo tribe, as they told us by pointing to themselves, and saying, 'Karroos', and then they pointed to us, and said 'Dutch'. We shot game, and gave it to them, which pleased them very much, and they remained with us for five or six days. We tried by signs to inquire of them, if there were any Dutch settlement about there; and they understood us, and said that there was, in a direction which they pointed out to us, to the north-east. We offered them a present if they would show us the way. Two of the men agreed to go with us; the rest of the tribe, with the women and children, went southward. The next day we arrived at a Dutch settlement of three or four farmhouses, called Graaff Reinet; but I must leave off now, for it is past bed-time."

Chapter Thirty Eight

The construction of the fish-pond proceeded rapidly, and on the third day it was nearly complete. As soon as all the walls were finished, Ready threw out sand and shingle, so as to make the part next to the beach nearly as deep as the other; so that there might be sufficient water to prevent the gulls and man-of-war birds from darting down, and striking the fish. While Ready was thus employed, Mr Seagrave and William collected more rocks, so as to divide the pond into four parts, at the same time allowing a communication between each part. These inside walls, as well as the outside, were made of sufficient width to walk upon; by which means they would have all the fish within reach of the spear, in case they wished to take them out. The day after the pond was completed the weather changed. The rain poured down with great force, but it was not accompanied with such terrific thunder and lightning, nor were the storms of so long continuance, as at the commencement of the rainy season. In the intervals of fine weather they caught a great many fish, which they put into the pond, so that it was well stocked. But a circumstance occurred, which was the occasion of great alarm to them all; which was, that one evening William was taken with a shivering, and complained very much of a pain in his head. Ready had promised to continue his narrative on that evening, but William was too ill to sit up. He was put into bed, and the next morning he was in a violent fever. Mr Seagrave was much alarmed, as the symptoms were worse every hour; and Ready, who had sat up with him during the night, called Mr Seagrave out of the house, and said, "This is a bad case, sir: William was working yesterday with his hat off, and I fear that he has been struck by the sun."

The poor boy was for many days in great danger; and the cheerful house was now one of gloom and silence. How fervent were now the morning and evening prayers; how often during the day did his parents offer up a petition to heaven for their dear boy's recovery. The weather became finer every day, and it was almost impossible to keep Tommy quiet: Juno went out with him and Albert every morning, and kept them with her while she cooked; and, fortunately, Vixen had some young ones, and when Juno could no longer amuse them, she brought them two of the puppies to play with. As for the quiet, meek little Caroline, she would remain during the whole day holding her mother's hand, and watching her brother, or working with her needle by the side of his bed.

Ready, who could not be idle, had taken the hammer and cold chisel to make the salt-pan, at which he worked during those portions of the day in which his services were not required indoors; and as he sat chipping away the rock, his thoughts were ever upon William, for he dearly loved the boy for his amiable disposition and his cleverness; and many a time during the day would he stop his work, and the tears would run down his cheeks as he offered up his petition to the Almighty that the boy might be spared to his afflicted parents. And those prayers were heard, for on the ninth day William was pronounced by Ready and Mr Seagrave to have much less fever, and shortly afterwards it left him altogether; but he was so weak that he could not raise himself in his bed for two or three days; and it was not till more than a fortnight after the fever had left him that he could go out of the house. The joy that was expressed by them all when the change took place may be imagined: nor were the thanksgivings less fervent than had been the prayers.

During his convalescence, as there was nothing else to do, Mr Seagrave and Ready, who now went gladly to their work, determined, as the salt-pan was finished, that they would make a bathing-place. Juno came to their assistance, and was very useful in assisting to drag the wheels which brought the rocks and stones; and Tommy was also brought down, that he might be out of the way while Mrs Seagrave and Caroline watched the invalid. By the time that William was able to go out of the house, the bathing-place was finished, and there was no longer any fear of the sharks. William came down to the beach with his mother, and looked at the work which had been done; he was much pleased with it, and said, "Now, Ready, we have finished everything at home for the present; all we have to do is to explore the island, and to go to the cove and examine our collection from the wreck."

"Very true, William; and the weather has been so fine, that I think we may venture upon one or the other in a few days more; but not till you are stronger."

"I shall soon be strong again, Ready."

"I have no doubt of it, William; and we have good reason to thank God, for we could ill spare you."

"It's a long while since you have gone on with your story, Ready," said William, after they had taken their supper; "I wish you would do so now, as I am sure I shall not be tired."

"With pleasure, William," replied Ready; "but can you remember where I left off, for my memory is none of the best?"

"Oh, yes; if you recollect, you had just arrived at a Dutch farmer's house, in company with the savages, at a place called Graaff Reinet, I think."

"Well then, the Dutch farmer came out when he saw us coming, and asked us who we were. We told him that we were English prisoners, and that we wished to give ourselves up to the authorities. He took away our arms and ammunition, and said that he was the authority in that part, which was true enough; and then he said, 'You'll not run away without arms and ammunition, that's certain. As for sending you to the Cape, that I may not be able to do for months; so if you wish to be fed well, you must work well while you're here.' We replied, that we should be very glad to make ourselves useful, and then he sent us some dinner by a Hottentot girl. But we soon found out that we had to deal with an ill-tempered, brutal fellow; and that he gave us plenty of hard work, but by no means plenty of food. He would not trust us with guns, so the Hottentots went out with the cattle, but he gave us plenty of work to do about the house; and at last he treated us very cruelly. When he was short of provisions for the Hottentots and other slaves, of whom he had a good many, he would go out with the other farmers who lived near him, and shoot quaggas for them to eat. Nobody but a Hottentot could live upon such flesh."

"What is quagga?"

"A wild ass, partly covered with stripes, but not so much as the zebra; a pretty animal to look at, but the flesh is very bad. At last he would give us nothing to eat but quaggas, the same as the Hottentots, while he and his family—for he had a wife and five children—lived upon mutton and the flesh of the antelope, which is very excellent eating. We asked him to allow us a gun to procure better food, and he kicked Romer so unmercifully, that he could not work for two days afterwards. Our lives became quite a burden to us; we were employed all day on the farm, and every day he was more brutal towards us. At last we agreed that we would stand it no longer, and one evening Hastings told him so. This put him into a great rage, and he called two of the slaves, and ordered them to tie him to the waggon wheel, swearing that he would cut every bit of skin off his body, and he went into his house to get his whip. The slaves had hold of Hastings, and were tying him up, for they dared not disobey their master, when he said to us, 'If I am flogged this way, it will be all over with us. Now's your time; run back behind the house, and when he comes out with the whip, do you go in and seize the muskets, which are always ready loaded. Hold him at bay till I get clear, and then we will get away somehow or other. You must do it, for I am sure he will flog me till I am dead, and he will shoot you, as runaway prisoners, as he did his two Hottentots the other day.' As Romer and I thought this very probable, we did as Hastings told us; and when the Dutchman had gone towards him where he was tied up, about fifty yards from the house, we went in. The farmer's wife was in bed, having just had an addition to her family, and the children we cared not for. We seized two muskets and a large knife, and came out just as the Dutchman had struck the first blow with the rhinoceros whip, which was so severe, that it took away poor Hastings' breath. We went up; he turned round and saw us: we levelled our muskets at him, and he stopped. 'Another blow, and we'll shoot you,' cried Romer. 'Yes,' cried I; 'we are only boys, but you've Englishmen to deal with.' When we came up, Romer kept his piece levelled at the Dutchman, while I passed him, and with the knife cut the thongs which bound Hastings. The Dutchman turned pale and did not speak, he was so frightened, and the slaves ran away. As soon as Hastings was free, he seized a large wooden mallet, used for driving in stakes, and struck the Dutchman down to the earth, crying out, 'That for flogging an Englishman, you rascal!'

"While the man lay senseless or dead—I didn't know which at the time—we tied him to the waggon wheels, and returning to the house, seized some ammunition and other articles which might be useful. We then went to the stables, and took the three best horses which the Dutchman had, put some corn in a sack for each of them, took some cord for halters, mounted, and rode away as fast as we could. As we knew that we should be pursued, we first galloped away as if we were going eastward to the Cape; and then, as soon as we were on ground which would not show the tracks of our horses' hoofs, we turned round to the northward, in the direction of the Bushman country. It was dark soon after we had altered our course; but we travelled all night, and although we heard the roaring of the lions at a distance, we met with no accident. At daylight we rested our horses, and gave them some corn, and then sat down to eat some of the provision we had brought with us."

"How long were you with the farmer at Graaff Reinet?"

"Nearly eight months, sir; and during that time we could not only speak Dutch, but we could make ourselves understood by the Hottentots and other natives. While we were eating we held a consultation how we should proceed. We were aware that the Dutchmen would shoot us if they came up with us, and that they would come out in strong force against us; and we were afraid that we had killed the man, and if so, they would hang us as soon as we got to the Cape; so we were at a great loss to know how to act. At last we decided that we would cross the country of the Bushmen, and get to the sea-side, to the northward of the Cape. We determined that it would be better to travel at night, as there would be less fear of the wild beasts, or of being seen; so we went fast asleep for many hours. Towards the evening, we found water for the horses, and then we fed them again, and proceeded on our journey. I won't tell what passed every day for a fortnight, by which time we had pretty well killed our horses, and we were compelled to stop among a tribe of Gorraguas, a very mild, inoffensive people, who supplied us with milk, and treated us very kindly. We had some adventures, nevertheless. One day as we were passing by a tuft of small trees, a rhinoceros charged upon my horse, which very narrowly escaped by wheeling short round and getting behind him; the beast then made off without meddling with us any more. Every day we used to shoot some animal or other, for provision: sometimes it was a gnu, something between an antelope and a bull; at other times it was one of the antelope kind.

"Well, we stayed for three weeks with these people, and gave our horses time to refresh themselves; and then we set off again, keeping more towards the coast as we went southward, for the Gorraguas told us that there was a fierce native tribe, called Kaffers, to the northward, who would certainly kill us if we went there. The fact is, we did not know what to do. We had left the Cape without any exact idea where we should go to, like foolish boys as we were, and we became more entangled with difficulties every day. At last we decided that it would be better to find our way back to the Cape, and deliver ourselves up as prisoners, for we were tired out with fatigue and constant danger. All that we were afraid of was that we had killed the Dutch farmer at Graaff Reinet, who had treated us so brutally; but Hastings said he did not care; that was his business, and he would take his chance: so when we bade adieu to the Gorraguas, we turned our horses' heads to the south-east, so as to make the sea and go to the southward at the same time.

"I have now to mention a most melancholy event which occurred. Two days after we had recommenced our travels, in passing through some high grass, we stumbled on a lion, which was devouring a gnu. Romer, who happened to be some ten yards foremost of the three, was so alarmed that he fired at the animal, which we had agreed never to do, as it was folly to enrage so powerful a beast, when our party was so small. The lion was slightly wounded; he gave a roar that might have been heard for a mile, sprang upon Romer, and with one blow of his paw knocked him off the saddle into the bushes. Our horses, which were frightened, wheeled round and fled, for the animal was evidently about to attack us. As it was, he did make one bound in our direction; we could not pull up until we had gone half a mile; and when we did, we saw the lion had torn down the horse which Romer had ridden, and was dragging away the carcass to the right at a sort of a canter, without any apparent effort on his part. We waited till he was well off, and then rode back to the spot where Romer had fallen: we soon found him, but he was quite dead; the blow with the lion's paw had fractured his skull.

"I ought to have said that the Gorraguas told us not to travel by night, but by day; and we had done so in consequence of their advice. I believe it was very good advice, notwithstanding this unfortunate accident, for we found that when we had travelled all night the lions had more than once followed us the whole time; and indeed I have often thought since that we were altogether indebted to his mercy who ordereth all things, both in heaven and earth, that we escaped so well as we did. Three days after poor Romer's death we first saw the wide ocean again. We kept near the coast, but we soon found that we could not obtain the supply of game, or fuel for our fires at night, so well as we could in the interior, and we agreed to get away from the coast again. We had a dreary plain to pass over, and we were quite faint for want of food—for we had been without any for nearly two days—when we came upon an ostrich. Hastings put his horse to his speed, but it was of no use—the ostrich ran much faster than the horse could. I remained behind, and, to my great joy, discovered his nest, with thirteen large eggs in it. Hastings soon came back, with his horse panting and out of wind. We sat down, lighted a fire, and roasted two of the eggs: we made a good dinner of them, and having put four more on our saddle-bows, we continued our journey. At last, one forenoon, we saw the Table Mountain, and were as glad to see it as if we had seen the white cliffs of Old England. We pushed on our horses with the hopes of being once more comfortably in prison before night; when, as we neared the bay, we noticed that English colours were flying on board of the vessels in the road. This surprised us very much; but soon after that we met an English soldier, who told us that the Cape had been taken by our forces more than six months ago. This was a joyful surprise, as you may suppose. We rode into the town, and reported ourselves to the main guard; the governor sent for us, heard our story, and sent us to the admiral, who took us on board of his own ship."

Chapter Thirty Nine

The next morning, as there was no particular work on hand, Ready and Mr Seagrave took the lines to add to the stock of the fish-pond. As the weather was fine and cool, William accompanied them, that he might have the benefit of the fresh air. As they passed the garden, they observed that the seeds sown had already sprung up an inch or two above the ground, and that, apparently none of them had missed. While Ready and Mr Seagrave were fishing, and William sitting near them, William said to his father—

"Many of the islands near us are inhabited; are they not, papa?"

"Yes, but not those very near us, I believe. At all events, I never heard any voyagers mention having seen inhabitants on the isles near which we suppose the one we are on to be."

"What sort of people are the islanders in these seas?"

"They are various. The New Zealanders are the most advanced in civilisation. The natives of Van Diemen's Land and Australia are some portions of them of a very degraded class—indeed, little better than the beasts of the field."

"I have seen them," said Ready; "and I think I can mention a people, not very numerous indeed, who are still more like the beasts of the field. I saw them once; and, at first, thought they were animals, and not human beings."

"Indeed, Ready; where may that be?"

"In the Great Andaman Isles, at the mouth of the Bay of Bengal. I once anchored in distress in Port Cornwallis, and the morning after we anchored, we saw some black things going upon all fours under the trees that came down to the water's edge. We got the telescope, and perceived then that they were men and women, for they stood upright."

"Did you ever come into contact with them?"

"No, sir, I did not; but I met, at Calcutta, a soldier who had; for at one time the East India Company intended making a settlement on the island, and sent some troops there. He said that they caught two of them; that they were not more than four feet high, excessively stupid and shy; they had no houses or huts to live in, and all that they did was to pile up some bushes to keep the wind off."

"Had they any arms?"

"Yes, sir, they had bows and arrows; but so miserably made, and so small, that they could not kill anything but very small birds."

"Where did the people come from who inhabited these islands, papa?"

"That is difficult to say, William; but it is supposed that they have become inhabited in much the same way as this our island has been—that is, by people in canoes or boats driven out to sea, and saving their lives by effecting a landing, as we have done."

"I believe that's the truth," replied Ready; "I heard say that the Andaman Isles were supposed to have been first inhabited by a slaver full of negroes, who were wrecked on the coast in a typhoon."

"What is a typhoon, Ready?"

"It is much the same as a hurricane, William; it comes on in India at the change of the monsoons."

"But what are monsoons?"

"Winds that blow regular from one quarter so many months during the year, and then change round and blow from another just as long."

"And what are the trade-winds, which I heard poor Captain Osborn talking about after we left Madeira?"

"The trade-winds blow on the equator, and several degrees north and south of it, from the east to the west, following the course of the sun."

"Is it the sun which produces these winds?"

"Yes, the extreme heat of the sun between the tropics rarefies the air as the earth turns round, and the trade-winds are produced by the rushing in of the less heated air."

"Yes, William; and the trade-winds produce what they call the Gulf Stream," observed Ready.

"How is that? I have heard it spoken of, papa."

"The winds, constantly following the sun across the Atlantic Ocean, and blowing from east to west, have great effect upon the sea, which is forced up into the Gulf of Mexico (where it is stopped by the shores of America), so that it is many feet higher in the Gulf than in the eastern part of the Atlantic. This accumulation of water must of course find a vent somewhere, and it does in what is called the Gulf Stream, by which the waters are poured out, running very strong to the northward, along the shores of America, and then (westward) eastward, passing not far from Newfoundland, until its strength is spent somewhere to the northward of the Azores."

"The Gulf Stream, William," said Ready, "is always several degrees warmer than the sea in general, which is, they say, owing to its waters remaining in the Gulf of Mexico so long, where the heat of the sun is so great."

"What do you mean by the land and sea breezes in the West Indies, and other hot climates, papa?"

"It is the wind first blowing off from the shore, and then blowing from the sea towards the shore, during certain hours of the day, which it does regularly every twenty-four hours. This is also the effect of the heat of the sun. The sea breeze commences in the morning, and in the afternoon it dies away, when the land breeze commences, which lasts till midnight."

"There are latitudes close to the trade-winds," said Ready, "where the wind is not certain, where ships have been becalmed for weeks; the crews have exhausted the water on board, and they have suffered dreadfully. We call them the Horse latitudes—why, I do not know. But it is time for us to leave off, and for Master William to go into the house."

They returned home, and after supper Ready went on with his narrative.

"I left off at the time that I was sent on board of the man-of-war, and I was put down on the books as a supernumerary boy. I was on board of her for nearly four years, and we were sent about from port to port, and from clime to clime, until I grew a strong, tall lad, and was put into the mizen-top. I found it very comfortable. I did my duty, and the consequence was, I never was punished; for a man may serve on board of a man-of-war without fear of being punished, if he only does his duty, and the duty is not very hard either; not like on board of the merchant vessels, where there are so few hands—there it is hard work. Of course, there are some captains who command men-of-war who are harsh and severe; but it was my good fortune to be with a very mild and steady captain, who was very sorry when he was obliged to punish the men, although he would not overlook any improper conduct. The only thing which was a source of constant unhappiness to me was, that I could not get to England again, and see my mother. I had written two or three letters, but never had an answer; and at last I became so impatient that I determined to run away the very first opportunity which might offer. We were then stationed in the West Indies, and I had very often consultations with Hastings on the subject, for he was quite as anxious to get away as I was; and we had agreed that we would start off together the very first opportunity. At last we anchored in Port Royal, Jamaica, and there was a large convoy of West India ships, laden with sugar, about to sail immediately. We knew that if we could get on board of one, they would secrete us until the time of sailing, for they were short-handed enough, the men-of-war having pressed every man they could lay their hands upon. There was but one chance, and that was by swimming on board of one of the vessels during the night-time, and that was easy enough, as they were anchored not a hundred yards from our own ship. What we were afraid of was the sharks, which were so plentiful in the harbour. However, the night before the convoy was to sail we made up our minds that we would run the risk, for we were so impatient to escape that we did not care for anything. It was in the middle watch—I recollect it, and shall recollect it all my life, as if it were last night—that we lowered ourselves down very softly from the bows of the ship, and as soon as we were in the water we struck out for one of the West Indiamen close to us. The sentry at the gangway saw the light in the water made by our swimming through it, and he hailed, of course; we gave no answer, but swam as fast as we could; for after he had hailed we heard a bustle, and we knew that the officer of the watch was manning a boat to send after us. I had just caught hold of the cable of the West Indiaman, and was about to climb up by it, for I was a few yards before Hastings, when I heard a loud shriek, and, turning round, perceived a shark plunging down with Hastings in his jaws. I was so frightened, that for a short time I could not move: at last I recovered myself, and began to climb up by the cable as fast as I could. I was just in time, for another shark made a rush at me; and although I was clear out of the water more than two feet, he sprung up and just caught my shoe by the heel, which he took down with him. Fear gave me strength, and in a second or two afterwards I was up at the hawse-holes, and the men on board, who had been looking over the bows, and had witnessed poor Hastings' death, helped me on board, and hurried me down below, for the boat from our ship was now nearly alongside. When the officer of the boat came on board, they told him they had perceived us both in the water, close to their vessel, and that the sharks had taken us down. As the shriek of Hastings was heard by the people in the boat, the officer believed that it was the case, and returned to the ship. I heard the drum beat to quarters on board of the man-of-war, that they might ascertain who were the two men who had attempted to swim away, and a few minutes afterwards they beat the retreat, having put down D.D. against my name on the books, as well as against that of poor Hastings."

"What does D.D. mean?"

"D stands for discharged from the service; D.D. stands for dead," replied Ready; "and it was only through the mercy of Providence that I was not so."

"It was a miraculous escape indeed," observed Mr Seagrave.

"Yes, indeed, sir; I can hardly describe my sensations for some hours afterwards. I tried to sleep, but could not—I was in agony. The moment I slumbered, I thought the shark had hold of me, and I would start up and shriek; and then I said my prayers and tried to go to sleep again, but it was of no use. The captain of the West Indiaman was afraid that my shrieks would be heard, and he sent me down a tumbler of rum to drink off; this composed me, and at last I fell into a sound sleep. When I awoke, I found that the ship was under weigh and with all canvas set, surrounded by more than a hundred other vessels; the men-of-war who took charge of the convoy, firing guns and making signals incessantly. It was a glorious sight, and we were bound for Old England. I felt so happy, that I thought I would risk the jaws of another shark to have regained my liberty, and the chance of being once more on shore in my own country, and able to go to Newcastle and see my poor mother."

"I am afraid that your miraculous escape did you very little good, Ready," observed Mrs Seagrave, "if you got over it so soon."

"Indeed, madam, it was not so; that was only the feeling which the first sight of the vessels under weigh for England produced upon me. I can honestly say that I was a better and more serious person. The very next night, when I was in my hammock, I prayed very fervently; and there happened to be a very good old Scotchman on board, the second mate, who talked very seriously to me, and pointed out how wonderful had been my preservation, and I felt it. It was he who first read the Bible with me, and made me understand it, and, I may say, become fond of it. I did my duty on our passage home as a seaman before the mast, and the captain was pleased with me. The ship I was in was bound to Glasgow, and we parted company with the convoy at North Foreland, and arrived safe in port. The captain took me to the owners, who paid me fifteen guineas for my services during the voyage home; and as soon as I received the money, I set off for Newcastle as fast as I could. I had taken a place on the outside of the coach, and I entered into conversation with a gentleman who sat next to me. I soon found out that he belonged to Newcastle, and I first inquired if Mr Masterman, the ship-builder, was still alive. He told me that he had been dead about three months. 'And to whom did he leave his money?' I asked, 'for he was very rich, and had no kin.' 'He had no relations,' replied the gentleman, 'and he left all his money to build an hospital and almshouses. He had a partner in his business latterly, and he left the yard and all the stores to him, I believe, because he did not know whom to leave it to. There was a lad whom I knew for certain he intended to have adopted and to have made his heir—a lad of the name of Ready; but he ran away to sea, and has never been heard of since. It is supposed that he was lost in a prize, for he was traced so far. Foolish boy that he was. He might now have been a man of fortune.'

"'Very foolish indeed,' replied I.

"'Yes; but he has harmed more than himself. His poor mother, who doted upon him, as soon as she heard that he was lost, pined away by degrees, and—'

"'You don't mean to say that she is dead?' interrupted I, seizing the gentleman by the arm.

"'Yes,' replied he, looking at me with surprise; 'she died last year of a broken heart.'

"I fell back on the luggage behind me, and should have fallen off the coach if the gentleman had not held me. He called to the coachman to pull up the horses, and they took me down, and put me inside; and as the coach rolled on, I cried as if my heart would break."

Ready appeared so much affected, that Mr Seagrave proposed that he should leave off his history for the present.

"Thank you, sir, it will be better; for I feel my old eyes dim with tears, even now. It's a dreadful thing in after-life to reflect upon, that your foolish conduct has hastened the death of a most kind mother; but so it was, William, and I give you the truth for your advantage."

Chapter Forty

A few mornings afterwards, Juno came in before breakfast with six eggs in her apron, which she had found in the hen-house.

"Look, Missy Seagrave—fowls lay eggs—soon have plenty—plenty for Master William—make him well again—and plenty for chickens by and by."

"You haven't taken them all out of the nests, Juno; have you?"

"No; leave one in each nest for hen to see."

"Well, then, we will keep them for William, and I hope, as you say, they will make him strong again."

"I am getting quite strong now, mother," replied William; "I think it would be better to leave the eggs for the hens to sit upon."

"No, no, William; your health is of more consequence than having early chickens."

For a few days Mr Seagrave and Ready were employed at the garden clearing away the weeds, which had begun to sprout up along with the seeds which had been sown; during which time William recovered very fast. The two first days, Juno brought in three or four eggs regularly; but on the third day there were none to be found. On the fourth day the hens appeared also not to have laid, much to the surprise of Mrs Seagrave; as when hens commence laying eggs they usually continue. On the fifth morning, when they sat down to breakfast, Master Tommy did not make his appearance, and Mrs Seagrave asked where he was.

"I suspect, madam," said Old Ready, laughing, "that Tommy will not come either to his breakfast or his dinner to-day."

"What can you mean, Ready?" said Mrs Seagrave.

"Why, madam, I will tell you. I thought it very odd that there were no eggs, and I thought it probable that the hens might have laid astray; so I went about yesterday evening to search. I could not find any eggs, but I found the egg-shells, hid under some cocoa-nut leaves; and I argued, that if an animal, supposing there was any on the island, had taken the eggs, it would not have been so careful to hide the egg-shells. So, this morning, I fastened up the door of the hen-house, and only left open the little sliding door, by which the fowls go in to roost; and then, after you were up, I watched behind the trees, and saw Tommy come out, and go to the hen-house. He tried the door, and finding it fast, crept into the hen-house by the little sliding-door. As soon as he was in I let down the slide, and fastened it with a nail; so there he is, caught in his own trap."

"And there shall he remain all day, the little glutton!" said Mr Seagrave.

"Yes, it will serve him right," replied Mrs Seagrave; "and be a lesson to him."

Mr Seagrave, Ready, and William, as usual, went down to their work; Mrs Seagrave and Juno, with little Caroline, were busy indoors. Tommy remained very quiet for an hour, when he commenced roaring; but it was of no use, no one paid any attention to him. At dinner-time he began to roar again, but with as little success: it was not till the evening that the door of the hen-house was opened, and Tommy permitted to come out. He looked very foolish; and sat down in a corner without speaking.

"Well, Tommy, how many eggs did you suck to-day?" said Ready.

"Tommy won't suck eggs any more," said the urchin.

"No, you had better not," replied Mr Seagrave, "or you will find, in the end, that you will have less to eat, instead of more, as you have this day."

Tommy waited very quietly and very sulkily till supper was ready, when he made up for lost time. After which Ready continued his narrative.

"I told you, William, that I was informed by the gentleman on the coach that my mother had died of a broken heart, in consequence of my supposed death. I was in agony until I arrived at Newcastle, where I could ascertain all the facts connected with her decease. When the coach stopped, the gentleman, who had remained outside, came to the coach door, and said to me, 'If I mistake not, you are Masterman Ready, who ran away to sea; are you not?' 'Yes, sir,' replied I, very sorrowfully, 'I am.' 'Well, my man,' said he, 'cheer up; when you went away you were young and thoughtless, and certainly had no idea that you would have distressed your mother as you did. It was not your going to sea, but the report of your death, which preyed so much upon her mind; and that was not your fault. You must come with me, as I have something to say to you.'

"'I will call upon you to-morrow, sir,' replied I; 'I cannot do anything until I talk to the neighbours and visit my poor mother's grave. It is very true that I did not intend to distress my mother; and that the report of my death was no fault of mine. But I cannot help feeling that, if I had not been so thoughtless, she would be still alive and happy.' The gentleman gave me his address, and I promised to call upon him next morning. I then went to the house my mother used to live in. I knew that she was not there; yet I was disappointed and annoyed when I heard merry laughter within. I looked in, for the door was open; in the corner where my mother used to sit, there was a mangle, and two women busily at work; others were ironing at a large table; and when they cried out to me, 'What do you want?' and laughed at me, I turned away in disgust, and went to a neighbouring cottage, the inmates of which had been very intimate with my mother. I found the wife at home, but she did not know me; and I told her who I was. She had attended my mother during her illness, till the day of her death; and she told me all I wished to know. It was some little relief to my mind to hear that my poor mother could not have lived, as she had an incurable cancer; but at the same time the woman told me that I was ever in her thoughts, and that my name was the last word on her lips. She also said that Mr Masterman had been very kind to my mother, and that she had wanted nothing. I then asked her to show me where my mother had been buried. She put on her bonnet, and led me to the grave, and then, at my request, she left me. I seated myself down by the mound of turf which covered her, and long and bitterly did I weep her loss and pray for forgiveness.

"It was quite dark when I left the spot and went back to the cottage of the kind woman who had attended my mother. I conversed with her and her husband till late, and then, as they offered me a bed, I remained with them that night. Next morning I went to keep my appointment with the gentleman whom I had met in the coach: I found by the brass plate on the door that he was a lawyer. He desired me to sit down, and then he closed the door carefully, and having asked me many questions, to ascertain if I was really Masterman Ready, he said he was the person employed at Mr Masterman's death, and that he had found a paper which was of great consequence, as it proved that the insurance of the vessel which had belonged to my father and Mr Masterman, and which had been lost, had not been made on Mr Masterman's share only, but upon my father's as well, and that Mr Masterman had defrauded my mother. He said he had found the paper in a secret drawer some time after Mr Masterman's death, and that my mother being dead, and I being supposed to be dead, he did not see any use in making known so disagreeable a circumstance; but that, now I had re-appeared, it was his duty so to do, and that he would arrange the matter for me, if I pleased, with the corporation of the town, to whom all Mr Masterman's property had been left in trust to build an hospital and almshouses. He said that the insurance on the vessel was three thousand pounds, and that one-third of the vessel belonged to my father, so that a thousand pounds were due to him, which the interest for so many years would increase to above two thousand pounds. This was good news for me, and you may suppose I readily agreed to all he proposed. He set to work at once, and having called together the mayor and corporation of the town, and proved the document, they immediately agreed that I was entitled to the money, and that it should be paid to me without any contest. Thus you see, Master William, was a new temptation thrown in my way."

"How do you mean a temptation? It surely was very fortunate, Ready," said William.

"Yes, William, it was, as people say, fortunate, according to the ideas of the world; every one congratulated me, and I was myself so inflated with my good fortune, that I forgot all the promises of amendment, all the vows of leading a good life, which I made over my poor mother's grave. Now do you perceive why I called it a temptation, Master William?"

"My dear child," said Mr Seagrave, "riches and prosperity in this world prove often the greatest of temptations; it is adversity that chastens and amends us, and which draws us to God."

"As soon as the money was in my own hands," continued Ready, "I began to squander it away in all manner of folly. Fortunately, I had not received it more than ten days, when the Scotch second mate came like a guardian angel to save me. As soon as I had made known to him what had taken place, he reasoned with me, pointed out to me that I had an opportunity of establishing myself for life, and proposed that I should purchase a part of a vessel, on condition that I was captain of her. I liked this idea very much, and being convinced that I had been making a fool of myself, I resolved to take his advice; but one thing only restrained me: I was still very young, not more than twenty years old; and although I could navigate at one time, I had latterly paid no attention. I told Sanders this, and he replied, that if I would take him as my first mate, that difficulty would be got over, as he could navigate well, and that I could learn to do so in the first voyage; so all was arranged.

"Fortunately, I had not spent above one hundred pounds of the money. I set off for Glasgow in company with Sanders, and he busied himself very hard in looking about for a vessel that would suit. At last, he found that there was one ready for launching, which, in consequence of the failure of the house for which it was built, was to be sold. He made inquiries, and having found who was likely to purchase her—that it was a very safe and respectable firm—he made a proposal for me that I should take one-fourth share of her, and command her. As Sanders was very respectable, and well known to be a steady man, his recommendation was attended to so far that the parties wished to see and speak to me. They were satisfied with me, young as I was, and the bargain was made. I paid down my two thousand pounds for my share, and as soon as the vessel was launched, was very busy with Sanders, whom I had chosen as first mate, in fitting her out. The house which had purchased her with me was a West India firm, and the ship was of course intended for the West India trade. I had two or three hundred pounds left, after I had paid my share of the vessel, and this I employed in purchasing a venture on my own account, and providing nautical instruments, etcetera. I also fitted myself out, for you see, William, although Sanders had persuaded me to be rational, I was still puffed up with pride at the idea of being captain of my own ship; it was too great a rise for one who had just before been a lad in the mizen-top of a man-of-war. I dressed myself very smart—wore white shirts, and rings on my fingers. Indeed, as captain and part owner of a fine vessel, I was considered as somebody, and was often invited to the table of the other owners of the vessel. I was well off, for my pay was ten pounds a month, independent of what my own venture might produce, and my quarter-share of the profits of the vessel. This may be considered as the most prosperous portion of my life; and so, if you please, we will leave off here for to-night, for I may as well tell you at once that it did not last very long."

Chapter Forty One

For several days after, they were employed in clearing away the stumps of the cocoa-nut trees in the winding path to the storehouse; and as soon as that work was finished, Ready put up a lightning-conductor at the side of the storehouse, like the one which he had put up near to the cottage. They had now got through all the work that they had arranged to do during the rainy season. The ewes had lambed, but both the sheep and the goats began to suffer for want of pasture. For a week they had no rain, and the sun burst out very powerfully; and Ready was of opinion that the rainy season was now over. William had become quite strong again, and he was very impatient that they should commence the survey of the island. After a great deal of consultation, it was at last settled, that Ready and William should make the first survey to the southward, and then return and report what they had discovered. This was decided upon on the Saturday evening, and on the Monday morning they were to start. The knapsacks were got ready, and well filled with boiled salt pork, and flat cakes of bread. They were each to have a musket and ammunition, and a blanket was folded up to carry on the shoulders, that they might sleep on it at night. Ready did not forget his compass, or the small axes, for them to blaze the trees as they went through the wood.

The whole of Saturday was occupied in making their preparations. After supper, Ready said, "Now, William, before we start on our travels, I think I may as well wind up my history. I haven't a great deal more to tell, as my good fortune did not last long; and after my remaining so long in a French prison, my life was one continued chapter of from bad to worse. Our ship was soon ready, and we sailed with convoy for Barbadoes. Sanders proved a good navigator, and from him, before we arrived at Barbadoes, I gained all the knowledge which I required to enable me to command and navigate my vessel. Sanders attempted to renew our serious conversation, but my property had made me vain; and now that I felt I could do without his assistance, I not only kept him at a distance, but assumed the superior. This was a very ungrateful return for his kindness to me; but it is too often the case in this world. Sanders was very much annoyed, and on our arrival at Barbadoes, he told me that it was his intention to quit the vessel. I replied very haughtily, that he might do as he pleased; the fact is, I was anxious to get rid of him, merely because I was under obligations to him. Well, sir, Sanders left me, and I felt quite happy at his departure. My ship was soon with a full cargo of sugar on board of her, and we waited for convoy to England. When at Barbadoes, I had an opportunity to buy four brass guns, which I mounted on deck, and had a good supply of ammunition on board. I was very proud of my vessel, as she had proved in the voyage out to be a very fast sailer: indeed, she sailed better than some of the men-of-war which convoyed us; and now that I had guns on board, I considered myself quite safe from any of the enemies' privateers. While we were waiting for convoy, which was not expected for a fortnight, it blew a very heavy gale, and my ship, as well as others, dragged their anchors, and were driven out of Carlisle Bay. We were obliged to make sail to beat into the bay again, it still blowing very fresh. What with being tired waiting so long for convoy, and the knowledge that arriving before the other West Indiamen would be very advantageous, I made up my mind that, instead of beating up into the bay again, I would run for England without protection, trusting to the fast sailing of my vessel and the guns which I had on board. I forgot at the time that the insurance on the vessel was made in England as 'sailing with convoy,' and that my sailing without would render the insurance void, if any misfortune occurred. Well, sir, I made sail for England, and for three weeks everything went on well. We saw very few vessels, and those which did chase us could not come up with us; but as we were running with a fair wind up channel, and I had made sure of being in port before night, a French privateer hove in sight and gave chase. We were obliged to haul our wind, and it blowing very fast, we carried away our main-top mast. This accident was fatal; the privateer came alongside of us and laid us by the board, and that night I was in a French prison, and, I may say, a pauper; for the insurance of the vessel was void, from my having sailed without convoy. I felt that I had no one to thank but myself for the unfortunate position I was in; at all events, I was severely punished, for I remained a prisoner for nearly six years. I contrived to escape with three or four others; we suffered dreadfully, and at last arrived in England, in a Swedish vessel, without money, or even clothes that would keep out the weather. Of course, I had nothing to do but to look out for a berth on board of a ship, and I tried for that of second mate, but without success; I was too ragged and looked too miserable; so I determined, as I was starving, to go before the mast. There was a fine vessel in the port; I went on board to offer myself; the mate went down to the captain, who came on deck, and who should he be but Sanders? I hoped that he would not remember me, but he did immediately, and held out his hand. I never did feel so ashamed in my life as I did then. Sanders perceived it, and asked me down into the cabin. I then told him all that had happened, and he appeared to forget that I had behaved so ill to him; he offered me a berth on board, and money in advance to fit me out. But if he would not remember my conduct, I could not forget it, and I told him so, and begged his forgiveness. Well, sir, that good man, as long as he lived, was my friend. I became his second mate before he died, and we were again very intimate. My misfortunes had humbled me, and I once more read the Bible with him; and I have, I trust, done so ever since. When he died, I continued second mate for some time, and then was displaced. Since that, I have always been as a common seaman on board of different vessels; but I have been well treated and respected, and I may add, I have not been unhappy, for I felt that property would have only led me into follies, and have made me forget, that in this world we are to live so as to prepare ourselves for another. Now, William, you have the history of Masterman Ready; and I hope that there are portions of it which may prove useful to you. To-morrow we must be off betimes, and as we are all to breakfast early together, why, I think the sooner we go to bed the better."

"Very true," replied Mr Seagrave, "William, dear, bring me the Bible."

Chapter Forty Two

They were all up early the next morning, and breakfasted at an early hour. The knapsacks and guns, and the other requisites for the journey, were all prepared; William and Ready rose from the table, and taking an affectionate leave of Mr and Mrs Seagrave, they started on their journey. The sun was shining brilliantly, and the weather had become warm; the ocean in the distance gleamed brightly, as its waters danced, and the cocoa-nut trees moved their branches gracefully to the breeze. They set off in high spirits, and having called the two shepherd dogs, and driven back Vixen, who would have joined the party, they passed the storehouse, and ascending the hill on the other side, they got their hatchets ready to blaze the trees; and Ready having set his course by his pocket compass, they were fairly on their way. For some time they continued to cut the bark of the trees with their hatchets, without speaking, and then Ready stopped again to look at his compass.

"I think the wood is thicker here than ever, Ready," observed William.

"Yes, sir, it is; but I suspect we are now in the thickest part of it, right in the middle of the island; however, we shall soon see. We must keep a little more away to the southward. We had better get on as fast as we can. We shall have less work by and by, and then we can talk better."

For half-an-hour they continued their way through the wood, and, as Ready had observed, the trees became more distant from each other; still, however, they could not see anything before them but the stems of the cocoa-nuts. It was hard work, chopping the trees every second, and their foreheads were moist with the exertion.

"I think we had better pull up for a few minutes, William; you will be tired."

"I have not been so used to exercise, Ready, and therefore I feel it more," replied William, wiping his face with his handkerchief. "I should like to stop a few minutes. How long do you think it will be before we are out of the wood?"

"Not half-an-hour more, sir, I should think; even before that, perhaps."

"What do you expect to find, Ready?"

"That's a difficult question to answer. I can tell you what I hope to find, which is, a good space of clear ground between the beach and the wood, where we may pasture our sheep and goats; and perhaps we may find some other trees besides cocoa-nuts: at present, you know, we have seen only them and the castor-oil beans, that Tommy took such a dose of. You see, William, there is no saying what new seeds may have been brought here by birds, or by the winds and waves."

"But will those seeds grow?"

"Yes, William; I have been told that seeds may remain hundreds of years under-ground, and come up afterwards when exposed to the heat."

They continued their way, and had not walked for more than a quarter of an hour, when William cried out, "I see the blue sky, Ready; we shall soon be out; and glad shall I be, for my arm aches with chopping."

"I dare say it does, sir. I am just as glad as you are, for I'm tired of marking the trees; however, we must continue to mark, or we shall not find our way back when we want it."

In ten minutes more they were clear of the cocoa-nut grove, and found themselves among brushwood higher than their heads; so that they could not see how far they were from the shore.

"Well," said William, throwing down his hatchet, "I'm glad that's over; now let us sit down a little before we go any further."

"I'm of your opinion, sir," replied Ready, sitting down by the side of William; "I feel more tired to-day than I did when we first went through the wood, after we set off from the cove. I suppose it's the weather. Come back, dogs; lie down."

"The weather is very fine, Ready."

"Yes, now it is; but I meant to have said that the rainy season is very trying to the health, and I suppose I have not recovered from it yet. You have had a regular fever, and, of course, do not feel strong; but a man may have no fever, and yet his health suffer a great deal from it. I am an old man, William, and feel these things now."

"I think that before we go on, Ready, we had better have our dinner; that will do us good."

"Well, we will take an early dinner, and we shall get rid of one bottle of water, at all events; indeed, I think that, as we must go back by the same way we came, we may as well leave our knapsacks and everything but our guns under these trees; I dare say we shall sleep here too, for I told Mr Seagrave positively not to expect us back to-night. I did not like to say so before your mother, she is so anxious about you."

They opened their knapsacks, and made their meal, the two dogs coming in for their share; after which they again started on their discoveries. For about ten minutes they continued to force their way through the thick and high bushes, till at last they broke out clear of them, and then looked around them for a short time without speaking. The sea was about half a mile distant, and the intervening land was clear, with fresh blades of grass just bursting out of the earth, composing a fine piece of pasture of at least fifty acres, here and there broken with small patches of trees and brushwood; there was no sandy beach, but the rocks rose from the sea about twenty to thirty feet high, and were in one or two places covered with something which looked as white as snow.

"Well, Ready," said William, "there will be no want of pasture for our flock, even if it increases to ten times its number."

"No," replied Ready, "we are very fortunate, and have great reason to be thankful; this is exactly what we required; and now let us go on a little, and examine these patches of wood, and see what they are. I see a bright green leaf out there, which, if my eyes do not fail me, I have seen many a time before." When they arrived at the clump of trees which Ready had pointed out, he said, "Yes, I was right. Look there, this is the banana; it is just bursting out now, and will soon be ten feet high, and bearing fruit which is excellent eating; besides which the stem is capital fodder for the beasts."

"Here is a plant I never saw before," said William, pulling off a piece of it, and showing it to Ready.

"But I have, William. It is what they call the bird's-eye pepper; they make Cayenne pepper out of it. Look, the pods are just formed; it will be useful to us in cooking, as we have no pepper left. You see, William, we must have some birds on the island; at least it is most probable, for all the seeds of these plants and trees must have been brought here by them. The banana and the pepper are the food of many birds. What a quantity of bananas are springing up in this spot; there will be a little forest of them in a few weeks."

"What is that rough-looking sort of shrub out there, Ready?"

"I can't see so well as you, William, so let us walk up to it. Oh, I know it now; it is what they call the prickly pear in the West Indies. I am very glad to have found that, for it will be very useful to us."

"Is it good eating, Ready?"

"Not particularly; and the little spikes run into your fingers, and are very difficult to get rid of; but it is not bad by way of a change. No, the use it will be to us is to hedge in our garden, and protect it from the animals; it makes a capital fence, and grows very fast, and without trouble. Now let us go on to that patch of trees, and see what they are."

"What is this plant, Ready?"

"I don't know, William."

"Then I think I had better make a collection of all those you don't know, and take them back to father; he is a good botanist."

William pulled a branch of the plant off, and carried it with him. On their arrival at the next patch of trees, Ready looked at them steadfastly for some time.

"I ought to know that tree," said he. "I have often seen it in hot countries. Yes, it's the guava."

"What! is it the fruit they make guava jelly of?" said William.

"Yes, the very same."

"Let us now walk in the direction of those five or six trees," said William; "and from there down to the rocks; I want to find out how it is that they are so white."

"Be it so, if you wish," replied Ready.

"Why, Ready, what noise is that? Hark! such a chattering, it must be monkeys."

"No, they are not monkeys; but I'll tell you what they are, although I cannot see them; they are parrots—I know their noise well. You see, William, it's not very likely that monkeys should get here, but birds can, and it is the birds that we have to thank for the bananas and guavas, and other fruits we may find here."

As soon as they came under the trees, there was a great rioting and fluttering, and then away flew, screaming as loud as they could, a flock of about three hundred parrots, their beautiful green and blue feathers glistening in the beams of the sun.

"I told you so; well, we'll have some capital pies out of them, William."

"Pies! do they make good pies, Ready?"

"Yes, excellent; and very often have I had a good dinner from one in the West Indies, and in South America. Stop, let us come a little this way; I see a leaf which I should like to examine."

"The ground is very swampy just here, Ready; is it not?"

"Yes; there's plenty of water below, I don't doubt. So much the better for the animals; we must dig some pools when they come here.

"Oh! I thought I was not wrong. Look! this is the best thing I have found yet—we now need not care so much about potatoes."

"Why, what are they, Ready?"

"Yams, which they use instead of potatoes in the West Indies. Indeed, potatoes do not remain potatoes long, when planted in hot climates."

"How do you mean, Ready?"

"They turn into what they call sweet-potatoes, after one or two crops: yams are better things, in my opinion."

At this moment the dogs dashed among the broad yam leaves, and commenced baying; there was a great rustling and snorting.

"What's that?" cried William, who had been stooping down to examine the yam plant, and who was startled at the noise.

Ready laughed heartily. "It isn't the first time that they've made you jump, William."

"Why, it's our pigs, isn't it?" replied William.

"To be sure; they're in the yam patch, very busy feeding on them, I'll be bound."

Ready gave a shout, and a grunting and rushing were heard among the broad leaves, and, very soon, out rushed, instead of the six, about thirty pigs large and small; who, snorting and twisting their tails, galloped away at a great rate, until they gained the cocoa-nut grove.

"How wild they are, Ready!" said William.

"Yes, and they'll be wilder every day; but we must fence these yams from them, or we shall get none ourselves."

"But they'll beat down the fence before it grows up."

"We must pale it with cocoa-nut palings, and plant the prickly pears outside. Now, we'll go down to the sea-side."

As they neared the rocks, which were bare for about fifty yards from the water's edge, Ready said, "I can tell you now what those white patches on the rocks are, William; they are the places where the sea-birds come to every year to make their nests, and bring up their young. They always come to the same place every year, if they are not disturbed." They soon arrived at the spot, and found it white with the feathers of birds, mixed up with dirt.

"I see no nests, Ready, nor the remains of any."

"No, they do not make any nests, further than scratching a round hole, about half an inch deep, in the soil, and there they lay their eggs, sitting quite close to one another; they will soon be here, and begin to lay, and then we will come and take the eggs, if we want any, for they are not bad eating."

"Why, Ready, what a quantity of good things we have found out already! This has been a very fortunate expedition of ours."

"Yes, it has; and we may thank God for his goodness, who thus provides for us so plentifully in the wilderness."

"Do you know, Ready, I cannot help thinking that we ought to have built our house here."

"Not so, William; we have not the pure water, recollect, and we have not the advantages of the sandy beach, where we have our turtle- and fish-pond. No; we may feed our stock here; we may gather the fruit, taking our share of it with the poor birds; we may get our yams, and every other good provided for us; but our house and home must be where it is now."

"You are right, Ready; but it will be a long walk."

"Not when we are accustomed to it, and have made a beaten path; besides, we may bring the boat round, perhaps."

Then they walked along the sea-side for about a quarter of a mile, until they came to where the rocks were not so high, and there they discovered a little basin, completely formed in the rocks, with a narrow entrance.

"See, William, what a nice little harbour for our boat! we may here load it with yams and take it round to the bay, provided we can find an entrance through the reefs on the southern side of it, which we have not looked for yet, because we have not required it."

"Yes, Ready—it is, indeed, a nice, smooth little place for the boat. What is that thing on the bottom, there?" said William, pointing in the direction.

"That is a sea crawfish, quite as good eating as a lobster. I wonder if I could make a lobster-pot; we should catch plenty, and very good they are."

"And what are those little rough things on the rock?"

"They are a very nice little sort of oyster; not like those we have in England, but much better—they are so delicate."

"Why, Ready, we have two more good things for our table, again," replied William; "how rich we shall be!"

"Yes; but we have to catch them, recollect: there is nothing to be had in this world without labour."

"Ready," said William, "we have good three hours' daylight; suppose we go back and tell what we have seen: my mother will be so glad to see us."

"I agree with you, William. We have done well for one day; and may safely go back again, and remain for another week. There are no fruits at present, and all I care about are the yams; I should like to protect them from the pigs. But let us go home and talk the matter over with Mr Seagrave."

They found out the spot where they had left their knapsacks and hatchets, and again took their path through the cocoa-nut trees, following the blaze which they had made in the morning. One hour before sunset they arrived at the house, where they found Mr and Mrs Seagrave sitting outside, and Juno standing on the beach with the two children, who were amusing themselves with picking up the shells which were strewed about. William gave a very clear account of all they had seen, and showed his father the specimens of the plants which he had collected.

"This," said Mr Seagrave, "is a well-known plant; and I wonder Ready did not recognise it; it is hemp."

"I never saw it except in the shape of rope," replied Ready. "I know the seed well enough."

"Well, if we require it, I can tell you how to dress it," replied Mr Seagrave. "Now, William, what is the next?"

"This odd-looking, rough thing."

"That's the egg-plant: it bears fruit of a blue colour. I am told they eat it in the hot countries."

"Yes, sir, they do; they fry it with pepper and salt; they call it bringal. I think it must be that."

"I do not doubt but you are right," replied Mr Seagrave. "Why, William, you should know this."

"It is like the grape-vine."

"Yes, and it is so; it is the wild grape; we shall eat them by and bye."

"I have only one more, papa: what is this?"

"You don't know it, because it has sprung up so high, William; but it is the common mustard plant,—what we use in England, and is sold as mustard and cress. I think you have now made a famous day's work of it; and we have much to thank God for."

As soon as they had returned to the house, a consultation was held as to their future proceedings; and, after some debate, it was agreed that it would be advisable that they should take the boat out of the sand; and, as soon as it was ready, examine the reef on the southward, to see if they could find a passage through it, as it would take a long while to go round it; and, as soon as that was accomplished, Mr Seagrave, Ready, William, and Juno should all go through the wood, carrying with them a tent to pitch on the newly-discovered piece of ground: and that they should set up a flag-staff at the little harbour, to point out its position. Of course, that would be a hard day's work; but that they would, nevertheless, return the same night, and not leave Mrs Seagrave alone with the children. Having accomplished this, Ready and William would then put the wheels and axle in the boat, and other articles required, such as saw, hatchets, and spades, and row round to the south side of the island, to find the little harbour. As soon as they had landed them, and secured the boat, they would then return by the path through the wood.

The next job would be to rail in the yam plantation to keep off the pigs, and, at the same time, to drive the sheep and goats through the wood, that they might feed on the new pasture ground. Ready and William were then to cut down cocoa-nut trees sufficient for the paling, fix up the posts, and when that was done, Mr Seagrave was to come to them and assist them in railing it in, and drawing the timber. This they expected would be all done in about a month; and during that time, as Mrs Seagrave and Juno would be, for the greatest part of it, left at the house, they were to employ themselves in clearing the garden of weeds, and making preparation for fencing it in.

As soon as this important work had been completed, the boat would return to the bay with a load of prickly pears for the garden fence, and then they were to direct their attention to the stores which had been saved from the wreck, and were lying in the cove where they had first landed. When they had examined them, and brought round what were required, and secured them in the storehouse, they would then have a regular survey of the island by land and by water. But man proposes and God disposes, as will be shown by the interruption of their intended projects which we shall have to narrate in the ensuing chapter.

Chapter Forty Three

As usual, Ready was the first up on the following morning, and having greeted Juno, who followed him out of the house, he set off on his accustomed rounds, to examine into the stock and their other possessions. He was standing in the garden at the point. First he thought that it would be necessary to get ready some sticks for the peas, which were now seven or eight inches out of the ground; he had proceeded a little farther, to where the calivances, or French haricot beans, had been sown, and had decided upon the propriety of hoeing up the earth round them, as they were a very valuable article of food, that would keep, and afford many a good dish during the rainy or winter season. He had gone on to ascertain if the cucumber seeds had shown themselves above-ground, and was pleased to find that they were doing well. He said to himself, "We have no vinegar, that I know of, but we can preserve them in salt and water, as they do in Russia; it will be a change, at all events;" and then he raised his eyes and looked out to the offing, and, as usual, scanned the horizon. He thought he saw a ship to the north-east, and he applied his telescope to his eye. He was not mistaken—it was a vessel.

The old man's heart beat quick; he dropped his telescope on his arm, and fetched some heavy breaths before he could recover from the effect of this unexpected sight. After a minute, he again put his telescope to his eye, and then made her out to be a brig, under top-sails and top-gallant sails, steering directly for the island.

Ready walked to the rocky point, from which they fished, and sat down to reflect. Could it be that the vessel had been sent after them, or that she had by mere chance come among the islands? He decided after a short time that it must be chance, for none could know that they were saved, much less that they were on the island. Her steering towards the island must then be either that she required water or something else; perhaps she would alter her course and pass by them. "At all events," thought the old man, "we are in the hands of God, who will, at his own time and in his own way, do with us as he thinks fit. I will not at present say anything to Mr and Mrs Seagrave. It would be cruel to raise hopes which might end in disappointment. A few hours will decide. And yet I cannot do without help—I must trust William."

Ready rose, examined the vessel with his telescope, and then walked towards the house. William was up, and the remainder of the family were stirring.

"William," said Ready to him, as they walked away from the house, "I have a secret to tell you, which you will at once see the necessity of not telling to anyone at present. A few hours will decide the question." William readily gave his promise. "There is a vessel off the island; she may be the means of rescuing us, or she may pass without seeing us. It would be too cruel a disappointment to your father and mother, if the latter were the case."

William stared at Ready, and for a moment could not speak, his excitement was so great.

"Oh, Ready, how grateful I am! I trust that we may be taken away, for you have no idea how my poor father suffers in silence—and so does my mother."

"I know it, William, I know it, and it is natural; they do their best to control their yearnings, and they can do no more. But now we must be quick, and at work before breakfast. But stop, I will show you the vessel."

Ready caught the vessel in the field of the telescope, which he leant against the trunk of a cocoa-nut, and William put his eye to the glass.

"Do you see her?"

"Oh yes, Ready, and she is coming this way."

"Yes, she is steering right for the island. I will put the telescope down here, and we will go about our work."

William and Ready went to the storehouse for the axe. Ready selected a very slight cocoa-nut tree nearest to the beach, which he cut down, and as soon as the top was taken off with the assistance of William he carried it down to the point.

"Now, William, go for a shovel and dig a hole here, that we may fix it up as a flag-staff. When all is ready, I will go for a small block and some rope for halyards to hoist up the flags as soon as the vessel is likely to see them. At breakfast-time, I shall propose that you and I get the boat out of the sand and examine her, and give Mr Seagrave some work indoors."

"But the flags, Ready; they are round my mother's bed. How shall we get them?"

"Suppose I say that it is time that the house should be well cleaned, and that the canvas hangings of the beds should be taken out to be aired this fine day. Ask your father to take the direction of the work while we dig out the boat; that will employ them all inside the house."

"Yes, that will do, Ready."

During breakfast-time, Ready observed that he intended to get the boat out of the sand, and that William should assist him.

"And what am I to do, Ready?" said Mr Seagrave.

"Why, sir, I think, now that the rains are over, it would not be a bad thing if we were to air bedding, as they say at sea; it is a fine, warm day; and if all the bedding was taken out of the house and well shaken, and then left out to air, it would be a very good job over; for you see, sir, I have thought more than once that the house does smell a little close."

"It will be a very good thing, Ready," observed Mrs Seagrave; "and, at the same time, Juno and I will give the house a thorough cleaning and sweeping."

"Had we not better have the canvas screens down, and air them too?"

"Yes," replied Ready; "we had better air everything. We will assist in taking down the screens and flags, and spread them out to air, and then, if Mr Seagrave has no objection, we will leave him to superintend and assist Madam and Juno."

"With all my heart," replied Mr Seagrave. "We have done breakfast, and will begin as soon as you please."

Ready and William took down the canvas screens and flags, and went out of the cottage with them; they spread out the canvas at some distance from the house, and then William went down to the beach with the flags, while Ready procured the block and small rope to hoist them up with.

Ready's stratagem answered well. Without being perceived by those in the cottage, the flag-staff was raised, and fixed in the ground, and the flags all ready for hoisting; then Ready and William returned to the fuel-stack, and each carried down as much stuff as they could hold, that they might make a smoke to attract the notice of those on board of the vessel. All this did not occupy much more than an hour, during which the brig continued her course steadily towards the island. When Ready first saw her the wind was light, but latterly the breeze had increased very much, and at last the brig took in her top-gallant sails. The horizon behind the vessel, which had been quite clear, was now banked up with clouds, and the waves curled in white foam over the reefs of rocks extending from the island.

"The breeze is getting up strong, William," said Ready, "and she will soon be down, if she is not frightened at the reefs, which she can see plainer now the water is rough, than she could before."

"I trust she will not be afraid," replied William. "How far do you think she is off now?"

"About five miles; not more. The wind has hauled round more to the southward, and it is banking up fast, I see. I fear that we shall have another smart gale; however, it won't last long. Come, let us hoist the flags; we must not lose a chance; the flags will blow nice and clear for them to see them."

William and Ready hoisted up the ensign first, and below it the flag, with the ship's name, Pacific, in large letters upon it. "Now then," said Ready, as he made fast the halyards, "let us strike a light and make a smoke; that will attract their notice."

As soon as the cocoa-nut leaves were lighted, Ready and William threw water upon them, so as to damp them and procure a heavy column of smoke. The vessel approached rapidly, and they were watching her in silent suspense, when they perceived Mr and Mrs Seagrave, Juno carrying Albert, with Tommy and Caroline running down as fast as they could to the beach. The fact was, that Tommy, tired of work, had gone out of the house and walked towards the beach; there he perceived, first, the flags hoisted, and then he detected the vessel off the island. He immediately ran back to the house, crying out, "Papa! Mamma! Captain Osborn come back—come back in a big ship." At this announcement, Mr and Mrs Seagrave ran out of the house, perceived the vessel and the flags flying, and ran as fast as they could down to where William and Ready were standing by the flag-staff.

"Oh! Ready, why did you not tell us this before?" exclaimed Mr Seagrave.

"I wish you had not known it now, sir," replied Ready; "but, however, it can't be helped; it was done out of kindness, Mr Seagrave."

"Yes, indeed it was, papa."

Mrs Seagrave dropped down on the rock, and burst into tears. Mr Seagrave was equally excited.

"Does she see us, Ready?" exclaimed he at last.

"No, sir, not yet, and I waited till she did, before I made it known to you," replied Ready.

"She is altering her course, Ready," said William.

"Yes, sir, she has hauled to the wind; she is afraid of coming too near to the reefs."

"Surely she is not leaving us!" exclaimed Mrs Seagrave.

"No, madam; but she does not see us yet."

"She does! she does!" cried William, throwing up his hat; "see, she hoists her ensign."

"Very true, sir; she does see us. Thanks be to God!"

Mr Seagrave embraced his wife, who threw herself sobbing into his arms, kissed his children with rapture, and wrung old Ready's hand. He was almost frantic with joy. William was equally delighted.

As soon as they were a little more composed, Ready observed: "Mr Seagrave, that they have seen us is certain, and what we must now do is to get our own boat out of the sand. We know the passage through the reefs, and they do not. I doubt if they will, however, venture to send a boat on shore, until the wind moderates a little. You see, sir, it is blowing up very strong just now."

"But you don't think it will blow harder, Ready?"

"I am sorry to say, sir, that I do. It looks very threatening to the southward, and until the gale is over, they will not venture near an island so surrounded with rocks. It would be very imprudent if they did. However, sir, a few hours will decide."

"But, surely," said Mrs Seagrave, "even if it does blow, they will not leave the island without taking us off. They will come after the gale is over."

"Yes, madam, if they can, I do think they will; but God knows, some men have hard hearts, and feel little for the misery of others."

The brig had, in the meantime, kept away again, as if she was running in; but very soon afterwards she hauled to the wind, with her head to the northward, and stood away from the island.

"She is leaving us," exclaimed William, mournfully.

"Hard-hearted wretches!" said Mr Seagrave, with indignation.

"You are wrong to say that, sir," replied Ready: "excuse me, Mr Seagrave, for being so bold; but the fact is, that if I was in command of that vessel, I should do just as they have done. The gale rises fast, and it would be very dangerous for them to remain where they now are. It does not at all prove that they intend to leave us; they but consult their own safety, and, when the gale is over, we shall, I trust, see them again."

No reply was made to Ready's judicious remarks. The Seagraves only saw that the vessel was leaving them, and their hearts sank. They watched her in silence, and as she gradually diminished to the view, so did their hopes depart from them. The wind was now fierce, and a heavy squall, with rain, obscured the offing, and the vessel was no longer to be distinguished. Mr Seagrave turned to his wife, and mournfully offered her his arm. They walked away from the beach without speaking; the remainder of the party, with the exception of old Ready, followed them. Ready remained some time with his eyes in the direction where the vessel was last seen. At last he hauled down the ensign and flag, and, throwing them over his shoulder, followed the disconsolate party to the house.

Chapter Forty Four

When Ready arrived, he found them all plunged in such deep distress, that he did not consider it advisable to say anything. The evening closed in; it was time to retire. The countenance of Mr Seagrave was not only gloomy, but morose. The hour for retiring to rest had long passed when Ready broke the silence by saying, "Surely, you do not intend to sit up all night, Mr Seagrave?"

"Oh, no! there's no use sitting up now," replied Mr Seagrave, rising up impatiently. "Come, my dear, let us go to bed."

Mrs Seagrave rose, and retired behind the canvas screen. Her husband seemed as if he was about to follow her, when Ready, without speaking, laid the Bible on the table before him. Mr Seagrave did not appear to notice it; but William touched his father's arm, pointed to the book, and then went inside of the screen, and led out his mother.

"God forgive me!" exclaimed Mr Seagrave. "In my selfishness and discontent I had forgotten—"

"Yes, sir, you had forgotten those words, 'Come unto me, all ye who are weary and heavy laden, and I will give you rest.'"

"I am ashamed of myself," said Mrs Seagrave, bursting into tears.

Mr Seagrave opened the Bible, and read the psalm. As soon as he had closed the book, "good night" were all the words that passed, and they all retired to rest.

During the night, the wind howled and the rain beat down. The children slept soundly, but Mr and Mrs Seagrave, Ready, and William were awake during the whole of the night, listening to the storm, and occupied with their own thoughts.

Ready was dressed before daylight, and out on the beach before the sun had risen. The gale was at its height; and after a careful survey with his telescope, he could see nothing of the vessel. He remained on the beach till breakfast-time, when he was summoned by William, and returned to the house. He found Mr and Mrs Seagrave up, and more composed than they were the evening before; and they welcomed him warmly.

"I fear, Ready," said Mr Seagrave, "that you have no good news for us."

"No, sir; nor can you expect any good news until after the gale is over. The vessel could not remain here during the gale—that is certain; and there is no saying what the effects of the gale may be. She may lie to, and not be far from us when the gale is over; or she may be obliged to scud before the gale, and run some hundred miles from us. Then comes the next chance. I think, by her running for the island, that she was short of water; the question is, then, whether she may not find it necessary to run for the port she is bound to, or water at some other place. A captain of a vessel is bound to do his best for the owners. At the same time I do think, that if she can with propriety come back for us she will. The question is, first, whether she can; and, secondly, whether the captain is a humane man, and will do so at his own inconvenience."

"There is but poor comfort in all that," replied Mr Seagrave.

"It is useless holding out false hopes, sir," replied Ready; "but even if the vessel continues her voyage, we have much to be thankful for."

"In what, Ready?"

"Why, sir, no one knew whether we were in existence or not, and probably we never should have been searched for; but now we have made it known, and by the ship's name on the flag they know who we are, and, if they arrive safe in port, will not fail to communicate the intelligence to your friends. Is not that a great deal to be thankful for? We may not be taken off by this vessel, but we have every hope that another will be sent out to us."

"Very true, Ready; I ought to have seen that before; but my despair and disappointment were yesterday so great, that it almost took away my reason."

The gale continued during the day, and showed no symptoms of abatement, when they again retired for the night. The following day Ready was up early, as usual, and William accompanied him to the beach.

"I don't think that it blows so hard as it did, Ready."

"No, William, it does not; the gale is breaking, and by night, I have no doubt, will be over. It is, however, useless looking for the vessel, as she must be a long way from this. It would take her a week, perhaps, to come back to us if she was to try to do so, unless the wind should change to the northward or westward."

"Ready! Ready!" exclaimed William, pointing to the south-east part of the reef; "what is that? Look! it's a boat."

Ready put his telescope to his eye. "It's a canoe, William, and there are people in it."

"Why, where can they have come from? See! they are among the breakers; they will be lost. Let us go towards them, Ready."

They hastened along the beach to the spot nearest to where the canoe was tossing on the surf, and watched it as it approached the shore.

"William, this canoe must have been blown off from the large island, which lies out there;" and Ready again looked through his telescope: "there are two people in it, and they are islanders. Poor things! they struggle hard for their lives, and seem much exhausted; but they have passed through the most dangerous part of the reef."

"Yes," replied William, "they will soon be in smoother water; but the surf on the beach is very heavy."

"They won't mind that, if their strength don't fail them—they manage the canoe beautifully."

During this conversation the canoe had rapidly come towards the land. In a moment or two afterwards, it passed through the surf and grounded on the beach. The two people in it had just strength enough left to paddle through the surf, and then they dropped down in the bottom of the canoe, quite exhausted.

"Let's drag the canoe higher up, William. Poor creatures! they are nearly dead."

While dragging it up, Ready observed that the occupants were both women: their faces were tattooed all over; otherwise they were young, and might have been good-looking.

"Shall I run up and get something for them, Ready?"

"Do, William; ask Juno to give you some of whatever there is for breakfast; anything warm."

William soon returned with some thin oatmeal porridge, which Juno had been preparing for breakfast; and a few spoonfuls being forced down the throats of the two natives they gradually revived. William then left Ready, and went up to acquaint his father and mother with this unexpected event.

William soon returned with Mr Seagrave, and as the women were now able to sit up, they hauled up the canoe as far as they could, to prevent her being beat to pieces. They found nothing in the canoe, except a piece of matting and the two paddles which had been used by the natives.

"You see, sir," said Ready, "it is very clear that these two poor women, having been left in charge of the canoe, have been blown off from the shore of one of the islands to the south-east; they must have been contending with the gale ever since the day before yesterday, and, as it appears, without food or water. It's a mercy that they gained this island."

"It is so," replied Mr Seagrave; "but to tell the truth, I am not over pleased at their arrival. It proves what we were not sure of before, that we have very near neighbours, who may probably pay us a very unwelcome visit."

"That may be, sir," replied Ready; "still these two poor creatures being thrown on shore here does not make the matter worse, or the danger greater. Perhaps it may turn to our advantage; for if these women learn to speak English before any other islanders visit us, they will interpret for us, and be the means, perhaps, of saving our lives."

"Would their visit be so dangerous, then, Ready?"

"Why, sir, a savage is a savage, and, like a child, wishes to obtain whatever he sees; especially he covets what he may turn to use, such as iron, etcetera. If they came, and we concealed a portion, and gave up the remainder of our goods, we might escape; but still there is no trusting to them, and I would infinitely prefer defending ourselves against numbers to trusting to their mercy."

"But how can we defend ourselves against a multitude?"

"We must be prepared, sir: if we can fortify ourselves, with our muskets we would be more than a match for hundreds."

Mr Seagrave turned away. After a pause he said, "It is not very pleasant to be now talking of defending ourselves against savages, when we hoped two days ago to be leaving the island. Oh, that that brig would make its appearance again!"

"The wind is going down fast, sir," observed Ready; "it will be fine weather before the evening. We may look out for her; at all events, for the next week I shall not give up all hopes."

"A whole week, Ready! Alas! how true it is, that hope deferred maketh the heart sick."

"It is a severe trial, Mr Seagrave; but we must submit when we are chastened. We had better get these poor creatures up to the house, and let them recover themselves."

Ready then beckoned to them to get on their feet, which they both did, although with some difficulty. He then went in advance, making a sign for them to follow; they understood him, and made the attempt, but were so weak, that they would have fallen if they had not been supported by Mr Seagrave and William.

It required a long time for them to arrive at the house. Mrs Seagrave, who knew what had happened, received them very kindly, and Juno had a mess ready, which she put before them. They ate a little and then lay down, and were soon sound asleep.

"It is fortunate for us that they are women," observed Mr Seagrave: "we should have had great difficulty had they been men."

"Yes, sir," replied Ready; "but still we must not trust women too much at first, for they are savages."

"Where shall we put them to-night, Ready?"

"Why, sir, I have been thinking about that. I wish we had a shed close to us; but as we have not, we must let them sleep in the storehouse."

We must now pass over a space of fifteen days, in which there was nothing done. The expectation of the vessel returning was still alive, although each day decreased these hopes. Every morning Ready and William were at the beach with the telescope, and the whole of the day was passed in surmises, hopes, and fears. In fact, the appearance of the vessel and the expectation of leaving the island had completely overturned all the regularity and content of our island party. No other subject was broached— not any of the work proposed was begun, as it was useless to do anything if they were to leave the island. After the first week had passed, they felt that every day their chances were more adverse, and at the end of the fortnight all hopes were very unwillingly abandoned.

The Indian women had, in the meantime, recovered their fatigues, and appeared to be very mild and tractable. Whatever they were able to do, they did cheerfully, and had already gained a few words of English. The party to explore was again talked over, and arranged for the following Monday, when a new misfortune fell on them, which disconcerted all their arrangements.

On the Saturday morning, when Ready, as usual, went his rounds, as he walked along the beach, he perceived that the Indian canoe was missing. It had been hauled up clear of the water, so that it could not have floated away. Ready's heart misgave him; he looked through his telescope in the direction of the large island, and thought he could distinguish a speck on the water at a great distance. As he was thus occupied, William came down to him.

"William," said Ready, "I fear those island women have escaped in their canoe. Run up, and see if they are in the outhouse, or anywhere else, and let me know as soon as you can."

William in a few minutes returned, breathless, stating that the women were not to be found, and that they had evidently carried away with them a quantity of the large nails and other pieces of iron which were in the small kegs in the storehouse.

"This is bad, William; this is worse than the vessel not coming back."

"Why, we can do without them, Ready."

"Yes; but when they get back to their own people, and show them the iron they have brought with them, and describe how much more there is to be had, depend upon it, we shall have a visit from them in numbers, that they may obtain more. I ought to have known better than to leave the canoe here. We must go and consult with Mr Seagrave, for the sooner we begin to work now, the better."

They communicated the intelligence to Mr Seagrave when they were outside. He at once perceived their danger, so they held a council, and came to the following resolutions:—

That it would be necessary that they should immediately stockade the storehouse, so as to render it impossible for any one to get in; and that, as soon as the fortification was complete, the storehouse should be turned into their dwelling-house; and such stores as could not be put within the stockade should be removed to their present house, or concealed in the cocoa-nut grove.

It was decided that nothing should be begun on that day, Saturday; that Sunday should be spent in devout prayer for help and encouragement from the Almighty, who would do towards them as his wisdom should ordain; and that on Monday, with the blessing of God, they would recommence their labour.

"I don't know why, but I feel more courage now that there is a prospect of danger, than I felt when there was little or none," said Mrs Seagrave.

"How little do we know what the day may bring forth!" exclaimed Mr Seagrave. "How joyful were our anticipations when the vessel hoisted her colours! we felt sure that we were to be taken off the island. The same gale that drove the vessel away brought down to us the island women. The fair weather after the gale, which we hoped would have brought back the vessel to our succour, on the contrary enabled the women to escape in the canoe, and make known our existence to those who may come to destroy us. How true it is that man plans in vain; and that it is only by the Almighty will and pleasure that he can obtain his ends!"

Chapter Forty Five

But although they resolved as stated in the last chapter, nothing was done. Finally, one morning at sunrise, as they were looking round with the telescope, close to the turtle-pond, Masterman Ready said to Mr Seagrave, "Indeed, sir, we must no longer remain in this state of idleness; I have been thinking a great deal of our present position and prospects; as to the vessel coming back, we must, at present, give up all hopes of it. I only wish that we were quite as sure that we shall not have a visit from the savages: that is my great fear, and it really haunts me; the idea of our being surprised some night, and Mrs Seagrave and the dear children, perhaps, murdered in their beds, is awful to reflect upon."

"God help us!" exclaimed Mr Seagrave, covering up his face.

"God will help us, Mr Seagrave, but at the same time it is necessary that we should help ourselves; he will give his blessing to our exertions, but we cannot expect that miracles will be performed for us; and if we remain as we now are, inactive, and taking no steps to meet the danger which threatens us, we cannot expect the divine assistance. We have had a heavy shock, but it is now time that we recover from it, and put our own shoulders to the wheel."

"I agree with you, Ready," replied William; "indeed I have been thinking the same thing for many days past."

"We have all been thinking of it, I believe," said Mr Seagrave; "I'm sure I have lain awake night after night, considering our position and what we ought to do, but I have never been able to come to any satisfactory resolution."

"No more have I till last night, Mr Seagrave, but I think that I have now something to propose which, perhaps, will meet with your approval," replied Ready; "so now, sir, suppose we hold another council, and come to a decision."

"I am most willing, Ready," said Mr Seagrave, sitting down upon a rock; "and as you are the oldest, and moreover the best adviser of the three, we will first hear what you have to propose."

"Well then, Mr Seagrave, it appears to me that it will not do to remain in the house, for we may, as I have said, be surprised by the savages at any hour in the night, and we have no means of defence against numbers."

"I feel that, and have felt it for some time," replied Mr Seagrave. "What shall we do, then; shall we return to the cove?"

"I should think not, sir," said Ready; "what I propose is this: we have made a discovery on the south of the island, which is of great importance to us; not that I consider the fruit and other plants of any great value, as they will only serve to increase our luxuries, if I may so call them, during the summer season. One great advantage to us, is the feed which we have found for our live stock, and the fodder for them during the rainy season; but principally, the patch of yams, which will afford us food during the winter. They are of great importance to us, and we cannot too soon protect them from the pigs, which will certainly root them all up, if we do not prevent them. Now, sir, you know what we had arranged to do, but which we have not done; I think the cocoa-nut rails will take too much time, and it will be sufficient to make a ditch and hedge round the yams; but it will be very tedious if we are to go backwards and forwards to do the work, and Mrs Seagrave and the children will be left alone. I therefore propose, as the weather is now set in fair, and will remain so for months, that we pitch our tents on that part of the island, and remove the whole family there; we shall soon be very comfortable, and at all events much safer there than if we remain here, without any defence."

"It is an excellent plan, Ready; we shall, as you say, be removed from danger for the time, and when there, we may consider what we had best do by and by."

"Yes, sir. Those women may not have gained the other island, it is true, for they had the wind right against them for several days after they went away in the canoe, and, moreover, the current sets strong this way; but if they have, we must expect that the savages will pay us a visit; they will, of course, come direct to the house, if they do come."

"But, Ready, you don't mean to say that we are to leave this side of the island altogether, and all our comfortable arrangements?" said William.

"No, William, not altogether; for now I come to the second part of my proposition. As soon as we have done our work at the yam plantation, and made everything as comfortable there as we can, I think we may then leave Mrs Seagrave and the children in the tents, and work here. As we before agreed, let us abandon the house in which we live at present, and fit out the outhouse which is concealed in the cocoa-nut grove, as a dwelling-house, and fortify it so as to be secure against any sudden attack of the savages: for, return here we must, to live, as we cannot remain in the tents after the rainy season sets in."

"How do you propose to fortify it, Ready?" said Mr Seagrave; "I hardly know."

"That I will explain to you by and by, sir. Then, if the savages come here, at all events we should be able to defend ourselves with fire-arms; one man behind a stockade is better than twenty who have no other arms but spears and clubs; and we may, with the help of God, beat them off."

"I think your plan is excellent, Ready," said Mr Seagrave, "and that the sooner we begin, the better."

"That there is no doubt of, sir. Now, the first job is for William and me to try for the passage through this side of the reef with the boat, and then we will look for the little harbour which we discovered; as soon as that is done, we will return and take the tents and all we require round in the boat, and when we have pitched the tents and all is arranged, Mrs Seagrave and the children can walk through the wood with us, and take possession."

"Let us not lose an hour, Ready; we have lost too much time already," replied Mr Seagrave. "What shall we do to-day?"

"After breakfast, William and I will take the boat, and try for the passage. You can remain here, packing up the tents and such articles as must first be carried round. We shall be back, I hope, by dinner-time."

They then rose, and walked towards the house; all felt relieved in their minds, after they had made this arrangement, satisfied that they would be using all human endeavours to ward off the danger which threatened them, and might then put their confidence in that Providence who would, if he thought fit, protect them in their need.

Chapter Forty Six

The subject was introduced to Mrs Seagrave, while they were at breakfast, and as she perceived how much more secure they would be, she cheerfully consented. In less than an hour afterwards, William and Ready had prepared the boat, and were pulling out among the rocks of the reef to find a passage, which, after a short time, and by keeping two or three cables from the point, they succeeded in doing.

"This is very fortunate, William," observed Ready; "but we must now take some marks to find our way in again. See, the large black rock is on a line with the garden point: so, if we keep them in one, we shall know that we are in the proper channel; and now for a mark abreast of us, to find out when we enter it."

"Why, Ready, the corner of the turtle-pond just touches the right wall of the house," replied William.

"So it does; that will do; and now let us pull away as hard as we can, so as to be back in good time."

They soon were on the south side of the island, and pulling up along the shore.

"How far do you think that it is by water, Ready?"

"I hardly know; but at least four or five miles, so we must make up our minds to a good hour's pull. At all events, we shall sail back again with this wind, although there is but little of it."

"We are in very deep water now," observed William, after a long silence.

"Yes, on this side of the island we must expect it; the coral grows to leeward only. I think that we cannot be very far from the little harbour we discovered. Suppose we leave off rowing for a minute, and look about us."

"There are two rocks close to the shore, Ready," said William, pointing, "and you recollect there were two or three rocks outside of the harbour."

"Very true, William, and I should not wonder if you have hit upon the very spot. Let us pull in."

They did so; and, to their satisfaction, found that they were in the harbour, where the water was as smooth as a pond.

"Now, then, William, we will step the mast, and sail back at our leisure."

"Stop one moment, Ready; give me the boat-hook. I see something between the clefts of the rocks."

Ready handed the boat-hook to William, who, lowering it down into the water, drove the spike of iron at the end of it into a large crayfish, which he hauled up into the boat.

"That will be an addition to our dinner," said Ready; "we do not go back empty-handed, and, therefore, as the saying is, we shall be more welcome; now, then, let us start, for we must pull here again this afternoon, and with a full cargo on board."

They stepped the mast, and as soon as they had pulled the boat clear of the harbour, set sail, and in less than an hour had rejoined the party at the house.

William had brought up the crayfish, which had only one claw, and Juno put on another pot of water to boil it, as an addition to the dinner, which was nearly ready. Tommy at first went with his sister Caroline to look at the animal, and as soon as he had left off admiring it, he began, as usual, to tease it; first he poked its eyes with a stick, then he tried to unfold his tail, but the animal flapped, and he ran away. At last he was trying to put his stick into the creature's mouth, when it raised its large claw, and caught him by the wrist, squeezing him so tight that Tommy screamed and danced about as the crayfish held on. Fortunately for him, the animal had been so long out of water, and had been so much hurt by the iron spike of the boat-hook, that it was more than half-dead, or he would have been severely hurt. Ready ran to him, and disengaged the crayfish; but Tommy was so frightened, that he took to his heels, and did not leave off running until he was one hundred yards from the house, while Juno and Ready were laughing at him till the tears came into their eyes. When he saw the crayfish on the table, he appeared to be afraid of it, although it was dead.

"Well, Tommy," said Mr Seagrave, "I suppose you won't eat any of the crayfish?"

"Won't I?" replied Tommy. "I'll eat him, for he tried to eat me."

"Why did you not leave the animal alone, Tommy?" said Mr Seagrave; "if you had not tormented it, it would not have bitten you; I don't know whether you ought to have any."

"I don't like it; I won't have any," replied Tommy. "I like salt pork better."

"Well, then, if you don't like it, you shall not have it forced upon you, Tommy," replied Mr Seagrave; "so now we'll divide it among the rest of us."

Tommy was not very well pleased at this decision, for he really did wish to have some of it, so he turned very sulky for the rest of the dinner-time, especially when old Ready told him that he had had his share of the crayfish before dinner.

Chapter Forty Seven

As soon as the meal was over, Mr Seagrave and Juno assisted them in carrying down the canvas and poles for the tent, with shovels to clear away, and the pegs to fix the tents up properly. Before they started, William observed, "I think it would be a good thing, if Ready and I were to take our bedding with us, and then we could fix up one tent this evening, and sleep there; to-morrow morning we might set up the other, and get a good deal of work over before we come back."

"You are right, William," replied Ready; "let us see what Juno can give us to eat, and then we will do as you say, for the sooner we are all there the better."

As Mr Seagrave was of the same opinion, Juno packed up a piece of salt pork and some flour-cakes, which, with three or four bottles of water, they took down to the boat. Ready having thrown in a piece of rope to moor the boat with, they shoved off and were soon through the reef, and, after a smart pull, they arrived again at the small harbour.

As soon as they had landed all the things, they made the boat fast by the rope, and then carried a portion of the canvas and tent-poles up to the first copse of trees, which were the guavas; they then returned for the remainder, and after three trips everything was up.

"Now, William, we must see where to pitch the tent; we must not be too near the cocoa-nut grove, or we shall have too far to go for water."

"Don't you think that the best place will be close to the bananas? the ground is higher there, and the water is, you know, between the bananas and the yams."

"Very true, I think it will not be a bad place; let us walk there first, and reconnoitre the ground."

They walked to where the bananas were now throwing out their beautiful large green leaves, and decided that they would fix the tents upon the north side of them.

"So here let it be," said Ready; "and now let us go and fetch all the things; it is a nice dry spot, and I think will do capitally."

They were soon hard at work, and long before sunset one tent was ready, and they had put their bedding in it.

"Well, now, I suppose you are a little tired," said Ready; "I'm sure you ought to be, for you have worked hard to-day."

"I don't feel very tired, Ready, but it's not time to go to bed yet."

"No; and I think we had better take our shovels and dig the pits for the water, and then we shall know by to-morrow morning whether the water is good or not."

"Yes, Ready, we can do that before we get our supper."

They walked to where the ground between the bananas and yam patch was wet and swampy, and dug two large holes about a yard deep and square; the water trickled in very fast, and they were up to their ankles before they had finished.

"There'll be no want of water, Ready, if it is only fit to drink."

"I've no fear of that," replied Ready.

They returned to the tent and made their supper off the salt pork and flour-cakes, and then lay down on the mattresses. They were soon fast asleep, for they were tired out with the hard work which they had gone through.

The next morning, at sunrise, they were up again; the first thing they did was to go and examine the holes they had dug for water; they found them full and running over, and the water had settled quite clear; they tasted it, and pronounced it very good.

As soon as they had washed themselves, they went back and made their breakfast, and then set to work to get up the other tent. They then cleared all the ground near the tents of brushwood and high grass, and levelled it nicely with their shovels inside.

"Now, William, we have another job, which is to prepare a fireplace for Juno: we must go down to the beach for stones."

In another hour the fireplace was completed, and Ready and William looked at their work.

"Well, I call this a very comfortable lodging-house," said Ready.

"And I am sure," replied William, "it's very pretty. Mamma will be delighted with it."

"We shall have no want of bananas in a few weeks," said Ready; "look, they are all in blossom already. Well, now I suppose we had better leave everything here, and go back. We must have another trip this afternoon, and sleep here to-night."

They went down to the boat, and sailed back as before; by ten o'clock in the morning they had regained the house, and then they made arrangements for their work during the remainder of the day. It was agreed that the provisions necessary for a day or two, the table and chairs, the cooking utensils, and a portion of their clothes, should be taken round that afternoon, that Ready and William should come back early the next morning, and then they should all set off together through the wood to the new location. The sheep and lambs (for they had four lambs), the goats and kids, were to be driven through the wood by Mr Seagrave; William and Ready and the dogs would be very useful in driving them. As for the fowls and chickens, it was decided they should be left, as Ready and William could look after them on their occasional visits.

Chapter Forty Eight

The boat was well loaded that afternoon, and they had a heavy pull round, and hard work afterwards to carry all the articles up. William and Ready were, therefore, not sorry when their work was done, and they went to bed as soon as they had taken their supper.

At sunrise, they went back to the bay in the boat, which they hauled up, and then proceeded to the house, where they found that everyone was ready to start. Mr Seagrave had collected all the animals, and they set off; the marks on the trees were very plain, and they had no difficulty in finding their way; but they had a good deal of trouble with the goats and sheep, and did not get on very fast. It was three hours before they got clear of the cocoa-nut grove, and Mrs Seagrave was quite tired out. At last they arrived, and Mr and Mrs Seagrave could not help exclaiming "How beautiful!"

When they came to where the tents were pitched by the side of the bananas, they were equally pleased: it was quite a fairy spot. Mrs Seagrave went into her tent to repose after her fatigue; the goats and sheep were allowed to stray away as they pleased; the dogs lay down, panting with their long journey; Juno put Albert on the bed while she went with William to collect fuel to cook the dinner; Ready went to the pits to get some water, while Mr Seagrave walked about, examining the different clumps of trees with which the meadow was studded.

When Ready returned with the water, he called the dogs, and went back towards the yam plantation. Tommy followed them; the dogs went into the yams, and were soon barking furiously, which pleased Tommy very much; when, of a sudden, out burst again in a drove all the pigs, followed by the dogs, and so close to Tommy that he screamed with fright, and tumbled head over heels.

"I thought you were there, my gentlemen," said Ready, looking after the pigs; "the sooner we fence you out the better."

The pigs scampered away, and went into the cocoa-nut grove as they had done before. The dogs followed the pigs, and did not return for a long while afterwards.

It was late before the dinner was ready, and they were all very glad to go early to bed.

At day dawn, William and Ready had again started, and walked through the cocoa-nut grove back to the house, to bring round in the boat the articles of furniture and the clothes which had been left. Having collected everything in the house, and procured some more pork and flour from the storehouse, they completed the load by spearing one of the turtles which remained, and putting it into the bottom of the boat; they then set off again for their new residence, and arrived in time for breakfast.

"What a delightful spot this is!" said Mrs Seagrave. "I think we ought always to make it our summer residence, and only go back to the house during the rainy season."

"It is much cooler here, madam, during the summer, and much more pleasant; but we are more protected in the house by the cocoa-nut grove."

"Yes; that is true, and it is very valuable during the rainy season; but it makes it warmer in the summer time. I like the change, Ready, and shall be sorry when we have to go back again."

"Now I must go, and help Juno to cut up the turtle," said Ready. "We must make our larder among the banana trees."

"But what are we all to do, Ready?" said Mr Seagrave. "We must not be idle."

"No, sir; but I think we must give up this day to putting everything to rights, and making everything comfortable inside the tents; to-morrow we will commence the ditch and hedge round the yam plantation. We need not work very hard at it, for I don't think the pigs will venture here again, as I mean to tie up all the dogs round the yam patch every night, and their barking will keep them off."

"That will be a very good plan, Ready. What beautiful food there is for the sheep and goats!"

"Yes; this must be their future residence for the best part of the year. I think to-morrow we will begin a piece of the ditch, and show William how to put in the cuttings of prickly pear for the hedge, and then, I should propose that you and I go to the cove to examine the stores and select what it will be necessary to bring round. I think you said that you must go yourself?"

"Yes, Ready, I wish to go. When we have made our selection, I will return, and then you and William, who is more used to the boat than I am, can bring the stores round. I presume we shall not bring them here?"

"No, sir, we will take them round to the storehouse. When we have done that job, we must then commence our alterations and our stockade."

Chapter Forty Nine

The next morning they went with their shovels to the yam plantation, and commenced their work. As the ground was soft and swampy, the labour was very easy. The ditch was dug nearly a yard wide, and the earth thrown up on a bank inside. They then went to where the large patch of prickly pears grew, and cut a quantity, which they planted on the top of the bank. Before night, they had finished about nine or ten yards of the hedge and ditch.

"I don't think that the pigs will get over that when it is finished," said Ready, "and William will be able to get on by himself when we are gone, as well as if we were with him."

"I'll try if I cannot shoot a pig or two," said William.

"Let it be a young one, then; we must not kill the old ones. Now I think we may as well go back. Juno is carrying in the supper."

Before Mr Seagrave and Ready started on the following morning, the latter gave William directions as to the boat. The provisions and the knapsack having been already prepared, they took leave of Mrs Seagrave, and set off, each armed with a musket, and Ready with his axe slung over his shoulder. They had a long walk before them, as they had first to find their way back to the house, and from thence had to walk through the wood to the cove.

In two hours after leaving the house they reached the spot where they had first landed. The rocks near to it were strewed with timber and planks, which lay bleaching in the sun, or half-buried in the sand. Mr Seagrave sat down, and sighed deeply as he said, "Ready, the sight of these timbers, of which the good ship Pacific was built, recalls feelings which I had hoped to have dismissed from my mind; but I cannot help them rising up. The remains of this vessel appear to me as the last link between us and the civilised world, which we have been torn from, and all my thoughts of home and country, and I may say all my longing for them, are revived as strong as ever."

"And very natural that they should, Mr Seagrave; I feel it also. I am content, it is true, because I have nothing to wish or look forward to; but still I could not help thinking of poor Captain Osborn and my shipmates, as I looked upon the wreck, and wishing that I might take them by the hand again. It is very natural that one should do so. Why, sir, do you know that I feel unhappy even about the poor ship. We sailors love our vessels, especially when they have good qualities, and the Pacific was as fine a vessel as ever was built. Now, sir, I feel quite melancholy when I see her planks and timbers lying about here. But, sir, if we cannot help feeling as we do, it is our duty to check the feeling, so that it does not get the mastery over us. We can do no more."

"Very true, Ready," said Mr Seagrave, rising up; "it is not only useless, but even sinful to indulge in them, as they only can lead to our repining at the decrees of heaven. Let us now examine the rocks, and see if anything has been thrown up that may be of use to us."

They walked round, but, with the exception of spars and a barrel or two of tar, they could find nothing of value. There was no want of staves and iron hoops of broken casks, and these, Ready observed, would make excellent palings for the garden when they had time to bring them round.

After they had returned, they sat down to rest themselves, and then they went to the tents in the cocoa-nut grove, in which they had collected the articles thrown up when the ship went to pieces.

"Why, the pigs have been at work here!" said Ready; "they have contrived to open one cask of flour somehow or another; look, sir—I suppose it must have been shaky, or they could not have routed into it; the canvas is not good for much, I fear; fortunately, we have several bolts of new, which I brought on shore. Now, sir, we will see what condition the stores are in. All these are casks of flour, and we run no risk in opening them, and seeing if they are in good order."

The first cask which was opened had a cake round it as hard as a board; but when it was cut through with the axe, the inside was found in a good state.

"That's all right, sir; and I presume the others will be the same; the salt water has got in so far and made a crust, which has preserved the rest. But now let us go to dinner, and to work afterwards."

Chapter Fifty

After dinner they resumed their labour. "I wonder what's in this case?" said Mr Seagrave, pointing to the first at hand. Ready set to work with his axe, and broke off the lid, and found a number of pasteboard boxes full of tapes, narrow ribbons, stay-laces, whalebones, and cottons on reels.

"This has been sent out for some Botany Bay milliner," said Mr Seagrave. "I presume, however, we must confiscate it for the benefit of Mrs Seagrave and Miss Caroline. We will take them to them as soon as we have time."

The next was a box without a lock; the lid was forced up, and they found a dozen half-gallon square bottles of gin stored in divisions.

"That's Hollands, sir, I know," said Ready; "what shall we do with it?"

"We will not destroy it, Ready, but at the same time we will not use it but as a medicine," replied Mr Seagrave; "we have been so long used to spring-water, that it would be a pity to renew a taste for spirituous liquors."

"I trust we shall never want to drink a drop of it, sir, either as a medicine or otherwise. Now for this cask with wooden hoops."

The head was soon out, and discovered a dinner set of painted china with gold edges.

"This, Mr Seagrave, may be useful, for we are rather short of plates and dishes. Common white would have served as well."

"And be more suitable with our present outfit," replied Mr Seagrave.

"Here's a box with your name on it, sir," said Ready; "do you know what is in it?"

"I have no idea, Ready; but your axe will decide the point."

When the box was opened, everything appeared in a sad mouldy state from the salt water which had penetrated; but on removing the brown paper and pasteboard, it was found to contain stationery of all sorts, and, except on the outside, it was very little injured.

"This is indeed a treasure, Ready. I recollect now; this is paper, pens, and everything requisite for writing, besides children's books, copy-books, paint-boxes, and a great many other articles in the stationery line."

"Well, sir, that is fortunate. Now we may set up our school, and as the whole population of the island will attend it, it will really be a National School."

"Very true, Ready. Now for that cask."

"I can tell what that is by the outside; it is oil, and very acceptable, for our candles are nearly out. Now we come to the most valuable of all our property."

"What is that, Ready?"

"All the articles which I brought on shore in the different trips I took in the boat before the ship went to pieces; for you see, sir, iron don't swim, and, therefore, what I looked after most was ironware of all sorts, and tools. Here are three kegs of small nails, besides two bags of large, and there are several axes, hammers, and other tools, besides hanks of twine, sailing needles, and bees'-wax."

"They are indeed valuable, Ready."

"Here's some more of my plunder, as the Americans say. All these are wash-deck buckets, this a small harness cask for salting meat, and here's the cook's wooden trough for making bread, which will please Miss Juno; and in it, you see, I have put all the galley-hooks, ladles, and spoons, and the iron trivets, and here's two lamps. I think I put some cotton wicks somewhere—I know I did; we shall find them by and by. Here's the two casks, one of cartridges made up, and the other of gunpowder, and the other six muskets."

"These are really treasures, Ready, and yet how well we have done without them."

"Very true, sir, but we shall do better with them, and when we fit up the storehouse for a dwelling, Mr Seagrave, we shall be able to make it a little more comfortable in every respect than the present one; for you see there, all the fir-planking and deals, which William and I buried in the sand."

"I really had quite forgotten them, Ready. If I could but get the fear of the savages coming over out of my head, I really think we might live very comfortably even on this island."

"Do you know, Mr Seagrave, I am glad to hear you say that, for it proves that you are more contented and resigned than you were."

"I am so, Ready—at least I think so; but perhaps it is, that the immediate danger from the savages so fills my thoughts, that I no longer dwell so much upon our being taken off the island."

"I dare say it is as you state, sir; but now let us go on with our search. Here are the ship's compasses, and deep sea line and reel, also the land lead. The stuff will be very useful for our little boat."

"And I am very glad of the compasses, Ready; for with them I shall be able to make a sort of survey of the island, when I have a little time. Your pocket compass is too small for surveying. I shall take some bearings now, while I am here, as I may not be back again very soon."

"Well, sir, I think if we open this other case, which I perceive has your name on it, it will be as much as we need do to-day, for the sun is going down; we can then make up some kind of bed, eat our suppers, and go to sleep."

"I am very tired, Ready, and shall be glad to do as you propose. That case contains books; but what portion of my library I do not know."

"But you soon will, sir," replied Ready, wrenching it open with his axe. "They are a little stained on the outside, but they are jammed so tight that they do not appear to have suffered much. Here are one or two, sir."

"Plutarch's Lives. I am glad I have them: they are excellent reading for young or old; there is no occasion to open any more, as I know all the other books in the case are 'History'; perhaps the best case which could have been saved."

Chapter Fifty One

Mr Seagrave and Ready then set to work, and made a rough sort of bed of cocoa-nut branches; and, after eating their supper, committed themselves to the divine protection, and went to sleep. The next morning they resumed their labour, and opened every other case and package that had been saved from the wreck; they found more books, four boxes of candles, three casks of rice, and several other useful articles, besides many others which were of no value to them.

A chest of tea, and two bags of coffee, which Ready had brought on shore, were, much to their delight, found in good order; but there was no sugar, the little which they had saved having been melted away.

"That's unfortunate, sir."

"We cannot expect to get things here, as though we were a hundred yards from a grocer's shop. Now let us go to where we covered up the other articles with sand."

The sand was shovelled up, and the barrels of beef and pork and the deal boards found in good order, but many other things were quite spoilt. About noon they had finished, and as they had plenty of time, Mr Seagrave took the bearings of the different points of land with the compasses. They then shouldered their muskets, and set off on their return.

They gained the house in the bay, and having rested a little while at the storehouse, they proceeded on their way to the tents in the meadow. They had about half a mile to go, when Ready heard a noise, and made a sign to Mr Seagrave to stop. Ready, whispering to Mr Seagrave that the pigs were all close to them, loaded his musket; Mr Seagrave did the same, and they walked very softly to where they now heard their grunting; they did not see them till they were within twenty yards, and then they came upon the whole herd; the pigs raised their heads; the old ones gave a loud grunt, and then, just as Ready fired his musket, they all set off at full speed. Mr Seagrave had no opportunity of firing, but Ready had shot one, which lay kicking and struggling under a cocoa-nut tree.

"A piece of fresh pork will be quite a treat, Mr Seagrave," said Ready, as they walked up to where the animal was lying.

"It will, indeed, Ready," replied Mr Seagrave; "we must contrive to carry the beast home between us."

"We will sling it on the musket, sir, and it will not be very heavy. It is one of those born on the island, and a very fine fellow for his age."

The pig was soon slung, and they carried it between them. As they cleared the wood, they perceived Mrs Seagrave and William, who had heard the report of the musket, and had come out to meet them.

William took the load from his father, who walked on with Mrs Seagrave.

"Well, William, what news have you?" said Ready.

"Why, very good, Ready. Yesterday evening, when I was tired of work, I thought I would take the boat, and try if there was any fish to be caught on this side of the island in the deep water, and I caught three large ones, quite different from those we took among the reefs. We had one for breakfast and dinner to-day, and it was excellent."

"Did you go out in the boat by yourself?"

"No; I took Juno with me. She pulls very well, Ready."

"She is a handy girl, William. Well, we have had our survey, and there will be plenty of work for you and me, I can tell you; I don't think we can bring everything round in a week; so I suppose to-morrow we had better be off."

"Well, I like boating better than ditching, I can tell you, Ready," replied William. "I shan't be sorry to leave that work to my father."

"I suppose it must fall to him; as he will, of course, prefer staying with Mrs Seagrave and the children."

As soon as they were at the tents, Ready hung up the pig to the cross pole of the tent in which he and William and Mr Seagrave slept, and having propped the muskets up against the side of the tent, he went with William to get his knife and some stretchers of wood to open the pig with. While he and William were away, Caroline and Tommy came out to look at it, and Tommy, after telling Caroline how glad he was that they were to have roast pig for dinner, took up one of the muskets, and said, "Now, Caroline, I'll shoot the pig."

"Oh! Tommy, you must not touch the gun," cried Caroline; "papa will be very angry."

"I don't care," replied Tommy. "I'll show you how to shoot the pig."

"Don't, Tommy," cried Caroline; "if you do, I'll go and tell mamma."

"Then I'll shoot you," replied Tommy, trying to point the musket at her.

Caroline was so frightened, that she ran away as fast as she could, and then Tommy, using all his strength, contrived to get the musket up to his shoulder, and pulled the trigger.

It so happened that Tommy had taken up Mr Seagrave's musket, which had not been fired, and when he pulled the trigger it went off, and as he did not hold it tight to his shoulder, it recoiled, and hit him with the butt right on his face, knocking out two of his teeth, besides making his nose bleed very fast.

Tommy was so astonished and frightened at the musket going off, and the blow which he received, that he gave a loud yell, dropped the musket, and ran to the tent where his father and mother were, just as they had started up and had rushed out at hearing the report.

When Mrs Seagrave saw Tommy all covered with blood, and screaming so loud, she was so alarmed that she could not stand, and fell fainting in Mr Seagrave's arms. Ready and William, on hearing the musket go off, had run as fast as they could, fearing that some accident had happened; and while Mr Seagrave supported his wife, Ready went to Tommy, and wiping the blood off his face with the palm of his hand, perceived that there was no wound or serious mischief, and cried out to Mr Seagrave, "He's not hurt, sir; it's only his nose bleeding."

"Musket knocked me down," cried Tommy, sobbing as the blood ran out of his mouth.

"Serve you right, Tommy; you'll take care not to touch the musket again."

"I won't touch it again," cried Tommy, blubbering.

Juno now came up with some water to wash his face; Mrs Seagrave had recovered, and gone back into the tent, on Mr Seagrave telling her that it was only Tommy's nose which was bleeding.

In about half-an-hour Tommy had ceased crying, and his nose had left off bleeding; his face was washed, and then it was discovered that he had lost two front teeth, and that his cheek and lips were very much bruised. He was undressed, and put to bed, and was soon fast asleep.

"I should not have left the muskets," said Ready to William; "it was my fault; but I thought Tommy had been told so often not to touch fire-arms, that he would not dare to do so."

"He pointed it at me, and tried to shoot me," said Caroline, "but I ran away."

"Merciful heavens! what an escape!" cried Mrs Seagrave.

"He has been well punished this time, madam, and I'll venture to say he will not touch a musket again in a hurry."

"Yes; but he must be punished more," said Mr Seagrave. "He must remember it."

"Well, sir, if he is to be punished more, I think you cannot punish him better than by not allowing him to have any of the pig when it is cooked."

"I think so too, Ready; and therefore that is a settled thing—no pig for Tommy."

Chapter Fifty Two

The next morning Tommy's face presented a very woeful appearance. His cheek and lips were swelled and black, and the loss of his two front teeth made him look much worse.

Tommy looked very glum when he came to breakfast. There was the pig's fry for breakfast, and the smell of it had been very inviting to Tommy; but when his father scolded him, and told him that he was not to have one bit of the pig, he began to cry and roar so loud, that he was sent away from the tents till he had left off.

After breakfast, Ready proposed that he and William should take the boat, and begin their labour of carrying the articles round from the cove to the bay where the house was, pointing out that there was not a day to be lost. Juno had, at his request, already baked a large piece of the pig for them to take with them, and boiled a piece of salt pork, so that they were all ready to start.

"But, Ready," said Mrs Seagrave, "how long do you intend to remain absent with William?"

"Why, madam, this is Wednesday; of course we shall be back on Saturday night."

"My dear William, I cannot bear the idea of your being absent so long, and as you will be on the water every day, I shall be in a continual fright until I see you again."

"Well, mamma, I suppose I must write by the penny post, to let you know how I am."

"Don't laugh at me, William. I do wish there was a penny post, and that you could write every day."

Ready and William made every preparation for a continued absence. They took their blankets with them, and a small pot for cooking, and when all was prepared they bade Mr and Mrs Seagrave farewell. They were now to pull to the bay, and leave their luggage, and then go round to the cove. As they shoved off, William took the dog Remus into the boat.

"Why do you take the dog, William? he will be of use here in keeping the pigs away, but of no use to us."

"Yes, he will, Ready; I must take him; for I have an idea come into my head, so let me have my own way."

"Well, William, you can always have your own way, as far as I'm concerned; if you wish to take the dog, there is an end of the matter."

They hoisted the sail, and as the breeze was fresh, were round to the bay in a very short time. They took their provisions and stores up to the house, and made fast the door, called the fowls, and gave them some damaged rice which Ready had brought from the cove, and found, to their great delight, that they had now upwards of forty chickens; some, indeed, quite grown, and large enough to kill.

They then got into the boat again, and pulled away for the cove; the wind was fresh, and against them, so they had a long pull; but, as Ready observed, it was much better that it should be so, as, when the boat was loaded, they could very quickly sail back again to the bay.

As soon as they arrived at the cove, they lost no time in loading the boat; the nails, and iron work of every description, with the twine and tools, composed the major part of the first cargo; and calling Remus, who was lying on the sandy beach, they shoved off, hoisted their sail, and in an hour had regained the bay, and passed through the reef.

"I am glad that this cargo has arrived safe, William, for it is very valuable to us. Now we will take them all up, and that will be sufficient for to-day; to morrow, if we can, we will make two trips."

"We can, if we start early," replied William; "but now let us have our dinner, and carry the remainder of the things up afterwards."

As they were eating their dinner, and William was giving the bones to the dog, Ready said, "Pray, William, what was the idea in your head which made you bring Remus with you?"

"I will tell you, Ready; I mean him to carry a letter to mamma; you know that he always goes back when he is ordered, and now I wish to see if he will not go back to the tents, if he is told. I have brought a piece of paper and pencil with me."

William then wrote on the paper:

"Dear Mamma:— We are quite well, and just returned with the first cargo quite safe. Your affectionate son, *William* ."

William tied the paper round the dog's neck with a piece of twine, and then calling him out of the house, said to him, "Remus, go back, sir—go back, sir;" the dog looked wistfully at William, as if not sure of what he was to do, but William took up a stone, and pretended to throw it at the dog, who ran away a little distance, and then stopped.

"*Go back*, Remus—*go back*, sir." William again pretended to throw the stone, repeating the order, and then the dog set off as fast as his legs could carry him through the cocoa-nut grove.

"He is gone at all events," said William; "I think he will go home."

"We shall see, sir," replied Ready; "and now that we have finished our dinner, we will bring up the things, and put them in the storehouse."

Chapter Fifty Three

As soon as they had carried up the whole of the cargo, they secured the boat, and went up to the house to sleep. Just as they went in, Remus came bounding up to them with a letter round his neck.

"Here's the dog, William," said Ready; "he won't go home after all."

"How provoking! I made sure he would go back; I really am disappointed. We will give him nothing to eat, and then he will; but, dear me, Ready! this is not the paper I tied round his neck. I think not. Let me see." William took the paper, opened it, and read—

"Dear William:— Your letter arrived safe, and we are glad you are well. Write every day, and God bless you; it was very clever of you and Remus. Your affectionate mother, *Selina Seagrave* ."

"Well, it is clever," said Ready; "I'm sure I had no idea he had gone; and his coming back again, too, when he was ordered."

"Dear Remus, good dog," said William, caressing it: "now I'll give you a good supper, for you deserve it."

"So he does, sir. Well, you've established a post on the island, which is a great improvement. Seriously, William, it may prove very useful."

"At all events it will be a great comfort to my mother."

"Yes, especially as we shall be obliged all three to be here when we fit up the storehouse, and make the proposed alterations. Now I think we had better go to bed, for we must be up with the lark to-morrow."

"Here I suppose we ought to say, up with the parrots; for they are the only land birds on the island."

"You forget the pigeons; I saw one of them in the wood the other day. Good night!"

The next morning, they were off before breakfast. The boat was soon loaded, and they returned under sail. They then breakfasted, and having left the things they had brought on the beach, that they might lose no time, they set off again, and returned with another cargo two hours before dusk; this they landed, and then secured the boat. As soon as they were in the house, William wrote on a piece of paper:—

"Dear Mamma:— We have brought round two cargoes to-day. All well, and very tired. Yours, *William* ."

Remus did not require any teaching this time. William patted him, and said, "Good dog. Now, Remus, go back—go home, sir;" and the dog wagged his tail, and set off immediately.

Before they were in bed, the dog returned with the answer.

"How fast he must run, Ready! he has not been away more than two hours."

"No. So, now, Remus, you shall have plenty of supper, and plenty of patting and coaxing, for you are a clever, good little dog."

The next day, as they had to take the two cargoes up to the house, they could only make one trip to the cove. On Saturday they only made one trip, as they had to return to the tents, which they did by water, having first put a turtle into the boat; on their arrival, they found them all at the little harbour, waiting to receive them.

"Well, William, you did keep your promise and send me a letter by post," said Mrs Seagrave. "How very delightful it is! I shall have no fear now when you are all away."

"I must teach Romulus and Vixen to do the same, mamma."

"And I'll teach the puppies," said Tommy.

"Yes, Tommy; by the time you can write a letter, the puppies will be old enough to carry it," said Ready. "Come, Albert, I'll carry you up; you and I haven't had a game of play for a long while. How does the ditch and hedge get on, Mr Seagrave?"

"Pretty well, Ready," replied Mr Seagrave; "I have nearly finished two sides. I think by the end of next week I shall have pretty well inclosed it."

"Well, sir, you must not work too hard, there is no great hurry; William and I can get through a great deal together."

"It is my duty to work, Ready; and I may add, it is a pleasure."

As they were at supper the conversation turned upon the cleverness shown by the dog Remus.

Mr Seagrave narrated many instances of the sagacity of animals, when William asked the question of his father: "What is the difference then between reason and instinct?"

"The difference is very great, William, as I will explain to you; but I must first observe, that it has been the custom to say that man is governed by reason, and animals by instinct, alone. This is an error. Man has instinct as well as reason; and animals, although chiefly governed by instinct, have reasoning powers."

"In what points does man show that he is led by instinct?"

"When a child is first born, William, it acts by instinct only: the reasoning powers are not yet developed; as we grow up, our reason becomes every day more matured, and gains the mastery over our instinct, which decreases in proportion."

"Then when we have grown to a good old age, I suppose we have no instinct left in us?"

"Not so, my dear boy; there is one and a most powerful instinct implanted in man which never deserts him on this side of the grave. It is the fear, not of death, but of utter annihilation, that of becoming nothing after death. This instinctive feeling could not have been so deeply implanted in us, but as an assurance that we shall not be annihilated after death, but that our souls shall still exist, although our bodies shall have perished. It may be termed the instinctive evidence of a future existence."

"That is very true, Mr Seagrave," observed Ready.

"Instinct in animals, William," continued Mr Seagrave, "is a feeling which compels them to perform certain acts without previous thought or reflection; this instinct is in full force at the moment of their birth; it was therefore perfect in the beginning, and has never varied. The swallow built her nest, the spider its web, the bee formed its comb, precisely in the same way four thousand years ago, as they do now. I may here observe, that one of the greatest wonders of instinct is the mathematical form of the honeycomb of the bee, which has been proved by demonstration to be that by which is given the greatest possible saving of time and labour."

"But that is all pure instinct, papa; now you said that animals had reasoning powers. Will you point out to me how they show that they have?"

"I will, my dear boy; but we had better defer it till another evening. It is now time to go to bed."

Chapter Fifty Four

The following day, being Sunday, was devoted to the usual religious exercises. Tommy stole away out of the tent, while Mr Seagrave was reading a sermon, to have a peep at the turtle-soup, which was boiling on the fire; however, Juno suspected him, and had hold of him just as he was taking the lid off the pot. He was well scolded, and very much frightened lest he should have no soup for his dinner; however, as it was not a very heavy offence, he was forgiven.

In the evening, William requested his father to renew the conversation about the reasoning powers of animals.

"With pleasure, William," replied Mr Seagrave; "it is a fit discourse for a Sunday evening. Let us, however, first examine the various mental faculties discoverable in animals. In the first place, they have memory, especially memory of persons and places, quite as tenacious as our own. A dog will recognise an old master after many years absence. An elephant, who had again escaped into the woods, after twenty years remaining in a wild state, recognised his old mahoot, or driver. A dog will find his way back when taken more than a hundred miles from his master's residence. Another proof of memory in animals, were it required, is that they dream. Now, a dream is a confused recollection of past events; and how often do you not hear Romulus and Remus growling, barking, and whining in their sleep!"

"Very true, papa."

"Well, then, they have attention. See how patiently a cat will remain for hours before a hole, in watch for the mouse to come out. A spider will remain for months watching for the fly to enter its web; but this quality is to be observed in every animal in the pursuit of its prey. They have also association of ideas, which is, in fact, reasoning. A dog proves that; he will allow a gentleman to come up to the door, but fly at a beggar. When he is in charge of any property he will take no notice of a passer-by; but if a man stops, he barks immediately. In the elephant this association of ideas is even more remarkable; indeed, he understands what is said to him better than any other animal; his reasoning powers are most extraordinary. Promise him rewards, and he will make wonderful exertion. He is also extremely alive to a sense of shame. The elephants were employed to transport the heavy artillery in India. One of the finest attempted in vain to force a gun through a swamp. 'Take away that lazy beast,' said the director 'and bring another.' The animal was so stung with the reproach, that it used so much exertion to force the gun on with its head, as to fracture its skull, and it fell dead. When Chunee, the elephant which was so long in Exeter Change, was ordered as usual to take up a sixpence with his trunk, it happened one day that the sixpence rolled against the skirting-board, out of his reach. Chunee stopped, and reflected a little while, and then, drawing the air into his trunk, he threw it out with all his force against the skirting-board; the rebound of the air from the skirting-board blew the sixpence towards him, and he was enabled to reach it."

"That was very clever of him," replied William.

"Yes; it was a proof of thought, with a knowledge of cause and effect. There was a curious instance of a horse, which, by the bye, I consider the most noble animal of creation, which was ridden round by his master, to deliver newspapers. He invariably stopped at the doors where papers were to be left; but it happened that two people, living at different houses, took in a weekly newspaper between them; and it was agreed, that one should have the first reading of it on one week, and the other on the following. After a short time the horse became accustomed to this arrangement, and stopped at the one house on the one week, and at the other house on the following, never making a mistake."

"That was very curious; what a sagacious animal he must have been!" observed William.

"Animals also are, as you know, capable of receiving instruction, which is another proof of reasoning powers. The elephant, the horse, the dog, the pig, even birds may be taught a great deal."

"But then, papa, I still wish to know where the line is to be drawn between reason and instinct."

"I was about to come to that very point, William. When animals follow their instinct in providing their food, bringing up their young, and in their precautions against danger, they follow certain fixed rules, from which they never deviate. But circumstances may occur against which their instinct can afford them no regular provision; then it is that their reasoning powers are called into action. I will explain this by stating a fact relative to the bee, one of the animals upon which instinct is most powerful in its action. There is a certain large moth, called the Death's-head moth, which is very fond of honey. It sometimes contrives to force its way through the aperture of the hive, and gain an entrance. The bees immediately attack it, and it is soon destroyed by their stings; but the carcass is so large, that they cannot carry it out of the hive, as they invariably do the bodies of the smaller insects which may have intruded, and it appears that their sense of smell is very acute. What, then, do they do to avoid the stench arising from the dead body of this large moth? Why, they embalm it, covering it entirely with wax, by which it no longer becomes offensive to them."

"But, papa, might not their instinct have provided for such an event?" observed William.

"If such an event could have occurred to the bees in their wild state, you certainly might have raised the question; but recollect, William, that bees in their wild state live in the hollows of trees, and that the hole by which they enter is never more than sufficiently large to admit one bee at a time; consequently, no animal larger than a bee could gain entrance, and if it did, could of course have been easily removed from the hive; but the bees were here in a new position, in an artificial state, in a hive of straw with a large aperture, and therefore met with an exigence they were not prepared for, and acted accordingly."

"Yes, papa, I perceive the difference."

"I will conclude my observations with one remark. It appears to me, that although the Almighty has thought proper to vary the intellectual and the reasoning powers of animals in the same way that he has varied the species and the forms, yet even in this arrangement he has not been unmindful of the interest and welfare of man. For you will observe, that the reasoning powers are chiefly, if not wholly, given to those animals which man subjects to his service and for his use—the elephant, the horse, and the dog; thereby making these animals of more value, as the powers given to them are at the service and under the control of man."

Chapter Fifty Five

On the Monday morning, William and Ready went away in the boat, as before, to bring round the various articles from the cove. It had been arranged that they were not to return till the Saturday evening, and that the dog Remus was to bring intelligence of them and their welfare every afternoon. They worked hard during the week, and on Saturday they had completed their task; with the exception of a portion of the timbers of the ship, everything had been brought round, but had not been carried up to the storehouse, as that required more time.

On Saturday morning, they went for the last time to the cove, and Ready selected some heavy oak timber out of the quantity which was lying on the beach, part of which they put into the boat, and the remainder they towed astern. It was a heavy load, and although the wind was fair to sail back again to the bay, the boat went but slowly through the water.

"Well, William," said Ready, "we have done a good week's work, and I must say it is high time that it is done; for the boat is in rather a crazy condition, and I must contrive to patch her up by and by, when there is time."

"We shall not want to use her very much after this, Ready," replied William; "a few trips round to the little harbour will be all that will be required before we come back again to our old quarters."

"That's true, William; but she leaks very much, and at all events I'll give her a coat of pitch as soon as possible. For a slight-built little thing as she is, she has done hard duty."

"Pray, Ready, why, when you speak of a ship or boat, do you always call it she?"

"Well, William, I don't know why, but it is certain that we sailors always do so. I believe it is because a sailor loves his ship. His ship is his wife, is a very common saying with us; and then you see, Master William, a vessel is almost a thing of life in appearance. I believe that's the reason, and of course if a vessel is she, a little boat must be a she also."

"Well, I think you have explained it very well, Ready. I suppose on Monday we shall set to at the storehouse, and alter it for our future residence?"

"Can't begin too soon, William," replied Ready; "I don't doubt but Mr Seagrave has finished the hedge and ditch round the yams by this time, and if so, I expect Madam will not like to be left in the tents alone with Juno and the children, and so we shall all move back to the house again until we have altered the storehouse; I must say that I would rather your mamma remained in the tents until all was finished."

"Because you are afraid of a visit from the savages, Ready?"

"I am, sir, and that's the truth."

"But, Ready, if they do come, we shall see them coming, and would it not be better that we should all be together, even if we are obliged to conceal ourselves in consequence of not being prepared? Suppose the savages were to overrun the island, and find my mother, my little brother, and sister, defenceless, at the time we were obliged to retreat from our house; how dreadful that would be!"

"But I counted upon retreating to the tents."

"So we can all together, unless we are surprised in the night."

"That we must take care not to be. There's not three hours' dark in this season of the year. Well, William, I doubt not you may be right, and if they are all with us, Juno will be a great help, and we shall get through our work the faster."

"We had better let the question be decided by my father and mother."

"Very true, William; here's the point at last. We will haul the timber on the beach, and then be off as fast as we can, for it is getting late."

It was, indeed, much later than they had usually arrived at the little harbour, owing to the heavy load, which made the boat so long in coming round from the cove; and when they pulled in, they found Mr and Mrs Seagrave and the children all waiting for them.

"You are very late, William," said Mrs Seagrave. "I was quite uneasy till I saw the boat at a distance."

"Yes, mamma; but we could not help it; we had a heavy load to bring round, and now our work is done."

"I am delighted to hear it, William; for I cannot bear you being away so long."

"And my work is done," said Mr Seagrave; "the hedge and ditch were finished this morning."

"Well, then," observed Ready, "we must hold another council, but I presume it will not take very long."

"No; I expect not; it seldom does when people are of the same mind. Mrs Seagrave won't be left here, Ready, and I don't want to leave her, so I presume on Monday we all start home again."

"Yes, sir; if you please," replied Ready.

"Juno, I hope you have a good supper," said William; "for I'm very hungry."

"Yes, Massa William; plenty fried fish; Massa catch 'em this morning."

Chapter Fifty Six

The next day being Sunday was a day of repose, and as they had all worked so hard, they felt the luxury of a day of rest. In the afternoon, they agreed that on Monday they should make every preparation for quitting the tents, and returning to the house at the bay. They decided that the live stock should all be left there, as the pasturage was so plentiful and good, with the exception of one goat, which they would take back with them, to supply them with milk; and they also agreed that the tents should be left standing, with some cooking utensils, that in case William and Ready went round for the bananas or yams, or to examine the live stock, they should not be compelled to sleep in the open air, and should have the means of dressing their dinner. William and Ready were to carry the beds, etcetera, round to the bay in the boat, which they could do in two trips, and Mr and Mrs Seagrave, with the family, were to walk through the woods after taking a very early breakfast.

All these points being arranged, they had finished their supper, when William again brought up the conversation about animals, as he was delighted to bear Mr Seagrave talk on the subject. The conversation had not commenced more than a few minutes, when William said—

"Papa, they always say 'as stupid as an ass.' Is an ass such a stupid animal?"

"No, William; it is a very sagacious one; but the character has been given to the animal more on account of its obstinacy and untractableness, than on any other account. It is usual to say, as stupid as an ass, or as stupid as a pig, or a goose. Now, these three animals are very much maligned, for they are all sagacious animals. But the fact is that, as regards the ass, we have only very sorry specimens of the animal in England; they are stunted and small, and, from want of corn and proper food, besides being very ill-treated, are slow and dull-looking animals. The climate of England is much too cold for the ass; in the south of France and the Mediterranean, where it is much warmer, the ass is a much finer animal; but to see it in perfection we must go to the Torrid Zone in Guinea, right on the equator, the hottest portion of the globe, where the ass, in its native state and in its native country, is a handsome creature and as fleet as the wind; indeed, supposed to be, and mentioned in the Scriptures as the fleetest animal in creation. The fact is, that in Asia, especially in Palestine and Syria, asses were in great repute, and used in preference to horses. We must see an animal in its own climate to form a true estimate of its value."

"Does climate, then, make so great a difference?" said William.

"Of course it does, not only with animals, but with trees, plants, and even man, until he is accustomed to the change. With respect to animals, there are some which can bear the different varieties of climate, and even change of food. The horse, for instance, although originally indigenous to Arabia, lives as well in the Temperate, and even in the Frigid Zones it may be said, for they endure the hard winters of Russia and North America; so will domestic cattle, such as cows, sheep, pigs, etcetera. It is a curious fact that, during the winter in Canada, a large proportion of the food of cattle consists of *fish*."

"Fish, papa! Cows eat fish?"

"Yes, my dear boy, such is the fact. It is a remarkable instance of a graminivorous or grass-eating animal being changed for a time into a flesh-eating, or rather into fish-eating animal. But there are other animals which can live under any temperature, as the wolf, the fox, the hare, and rabbit. It is a curious provision,—that the sheep and goats in the hottest climates throw off their warm covering of wool, and retain little better than hair; while, removed to a cold climate, they recover their warm covering immediately."

"But a goat has no wool, papa."

"What are Cashmere shawls made of, William?"

"Very true, papa."

"Most animals have a certain increase of covering as they recede further from the warm climates to the cold ones. Wolves and foxes, hares and rabbits, change the colour of their skins to white when they get far north. The little English stoat, which is destroyed by the gamekeepers, becomes the beautiful snow-white ermine in Russia and other cold countries."

"Well, papa, I think it a great advantage to man, and a proof of the Almighty's care of him and kindness to him, in permitting all the animals most useful to him to be able to live in any country; but I don't know whether I am wrong in saying so, papa: I cannot see why an animal like the wolf should not have been kept to his own climate, like the lion and tiger, and other ferocious animals."

"You have started a question, William, which I am glad you have done, rather than it should have remained on your mind, and have puzzled you. It is true that the shepherd might agree with you, that the wolf is a nuisance; equally true that the husbandman may exclaim, What is the good of thistles, and the various weeds which choke the soil? But, my dear boy, if they are not, which I think they are, for the benefit of man, at all events they are his doom for the first transgression. 'Cursed is the ground for thy sake—thorns and thistles shall it bring forth to thee—and by the sweat of thy brow shalt thou eat bread,' was the Almighty's sentence; and it is only by labour that the husbandman can obtain his crops, and by watchfulness that the shepherd can guard his flocks. Labour is in itself a benefit: without exercise there would be no health, and without health there would be no enjoyment."

"I see now, papa. You have mentioned the animals which can live in all climates; will you not tell us something about other animals?"

"There is but one remark to make, William, which is, that animals indigenous to, that is, originally to be found in, any one portion of the globe, invariably are so fashioned as to be most fit for that country, and have the food also most proper for them growing or to be obtained in that country. Take, for instance, the camel, an animal fashioned expressly for the country to which he is indigenous, and without whose aid all communication must have been stopped between Asia and Africa. He is called the 'Ship of the Desert;' for the desert is a 'sea of sand.' His feet are so fashioned that he can traverse the sands with facility; he can live upon the coarsest vegetable food and salt plants which are found there, and he has the capacity of carrying water in a sort of secondary stomach, for his own supply where no water is to be found. Here is an animal wonderfully made by the Almighty for an express locality, and for the convenience of man in that country; for, in England, or elsewhere, he would be of no value. But it is late, my dear William; so we will first thank Him for all his mercies, and then to bed."

Chapter Fifty Seven

The next morning was one of bustle; there was packing up and every preparation for departure. Juno was called here and called there, and was obliged to ask little Caroline to look after the kettle and call to her if it boiled over. Master Tommy, as usual, was in every one's way, and doing more harm than good in his attempts to assist.

At last, Ready, to get rid of him, sent him down with a large bundle to the beach. Tommy shouldered it with great importance, but when he came back, looking rather warm with the exertion, and Ready asked him to take down another, he said he was too tired, and sat down very quietly till breakfast-time, before which everything was ready.

Mrs Seagrave and Juno packed up the breakfast and dinner things in a basket after breakfast was over, and then Mr and Mrs Seagrave and the family set off on their journey, accompanied by the dogs, through the cocoa-nut grove.

William and Ready lost no time in getting through their work; the crockery, kitchen utensils, table, and chairs, were the first articles put into the boat. The goat was then led down, and they set off with a full load, and arrived at the bay long before the party who were walking through the wood. They landed the things on the beach, and then shoved off again to bring round the bedding, which was all that was left. By three o'clock in the afternoon they had arrived at the bay with their second and last load, and found that the other party had been there about an hour, and Mr Seagrave and Juno were very busy taking the articles up from the beach.

"Well, William," said Ready, "this is our last trip for some time, I expect; and so much the better, for our little boat must have something done to her as soon as I can find time."

"Yes, indeed, Ready, she has done her work well. Do you know I feel as if I were coming home, now that we are back to the bay. I really feel quite glad that we have left the tents. I found the pigeons among the peas, Ready, so we must pick them as soon as we can. I think there were near twenty of them. We shall have pigeon pies next year, I expect."

"If it pleases God that we live and do well," replied Ready, who had his eyes fixed upon the sea.

Before night everything was in its place again in the house, and as comfortable as before, and as they were very tired, they went very early to bed, having first arranged what they should do in the morning. At daylight Ready and William went down to the turtle-pond and speared a turtle, for now the time was coming on for turning the turtle again, and the pond would soon be filled. Having cut it up and put a portion of it into the pot, all ready for Mrs Seagrave, as soon as breakfast was over they proceeded to the storehouse.

After a little consultation with Mr Seagrave, Ready marked out a square of cocoa-nut trees surrounding the storehouse, so as to leave a space within them of about twenty yards each side, which they considered large enough for the inclosure. These cocoa-nut trees were to serve as the posts between which were to be fixed other cocoa-nut trees cut down, and about fourteen feet high, so as to form a palisade or stockade, which could not be climbed over, and would protect them from any attack of the savages.

As soon as the line of trees had been marked out, they set to work cutting down all the trees within the line, and then outside to a distance of ten yards, so as to give them room for their work. Ready cut out cross-pieces, to nail from tree to tree, and now they found the advantage of having saved so many of the large spike nails, without which they never could have made so good or so quick a job of it. Mr Seagrave cut down trees, William and Juno sawed them off at a proper length with one of the cross-cut saws, and then carried them to Ready. They soon had more cut out than he could use, and then they dragged away the tops and branches, and piled them at a distance on the ground, to use as winter fuel, while Mr Seagrave helped Ready in fixing up the palisades. They worked very hard that day, and were not sorry to go to bed. Ready, however, took an opportunity to speak to William.

"I think," said he, "that now we are here again, it will be necessary to keep a sort of night-watch, in case of accident. I shall not go to bed till it is quite dark, which it will be by nine o'clock, and shall have my glass to examine the offing the last thing. You see, there is little fear of the savages coming here in the night-time, but they may just before night or very early in the morning, so one of us must be up again before daybreak, that is between two and three o'clock in the morning, to see if there is anything to be seen of them; if there is not, of course we may go to bed again, as they cannot arrive till many hours afterwards; and we must watch the wind and weather, if it is favourable for them to come to us, which, indeed, the wind will not be except at the commencement of the rainy season but it may be very light, and then they would not care for its being against them. I've been thinking of it, William, a great deal, and my idea is, that it will be at the beginning of the rainy season that we shall have a visit, if we have one at all; for you see that the wind don't blow regular from one quarter, as it does now, but is variable, and then they can make sail in their canoes, and come here easily, instead of pulling between thirty and forty miles, which is hard work against wind and current. Still, we must not be careless and we must keep a good look-out even now. I don't want to fret your father and Mrs Seagrave with my fears on the subject, but I tell you what I really think, and what we ought to do."

"I agree with you, Ready, and I will take care to be up before daybreak, and examine very carefully with the spy-glass as soon as the day dawns. You take the night part, and I will do the morning part of the watching."

Chapter Fifty Eight

For nearly a fortnight, the work upon the stockade continued without any intermission, when a circumstance occurred which created the greatest alarm and excitement. One day, as the party returned to dinner, Mrs Seagrave said with surprise, "Why, was not Tommy with you?"

"No," replied Mr Seagrave; "he has not been near us all day; he went with us after breakfast, but did not remain a quarter of an hour."

"No, Missy; I tell Massa Tommy to help carry cocoa-nut leaves, and then he go away directly."

"Goodness! where can he be?" exclaimed Mrs Seagrave, alarmed.

"I dare say he is picking up shells on the beach, ma'am," replied Ready, "or perhaps he is in the garden. I will go and see."

"I see him—oh, mercy!—I see him," said Juno, pointing with her finger; "he in the boat, and boat go to sea!"

It was but too true: there was Tommy in the boat, and the boat had drifted from the beach, and was now a cable's length away from it, among the breakers.

William ran off like the wind, followed close by Mr Seagrave and Ready, and at a distance by Mrs Seagrave and Juno; indeed, there was no time to be lost, for the wind was off the shore, and in a short time the boat would have been out to sea.

William, as soon as he arrived at the beach, threw off his hat and jacket and dashed into the water. He was already up to his middle, when old Ready, who had followed him, caught him by the arm and said:

"William, go back immediately. I insist upon it. Your going can do no good, as you do not understand the thing so well as I do; and go I will, so there will be double risk for nothing. Mr Seagrave, order him back. He will obey you. I insist upon it, sir."

"William," said Mr Seagrave, "come back immediately, I command you."

William obeyed, but before he was clear of the water Ready had swam across to the first rocks on the reef, and was now dashing through the pools between the rocks, towards the boat.

"Oh, father!" said William, "if that good old man is lost, I shall never forgive myself. Look, father, one—two—three sharks, here, close to us. He has no chance. See, he is again in deep water. God protect him!"

In the meantime, Mr Seagrave, whose wife was now by his side, after glancing his eye a moment at the sharks, which were within a few feet of the beach, had kept his gaze steadily upon Ready's movements. If he passed through the passage of deep water between the rocks he might be considered safe, as the boat was now beating on a reef on the other side, where the water was shallow. It was a moment of intense anxiety. At last Ready had gained the reef, and had his hands upon the rocks, and was climbing on them.

"He is safe, is he not?" whispered Mrs Seagrave faintly.

"Yes; now I think he is," replied Mr Seagrave, as Ready had gained a footing on the rocks, where the water was but a little above his ankles. "I think there is no deep water between him and the boat."

In another minute Ready was over the rocks, and had seized the gunnel of the boat.

"He is in the boat," cried William. "Thank God!"

"Yes, we must thank God, and that fervently," replied Mr Seagrave. "Look at those monsters," continued he, pointing to the sharks; "how quick they swim to and fro; they have scented their prey on the water. It is fortunate they are here."

"See, he has the boat-hook, and is pushing the boat off the reef into the deep water. Oh! he is quite safe now."

Such, however, was not the case. The boat had been beating on the rocks of the reef, and had knocked a hole in her bottom, and as soon as Ready had forced the boat into deep water, she began to fill immediately. Ready pushed as hard as he could with the boat-hook, and tearing off his neck-cloth, forced as much as he could of it into the hole. This saved them; but the boat was up to the thwarts with water, and the least motion on the part of Ready, or even Tommy, would have upset her immediately, and they had still to pass the deep water between the reef and the beach, where the sharks were swimming. Ready, who perceived his danger, called out to them to throw large stones at the sharks as fast as they could, to drive them away. This was immediately done by Mr Seagrave and William, aided by Juno and Mrs Seagrave.

The pelting of the stones had the desired effect. The sharks swam away, and Ready passed through to the beach, and the boat grounded just as she was up to the gunnel in water, and about to turn over. He handed out Tommy, who was so dreadfully frightened that he could not cry.

As soon as Ready landed, William sprang into his arms, crying, "Thank God, you are safe, Ready!" Mrs Seagrave, overpowered by her feelings, sank her head upon William's shoulder, and burst into tears.

"It was touch and go, William," observed Ready, as they walked up to the house, preceded by Mr and Mrs Seagrave. "How much mischief may be created by a thoughtless boy! However, one can't put old heads on young shoulders, and so Tommy must be forgiven."

"He has been punished enough, as far as fright goes," replied William; "I'll answer for it, he'll never get into the boat again by himself."

"No, I think not. But now, William, you saw how nearly I was swamped in the boat; indeed, it was only by his mercy that I was preserved; but taking the question merely as far as our endeavours could help us, do you think that if you had gained the boat instead of me, you would have brought her to the beach as I did?"

"No, Ready; I never could have managed her so skilfully as you did, and therefore I must have been swamped before I got on shore."

"Well, William, as I am an old sailor and you are not, therefore it is not vanity which makes me say that you could not have managed the boat so well as I did. Now, as I had not three or four seconds to spare, you, as you say, must have been swamped. I mention this to prove to you that I was right in desiring your father to order you back."

"Certainly, Ready; but Tommy is my brother, and I felt that it was more my duty than yours to risk my life for him."

"A very proper feeling, William; but you have other duties, which are, to look after your father and mother, and be a comfort and solace to them. Your life is more valuable than mine. I am an old man on the brink of the grave, and a year or two makes no difference, but your life is, I hope, of more consequence."

That evening the prayers were more than usually solemn, and the thanksgivings more heartfelt and sincere. Exhausted with the exciting scene of the day, they all retired early to bed.

Chapter Fifty Nine

When Tommy was questioned on the following morning as to his inducement to get into the boat, to their great surprise he replied, that he wanted to go round to the tents again, to see if the bananas were ripe; that he intended to eat some of them and be back before dinner-time, that he might not be found out.

"I suspect, Tommy, you would have been very hungry before you ate any bananas if we had not perceived you," said Ready.

"I won't go into the boat any more," said Tommy.

"I rather think you will keep to that resolution, Tommy," replied Mr Seagrave; "however, I must leave your mother to point out to you the danger you were in yourself, and in which you placed others by your folly."

The stockade was now almost finished; the door was the occasion of a good deal of consultation; at last, it was agreed that it would be better to have a door of stout oak plank, but with second door-posts inside, about a foot apart from the door, between which could be inserted short poles one above the other, so as to barricade it within when required. This would make the door as strong as any other portion of the stockade. As soon as this was all complete, the storehouse was to be altered for a dwelling-house, by taking away the wattles of cocoa-nut boughs on the sides, and filling them up with logs of cocoa-nut trees.

Before the week was ended the stockade and door were complete, and they now began to fell trees, to form the sides of the house. This was rapid work; and while Mr Seagrave, William, and Juno felled the trees, and brought them on the wheels to the side of the stockade, all ready cut to their proper lengths, Ready was employed in flooring the house with a part of the deal planks which they had brought round from the cove. But this week they were obliged to break off for two days, to collect all their crops from the garden.

A fortnight more passed away in continual hard work, but the house was at last finished, and very complete, compared to the one they were residing in. It was much larger, and divided into three rooms by the deal planking: the middle room which the door opened into was the sitting and eating room, with a window behind; the two side rooms were sleeping-rooms, one for Mrs Seagrave and the children, and the other for the male portion of the family.

"See, William," said Ready, when they were alone, "what we have been able to do by means of those deal planks; why, to have floored this house, and run up the partitions, would have taken us half a year if we had had to saw the wood."

"Yes; and what a comfort it is to have so many shelves about. When shall we shift into this house?"

"The sooner the better. We have plenty of work still to do, but we can work outside of the stockade."

"And what do you propose to do with the old house?" said William.

"We had better put some of our stores of least value in it for the present, until we can fit up another storehouse inside the stockade."

"Then we'll put those casks in, for they take up a great deal of room."

"All but that large one, William; we shall want that. I shall fix it up in a corner."

"What for, Ready?"

"To put water in."

"But we are closer to the spring than we were at the other house."

"I know that; but, perhaps, we may not be able to go out of the stockade, and then we shall want water."

"I understand, Ready; how thoughtful you are!"

"If at my age I did not think a little, William, it would be very odd. You don't know how anxious I am to see them all inside of this defence."

"But why should we not come in, Ready?"

"Why, sir, as there is still plenty of work, I do not like to press the matter, lest your mamma should be fidgeted, and think there was danger; but danger there is; I have a kind of forewarning of it. I wish you would propose that they should come in at once; the standing-bed places are all ready, except the canvas, and I shall nail on new by to-night."

In consequence of this conversation, William proposed at dinnertime that the next day they should go into the new house, as it was so much more handy to work there and live there at the same time. Mr Seagrave was of the same opinion, but Mrs Seagrave thought it better that everything should be tidy first.

"Why, ma'am," said Ready, "the only way to get things tidy is to go yourself and make them so. Nothing will ever be in its place unless you are there to put it in."

"Well, Ready," said Mrs Seagrave, "since you are against me as well as all the rest, I give it up, and if you please we will shift over to-morrow."

"Indeed, ma'am, I think it will be better; this is the last month of fine weather, and we shall have plenty to do."

"Be it so, Ready; you are the best judge; to-morrow we will take up our quarters in the stockade."

"Thank God!" muttered Ready very softly.

The next day was fully employed in changing their residence, and shifting over the bedding and utensils; and that night they slept within the stockade. Ready had run up a very neat little outhouse of plank, as a kitchen for Juno, and another week was fully employed as follows: the stores were divided; those of least consequence, and the salt provisions, flour, and the garden produce, etcetera, were put into the old house; the casks of powder and most of the cartridges were also put there for security; but a cask of beef, of pork, and flour, all the iron-work and nails, canvas, etcetera, were stowed away for the present under the new house, which had, when built as a storehouse, been raised four feet from the ground to make a shelter for the stock. This was very spacious, and, of course, quite dry, and contained all they wished to put in. Ready also took care, by degrees, to fill the large water-butt full of water, and had fixed into the bottom a spigot for drawing the water off.

"Well, Mr Seagrave," said Ready on the Saturday, "we have done a good many hard weeks' work lately, but this is the last of them. We are now comfortably settled in our new house: our stores are all under cover, and safe from the weather, and so we may now take things a little easier. William and I must repair the boat, so that we may take a trip round to examine how the stock and yams get on."

"And the bananas and the guavas," said Tommy.

"Why, we have quite forgotten all about them," observed Mrs Seagrave.

"Yes, ma'am; we have been so busy, that it is no wonder; however, there may be some left yet, and I will go round as soon as the boat is able to swim, and bring all I can find."

"We must put our seeds and potatoes in before the rainy season, Ready."

"It will be better, sir, if we can find time, as we shall not have much more fine weather now; at all events, we can get them in at intervals when the weather is fine. Now I shall go my rounds for turtle. Good-night, ma'am,— good-night, sir. Come, William."

William and Ready succeeded in turning six more turtles to add to their stock, and having taken a careful survey with the telescope, they came back, fastened the door of the stockade, and went to bed.

Chapter Sixty

Another week passed away, during which Ready repaired the boat, and William and Mr Seagrave were employed in digging up the garden. It was also a very busy week at the house, as they had not washed linen for some time. Mrs Seagrave and Juno, and even little Caroline were hard at work, and Tommy was more useful than ever he had been, going for the water as they required it, and watching little Albert. Indeed, he was so active, that Mrs Seagrave praised him before his papa, and Tommy was quite proud.

On the Monday William and Ready set off in the boat to the little harbour, and found all the stock doing well. Many of the bananas and guavas had ripened and withered, but there were enough left to fill the boat half full.

"We cannot do better than to leave the stock where it is at present, William; they can run into the cocoa-nut grove for shelter if there is a storm, and there is feed enough for ten times as many."

"Yes; but will you not dig up a few yams first?"

"I had quite forgotten it, William. I will go for the spade."

Having procured the yams, they set off on their return. Before they arrived at the bay, the sky clouded over and threatened a storm. It did not, however, rain till after they had landed, when a small shower announced the commencement of the rainy season. The fruit was very welcome to all of them, it was so long since they had tasted any.

The following day was beautifully fine, and everything appeared refreshed by the rain which had fallen. It was, however, agreed, that Ready and William should go round the next morning, bring home the tents, and as many yams as the boat could carry. William and Ready went out at night as usual, when Ready observed that the wind had chopped round to the eastward.

"That will be bad for us to-morrow, Ready," replied William. "We may sail to the harbour, but we shall have to pull back with the loaded boat."

"I trust it will be no worse than that, at all events," replied Ready; "but we must now return, and go to bed. I shall be up by daylight, so you need not wake without you like."

"I can't help waking," replied William, "and I shall, therefore, be up with you."

"Very well, I am always glad of your company."

The next morning, just before the day dawned, Ready and William unfastened the door of the stockade, and went down to the beach. The wind was still to the eastward, and blowing rather fresh, and the sky was cloudy. As the sun rose, Ready, as usual, had his telescope with him, and looked through it at the offing to the eastward. As he kept the spy-glass to his eye for some time without speaking, William said:

"Do you see anything, Ready, that you look so long in that direction?"

"Either my old eyes deceive me, or I fear that I do," replied Ready; "but a few minutes more will decide."

There was a bank of clouds on the horizon to the eastward, but as soon as the sun had risen above them, Ready, who had the telescope fixed in the same direction, said:

"Yes, William, I am right. I thought that those dark patches I saw there were brown grass sails."

"Sails of what, Ready?" said William, hastily.

"Of the Indian canoes; I knew that they would come. Take the glass and look yourself; my eye is quite dim from straining it so long."

"Yes, I have them now," replied William, with his eye to the glass. At last he said:

"Why, there are twenty or thirty of them, Ready, at least."

"And with twenty or thirty men in each too, William."

"What must we do, Ready? How frightened my poor mother will be! I'm afraid we can do nothing against such a number."

"Yes, William, we can do a great deal, and we must do a great deal. That there are hundreds of savages there is no doubt; but recollect that we have a stockade, which they cannot easily climb over, and plenty of firearms and ammunition, so that we can make a good fight of it, and perhaps beat them off, for they have nothing but clubs and spears."

"How fast they come down, Ready; why, they will be here in an hour."

"No, sir, nor in two hours either; those are very large canoes. However, there is no time to be lost. While I watch them for a few minutes till I make them more clearly out, do you run up to the house and beckon your father to come down to me; and then, William, get all the muskets ready, and bring the casks of powder, and of made-up cartridges, from the old house into the stockade. Call Juno, and she will help you. We shall have time enough to do everything. After you have done that, you had better come down and join us."

In a very few minutes after William ran up to the house, Mr Seagrave made his appearance.

"Ready, there is danger, I'm sure; William would not tell me, I presume, because he was afraid of alarming his mother. What is it?"

"It is, Mr Seagrave, that the savages are now coming down upon us in large force; perhaps five or six hundred of them; and that we shall have to defend ourselves with might and main."

"Do you think we have any chance against such a force?"

"Yes, sir, with God's help I have no doubt but that we shall beat them off; but we must fight hard, and for some days, I fear."

Mr Seagrave examined the fleet of canoes with the glass. "It is, indeed, dreadful odds to contend against."

"Yes, sir, but three muskets behind a stockade are almost a match for all their clubs and spears, provided none of us are wounded."

"Well, Ready, we must put our trust in the Lord, and do our best; I will second you to the utmost of my power, and William, I'm sure, will do his duty."

"I think, sir," said Ready, "we had better not wait here any more, as we have not long to prepare for them. We have only to fix up some of our strong deal planks on the inside of the stockade for us to stand upon when we are attacked, that we may see what the enemy is about, and be able to fire upon them. But first we had better go to the old house, and take out what provisions and other articles we shall most want, and roll the casks into the stockade, for to the old house they will go first, and perhaps destroy everything in it. The casks they certainly will, for the sake of the iron hoops. An hour's work will do a great deal. I believe we have everything we want in the stockade; Juno has her fuel, the large butt of water will last us two or three weeks at least, and if we have time, we will get the wheels down, and spear a couple of turtles for fresh provisions."

These observations were made as they walked up to the house. As soon as they arrived, they found William and Juno had just brought in the powder and cartridges. Mr Seagrave went in to break the matter to his wife.

"I was told that I had to expect this, my dear," replied Mrs Seagrave, "so that it has not come upon me altogether unawares, and anything that a poor weak woman can do, I will."

"I am indeed greatly relieved," said Mr Seagrave, "by finding you thus prepared and supported. I shall feel no anxiety—but we have work to be done."

Mr and Mrs Seagrave then joined William, Ready, and Juno, who had already proceeded to the old house. The children were all still in bed and asleep, so that there was no occasion for any one to watch them.

Chapter Sixty One

As they could have a very good view of the canoes from where the old house stood, Ready examined them with his glass every time that he returned from rolling up a cask to the stockade. Every one worked hard; even Mrs Seagrave did all she could, either assisting in rolling the casks, or carrying up what she was able to lift. In an hour they had got into the stockade all that they most cared for, and the canoes were still about six or seven miles off.

"We have a good hour before they arrive, sir," said Ready, "and even then the reefs will puzzle them not a little; I doubt if they are disembarked under two hours. We have plenty of time for all we wish to do. Juno, go for the wheels, and William, come down with the spear, and we will have some of the turtle into the stockade. Mr Seagrave, I do not require your assistance, so if you will have the kindness to get out the muskets, and examine the flints, it will be as well."

"Yes; and then you have to load them," replied Mrs Seagrave. "Juno and I can do that at all events, ready for you to fire them."

"An excellent idea, madam," replied Ready.

In half an hour six turtles were brought up by Juno and William, and then Ready followed them into the stockade.

They then rolled the casks, and upheaded them by the sides of the stockade, and fixed up deal planks to stand upon, just high enough to enable them to see over the top of the palisades, and to fire at the enemy. Mrs Seagrave had been shown how to load a musket, and Juno was now taught the same.

"Now, sir, we are all prepared," said Ready, "and Madam and Juno can go and look a little after the children, and get breakfast."

As soon as the children were dressed, Mr Seagrave called Ready, who was outside, watching the canoes, and they went to their morning devotions, and prayed heartily for succour in this time of need. They then breakfasted in haste; for, as may be supposed, they were almost too anxious to eat.

"This suspense is worse than all," said Mrs Seagrave. "I wish now that they were come."

"Shall I go to Ready and hear his report, my dear?—I will not be away three minutes."

In a short time Mr Seagrave returned, saying that the canoes were close to the beach, that the savages evidently had a knowledge of the passages through the reefs, as they had steered right in, and had lowered their sails; that Ready and William were on the look-out, but concealed behind the cocoa-nut trees.

"I hope they will not stay out too long."

"No fear of that, my dear Selina; but they had better watch their motions to the last minute."

During this conversation between Mr and Mrs Seagrave within the stockade, William and Ready were watching the motions of the savages, a large portion of whom had landed out of ten of the canoes, and the others were following their example as fast as they could, forcing their way through the reefs. The savages were all painted, with their war-cloaks and feathers on, and armed with spears and clubs, evidently having come with no peaceable intentions.

William, who had taken the telescope to examine them more minutely, said to Ready, "What a fierce, cruel set of wretches they appear to be; if they overpower us they will certainly kill us!"

"Of that there is no doubt, William; but we must fight hard, and not let them overpower us. Kill us they certainly will, and I am not sure that they may not eat us afterwards; but that is of little consequence."

William replied in a determined tone, "I'll fight as long as I have breath in my body; but, Ready, they are coming up as fast as they can."

"Yes; we must wait no longer. Come, William."

"I thought I saw another vessel under sail, out away by the garden point, Ready, just as we turned away."

"Very likely, sir, a canoe which has separated from the others during the night. Come, quick, William, they have begun to yell."

Another half-minute, and they arrived at the door of the stockade; they entered, shut the door, and then barricaded it with the cocoa-nut poles which they had fitted to the inner door-posts.

Chapter Sixty Two

The loud yells of the savages struck terror into the heart of Mrs Seagrave; it was well that she had not seen their painted bodies and fierce appearance, or she would have been much more alarmed. Little Albert and Caroline clung around her neck with terror in their faces; they did not cry, but looked round and round to see from whence the horrid noise proceeded, and then clung faster to their mother. Tommy was very busy, finishing all the breakfast which had been left, for there was no one to check him as usual; Juno was busy outside, and was very active and courageous. Mr Seagrave had been employed making the holes between the palisades large enough to admit the barrels of the muskets, so that they could fire at the savages without being exposed; while William and Ready, with their muskets loaded, were on the look-out for their approach.

"They are busy with the old house just now, sir," observed Ready, "but that won't detain them long."

"Here they come," replied William; "and look, Ready, is not that one of the women who escaped from us in the canoe, who is walking along with the first two men? Yes, it is, I am sure."

"You are right, William, it is one of them. Ah! they have stopped; they did not expect the stockade, that is clear, and it has puzzled them; see how they are all crowding together and talking; they are holding a council of war how to proceed; that tall man must be one of their chiefs. Now, William, although I intend to fight as hard as I can, yet I always feel a dislike to begin first; I shall therefore show myself over the palisades, and if they attack me, I shall then fire with a quiet conscience."

"But take care they don't hit you, Ready."

"No great fear of that, William. Here they come."

Ready now stood upon the plank within, so as to show himself to the savages, who gave a tremendous yell, and as they advanced a dozen spears were thrown at him with so true an aim that, had he not instantly dodged behind the stockade, he must have been killed. Three or four spears remained quivering in the palisades, just below the top; the others went over it, and fell down inside of the stockade, at the further end.

"Now, William, take good aim;" but before William could fire, Mr Seagrave, who had agreed to be stationed at the corner so that he might see if the savages went round to the other side, fired his musket, and the tall chief fell to the ground.

Ready and William also fired, and two more of the savages were seen to drop amidst the yells of their companions. Juno handed up the other muskets which were ready loaded, and took those discharged, and Mrs Seagrave, having desired Caroline to take care of her little brother, and Tommy to be very quiet and good, came out, turned the key of the door upon them, and hastened to assist Juno in reloading the muskets.

The spears now rushed through the air, and it was well that they could fire from the stockade without exposing their persons, or they would have had but little chance. The yells increased, and the savages now began to attack on every quarter; the most active, who climbed like cats, actually succeeded in gaining the top of the palisades, but, as soon as their heads appeared above, they were fired at with so true an aim that they dropped down dead outside. This combat lasted for more than an hour, when the savages, having lost a great many men, drew off from the assault, and the parties within the stockade had time to breathe.

"They have not gained much in this bout, at all events," said Ready; "it was well fought on our side, and William, you certainly behaved as if you had been brought up to it."

"Do you think they will go away now?" said Mrs Seagrave.

"Oh, no, madam, not yet; they will try us every way before they leave us. You see these are very brave men, and it is clear that they know what gunpowder is, or they would have been more astonished."

"I should think so too," replied Mr Seagrave; "the first time that savages hear the report of firearms, they are usually thrown into great consternation."

"Yes, sir; but such has not been the case with these people, and therefore I reckon it is not the first time that they have fought with Europeans."

"Are they all gone, Ready?" said William, who had come down from the plank to his mother.

"No; I see them between the trees now; they are sitting round in a circle, and, I suppose, making speeches."

"Well, I'm very thirsty, at all events," said William; "Juno, bring me a little water."

Juno went to the water-tub to comply with William's request, and in a few moments afterwards came back in great consternation.

"Oh, Massa! oh, Missy! no water; water all gone!"

"Water all gone!" cried Ready and all of them in a breath.

"Yes; not one little drop in the cask."

"I filled it up to the top!" exclaimed Ready very gravely; "the tub did not leak, that I am sure of; how can this have happened?"

"Missy, I tink I know now," said Juno; "you remember you send Massa Tommy, the two or three days we wash, to fetch water from the well in little bucket. You know how soon he come back, and how you say what good boy he was, and how you tell Massa Seagrave when he come to dinner. Now, Missy, I quite certain Massa Tommy no take trouble go to well, but fetch water from tub all the while, and so he empty it."

"I'm afraid you're right, Juno," replied Mrs Seagrave. "What shall we do?"

"I go speak Massa Tommy," said Juno, running to the house.

"This is a very awkward thing, Mr Seagrave," observed Ready gravely.

Mr Seagrave shook his head.

The fact was, that they all perceived the danger of their position: if the savages did not leave the island, they would perish of thirst or have to surrender; and in the latter case, all their lives would most certainly be sacrificed.

Juno now returned: her suspicions were but too true. Tommy, pleased with the praise of being so quick in bringing the water, had taken out the spigot of the cask, and drawn it all off.

"Well," observed Mr Seagrave, "it is the will of Heaven that all our careful arrangements and preparations against this attack should be defeated by the idleness of a child, and we must submit."

"Very true, sir," replied Ready; "all our hopes now are that the savages may be tired out, and leave the island."

"If I had but a little for the children, I should not care," observed Mrs Seagrave; "but to see those poor things suffer—is there not a drop left, Juno, anywhere?"

Juno shook her head.

Mrs Seagrave said she would go and examine, and went away into the house accompanied by Juno.

"This is a very bad business, Ready," observed Mr Seagrave. "What would we give for a shower of rain now, that we might catch the falling drops!"

"There are no signs of it, sir," replied Ready; "we must, however, put our confidence in One who will not forsake us."

"I wish the savages would come on again," observed William; "for the sooner they come, the sooner the affair will be decided."

"I doubt if they will to-day; at night-time I think it very probable. We must make preparations for it."

"Why, what can we do, Ready?"

"In the first place, sir, by nailing planks from cocoa-nut tree to cocoa-nut tree above the present stockade, we may make a great portion of it much higher, and more difficult to climb over. Some of them were nearly in, this time. If we do that, we shall not have so large a space to watch over and defend; and then we must contrive to have a large fire ready for lighting, that we may not have to fight altogether in the dark. It will give them some advantage in looking through the palisades, and seeing where we are, but they cannot well drive their spears through, so it is no great matter. We must make the fire in the centre of the stockade, and have plenty of tar in it, to make it burn bright, and we must not, of course, light it until after we are attacked. We shall then see where they are trying for an entrance, and where to aim with our muskets."

"The idea is very good, Ready," said Mr Seagrave; "if it had not been for this unfortunate want of water, I really should be sanguine of beating them off."

"We may suffer very much, Mr Seagrave, I have no doubt; but who knows what the morrow may bring forth?"

"True, Ready. Do you see the savages now?"

"No, sir; they have left the spot where they were in consultation. I suppose they are busy with their wounded and their dead."

As Ready had supposed, no further attack was made by the savages on that day, and he, William, and Mr Seagrave, were very busy making their arrangements; they nailed the planks on the trunks of the trees above the stockade, so as to make three sides of the stockade at least five feet higher, and almost impossible to climb up; and they prepared a large fire in a tar-barrel full of cocoa-nut leaves mixed with wood and tar, so as to burn fiercely. Dinner or supper they had none, for there was nothing but salt pork and beef and live turtle, and, by Ready's advice, they did not eat, as it would only increase their desire to drink.

The poor children suffered much; and little Albert wailed and cried for "water, water." Ready remained on the look-out; indeed, everything was so miserable inside of the house, that they were all glad to go out of it; they could do no good, and poor Mrs Seagrave had a difficult and most painful task to keep the children quiet under such severe privation, for the weather was still very warm and sultry.

Chapter Sixty Three

But the moaning of the children was very soon after dusk drowned by the yells of the savages, who, as Ready had prognosticated, now advanced to the night attack.

Every part of the stockade was at once assailed, and their attempts now made were to climb into it; a few spears were occasionally thrown, but it was evident that the object was to obtain an entrance by dint of numbers. It was well that Ready had taken the precaution of nailing the deal planks above the original stockade, or there is little doubt but that the savages would have gained their object; as it was, before the flames of the fire, which Juno had lighted by Ready's order, gave them sufficient light, three or four savages had climbed up and had been shot by William and Mr Seagrave, as they were on the top of the stockade.

When the fire burnt brightly, the savages outside were more easily aimed at, and a great many fell in their attempts to get over. The attack continued more than an hour, when at last, satisfied that they could not succeed, the savages once more withdrew, carrying with them, as before, their dead and wounded.

"I trust that they will now re-embark, and leave the island," said Mr Seagrave.

"I only wish they may, sir; it is not at all impossible; but there is no saying. I have been thinking, Mr Seagrave, that we might be able to ascertain their movements by making a look-out. You see, sir, that cocoa-nut tree," continued Ready, pointing to one of those to which the palisades were fastened, "is much taller than any of the others: now, by driving spike-nails into the trunk at about a foot apart, we might ascend it with ease, and it would command a view of the whole bay; we then could know what the enemy were about."

"Yes, that is very true; but will not anyone be very much exposed if he climbs up?"

"No, sir; for you see the cocoa-nut trees are cut down clear of the palisades to such a distance, that no savage could come at all near without being seen by anyone on the look-out, and giving us sufficient time to get down again before he could use his spear."

"I believe that you are right there, Ready; but at all events I would not attempt to do it before daylight, as there may be some of them still lurking underneath the stockade."

"Certainly there may be, sir, and therefore until daylight we will not begin."

Mr Seagrave then went into the house; Ready desired William to lie down and sleep for two or three hours, as he would watch. In the morning, when Mr Seagrave came out, he would have a little sleep himself.

"I can't sleep, Ready. I'm mad with thirst," replied William.

"Yes, sir; it's very painful—I feel it myself very much, but what must those poor children feel? I pity them most."

"I pity my mother most, Ready," replied William; "it must be agony to her to witness their sufferings, and not be able to relieve them."

"Yes, indeed, it must be terrible, William, to a mother's feelings; but perhaps these savages will be off to-morrow, and then we shall forget our privations."

"I trust in God that they may, Ready, but they seem very determined."

"Yes, sir; iron is gold to them, and what will civilised men not do for gold?"

In the meantime, Mr Seagrave had gone into the house. He found the children still crying for water, notwithstanding the coaxing and soothing of Mrs Seagrave, who was shedding tears as she hung over poor little Albert. Little Caroline only drooped, and said nothing. Mr Seagrave remained for two or three hours with his wife, assisting her in pacifying the children, and soothing her to the utmost of his power; at last he went out and found old Ready on the watch.

"Ready, I had rather a hundred times be attacked by these savages and have to defend this place, than be in that house for even five minutes, and witness the sufferings of my wife and children."

"I do not doubt it, sir," replied Ready; "but cheer up, and let us hope for the best; I think it very probable that the savages after this second defeat will leave the island."

"I wish I could think so, Ready; it would make me very happy; but I have come out to take the watch, Ready. Will you not sleep for a while?"

"I will, sir, if you please, take a little sleep. Call me in two hours; it will then be daylight, and I can go to work, and you can get some repose yourself."

"I am too anxious to sleep; I think so, at least."

"William said he was too thirsty to sleep, sir, but, poor fellow, he is now fast enough."

"I trust that boy will be spared, Ready."

"I hope so too; but we are all in the hands of the Almighty."

Mr Seagrave took his station on the plank, and was left to his own reflections; that they were not of the most pleasant kind may easily be imagined. He prayed earnestly and fervently that they might be delivered from the danger and sufferings which threatened them, and became calm and tranquil; prepared for the worst, if the worst was to happen, and confidently placing himself and his family under the care of him who orders all as he thinks best.

At daylight Ready woke up and relieved Mr Seagrave, who did not return to the house, but lay down on the cocoa-nut boughs, where Ready had been lying by the side of William. As soon as Ready had got out the spike-nails and hammer, he summoned William to his assistance, and they commenced driving them into the cocoa-nut tree, one looking out in case of the savages approaching, while the other was at work. In less than an hour they had gained the top of the tree close to the boughs, and had a very commanding view of the bay, as well as inland. William, who was driving the last dozen spikes, took a survey, and then came down to Ready.

"I can see everything, Ready: they have pulled down the old house altogether, and are most of them lying down outside, covered up with their war-cloaks; some women are walking to and fro from the canoes, which are lying on the beach where they first landed."

"They have pulled down the house to obtain the iron nails, I have no doubt," replied Ready. "Did you see any of their dead?"

"No; I did not look about very much, but I will go up again directly. I came down because my hands were jarred with hammering, and the hammer was so heavy to carry. In a minute or two I shall go up light enough. My lips are burning, Ready, and swelled; the skin is peeling off. I had no idea that want of water would have been so dreadful. I was in hopes of finding a cocoa-nut or two on the tree, but there was not one."

"And if you had found one, it would not have had any milk in it at this season of the year. However, William, if the savages do not go away to-day, something must be done. I wish now that you would go up again, and see if they are not stirring."

William again mounted to the top of the tree, and remained up for some minutes; when he came down, he said, "They are all up now, and swarming like bees. I counted 260 of the men in their war-cloaks and feather head-dresses; the women are passing to and fro from the well with water; there is nobody at the canoes except eight or ten women, who are beating their heads, I think, or doing something of the kind. I could not make it out well, but they seem all doing the same thing."

"I know what they are about, William: they are cutting themselves with knives or other sharp instruments. It is the custom of these people. The dead are all put into the canoes, and these women are lamenting over them; perhaps they are going away, since the dead are in the canoes, but there is no saying."

Chapter Sixty Four

The second day was passed in keeping a look-out upon the savages, and awaiting a fresh attack. They could perceive from the top of the cocoa-nut tree that the savages held a council of war in the forenoon, sitting round in a large circle, while one got up in the centre and made a speech, flourishing his club and spear while he spoke. In the afternoon the council broke up, and the savages were observed to be very busy in all directions, cutting down the cocoa-nut trees, and collecting all the brushwood.

Ready watched them for a long while, and at last came down a little before sunset. "Mr Seagrave," said he, "we shall have, in my opinion, no attack this night, but to-morrow we must expect something very serious; the savages are cutting down the trees, and making large faggots; they do not get on very fast, because their hatchets are made of stone and don't cut very well, but perseverance and numbers will effect everything, and I dare say that they will work all night till they have obtained as many faggots as they want."

"But what do you imagine to be their object, Ready, in cutting down trees, and making the faggots?"

"Either, sir, to pile them up outside the palisades, so large as to be able to walk up upon them, or else to pile them up to set fire to them, and burn us out."

"Do you think they will succeed?"

"Not without very heavy loss; perhaps we may best them off, but it will be a hard fight; harder than any we have had yet. We must have the women to load the muskets, so that we may fire as fast as we can. I should not think much of their attempt to burn us, if it were not for the smoke. Cocoa-nut wood, especially with the bark on, as our palisades have, will char a long while, but not burn easily when standing upright; and the fire, when the faggots are kindled, although it will be fierce, will not last long."

"But suffering as we are now, Ready, for want of water, how can we possibly keep up our strength to meet them in a suffocating smoke and flame? we must drop with sheer exhaustion."

"We must hope for the best, and do our best, Mr Seagrave," replied Ready; "and recollect that should anything happen to me during the conflict, and if there is any chance of your being overpowered, you must take advantage of the smoke to escape into the woods, and find your way to the tents. I have no doubt that you will be able to do that; of course the attack will be to windward if they use fire, and you must try and escape to leeward; I have shown William how to force a palisade if necessary. The savages, if they get possession, will not think of looking for you at first, and, perhaps, when they have obtained all that the house contains, not even afterwards."

"Why do you say if any accident happens to you, Ready?" said William.

"Because, William, if they place the faggots so as to be able to walk to the top of the palisades, I may be wounded or killed, and so may you."

"Of course," replied William; "but they are not in yet, and they shall have a hard fight for it."

Ready then told Mr Seagrave that he would keep the watch, and call him at twelve o'clock. During these two days, they had eaten very little; a turtle had been killed, and pieces fried, but eating only added to their thirst, and even the children refused the meat. The sufferings were now really dreadful, and poor Mrs Seagrave was almost frantic.

As soon as Mr Seagrave had gone into the house, Ready called William, and said, "William, water we must have. I cannot bear to see the agony of the poor children, and the state of mind which your poor mother is in; and more, without water we never shall be able to beat off the savages to-morrow. We shall literally die of choking in the smoke, if they use fire. Now, William, I intend to take one of the seven-gallon barricos, and go down to the well for water. I may succeed, and I may not, but attempt it I must, and if I fall it cannot be helped."

"Why not let me go, Ready?" replied William.

"For many reasons, William," said Ready; "and the chief one is that I do not think you would succeed so well as I shall. I shall put on the war-cloak and feathers of the savage who fell dead inside of the stockade, and that will be a disguise, but I shall take no arms except his spear, as they would only be in my way, and increase the weight I have to carry. Now observe, you must let me out of the door, and when I am out, in case of accident put one of the poles across it inside; that will keep the door fast, if they attack it, until you can secure it with the others. Watch my return, and be all ready to let me in. Do you understand me?"

"Yes, perfectly, Ready; but I am now, I must confess, really frightened; if anything was to happen to you, what a misery it would be!"

"There is no help for it, William. Water must, if possible, be procured, and now is a better time to make the attempt than later, when they may be more on the watch; they have left off their work, and are busy eating; if I meet any one, it will only be a woman."

Ready went for the barrico, a little cask, which held six or seven gallons of water. He put on the head-dress and war-cloak of the savage; and, taking the barrico on his shoulder, and the spear in his hand, the poles which barred the door were softly removed by William, and after ascertaining that no one was concealed beneath the palisades, Ready pressed William's hand, and set off across the cleared space outside of the stockade, and gained the cocoa-nut trees. William, as directed, closed the door, passed one pole through the inner door-posts for security, and remained on the watch. He was in an awful state of suspense, listening to the slightest noise, even the slight rustling by the wind of the cocoa-nut boughs above him made him start; there he continued for some minutes, his gun ready cocked by his side.

It is time that he returned, thought William; the distance is not 100 yards, and yet I have heard no noise. At last he thought he heard footsteps coming very softly. Yes, it was so. Ready was returning, and without any accident. William had his hand upon the pole, to slip it on one side and open the door, when he heard a scuffle and a fall close to the door. He immediately threw down the pole, and opened it just as Ready called him by name. William seized his musket and sprang out; he found Ready struggling with a savage, who was uppermost, and with his spear at Ready's breast. In a second William levelled and fired, and the savage fell dead.

"Take the water in quick, William," said Ready in a faint voice. "I will contrive to crawl in if I can."

William caught up the barrico of water, and took it in; he then hastened to Ready, who was on his knees. Mr Seagrave, hearing the musket fired, had run out, and finding the stockade door open, followed William, and seeing him endeavouring to support Ready, caught hold of his other arm, and they led him tottering into the stockade; the door was then immediately secured, and they went to his assistance.

"Are you hurt, Ready?" said William.

"Yes, dear boy, yes; hurt to death, I fear: his spear went through my breast. Water, quick, water!"

"Alas! that we had some," said Mr Seagrave.

"We have, papa," replied William; "but it has cost us dearly."

William ran for a pannikin, and taking out the bung, poured some water out of the barrico and gave it to Ready, who drank it with eagerness.

"Now, William, lay me down on these cocoa-nut boughs; go and give some water to the others, and when you have all drunk, then come to me again. Don't tell Mrs Seagrave that I'm hurt. Do as I beg of you."

"Papa, take the water—do pray," replied William; "I cannot leave Ready."

"I will, my boy," replied Mr Seagrave; "but first drink yourself."

William, who was very faint, drank off the pannikin of water, which immediately revived him, and then, while Mr Seagrave hastened with some water to the children and women, occupied himself with old Ready, who breathed heavily, but did not speak.

Chapter Sixty Five

After returning twice for water, to satisfy those in the house, Mr Seagrave came to the assistance of William, who had been removing Ready's clothes to ascertain the nature of the wound he had received.

"We had better move him to where the other cocoa-nut boughs lie; he will be more comfortable there," said William.

Ready whispered, "More water." William gave him some more and then, with the assistance of his father, Ready was removed to a more comfortable place. As soon as they laid him there, Ready turned on his side, and threw up a quantity of blood.

"I am better now," said he in a low voice; "bind up the wound, William; an old man like me has not much blood to spare."

Mr Seagrave and William then examined the wound; the spear had gone deep into the lungs. William threw off his shirt, tore it up into strips, and then bound up the wound so as to stop the effusion of blood.

Ready, who at first appeared much exhausted with being moved about, gradually recovered so as to be able to speak in a low voice, when Mrs Seagrave came out of the house.

"Where is that brave, kind man?" cried she, "that I may bless him and thank him."

Mr Seagrave went to her, and caught her by the arm. "He is hurt, my dear; and very much hurt. I did not tell you at the time."

Mr Seagrave related what had occurred, and then led her to where Ready was lying. Mrs Seagrave knelt by his side, took his hand, and burst into tears.

"Don't weep for me," said Ready; "my days have been numbered; I'm only sorry that I cannot any more be useful to you."

"Dear good man," said Mrs Seagrave, "whatever may be our fates, and that is for the Almighty to decide for us, as long as I have life, what you have done for me and mine shall never be forgotten."

Mrs Seagrave then bent over him, and kissing his forehead, rose and retired weeping into the house.

"William," said Ready, "I can't talk now; raise my head a little, and then leave me. You have not looked round lately. Come again in about half an hour. Leave me now, Mr Seagrave; I shall be better if I doze a little."

They complied with Ready's request; went up to the planks, and examined carefully all round the stockade; at last they stopped.

"This is a sad business, William," said Mr Seagrave.

William shook his head. "He would not let me go," replied he; "I wish he had. I fear that he is much hurt."

"I should say that he cannot recover, William. We shall miss him tomorrow if they attack us."

"I hardly know what to say, papa; but I feel that since we have been relieved, I am able to do twice as much as I could have done before."

"I feel the same, but still with such a force against us, two people cannot do much."

"If my mother and Juno load the muskets for us," replied William, "we shall at all events do as much now as we should have been able to do if there were three, so exhausted as we should have been."

"Perhaps so; at all events we will do our best, for we fight for our lives and for those most dear to us."

William went softly up to Ready, and found that he was dozing; he therefore did not disturb him, but returned to his father. Now that their thirst had been appeased, they all felt the calls of hunger. Juno and William went and cut off steaks from the turtle, and fried them; they all made a hearty meal, and perhaps never had they taken one with so much relish in their lives.

It was nearly daylight, when William, who had several times been softly up to Ready, found him with his eyes open.

"How do you find yourself, Ready?" said William.

"I am quiet and easy, William, and without much pain; but I think I am sinking, and shall not last long. Recollect that if you are obliged to escape from the stockade, you take no heed of me, but leave me where I am. I cannot live, and were you to move me, I should only die the sooner."

"I had rather die with you, than leave you, Ready."

"No, that is wrong; you must save your mother, and your brothers and sister; promise me that you will do as I wish."

William hesitated.

"I point out to you your duty, William. I know what your feelings are, but you must not give way to them; promise me this, or you will make me very miserable."

William squeezed Ready's hand; his heart was too full to speak.

"They will come at daylight, William; you have not much time to spare; climb to the look-out, and wait there till day dawns; watch them as long as you can, and then come and tell me what you have seen."

Ready's voice became faint after this exertion of speaking so much.

William immediately climbed up the cocoa-nut tree, and waited there till daylight. At the dawn of day, he perceived that the savages were at work, that they had collected all the faggots together opposite to where the old house had stood, and were very busy in making arrangements for the attack. At last, every one shouldered a faggot, and commenced their advance towards the stockade; William immediately descended and called his father, who was talking with Mrs Seagrave. The muskets were all loaded, and Mrs Seagrave and Juno took their posts below the planking, to reload them as fast as they were fired.

"We must fire upon them as soon as we are sure of not missing, William," said Mr Seagrave, "for the more we check their advance, the better."

When the first savages were within fifty yards, they both fired, and two of the men dropped; they continued to fire as their assailants came up, with great success for the first ten minutes; after which the savages advanced in a larger body, and took the precaution to hold the faggots in front of them, for some protection as they approached. By these means they gained the stockade in safety, and commenced laying their faggots. Mr Seagrave and William still kept up an incessant fire upon them, but not with so much success as before.

Although many fell, the faggots were gradually heaped up, till they almost reached to the holes between the palisades, through which they pointed their muskets; and as the savages contrived to slope them down from the stockade to the ground, it was evident that they meant to mount up and take them by escalade. At last, it appeared as if all the faggots had been placed, and the savages retired farther back, to where the cocoa-nut trees were still standing.

"They have gone away, father," said William; "but they will come again, and I fear it is all over with us."

"I fear so too, my boy," replied Mr Seagrave; "they are only retreating to arrange for a general assault, and they now will be able to gain an entrance. I almost wish that they had fired the faggots; we might have escaped as Ready pointed out to us, but now I fear we have no chance."

"Don't say a word to my mother," said William; "let us defend ourselves to the last, and if we are overpowered it is the will of God."

"I should like to take a farewell embrace of your dear mother," said Mr Seagrave; "but, no; it will be weakness just now. Here they come, William, in a swarm. Well, God bless you, my boy; we shall all, I trust, meet in Heaven!"

The whole body of savages were now advancing from the cocoa-nut wood in a solid mass; they raised a yell, which struck terror into the hearts of Mrs Seagrave and Juno, yet they flinched not. The savages were again within fifty yards of them, when the fire was opened upon them; the fire was answered by loud yells, and the savages had already reached to the bottom of the sloping pile of faggots, when the yells and the reports of the muskets were drowned by a much louder report, followed by the crackling and breaking of the cocoa-nut trees, which made both parties start with surprise; another and another followed, the ground was ploughed up, and the savages fell in numbers.

"It must be the cannon of a ship, father," said William; "we are saved— we are saved!"

"It can be nothing else; we are saved, and by a miracle!" replied Mr Seagrave in utter astonishment.

The savages paused in the advance, quite stupefied; again, again, again, the report of the loud guns boomed through the air, and the round-shot and grape came whizzing and tearing through the cocoa-nut grove; at this last broadside, the savages turned, and fled towards their canoes: not one was left to be seen.

"We are saved!" cried Mr Seagrave, leaping off the plank and embracing his wife, who sank down on her knees, and held up her clasped hands in thankfulness to Heaven.

William had hastened up to the look-out on the cocoa-nut tree, and now cried out to them below, as the guns were again discharged:

"A large schooner, father; she is firing at the savages, who are at the canoes; they are falling in every direction: some have plunged into the water; there is a boat full of armed men coming on shore; they are close to the beach, by the garden-point. Three of the canoes have got off full of men; there go the guns again; two of the canoes are sunk, father; the boat has landed, and the people are coming up this way." William then descended from the look-out as fast as he could.

As soon as he was down, he commenced unbarring the door of the stockade. He pulled out the last pole just as he heard the feet of their deliverers outside. He threw open the door, and, a second after, found himself in the arms of Captain Osborn.

Chapter Sixty Six

Before we wind up this history, it will be as well to state to my young readers how it was that Captain Osborn made his appearance at so fortunate a moment. It will be recollected how a brig came off the island some months before this, and the great disappointment that the party on the island experienced in her not making her appearance again. The fact was, that those on board of the brig had not only seen their signals, but had read the name of the "*Pacific*" upon the flag hoisted; but the heavy gale which came on drove them so far to the southward, that the master of the brig did not consider that he should do his duty to his owners, if he lost so much time in beating up for the island again. He therefore decided upon making all sail for Sydney, to which port he was bound.

When Captain Osborn was put into the boat by Mackintosh and the seamen of the *Pacific*, he was still insensible; but he gradually recovered, and after a stormy night, Captain Osborn was so far recovered as to hear from Mackintosh what had taken place, and why it was that he found himself in an open boat at sea. The next morning the wind moderated, and they were fortunate enough to fall in with a vessel bound to Van Diemen's Land, which took them all on board.

From the account given by Mackintosh, Captain Osborn had no doubt in his mind but that the Seagrave family had perished, and the loss of the vessel, with them on board, was duly reported to the owners. When at Van Diemen's Land, Captain Osborn was so much taken with the beauty and fertility of the country, and perhaps not so well inclined to go to sea again after such danger as he had incurred in the last voyage, that he resolved to purchase land and settle there. He did so, and had already stocked his farm with cattle, and had gone round to Sydney in a schooner to await the arrival of a large order from England which he had sent for, when the brig arrived and reported the existence of some white people on the small island, and also that they had hoisted a flag with the name *Pacific* worked on it.

Captain Osborn, hearing this, went to the master of the brig, and questioned him. He found the latitude and longitude of the island to be not far from that of the ship when she was deserted, and he was now convinced that, by some miracle, the Seagrave family had been preserved. He therefore went to the Governor of New South Wales, and made him acquainted with the facts which had been established, and the Governor instantly replied, that the government armed schooner was at his service, if he would himself go in quest of his former shipmates. Inconvenient as the absence at that time was to Captain Osborn, he at once acquiesced, and in a few days the schooner sailed for her destination. She arrived off the island on the same morning that the fleet of canoes with the savages effected their landing, and when William made the remark to Ready as they were hastening into the stockade, that there was another vessel under sail off the garden-point, had Ready had time to put his eye to the telescope, he would have discovered that it was the schooner.

The schooner stood in to the reefs, and then hauled off again, that she might send her boat in to sound for an anchorage. The boat, when sounding, perceived the canoes and the savages, and afterwards heard the report of firearms on the first attack. On her return on board the schooner, they stated what they had seen and heard, and their idea that the white people on the island were being attacked by the savages. As the boat did not return on board till near dusk, they had not time to canvas, the question when the night attack was made, and they again heard the firing of the muskets. This made Captain Osborn most anxious to land as soon as possible, but as the savages were in such numbers, and the crew of the schooner did not consist of more than twenty-five men, the commander considered it was rash to make the attempt. He did, however, show the utmost anxiety to bring his schooner to an anchor, so as to protect his men, and then agreed that they should land.

The boat had reported deep water and good anchorage close to the garden-point, and every preparation was made for running at daylight on the following morning; but unfortunately, it fell calm for the best part of the day, and it was not until the morning after, just as the savages were making their last attack upon the stockade, that she could get in. As soon as she did, she opened the fire of her carronades, and the result is already known.

My readers must, if they can, imagine the joy of Mr and Mrs Seagrave when they beheld their old friend Captain Osborn. All danger was now over; the party who had landed with him went out under the command of the mate, to ascertain if there were any more of the savages to be found; but, except the dead and dying, all had escaped in some of the smaller canoes. Captain Osborn remained with the Seagraves, and they informed him of the state of poor old Ready, whom William had gone to attend as soon as Captain Osborn was engaged with his father and mother. Captain Osborn hurried out to see him; Ready knew his voice, for his eyes were already so dim that he could not see.

"That is Captain Osborn, I know," said Ready in a faint voice. "You have come in good time, sir; I knew you would come, and I always said so: you have the thanks of a dying man."

"I hope it is not so bad as that, Ready; we have a surgeon on board, and I will send for him at once."

"No surgeon can help me, sir," replied Ready; "another hour of time will not pass before I shall be in Eternity."

The old man then joined his hands across his breast, and remained for some time in silent prayer. Then he bade them farewell in a faint voice, which at last was changed to a mere whisper. They still remained, in silence and in tears, standing round him, William only kneeling and holding his hand, when the old man's head fell back, and he was no more!

"It is all over," said Mr Seagrave mournfully, "and he has, I have no doubt, gone to receive the reward of a good and just man. 'Happy are those who die in the Lord.'"

Mr Seagrave then led away his wife and children, leaving Juno and William. William closed his eyes, and Juno went and fetched the ship's ensign, which they laid over the body, after which they joined the rest of the party in the house.

It was decided that the following day should be passed in packing up and getting on board their luggage, and that the day after the family should embark. William then mentioned the wish of poor old Ready as to his burial. The commander of the schooner immediately gave directions for a coffin to be made, and for his men to dig the grave at the spot that William should point out.

Chapter Sixty Seven

The hurry and bustle of preparing for their departure from the island, and the rapid succession of events which had been crowded together within so very few days, had not allowed time for much thought or reflection to Mr and Mrs Seagrave and William; at length, however, every preparation had been made, and they were no longer urged by the commander of the schooner to hasten their packing up and arrangements; for everything had been sent on board during the afternoon, and it was proposed that they should sail on the following day.

Now they had time to feel, and bitterly did they lament the loss of their old friend, and deplore that he had not survived to sail with them to Sydney. They had always indulged the hope that one day they should be taken off the island, and in that hope they had ever looked forward to old Ready becoming a part of their future household. Now that their wishes had been granted—so much was the feeling of joy and gratitude mingled with regret—that could he have been restored to them, they felt as if they would have gladly remained on the island.

Captain Osborn, the commander, and the crew of the schooner had taken leave of them for the night, and had gone on board, having made arrangements for the interment of Ready, previous to their sailing, on the following day. The children had been put to bed, and Juno had quitted the house; Mr and Mrs Seagrave and William were sitting together in their now half-dismantled room, when Juno entered; the poor girl had evidently been weeping.

"Well, Juno," observed Mr Seagrave, with a view to break the silence which had continued for some time previous to her entrance, "are you not glad to leave the island?"

"One time I think I would be very glad, but now I not care much," replied Juno. "Island very nice place, all very happy till savage come. Suppose they not kill old Ready, I not care."

"Yes, indeed," said Mrs Seagrave, "it is a sad blow to us all; I did hope to have fostered the good old man, and to have been able to have shown him our gratitude, but—"

"It is the will of Heaven that it should be otherwise," continued Mr Seagrave; "I would give half that I am possessed of, that he had not perished."

"Oh, Massa!" said Juno, "I sit by him just now; I take off the flag and look at his face, so calm, look so happy, so good, I almost tink he smile at me, and then I cry. Oh! Massa Tommy, all because you idle boy."

"It adds much to my regret," replied Mr Seagrave, "that his life should have been sacrificed through the thoughtlessness of one of my own children; what a lesson it will be to Tommy when he is old enough to comprehend the consequences of his conduct."

"That he must not know, papa," said William, who had been leaning mournfully over the table; "one of Ready's last injunctions was that Tommy was never to be told of it."

"His last wishes shall be religiously attended to, my dear boy," replied Mr Seagrave; "for what do we not owe to that good old man? When others deserted us and left us to perish, he remained with us to share our fate. By his skill we were saved and landed in safety. He provided for our wants, added to our comforts, instructed us how to make the best use of our means. Without his precautions we should have perished by the spears of the savages. What an example of Christian fortitude and humility did he ever show us! and indeed, I may truly say, that by his example, sinful as I must ever be, I have become, I trust, a better man. Would that he were now sitting by us,—but the Lord's will be done!"

"I feel as if I had lost a stay or prop," replied Mrs Seagrave. "So accustomed have I been to look to him for advice since we have been on this island. Had he not been thus snatched from us—had he been spared to us a few years, and had we been permitted to surround his death-bed, and close his eyes in peace—" and Mrs Seagrave wept upon the shoulder of her husband.

After a time, Mrs Seagrave recovered herself; but silence ensued, only broken by an occasional sob from poor Juno. William's heart was too full; he could not for a long while utter a word; at last he said in a low voice:

"I feel that, next to my dear father and mother, I have lost my best friend. I cannot forgive myself for allowing him to go for the water; it was my duty to go, and I ought to have gone."

"And yet we could have ill spared you, my dear boy; you might have perished," replied Mrs Seagrave.

"It would have been as God willed," replied William; "I might have perished, or I might not."

"We never know what the morrow may bring forth," said Mr Seagrave, "or what may be in store for us. Had not this misfortune happened, had old Ready been spared to us, how joyfully should I and all of you have quitted this island, full of anticipation, and indulging in worldly prospects. What a check have I received! I now am all thought and anxiety. I have said to myself, 'we have been happy on this island; our wants have been supplied; even our comforts have been great. We have been under no temptations, for we have been isolated from the world; am I so sure that I shall be as happy in future as I have been? Am I confident, now my long-wished-for return to the world is about to take place, that I shall have no cause to lament that I ever quitted this peaceful, quiet spot?' I feel that it is a duty to my family that I should return to society, but I am far from feeling that our happiness may be increased. We have, however, a plain precept to follow, which is, to do our duty in that state of life to which it has pleased God to call us."

"Yes," replied Mrs Seagrave; "I feel the truth of all you have just said. We are in his hands; let us put our trust in him."

"We will," replied Mr Seagrave; "but it is late, and we have to rise early to-morrow morning. This is the last evening which we shall pass on this island; let us return our thanks for the happiness we have enjoyed here. We thought to have quitted this spot in joy,—it is his will that we should leave it in sorrow."

Mr Seagrave took down the Bible, and after he had read a chapter, he poured forth a prayer suited to their feelings, and they all retired to repose.

The next morning they were up early, and packed up the few articles which still remained to go on board. Mr Seagrave read the prayers, and they went to breakfast. Few words were exchanged, for there was a solemn grief upon all of them. They waited for the arrival of Captain Osborn and the crew of the schooner to attend the funeral of poor old Ready. William, who had gone out occasionally to look at the vessel, now came in, and said that two boats were pulling on shore. A few minutes afterwards, Captain Osborn and the commander of the schooner soon made their appearance. The coffin had been brought on shore; the body of Ready was put into it, and it was screwed down.

In half an hour all was prepared, and the family were summoned from the house. The coffin, covered with the Union Jack as a pall, was raised on the shoulders of six of the seamen, and they bore it to the grave, followed by Mrs Seagrave and the children, the commander of the schooner, and several of the men. Mr Seagrave read the funeral service, the grave was filled up, and they all walked back in silence. At the request of William, the commander of the schooner had ordered the carpenter to prepare an oak paling to put round the grave, and a board on which was written the name of the deceased and day of his death. As soon as this had been fixed up, William, with a deep sigh, followed the commander of the schooner to the house to announce that all was finished, and that the boat waited for them to embark.

"Come, my dear," said Mr Seagrave to his wife.

"I will, I will," replied Mrs Seagrave, "but I don't know how it is, now that the hour is come, I really feel such pain at quitting this dear island. Had it not been for poor Ready's death, I really do think I should wish to remain."

"I don't doubt but that you feel sorrow, my dear, but we must not keep Captain Osborn waiting."

As Mr Seagrave was aware that the commander of the schooner was anxious to get clear of the islands before night, he now led his wife down to the boat. They all embarked, and were soon on the deck of the schooner, from whence they continued to fix their eyes upon the island, while the men were heaving up the anchor. At last sail was made upon the vessel, the garden-point was cleared, and, as they ran away with a fair wind, each object on the shore became more indistinct. Still their eyes were turned in that direction.

As they ran down to the westward, they passed the cove where they had first landed, and Mr Seagrave directed Mrs Seagrave's attention to it. She remained for some time looking at it in silence, and then said as she turned away:

"We shall never be more happy than we were on that island, Seagrave."

"It will indeed be well, my dear, if we never are less happy," replied her husband.

The schooner now ran fast through the water, and the island was every minute less distinct; after a time, the land was below the horizon, and the tops of the cocoa-nut trees only to be seen; these gradually disappeared. Juno watched on, and when at last nothing could be seen, she waved her handkerchief in the direction of the island, as if to bid it farewell, and then went down below to hide her grief.

The wind continued fair, and, after a favourable passage of little more than four weeks, they arrived at Sydney Cove, the port to which they were bound when they embarked from England on board of the good ship Pacific.

PS. As my young readers will probably wish to know a little more about the Seagrave family, I will inform them that Mr Seagrave, like the patriarch Job after his tribulation, found his flocks and herds greatly increased on his arrival at Sydney. Mr and Mrs Seagrave lived to see all their children grown up. William inherited the greater part of the property from his father, after having for many years assisted him in the management of it. Tommy, notwithstanding all his scrapes, grew up a very fine fellow, and entered the army. Caroline married a young clergyman, and made him an excellent wife; little Albert went into the navy, and is at present a commander.

Juno is still alive, and lives at Seagrave plantation with William, and her greatest pleasure is to take his children on her knee, and tell them long stories about the island, and make them cry when she goes through the history of old Ready's death and burial.